Overlook

A Night Novel

Dustin Stevens

Overlook
Copyright © 2023, Dustin Stevens

Cover Art and Design: Christian Bentulan
Formatting: Jamie Davis

No beast is more savage than man when possessed with power answerable to his rage. —Plutarch

Chapter One

Now

"G, come in. Over."

The sound is from a standard two-way radio. A mechanized voice preceded by a burst of static, followed by a distinctive click. A clear end to the transmission, letting the receiver know the line is theirs to reply.

An answer the man standing on the beach thirty yards away from me seems in no hurry to provide. Intent on getting the last few drags of his cigarette, he stands with his automatic weapon cradled against his chest. A midsized rifle with a magazine curved away from the base.

A Kalashnikov, if I'm forced to guess, the thin moonlight overhead and my current position not exactly giving me the best viewing angle.

A red cherry appears as he inhales deeply before flicking the remaining butt out into the water before him. A move steeped in complete disdain, his every movement since the top of my head first crested the water four minutes ago letting it be known that he would rather be anywhere else in the world.

A sentry posted on the south end of Fawn Island, a tiny knob of earth rising out of Deer Harbor. Two and a half acres of dense pine forest resting atop a mass of boulders and rock beaches.

Space enough for just a single estate, purchased both ten and six years ago before being sold one last time to its current owner. A sprawling mansion flanked by a pair of smaller guesthouses.

Structures all arranged to the north and center of the island, making the lone gunman standing before me the sole line of defense on the south end. A football field of dense forestation separates him from where the party will take place tomorrow night.

No doubt the reason for the disdain he wears like a cloak. Contempt for drawing the proverbial short straw and being cast down here, forced to stare at nothing but the darkened waters of the open end of the harbor. Endless trips across the sun-bleached shells of mussels left behind by the natives who called this place home a century ago.

An omnipresent crunching sound, almost as distinct as the radio squawking from his belt. Noises that pass easily across the cold water, finding my ears resting just inches above it.

A tiny spike in a flat sea stretching out wide before him.

An aberration that would be almost impossible to see, even if he did give a damn about his job and bothered to look up every once in a while.

"Still here," the man known as G replies. Releasing the tab on the side of the radio for a moment, he lets a blast of static come in before adding, "Still not a damn thing to see out here in the dark."

Turning sideways to the shore, he begins his march anew. Another trek back across the gravel bar masquerading as a beach. An opening between two craggy outcroppings measuring no more than thirty yards across.

Rocky endcaps to the razored cliffs surrounding ninety percent of the island, arranged in an inverted horseshoe formation.

An opening I spotted on our scouting trip earlier in the day. A lazy jaunt with my daughter behind the steering wheel while I posed as a retired fisherman, right down to the fishing gear I carried and the oversized wave I'd offered to the guard watching from the eastern rock formation.

Another little bastard like the one before me. Young punks playing dress up, wearing tactical attire they saw in some movie and carrying pieces of shit rifles.

Guys holding themselves out as guns for hire, when in reality they are more like window dressing.

Damned ceramic owls resting atop a building, hoping to keep pigeons from shitting on it, but not able to actually do a damn thing to stop them.

"Look alive," the voice on the other end instructs. "Never know what could be out there in the dark."

The guard doesn't bother to reply. Returning the radio to his belt, I hear him mutter, "Yeah, yeah."

Words of dismissal just barely audible over the brittle shells being pulverized beneath his feet.

The signal I've been waiting for.

Floating with my body parallel to the surface, I grip the twin handles of the submersible that pulled me in from the same fishing boat currently floating somewhere in the darkness behind me. Close proximity that meant my arriving journey was less than a mile in total.

A short jaunt through the inky depths clutching the motorized thruster, a small can of compressed air clamped between my teeth, a full-body wetsuit protecting everything but my cheeks and jaw from the frigid water.

Icy cold that otherwise would have me succumb to hypothermia within minutes. Yet another cautionary tale, cast down into the waters surrounding the last bits of land separating the United States from Canada.

Flipping the accelerator switch with my right thumb, I nudge the underwater craft forward. Small hits pushing me closer to shore, with water passing across my oval dive mask and over the balaclava that is the top of my suit.

Silent progress that steadily cuts the distance between me and my landing spot by half.

And then half again.

A steady approach to the island rising before me. A darkened monolith formed from rocks and trees shooting straight up out of the water, towering high above.

A sight I allow myself to consider for only a moment before putting my focus on the guard continuing to move east across the shoreline. Short, choppy steps that take him to the boulders on the far end before he pauses, again going for his belt.

A reach that causes me to let up on the accelerator, expecting him to bring the radio back out. A call to whoever was on the line earlier, letting them know that they have an intruder.

I have been spotted.

My pulse picks up as I let my feet drift downward, my toes scraping across the rocky bottom beneath me. Semi-firm footing should I have to make a sudden move. A desperation heave I fully expect to need at some point tonight, though was hoping to put off until at least I'd made shore.

Hopefully, even located the reason why I am here.

The lone thing in the world strong enough to make a sixty-year-old man come out of retirement to do this sort of shit. Water landings and nighttime raids, to say nothing of the various other things I've resorted to in the last couple of days.

Stuff I haven't even attempted in damn near a decade. Successfully managed to pull off in even longer.

Chances taken now only because there is no other way.

A fact that was drilled into me before I went into the water a few minutes ago, as if I haven't been entirely aware of it since that moment on my dock a couple of days ago.

A charge that starts right here.

Now.

This little bastard playing soldier just the first of however many obstacles I need to overcome.

Chapter Two

Then

I gave up on actually paying attention to the lure on the end of my line more than five minutes ago. The instant I heard the faint whine of a car engine approaching in the distance, any focus I had on fishing faded away.

Not the feel of the rattletrap lure I was working a few feet below the navy-blue surface of the pond or even the speed with which I was reeling. Movements that became nothing more than background activity, my attention moving toward the approach of the V6 engine. Standard fare for a mid-sized American sedan, pushed in a way that hinted the driver was in a hurry to arrive.

A speedy approach just barely allowing me a complete visual of the vehicle once it finally made the turn into my driveway. A snapshot with blurred edges, taken by the cameras imbedded in the towering pine trees framing either side of the gravel lane.

An initial line of defense, completely undetectable from the road.

A first assessment, determining how far the rare visitor I ever received made it thereafter.

The instant the snapshot was taken, it was sent directly to my cellphone. An image paired with the alerts from the sensors buried in the ground. Visual and auditory warnings letting me know that my personal sanctum had been breached.

Sirens that sent small hits of adrenaline into my system, preparing me to act. Physiological responses beat into me both by training and experience.

Momentary spikes that made me glance to the tackle box resting on the dock by my feet and the hidden compartment that comprised the bottom of it. One of many such hiding places around the property and throughout my home.

Stash spots to ensure I was never far from a weapon.

Ingrained behavior, going back more than twenty-five years. A reflexive reaction, lasting only until I checked the screen of the phone before dissipating. A quick flare of long dormant synapses, receding back to stasis as my gaze returned to the sight of the vehicle coming my way on the screen of my phone.

An arrival not unwelcome, but certainly not expected.

A potential friend, or an enemy far worse than whatever my body was preparing for just a moment earlier.

Hitting a single button to open the gate nestled eighty yards further down the lane, I returned the phone back to the inside pocket of my fleece overcoat. Remaining fixed in position, I let my eyes glaze, listening as my guest came closer.

More of the same hurried pace, the sound passing easily along the line cut through the forest encircling my home. A slash amidst the heavy timber more than twice as wide as necessary, done with that distinct purpose in mind.

A means of turning it into a sound tunnel. One more way of alerting me to any visitors well before they arrived.

Not that there was an abundance of people seeking me out these days, the full list of people who had ventured down the gravel lane since I moved in able to be counted on three fingers.

The mailman, who had made the drive just twice before

requesting that any future packages be retrieved at the post office in town. Agnes Elder, a woman who insisted on bringing me baked goods every so often, claiming it was what neighbors were supposed to do, her definition of the word apparently extending across the two miles separating the homestead of her and her late husband from my own.

And the woman currently seated behind the gray Honda headed my way.

Continuing with the performative charade, I sat on the rough-hewn bench built directly into the dock overlooking my pond. A body of water more than ten acres in total, lined with cattails, dense pine forest rising behind them on either end.

A deep pool carved by nature's own hand, backdropped by the Cascade Mountains in the distance. Jagged peaks already kissed with the first snowfall of the year at the higher elevations.

Omens of the brutal Pacific Northwest winter that would soon be upon us at the lower levels.

A retirement destination that was not of my own choosing, though there were worse places to be.

A thought I had been having, staring at the afternoon sun splashed across the surface of the water, when the sound of the engine pulled it away. One more thing shoved to the periphery, forgotten as I heard the sedan slide to a stop within thirty yards of where I was sitting. Tires slinging gravel, ending with the engine cutting out and the metal hinges of a door whining as it was wrenched open.

Sounds that cut through the crisp Washington air while I hooked a finger into the filament line on my St. Croix rod. A means of holding it in place as I raised the tip toward the heavens before jerking it forward. A motion done thousands of times from that very spot, the cast sending the black and red lure onto a looping arc that ended with a small splash in the center of the marigold stripe resting atop the water.

A landing place I was content to leave it as I set the line and pretended to reel, listening to the thump of boot heels moving the length of the dock.

A percussive beat that was louder than necessary. Stomping meant to send shock waves down through the pillars and out into the water, effectively ending any chance of catching another fish for the day.

A little trick she picked up long ago, making it quite clear what she thought of the pastime.

"Used to be a time when someone couldn't even make it off the road before you knew they were there," the not-quite-familiar voice of my daughter Quinn opened. Words interspersed with more footsteps. Steady progress made in my direction. "Hell, now you don't even look up from the damn water."

A greeting clearly meant to goad me. Pick up right where we left things the last time we saw each other.

Exactly five hundred days ago.

A gap that, according to the last thing she said before leaving, was but a fraction of the time she hoped it would be before we crossed paths again.

What could have possibly drawn her out now, I could only guess at.

"Your left taillight is out," I replied. My own return barb, letting her know that just because I wasn't standing in the center of the driveway as I once had, she still wasn't able to sneak up on me.

Never would be.

Snorting softly, her pace slowed. The heft of her footfalls dropped. The heels of the hiking boots she wore scraped across the aged boards as she appeared in my periphery, her thumbs hooked in the rear loops of her jeans.

Her preferred pose, adopted when she was but seven years old.

One she had kept through the three-plus decades since.

"Still out here every afternoon?" she asked, staring across the pond. As easy a place as any for her to put her focus, making a point of avoiding eye contact.

"For as long as I can," I answered, "before winter hits."

Again, she snorted. Much deeper this time, forceful enough to rock her head back a couple of inches. "Jesus, sitting out here trying to catch fish until it gets too cold. When did you become such an old man?"

Much like her opening comment, I knew she was only trying to bait me. Repeated remarks that she wanted me to snap back at, proving that she could still get under my skin whenever she wanted.

Personal digs she knew weren't true, meant only to put me on the defensive. A tact she first adopted about the same time as the pose with her belt loops and the game of trying to scare away the fish.

A child older than her years who had grown into an adult refusing to act them.

My trips to the dock each day weren't out of boredom or a means to pass the time, but rather to collect dinner. Fresh fish that was far cheaper and safer than anything lining the shelves at the Safeway in town.

Just as my reticence to continue once the snows got down this low had nothing to do with the cold, but because the damned things stopped biting.

Responses I kept to myself as I lifted my focus her way, taking in the up-close profile of my daughter for the first time in well over a year. A length of time matching the gap before, these impromptu meetings apparently having become a biennial event.

Gaze pinched up against the sun, she stood facing straight ahead, her silhouette cutting a distinct contrast against the evergreen forest behind her. Sandy brown hair pulled back into a ponytail. Freckled skin bearing the last hints of a summer tan, making the fine lines around her mouth and eyes all the more pronounced.

Signs of her own ongoing battle with time, contributing in no small way to her insistence on pointing out my age each time we spoke.

In addition to the boots she'd used to announce her presence, she was dressed in faded jeans, the knees and thighs weathered to the point of threadbare. Shredding that could have been purchased or the result of hundreds of trips through the washer.

A matching denim jacket overlaid a purple and gray flannel, the slightest hint of a tank top peeking out beneath.

An ensemble just barely warm enough for the autumn air, especially with the sun sitting only a few inches above the horizon.

"You look well, Q."

For the third time since her arrival, she replied with a sniff. A sharp inhalation, culminating with her cutting her gaze my direction. A searching glance, her eyes flitting across my features.

Some, like the crystalline blue eyes and freckled skin, that matched hers.

Others, like the once chestnut hair that had trended to silver and been buzzed short, that were distinctly my own.

"And you look like shit."

A quip one would think was another jab, but was in reality probably the truth. The first fact spoken since her arrival.

"Like you said - I'm an old man."

Knowing that the answer was an admission she was not expecting, I returned my attention to the fishing pole. Gripping the base of the rod in my left hand, I worked the right in a slow clockwise progression. A steady pace that kept the metal loop of the spin reel rotating, tugging the line through the water.

An activity I was content to keep at for as long as it took, willing to wait her out no matter the myriad questions I carried.

Patience she was not nearly as equipped with, making it no more than a couple of moments before saying, "That's what I'm afraid of."

"What is?"

"That you've become an old man," she said, slowly rotating to take me in. "Because I need your help."

Pausing, she seemed to consider what she'd just said, how it sounded out loud, before revising it to say, "*Cailee* needs your help."

Chapter Three

It wasn't that I was opposed to killing.

Quite the opposite, actually.

The first life I ever took was from a duck blind with my father when I was just nine years old. A hunting trip to the woods of Arkansas where my grandparents owned a small cabin on the edge of a wetlands that was rife with game. Everything imaginable, ranging from whitetail deer to the full array of waterfowl.

A hunter's paradise that my old man had been slipping away to a couple times a year for as long as I could remember, having finally deemed me old enough to join. My first foray into the wilderness. The start of what he referred to as my passage into manhood, where he first started calling me by the nickname that had stuck in the fifty-one years since.

An opening to a trip that was marked by staying up late and cussing too much. All the other stuff he knew I wasn't allowed to get away with in front of my mother. Small liberties that delighted my young self to no end, but still paled compared to the thrill of aiming the front of my little single-shot Wingmaster at a live target for the first time and pulling the trigger.

The feel of absorbing the kinetic energy transferred from the stock of the gun into my shoulder. The sound of it penetrating the foam plugs wedged into my ears. The smell of gunpowder.

The sight of feathers exploding in the air and our old dog scrambling up from his seat beside us. Speed and energy I hadn't seen from him in years as he flung himself broadside into the water to go and retrieve my prize.

The start of a lifelong affinity for nature that had stretched for more than five decades. A nuanced relationship predicated not on wanton violence or decorating the walls of my home with past conquests, but of understanding the world and my place in it.

A totality so much bigger than one person, mine merely a role to be played. A position from which I could both give and extract, the most important rule my father ever imparted being to never take more than was needed.

To never, ever be wasteful with nature's gifts.

A maxim I'm certain was intended to reference any future trips into the woods, but that also came to serve me well later in life.

A career spent going on hunts of different kinds, seeking out prey of an infinitely different manner.

Hearing the last words from my daughter, that lesson again came to mind as I reeled in the few feet of line still extended into the pond before me. The only visible reaction to what she said, coming in the form of my right hand moving as fast as the reel would allow.

An increase in pace to signify I no longer had any interest in what rested beneath the surface of the water. Only in getting the lure up and out so I could fully focus on what was just shared.

Words that had spurred an initial thought of dropping the damned pole altogether. Simply opening my hands and letting it fall to the dock, landing with a clatter before coming to settle wherever it may. Same for everything in the tackle box resting on the weathered boards by my feet, save maybe the Beretta tucked away in the bottom compartment.

Otherwise, the rest were items I no longer had any interest in or use for, left behind as I wheeled away from the bench and tore down the length of the dock. Retracing the path Quinn had followed just minutes before, I could hit the gravel of the driveway within seven seconds.

Twenty-one after that, the concrete walk in front of my home.

Less than half a minute to get from resting on the end of the dock to my front door. Two more beyond that to change my shoes and coat. Another handful of seconds to grab the go-bag stowed away in the bottom of the hall closet and push through the side door of my kitchen, exiting into the garage.

A total of under five minutes before I was on the move, tearing off in pursuit of an unknown enemy. An adversary whose identity I had not the slightest inkling of, but at the same time had been expecting for decades.

An eventuality that came with the kind of life I'd lived. The things I'd done. The people I had crossed paths with.

One I had been able to avoid for the last twenty-five years, always with the certain knowledge that at some point, it would happen again.

My only hope being that that wasn't what this was about. The comment Quinn had just made about my granddaughter needing my help was merely referring to a hand in getting something into her apartment just off the edge of campus at the University of Washington. A problem with her heating or plumbing.

Even financial assistance of some kind.

Alternative outcomes that I knew were nothing more than wishful thinking – the girl not even knowing my name, let alone that I could turn a wrench - as I lifted the lure up out of the water. Letting it drop onto the dock between us, droplets of water staining the faded boards, I rose from my seat.

Stepping forward to the corner post, I hefted the stringer with three trout attached to it up from the water. Not even bothering to let the excess sluice away, I unclipped each one from the metal hooks securing them in place.

Their good luck, coming at the sake of my misfortune. A desire to not be wasteful, knowing that whatever else my daughter was about to share would radically redirect the rest of my day.

If not many more thereafter.

One at a time, I tossed them into the water, the resulting impacts sending ripples through the same golden stripe I was admiring just a few minutes earlier. Keeping the stringer hooked around the nail driven into the top of the corner post, I dropped it back into the icy depths.

An implement I would be back for later, my focus already well beyond the daily rite.

"What happened?" I asked, turning to face my daughter.

Looking at her square for the first time since her arrival, I could see that the faint creases marring her face weren't the result of aging, but rather exhaustion. Fatigue, coupled with extreme worry.

Fear, even.

A combination bad enough to make her do the unthinkable, going against her word and coming to seek me out.

A litany of information I filed away in an instant. Drawing my core tight, I balanced my weight evenly, preparing myself to move.

"Where is she?"

"I don't know," Quinn replied. Words that seeped out as barely more than a whisper. An admission that caused those same faint lines to become more pronounced as her features crinkled into a wince.

"But you know something is wrong?"

Dropping her chin, she replied, "You remember that stupid game you used to play with me? The one where you would let me choose a code word, and if anything was ever wrong, all I had to do was call and say it, or yell it out whenever you or mom came to pick me up?"

The system was something my colleagues and I all used with our families. A trick of the trade that I had contorted into a game for the sake of my daughter when she was just a child. A way to make it seem fun, rather than imparting fear.

A scheme she had taken to for a number of years, before eventually the combined natures of her and her mother began to win out. Self-righteousness and animosity mixing into a brew that made her turn even that into a way of ridiculing me.

Choices for safe words that were condescending, or silly, or even just plain vulgar.

More items in a checkered past that were best left there for the time being.

"Yes."

Reaching to the left pocket of her jean jacket, Quinn extracted her cellphone. Pulling it up in front of her, she began to tap at the screen with both thumbs.

"Don't you dare take this as some sort of victory," she said, "but when Cailee got old enough to start going places by herself, I instituted the same thing. Only difference was, I was smart enough not to let a child pick out the word."

Finishing whatever she was doing on the phone, she raised her attention my way.

"Thankfully, we never had to use it. Hell, it had been so long since we even talked about it, I'd almost forgotten what it was."

Turning the phone my way, she thrust it out to arm's length before her.

"Until I woke up to find this this morning."

Bending forward at the waist, I brought my nose to within a foot of the screen. A close enough vantage to plainly see the text message emblazoned across it.

Two words, totaling just nine letters.

Mom! Hungry!

Chapter Four

There were two distinct emotions permeating every word shared by my daughter. A pair of things that were present even before she arrived, pushing her to drive the way she was. Alternating pressure on the gas and brake, forcing her to disregard personal safety in the name of seeking help.

Things that I couldn't help but notice becoming more pronounced with each additional syllable uttered. The fear of stating things aloud, along with the constant pressure of a ticking clock.

Competing forces that stood in harsh contrast to one another. An ongoing battle that had waged to the point she had no choice but to make the drive out and ask for my help.

A search for aid that had in kind only heightened both of the underlying feelings. A vicious cycle that was feeding on itself. A threat to consume her from within, no matter how much she tried to pretend otherwise.

The first of those was something that was readily recognizable to any person who had ever been a parent. A realization of a worst fear that creeped in shortly after the child was wrapped in a hospital blanket and handed over for the very first time.

An understanding of the gift that was just received and the responsibility that came with it. The charge to always keep them safe and healthy, no matter the cost or consequences.

A personal vow that we have all made.

The fulfilling it part being where things varied wildly.

The second thing pulsating from my daughter in waves was the sheer hostility she carried. Anger over having to be in my presence. Self-loathing for having climbed into her car and making the drive out to a place she'd only been a couple of other times.

An initial visit that I had requested simply so she knew where to find me, should something ever happen, no matter what it might turn out to be. The promise of aid in whatever arose that I thought was interrupted by what took place the last time we interacted. A public fracas at Cailee's high school graduation, followed by her making a second trip out to tell me just what she thought of me and my unwanted presence.

A scathing dressing down that ended with her reminding me there was a reason she and her mother had moved across the country to get away from me. The very same one that was why I had never been formally introduced to my only grandchild, what little interaction I had had with Cailee being from afar.

"This has to make you happier than a pig in shit, huh?" Quinn muttered. Coming no closer than the doorway separating my living room from the kitchen, she stood with her shoulder pressed against the peeled log framing it.

A pose attempting to appear detached, even while nervous energy radiated from her.

More of that same internal war, pulling her in opposite directions.

"Why's that?" I asked without glancing up from the go-bag snatched out of the hallway closet just minutes before.

Resting on the island in the center of the kitchen, the zipper was pulled open, either side left gaping wide. Quick access for me to do one final check, ensuring that each item was exactly where I last packed it a couple weeks before.

Just as I did every month, ensuring that everything inside was still in good working condition.

A force of habit, always accompanied by the silent prayer that it would be nothing more than wasted time. Performative effort that would never be needed.

"Me coming to you like this," Quinn replied. "Asking for help."

The wrath my daughter had for me, I understood plenty well. A fractured relationship that could be traced back to a very specific incident on a very specific date, twenty-five years before.

The first – and only – time that my work life as a member of the FBI's Fugitive Task Force spilled over into my personal life. A late-night arrival from a man I was tracking named Marcel Bardette and his crew that extinguished the lives of two men and eventually landed Bardette in prison.

One that very nearly took the lives of my wife and daughter as well before ultimately claiming my marriage and any kind of lasting interaction with either of them.

A vicious incident that forever changed how they looked at me.

Hell, how they perceived and interacted with the world.

A single event that sent them both fleeing across the country just months later, seeking out the furthest possible location they could while still remaining in the continental United States.

An escape that was the reason why my home was now nestled deep in the Pacific Northwest, instead of back where I was born in Alabama. Or down on a ranch in Texas. Or even some remote island in the Caribbean.

A self-appointed position of overlook, even if it was never asked for nor wanted.

What I couldn't understand was how my daughter could think for an instant that anything she had shared in the last ten minutes would be a source of amusement. Some petty victory that I would revel in, even at the expense of my granddaughter.

Disbelief that I displayed through a single upturned eyebrow. A quick glance to her standing on the periphery of my vision before returning my focus back to the task before me.

Items that I shifted or removed as necessary, trying to envision what might be needed. How long we may be gone.

An unenviable task, my mind conjuring images both remembered and seen only in nightmares.

"The number the text came from," I replied, bypassing the topic entirely. A matter sure to nudge us into an argument for which neither of us had the time or energy. "I noticed it didn't have a name attached to it."

Taking a moment to bite back whatever initial barb rose to mind, my daughter replied, "No."

"Local area code," I said. "A friend? Roommate?"

"Definitely not her roommate," Quinn answered. "I have her number saved, and she hasn't seen or heard from Cailee all day."

"How many times have you tried the number?"

"At least a hundred," Quinn replied. "Damn thing has been off all day. Goes straight to voicemail. Same for Cailee's."

Grabbing the far strap of the bag in one hand to hold it still, I began to stuff the last few items back inside. Things that were going with me, included if there was even the slightest chance they might be needed.

All of the expected staples, such as a couple of changes of clothes and a toiletry kit, ranging on up to a sheathed MK3 knife. A couple of lengths of paracord.

Even a pair of night-vision goggles.

A distillation of damn near everything I had used in my previous career crammed into an oversized canvas bag.

The rest of whatever I might require, I knew was stowed in the truck waiting for me in the garage.

"I'm assuming you tried the police?"

For no less than the tenth time since she showed up, Quinn snorted, this one even more derisive than the rest. "Exactly what you'd imagine. Said she has to be gone at least forty-eight hours to be considered a missing person, which makes zero sense, because...well...you know."

I did know. I had spent decades trying to find people who were either missing or didn't want to be found and was more familiar than most how imperative those very same first hours were. Precious time that often dictated if a person made it home, and if they did, what kind of shape they were in.

Two full days during which the police often refused to even start looking.

"What about her car?"

"Not with her," Quinn answered. "There's no parking for under-classmen at her apartment."

"How does she get around?"

"I see all her Uber charges," Quinn answered. "There weren't any for last night, so she must have taken the bus or had someone pick her up."

Grunting softly, I considered the information for a moment. Things that didn't provide a ton on their own, but could be pursued later if nothing else presented itself.

"Who was the last person to see her?"

"For sure?" Quinn asked. "Her roommate. Yesterday. She was headed to class and Cailee was off to have dinner with her father for his birthday."

"Where?"

"Not sure," Quinn said. "I haven't been able to reach him either."

Content with what was wedged into the bag, I pulled the zipper closed across the top. Knowing precious little at the moment, there was no way to cull together every last item that might be needed.

Even trying to was only going to burn more time we didn't have.

Anything else required would have to be picked up along the way.

"Then that's where I'll start."

"*You're* not starting anywhere. I came to you for help, not to be left behind by you and your little bag of toys there, Rambo," Quinn said. "And I've already been by his place. He's not there."

Handfuls of retorts came to mind. Replies to her crack of my not going alone, and even her mention of Cailee's father not being at home.

More items that were again pushed aside in the name of protecting our most precious resource.

"Can we at least agree that I'm driving?"

Chapter Five

Now

Chancing one last pulse on the submersible, I move to where the textured soles of my wetsuit can touch firmly beneath me. Water shallow enough that I can push the SeaScooter without needing to use the throttle to nudge it toward the massive boulder serving as the cap on the west end of the beach.

A landmark that I can easily find if need be in the future.

A watery parking place, fully submerged, but at a depth shallow enough to be accessible if things really go sideways in the minutes ahead. A last resort for a quick escape if I come to discover that I have been set up.

Again.

Pushing it to arm's length before me, I release the craft, letting the combination of water and gravity carry it to the bottom just shy of the hulking stone.

Forward movement that I don't follow, coming to a stop with weight balanced to anchor me against the gentle ebb of the current coming to shore. Soft waves that try to nudge me on, having little effect against my heels dug into the sand and silt. Millenia of aquatic debris providing stable footing beneath me.

A stopping point for me to reach to the base of my spine and grasp the nylon cord holding my dive bag in place. Twisting it around so I can clutch it in both hands, I use my body to shield it from creating drag behind me.

For a moment, I make no attempt to go further. One final pause to collect myself, making sure everything is balanced, before starting anew through the shallow water. A heading aimed not for the guard still standing with his back to me, but around the back end of the boulder serving as a parking spot for the submersible.

A slow rise from the depths with my body bent forward at the waist. Effort to keep as much of myself hidden from view as possible.

Energy expenditure that causes my legs and lower back to burn. Water sluices down over me as I rise an inch at a time, like some sort of sea creature coming to shore.

Thirty yards away, the guard is oblivious to my presence. Between the cigarette clamped between his lips and the cellphone clutched in both hands, his senses are completely occupied.

Outside distractions, aided by the thin breeze passing over me, carrying away the slightest hints of sound from water droplets showering down around me.

A rare bit of good luck after what feels like two days of nothing but shit. A series of pitfalls and false starts finally coming to an end.

A goal I have been chasing since first leaving home, at last feeling like it may be within reach.

Or so I keep telling myself, not wanting to even consider the alternative.

With each step forward, I add a few extra inches of lateral movement. Additional distance toward the outer edge of the boulder placed there at the time of creation, having not moved more than a few inches from settling in the centuries since.

A darkened silhouette that is little more than a shadow. An ideal blind for me to press myself against, trusting that the neoprene suit covering all but my face will blend seamlessly against it.

An ideal place for me to spring a trap, sitting and waiting for my prey to come to me.

Little by little, the water level drops around me. Too low to be accommodated by any amount of hunch, my shoulders rise from the ocean, followed in order by my chest and torso.

Exposure that causes my pulse to increase and my teeth to clamp tighter on the nozzle of the air tank.

Flicking my gaze from the boulder to the guard and back again, I make sure I haven't been detected. A stealth incursion that he is completely unaware of as I make my way the last couple of feet.

Abandoning my abbreviated posture, I clutch the dive bag tight in both hands. My feet never rise from the silt beneath me.

Final precautions to ensure I make not a sound as I reach my destination and press myself flat against the cold stone. An ideal location to strip away the air tank and dive mask, stuffing them both into the bottom of the bag.

Items I hopefully won't need again, but don't want to discard just yet.

From it, I extract only a single item. Another from the stash in what my daughter keeps insisting on calling a tank.

A Taser X26C.

Otherwise known as a stun gun.

Chapter Six

Then

Everett Jory could not be classified as Quinn's ex-husband, because they were never married. He couldn't really even be considered an old boyfriend, as the two barely dated. Forced interaction after she turned up pregnant that lasted through much of Cailee's first year before finally the two of them both succumbed to their respective natures and became too much for one another.

In Everett's case, it was the extreme apathy with which he approached everything. A stoner's mentality without the stench of pot smoke constantly enveloping him.

A product of his upbringing, he was blessed with money and absentee parents who were far more interested in obtaining it than anything to do with him.

For my daughter, it was her residing at the opposite end of the spectrum. A tight grip on everything and everyone that could suffocate even the most relaxed person walking the planet, coupled with sudden bursts of tempestuousness.

A personality type it wasn't hard to determine was also a direct result of her formative years. A byproduct of what happened at the house that night as a singular redirecting event, along with the worst parts of both myself and my ex-wife, all manifesting inside a single form.

The most apt term to describe Everett was simply as Cailee's father. A co-parent who, to his credit, had stuck around and stayed involved. Paid his share. Even showed up at birthday parties and Christmases and put on the fake smile for the sake of his child.

Involvement I liked to think had nothing to do with a couple of visits I paid him not long after he and Quinn parted ways.

Subtle reminders that no matter how far away I might live, I was always around.

"Told you," Quinn said. A matter-of-statement that was her way of telling me I wasted time without having to say as much. A preference for brevity, paired with folding her arms as she stared out from the passenger seat. "He's not here."

Saying nothing in reply, I nudged my truck up through the center of the driveway. A tract of concrete wide enough to service the trio of garage doors abutting the south end of the house, though there were no vehicles present.

No signs of life anywhere for that matter.

No lights on behind any of the windows, blazing forth in the waning glow of late afternoon. No tendril of smoke curling upward from the chimney.

"Was he going anywhere for his birthday?" I asked. "Out of town for the weekend or something?"

Again, Quinn snorted. A favored means of communication, followed by her stating, "How the hell should I know? We coexist, but it's not like we're friends."

Accepting the reply without comment, I gave the front of the place one more sweep. A check over the brick façade rising two stories tall, and the towering trees having dropped most of their leaves on the front lawn.

Telltale features of the throes of autumn in the Pacific Northwest, right down to the trio of pumpkins resting on the front steps.

"C has a room here, right?" I asked.

"Cailee," Quinn snapped, jerking her gaze over my direction. "You might call me Q, but she has a name. An actual girl's name, unlike the damn thing you picked out for me."

Rotating back to face forward, she added, "And yes, she does. Doesn't use it much now, but she was here at least every other weekend until last year."

Saying nothing in reply, I pushed open the driver's side door. Silent hinges that gave way to a puff of crisp air sliding across me and filling the cab of the truck.

A brisk intrusion that caused Quinn's ponytail to flutter as I stepped out and went for the rear door to the cab. A second smaller door folded inward, providing access to the bench comprising the backseat for the vehicle.

Room enough for two or three additional people, currently consumed by the bag I just repacked not a half hour earlier. A parcel I wasn't as concerned with at the moment, instead reaching to the middle drawer built into the bottom of the bench.

Storage for items that always stayed with the truck. Necessary implements in line with the vehicle itself, stowed away for moments just such as this.

To say nothing of the other compartments surrounding it, containing items of a far more violent nature.

Two of the many reasons why I had insisted on driving, the rest concerning the vehicle itself. A roving fortress of sorts that had been reinforced down to the chassis, meant to serve as a mobile base should ever it come down to it.

Measures that I prayed wouldn't be necessary, even as every internal warning light already seemed to be indicating otherwise.

"Jesus, I knew coming to you was a bad idea," Quinn muttered. Turned sideways in the front seat, she stared into the back, the look on her face matching the tone of her voice.

Revulsion, without the slightest hint of a veil.

"I already told you, Everett didn't do this. You don't need to go all Danny Rivers on him and break his leg. Sure as hell don't need whatever you've got in your little toy box there."

The first part of her comment was a second barb in as many minutes. A reference to a guy she dated before even Everett, who succumbed to a broken leg while they were together.

Yet another thing – like her name – to have been attributed to me over the years.

The back half of her comment I let linger while going straight for the rear corner of the middle compartment. Pulling out the tool I needed, I held it up for her to see, pausing just long enough to ensure it registered.

A pick gun.

One of the least lethal objects in the vehicle, ideally suited to where we were and what we needed to do.

"I know Everett didn't do this, but Cailee might have stayed here last night, which means there may be something telling us where she is," I said. Retreating a step back, I placed a hand on the smaller rear door, preparing to fling it shut, "And unless you have a key, this is the fastest way inside."

Chapter Seven

I meant what I said when I told Quinn that the point in going inside Everett Jory's house was to take a look at Cailee's room. Twenty years ago, I might have had some interest in scouring through his home. Seeing what he was into. How he spent his time and who he spent it with.

Hell, I did do that.

More than once.

This far removed, though, there was no point. Any suspicion I had of the man had long since faded. If anything, it had even turned to a bit of respect. Given the lack of oversight throughout his child-hood and the amount of resources that were available, it was amazing that things hadn't gone worse than they did.

I knew we weren't going to walk in to find him passed out in a drug-induced coma somewhere. I also knew he didn't dabble in the sorts of things that might have pissed someone off and gotten himself killed or his daughter kidnapped.

He sure as hell didn't work in the type of field I used to, resulting in evil men with a worse crew showing up in the middle of the night.

What I really wanted was exactly what I told Quinn, which was to see if there was anything in Cailee's room that might give us a heading. Signs of recent passing that could tip us off where she might be, allowing us to bypass having to find her father first.

Photos of friends or places where she may be holed up. Hand-written notes with names or phone numbers we could reach out to.

Anything that might get us that much closer to her.

A goal that was never that realistic, but was worth the twelve minutes we spent pursuing it. Low-hanging fruit that turned out to be rotten, leaving us right where we were before pulling up in front of the home bordering somewhere between a house and a mansion.

A palatial spread plenty big enough for one man with a daughter as an occasional houseguest. A home made possible through an upfront lump sum gifted from his family's wealth, supplemented with monthly payments from his own work.

"Okay, now what?" Quinn asked. The first words since leaving the house, stated with no small amount of accusation.

An audience member at a magician's show, disbelieving every act while trying to figure out how it was done. A personal vendetta to ruin the big reveal, proving it was all a con.

As if what I spent a career doing, finding people who didn't want to be found, was a ruse. An act made possible through sleight of hand and a couple of fancy tricks.

Back in our respective seats in the front cab of my truck, I had already stowed the pick gun back into place. A return to its usual position between sleeves of cobra cuffs and a stun gun, figuring there was a decent chance it would be needed again before we were done.

Careful placement to ensure it could be found when needed.

Forced movements done through little more than muscle memory. Practiced behavior from a different time, allowing my active mind to focus on what we were up against. A scenario in which we still didn't have concrete evidence that anything heinous had taken place, but we sure as hell didn't know for sure that it hadn't either.

A situation that was already bad enough to cause Quinn to seek me out, growing worse with each additional moment. Time without further contact, during which Cailee could be getting further away, or unspeakable harms could be befalling her.

Acts that I had to force from my mind as I took my cellphone from the middle console.

"When was the last time you tried the number Cailee texted from?" I asked. A question posed with my head down, focus on the screen before me.

"While you were pilfering through her room," Quinn sniped. "Still off. Why?"

Ignoring both her comment and the question, I said, "Give me Everett's cellphone number."

"Why?" she asked again.

"Because as of right now, they've both vanished," I answered.

Glancing up, I was able to watch in real time as the explanation landed with her. A classic parent mistake of fixating only on Cailee, to the point that she hadn't considered that Everett was technically missing as well.

Radio silence that could be merely coincidental, a part of some elaborate birthday celebration, or could be very telling as to Cailee's disappearance.

Exhaling audibly, Quinn dropped her attention down to the device clutched tight in both hands. Just as she did on the dock earlier, she attacked it with either thumb, tapping out a series of commands before rattling off a string of digits.

Numbers I punched into the browser up on my own screen.

"What are you doing?" Quinn asked. Raising hers if a few inches in her seat, she leaned across the middle console to get a better view. "Tracing his freaking phone?"

"You'd be surprised how easy the damn things are to track," I answered, staring down at the glowing screen. A plain white background with a blue circle in the center, rotating to display progress.

An ongoing search that lasted the better part of a minute, ending with a visual schematic appearing on screen. An overhead view of a map with a red marker in the center, pointing to an address in Lake Stevens.

Muttering it to myself one time after another, I reversed out of the tracking program. A quick return to the internet home screen where I input the address, the site needing only a fraction of the previous one to spit out an answer for us.

"The Fireside Inn," I read aloud, tilting the screen so Quinn could see it from her raised perch in the passenger seat. "Ever heard of it?"

For the first time all day, the slightest hint of mirth creased her visage. A wan smile that died as fast as it appeared.

"Oh, yeah. That's a favorite of his." Falling back into her seat, she added, "Must be five hundred rooms in there, though. Your little trick get close enough to find which one he's in?"

"No," I replied, reaching out and twisting the keys in the ignition. "That's your job."

A few feet away, I heard her scoff. "My job? How the hell am I going to do that?"

"You two share a kid," I said, dropping the gearshift into reverse and beginning to back down the drive. "Be creative."

Chapter Eight

Even from my perch just inside the entrance of the Fireside Inn, I could see the red glow of the poor girl behind the counter. A woman young enough to still be in graduate school or even college, working the evening shift to help make ends meet while finishing her degree.

Someone who likely had a textbook or flashcards on the desk in front of her, just hoping to get through the interaction with Quinn as quickly as possible and get back to her studies. A simple following of procedure, denying the request for guest information, that quickly spiraled beyond her control.

A situation that would have been easier for her to handle during normal business hours, when there might be a security guard or a manager around for her to call out to, but left alone for the rest of the evening, she didn't really have a choice but to give in.

I had been on the receiving end of my daughter's threats before. An unpleasant experience even when deserved, let alone when taking punishment on behalf of someone else.

In this particular case, an imaginary cheating husband who Quinn knew was shacked up somewhere on the grounds with his little whore. A slight twist on reality that was played to dramatic effect, emphasizing all the right buzzwords.

Phrases that reverberated through the cavernous lobby as Quinn shouted them out, demanding the attention of the handful of guests passing through. A complete standstill that put all focus on the front desk.

And drew the vast majority of the receptionist's blood to her otherwise pale features.

"Subtle," I muttered as we stepped off the elevator on the tenth floor. The top level of the structure, providing ample views of the parking lot through the series of windows passing by on our right.

Building placement meant to maximize the view of the area's eponymous lake and the same mountains I was staring at earlier to paying guests behind the doors filing by on the left.

"Worked, didn't it?" Quinn fired back.

A question I took for rhetorical that she wasn't about to let go unanswered, muttering, "That's what I thought," before abruptly stopping at a door in the exact center of the floor. Placement no doubt affording the best vantage to the natural features outside.

One of the perks of the wealth Everett had been born into.

Not that I believed for an instant that what was going on behind the door had anything to do with admiring the view.

Activity that Quinn either didn't realize or didn't care about as she balled her hand into a fist and pounded the side of it against the door. Hammering it three times, she paused for just a moment, then unleashed another trio.

Six in short order that evoked some sort of response from the opposite side. A muffled answer that only made Quinn hit harder, giving up on her fist for an open-palmed slap.

"Dammit, Everett, I know you're in there! Open the-"

It wasn't hard to figure out how the rest of the line was going to go, even as it was cut short by the door swinging open to reveal the man we were there to see. Completely naked save the sheet that was wrapped around his waist, one hand clutched it tight at his hip while the other rested on the edge of the door.

Skin flush from previous exertion, his bare chest pulled in and out as he drew in sharp breaths. Plates supported by the faint outline of abs that grew more or less pronounced with each breath.

Curly hair askew, he stared out, his eyes wide.

"Quinn?! What the hell? How did you even..." The start of a question that was just as easy to determine the rest of, stopped short as his gaze landed on me.

Eyes widening, his jaw sagged. A bit of color receded from his cheeks, creating a stark contrast with his bare chest.

"Rand," he muttered. "I mean, Mr. Bryant."

"Like I told you last time, Everett, Bear is fine," I replied, handing him the nickname that had been my chosen moniker since my father first used it on that hunting trip when I was just a kid.

A birthright when born with the last name Bryant in the state of Alabama, even if there was no familial connection.

"Can we come in?"

Still visibly trying to process the shock of someone beating on the door and the equal surprise of seeing us both standing outside, he didn't immediately reply.

"It's about Cailee."

His entire body went rigid as he slid his gaze from me to my daughter. "Is she okay?"

"We don't know. We can't find her," Quinn said. "We thought she might still be with you, but based on what I'm staring at..."

"Still with me?" Everett repeated without registering her insinuation, his features finally shifting from his initial shock, this time moving into confusion. Folds of skin piled up around his eyes as he tilted his head to the side. "What do you mean-"

"Hey," I inserted, cutting off yet another obvious question. A painfully slow conversation that I attempted to hurry along, raising a hand and gesturing to the open hallway beside us. "Can we do this inside, please?"

"Oh, yeah, of course," Everett said. Taking a step back, he held the door wide, letting Quinn and me both pass through. Closing it in our wake, he added, "Just give me a second to get dressed," before ducking into the bathroom standing adjacent to the entrance.

Standard placement that was about the only thing consistent between the room we were in and most hotel fare, right down to the young Filipina woman with a curtain of glossy black hair standing between the sofa and flatscreen television. Hugging a pillow to cover her bare figure, she stared at us with wide eyes.

"Hi," she managed to get out. A single word, paired with a nervous giggle. "I'm Danila."

"You're naked," Quinn said without reciprocating the introduction. "Go get dressed."

Jerking her head upward, she pointed with her chin toward the door on the far end of the room. An entryway into the bedroom comprising the back half of a palatial suite. Multiple spaces all strung together, meant to best maximize the floor-to-ceiling windows lining the entire wall.

Optimal viewing for the lake already beginning to reflect the lights of town and the mountains resting beyond that. A sweeping panorama, to be enjoyed from the lavish trappings surrounding us. Thick carpeting on the floor. Artwork with gold frames on the walls. A crystal chandelier overhead and a stone fireplace spitting out gas-fed flames beside us.

A place that would easily rank as one of the nicer homes I'd ever been in, with a price tag that had to have been four figures a night.

"Sure as hell not how I spend my birthdays," Quinn muttered once the girl was gone and it was back to just the two of us.

One of the few statements made in our brief time together that was neither a question nor a derisive comment that I let linger as I padded across the room. Peering out through the windows, I put my focus on the assortment of lights dotting the top of the lake below.

Twinkling dots, each representing a dining establishment or apartment or even another hotel room just like this one. Thousands of possibilities as to where Cailee could be, with many millions more covering the greater Seattle area to the south.

An unfathomable number of spots where one lone girl could be hiding.

Or, even worse, held against her will.

A search that was nothing short of impossible, needing to start funneling inward fast.

"Sorry about that," Everett said, his voice arriving just an instant before his reflection appeared in the window beside me. Movement that pulled my focus the opposite direction to see him heading our way in a pair of gym shorts and dri-fit pullover.

Garments that were likely left behind after an earlier workout, grabbed up to save him from having to make the trip all the way to the bathroom.

If there was any lingering anger over our sudden intrusion, he didn't display it. Same for the bit of fear that graced his features at first spotting me in the hall.

Emotions that had fallen away, leaving only concern behind. Worry that creased his brow, made more obvious as he ran a hand through his hair, letting the curls fall back atop his scalp.

"You say Cailee is missing?"

"Worse than that," Quinn said. "We think she's in trouble."

Flicking his gaze between us, Everett moved for his phone on the coffee table in the center of the room. Snatching it up, he went at it the same way Quinn had earlier, frantically beating on the screen with his thumbs.

"Sorry about the missed calls. Phone was on silent," he muttered without looking up. An apology that didn't need further explanation from him or comment by us, both sides letting it go there.

His focus firmly on the device, he kept at it another moment, presumably searching for word from Cailee, before snapping his gaze up. "What makes you think she's in trouble?"

"She texted me that she was hungry from an unknown number," Quinn replied.

From where I was standing, I could see Everett's jaw sag. Enough of a reaction to reveal that he was familiar with the practice of using a safe word, and even knew what it was.

An extra bit of gravitas that landed hard as he held the phone before him, motionless until the faint call of a mechanized voice could be heard.

"Straight to voicemail," he whispered, tapping the screen once to end the call before slowly lowering the phone to his side. "When? What happened?"

"No clue," Quinn snapped, content to take the lead for us. "I woke up this morning and found the text, been running around like a bat out of hell ever since trying to find both of you."

Across from us, the bedroom door cracked open. A silent movement of no more than a foot, allowing the same young woman we had seen upon arrival to slip through.

Her diminutive frame wrapped in a fluffy robe, she took just a single step forward and came to a stop, folding her hands before her.

Forward movement that drew Everett's gaze her way, even as he asked, "This morning? Meaning she sent it after you guys had dinner last night?"

With just two short questions, I could feel my core draw tight. A clench in response to what I knew came next.

The realization that not only were we no closer to Cailee, but we had sacrificed a lot more than just the earlier twelve minutes this time.

"We didn't have dinner last night," Quinn replied, the confusion in her voice making it clear she hadn't yet put things together. "She said she was meeting you for your birthday."

Pulling his gaze away from his lady friend, Everett fixed his focus on Quinn. "She told me she was meeting you for Thursday dinner, like you guys do every week. She and I aren't getting together until Sunday."

Chapter Nine

"Who the hell are you?"

Now

The amateurs always lead with a question. The young ones brought up in a world where every thought they have ever had has been broadcast to the masses courtesy of the phone in their hands. A conduit to dozens of different media outlets, all just waiting to gobble up whatever bits of random jargon come to mind.

Availability that has long imbued them with the belief that the rest of the world doesn't just want, but *needs,* their opinion. Every thought they've ever had, given a platform and an audience.

Self-righteousness so ingrained that when the spindly jackass in black tactical attire opens the door to the guesthouse and sees the Taser X26C aimed at him, his first response isn't to reach for his own weapon. It isn't to go diving out of the way, looking for cover.

Hell, he doesn't even get mad or cuss at me or scream out into the night for help that might be patrolling the grounds nearby.

It's to ask me a damn question. Open a dialogue between the two of us as if we're dating and he's texting to ask what I want to do tonight.

A question that does the impossible, pissing me off even more than I already am. The thousandth infraction compiled and crammed into the last couple of days, leaving me with zero pause as I pull back on the trigger, sending the pair of barbed projectiles across the small gap between us.

Electrodes connected by coiled wire that unspools through the open doorway. Loops that extend like a snake striking, making it the better part of their fifteen-foot range before hitting their target.

Twin contact points easily penetrating the dark pullover he wears, piercing the skin of his chest plates. Conduits allowing more than fifty thousand volts to surge into his system, his entire body seizing on contact.

A marionette with the strings cut, balanced precariously as every muscle clenches involuntarily. An overload to the central nervous system causing every fiber and striation along his exposed neck and hands to stand out before gravity eventually takes over and he topples to the side.

His eyes bulge. Saliva pours from the corner of his mouth, streaking across his cheek.

The faint smell of burnt flesh wafts into the air.

A combination that is still far better than this asshole deserves. A non-lethal option chosen only for the sake of its silence, helping maintain my cover for the time being.

An outcome that the people he works for won't be so fortunate to share, should our paths cross in the short time I remain on this damned island.

Ten seconds after sending the electrodes hurtling between us, I release the trigger on the weapon. Ejecting the spent cartridge from the end of it, I pull the next in line from the bottom of the handle and jam it home.

The taser equivalent of switching to a new magazine. The best I can hope for with a weapon that only holds a single round at a time.

The third of six that I have available, the first used on the guard patrolling the rocky outcropping where I breached the shore nine minutes ago. Four more shots to be used as insurance for anyone else who might be lurking inside the structure.

Defenses I don't anticipate, most of the muscle already on the island tonight sure to be concentrated around the main house. A skeleton crew to sweep the grounds a day early, the rest set to either show up in the morning or – more likely – to arrive with the guests tomorrow.

A gathering of deplorables under the banner of an uneasy truce. The reason I chose to come now instead of waiting, looking to exploit the situation and be gone before anyone is the wiser.

Provided I get my ass moving in time to make that happen.

The front tip of the taser extended before me, I cross over the threshold into the guesthouse. Moving no more than a couple of inches inside, I put my back to the outer wall and sidestep to the right a single pace. Far enough to allow me to nudge the door closed, extinguishing the stripe of bright light thrown across the stone path behind me.

A vantage giving me a full view of the interior of the structure. A space outfitted to serve its intended purpose, with leather furniture arranged in a wide horseshoe and a stone fireplace along the back wall. Overhead, light is provided by a wrought iron chandelier.

A rustic vibe not a great deal unlike my own home or the cabin I spent last night in.

The obvious exceptions being the man lying prone on the floor at my feet and the very specific cargo I hope to find stored somewhere inside. Back bedrooms or a basement or something worse I'd rather not consider.

Not with my ire already redlined, my pulse thrumming in line with the clock ticking in my head.

The taser extended at shoulder height before me, I swing it in a complete arc. A pass from left to right and back again, ensuring that the man was the only one assigned to guard the entrance. Nobody else has heard his fall and is about to come running in. No one is hiding behind the sofa or the wet bar sprouting from the wall to my left.

A quick check to ensure I am alone before releasing my left hand from the weapon. Rushing forward a pair of steps, I drop to a knee beside my fallen adversary. Jerking my shoulders to the side, I allow the strap of the dive bag I am wearing like a pack to swing free.

A movement practiced thousands of times before, muscle memory taking over. A sequence that rushes back despite the years since it was last performed. Hands wrapped in the textured gloves of the wetsuit go straight for the bottom, feeling around but an instant before extracting a pair of cobra cuffs from within. Double locking restraints much stronger than the usual zip ties.

Another item selected with purpose from the cache in the backseat of my truck.

Another layer of precaution, ensuring me the time to escape without anybody else on the island being aware of my presence.

Shooting my left hand out before me, I mash the palm of it into the man's shoulder. An open-handed strike sufficient to force his weight over, rolling him from his shoulder onto his stomach.

A half revolution he goes through without offering resistance, despite being more than thirty years younger and weighing at least as many pounds more than me. The stun gun has created a complete confusion of his nervous system, making it impossible for him to even open his mouth to call out, let alone fight back.

An inability to control his faculties enabling me to twist his arms up behind him, his arms flopping helplessly as I slide the cuffs over his wrists and cinch them into place. Same for as I push him back over, grabbing up the roll of duct tape stowed inside the bag and use it to cover his mouth and encase his ankles.

Incapacitation that is not nearly as thorough as Mick just last night, but will do what I need it to. A means of sidelining him for the brief window between his recovery from the taser and my ass getting off this rock.

Never to return.

Leaving him laying right where he fell, I pull the top closed on the bag and swing it back up into position. Bouncing twice to center its weight along my spine, I grab up the X26C from the floor and extend it before me as I begin to rise, returning to my previous combat stance.

A conditioned pose as I again scan my surroundings. Sweat streams down over my features, settling into my brows and resting salty across my lips.

In my head, the clock continues to run, now up to twelve minutes and counting. A constant reminder of the situation I am in. The ongoing balancing act between urgency and prudence.

The need to not give in to my baser desires and descend upon the man at my feet. A physical manifestation of the evil I've spent the last couple days chasing.

A representative for the reason I am on this island, giving me something to begin unleashing some of the wrath I feel.

Precious release that will have to settle for a single stomp as I drive my heel into the side of the man's knee, the force of the impact traveling all the way to my hip. A shot that causes his eyes to again bulge as his entire body convulses.

The same exact response given by his cohort down along the rocky shoreline.

Again, far better than either one of these assholes deserves.

A beating they are lucky to be avoiding, my focus on bigger matters at the moment.

"Alright, C," I whisper, ignoring my daughter's previous correction as I step over the guard's sorry ass and out into the room, "where the hell are you?"

Chapter Ten

Then

"Turn left, over there," Quinn said, extending a hand from the passenger seat. Just four words, added to a tally that was barely more than a dozen since leaving The Fireside Inn. A second stop that yielded even less than the first, not only failing to provide any new information, but eliminating a secondary means of tracking Cailee.

A situation worsened by the fact that my granddaughter had lied to both sides, leaving us with no obvious answers as to who might have last seen her or where she could be.

Quite possibly the only thing that could have heightened the concentrated anxiousness inside the cab of the truck. Tension that was plainly obvious in the simple command from my daughter.

Urgency that was starting to rear within me as well, no matter how many times I told myself to keep it in check. Becoming emotional did absolutely nothing beyond blocking my ability to think clearly, that alone why Quinn had sought me out and what Cailee needed most right now.

Leaning forward, Quinn pointed across the intersection to the building on the corner that wasn't technically a dorm, but might as well have been. A structure that rose a half dozen floors above the pavement and was more windows than concrete, most of them glowing bright.

Basic interior lamps, supplemented with strings of decorative lights. Bulbs of varying sizes normally reserved for the holiday season, brought out early in the name of interior décor.

Personal touches, added on the cheap.

Located two blocks east of the University of Washington's main campus, the place held itself out to be a standard apartment complex. A building with hundreds of available units, ranging from studios all the way up to three bedrooms.

A potential hunting ground for pedophiles or predators, thwarted by the fact that only students were allowed to apply.

One of many facts I picked up during research when Cailee moved into the place just a couple of months ago. A relocation after a freshman year spent in the dorms, hoping – I assumed – to avoid the housing assignment process for something close by with her best friend.

Details I wasn't even sure if Quinn was aware of, not about to state them out loud and let it be known how much attention I had continued to pay, even after her tirade a year and a half before.

Not that it seemed to have done a lot of good, all of my preparation still resulting in the one thing in the world I wanted least.

"There are some visitor parking stalls down front, by the lobby," Quinn added. Information that I was also aware of but didn't bother pointing out, content to keep whatever emotion we both carried aimed outward.

Anxiety that was sure to grow worse moving forward as we chewed through hours we didn't have. Extra time on a tally that started sometime last night, fast approaching a full twenty-four. Halfway to the vaunted forty-eight-hour threshold, at which point the odds of finding a kidnap victim or even the people responsible dropped precipitously.

An invisible barrier I had spent a career trying to beat, mashing my head against it too many times to count.

One made to seem that much more daunting now by the fact that on the other side of it was a void threatening to consume one of my own. A girl I had never so much as spoken to beyond a few stray words. Manufactured meets in public places such as the Starbucks three blocks away that she loved to hit most mornings before class.

More information that I didn't dare share with my daughter as I swung the truck through the intersection and pulled in.

"How are we going to do this?" I asked, easing the truck into one of three slanted spots in front of the building.

The instant it became apparent that Everett knew even less than we did, our attention had turned to next steps. Leaving him and his most recent romantic dalliance to pack up and head home where they could keep an eye and ear out for Cailee, we had gone straight down to the truck, intent on following the most logical progression.

The place where Cailee spent most of her time and was known to have been at some point yesterday.

Where any stray bits of information that might be useful would be located.

"I'm about to-" Quinn said, her phone clutched in both hands before her. The start of an answer I assumed included telling me she was going to text Cailee's roommate to come get us, interrupted by the sight of a pair of young ladies exiting the building.

Girls in leggings and baggy sweatshirts with canvas bags thrown over a shoulder. Bright colors to match the yoga mats rolled tight and shoved down into the sacks.

Uttering not a syllable more, Quinn jerked open the door beside her. The start of a quick exit, her hand raised in the air.

"Hey there! Do you girls mind holding that for us?"

Delivered in a tone I had never once heard my daughter employ, I couldn't help but pause as I climbed out from behind the wheel. A quick check to ensure that singsong note was actually emitted from

Quinn as she jogged up onto the curb, her ponytail swinging behind her.

A momentary shedding of the panic and worry that had clung to her throughout the day.

Even the sheer animosity that had been aimed my way for the two and a half decades before.

A fleeting glimpse of what she might have been like if I had never heard the name Marcel Bardette. If I had decided to be a banker. Gone to law school.

Done damned near anything else in my life besides deciding to hunt down monsters, unintentionally inviting them to our door.

"Hey there, Ms. Coyle," the closest one said, employing the moniker my daughter had taken on when she and her mother moved west. A return to my ex-wife's maiden name that my daughter – and now her daughter – had glommed onto as well. "How are you?"

"Wonderful," Quinn replied, continuing the charade with a word I had never once heard her use. "What are you ladies up to this evening?"

"Just heading off to get in a quick class," the girl on the left said. A brunette with her hair pulled back into a ponytail, the rubber band at the base of her skull barely able to contain the tangle of curls.

"You know, have to look good before heading out later tonight," the first one added. A young woman who seemed a carbon copy in every way save the color of her hair, with locks so blonde they were almost white. "Homecoming weekend."

"How about you?" the brunette added. "You here for the festivities?"

"No, no," Quinn said, turning her body to the side and letting the girls drift past as she held the door. A subtle move, feigning interest while managing to switch positions with them. "We're just stopping by to say hi and drop off a few things for Cailee. Have you seen her?"

"Not today," the blonde answered. An oversized smile graced her features as she tilted her head back, letting the ponytail drag across her shoulder blades as they continued to inch further from the door. "Rough night last night, so this is my first time out today."

"Hey, that happens!" Quinn said, matching the luminosity of the girl's smile.

Performative art that I was unable to match with much more than a flicker at the corner of my mouth.

"Probably again tonight!" the brunette replied, setting all three to laughing as the gap between them widened even further.

Hearty chuckles that still hung in the air as Quinn fluttered her fingers at them in farewell and called, "You girls have fun this weekend!"

"Thanks!" they replied in unison, each raising a hand before turning as one and heading toward the parking lot.

An entire interaction lasting no more than a couple of moments. A rare bit of levity at a time when it felt woefully out of place.

Mirth that evaporated from my daughter as fast as it had arrived, ending with her motioning me inside. "Come on, let's get to the elevator before I have to talk to anybody else."

Saying nothing in reply – about her comment or the little display she'd just put on – I did as instructed. Silence that continued as we stepped into the elevator and made our way to the fifth floor, stepping out into a wide corridor with walls painted tan. Carpet with swirls of cranberry and gold covered the floors. Every so often, there were small additions made by the respective apartment residents.

Rugs lined with drying shoes. Small autumn spreads of pumpkins and gourds. Even a couple of side tables already bearing dishes filled with Halloween candy.

Items that mixed with the faint sounds of music and conversation behind many of the doors, even if there was nobody else visible. A lack of others that made it easy for us to race-walk the length of the floor, making it nearly to the far end before stopping at a door with a fall wreath framing the peephole and a rug on the floor instructing us to wipe our paws.

Details that I took in at a glance as Quinn stepped forward and knocked three times against the hardwood. Taps that weren't nearly as aggressive as those employed at the Fireside Inn earlier, but still could be heard reverberating within.

Contacts firm enough to draw out the sound of footsteps approaching on the opposite side, ending with the door swinging open to reveal a young girl with mocha skin and wavy hair held in a wide braid at the back of her skull.

Vivian Crane. A chemistry major from a good family in Tacoma who almost always went by the shortened Viv. A girl who Cailee met last year when they were assigned to the same freshman dorm and had been inseparable from ever since.

More information I wasn't supposed to know. Baseline data I had collected, even if my daughter's demands last spring had meant I took a far less active role in my oversight.

A conscious step back I was coming to regret more with each passing moment.

Eyes wide, Viv glanced between us. A quick look that bordered on hope before receding, her shoulders sagging as she said, "Hey, Ms. Coyle."

A greeting Quinn didn't bother reciprocating, instead replying, "I take it that means you still haven't heard from her either?"

Chapter Eleven

Outside of a couple of instances just like this, when I needed to question a potential witness about something I was working on, the last college dwelling I was in was damned near forty years ago. A different time and place when the rooms resembled military barracks and those of us who lived there all played one sport or another.

A separate living space that other students liked to whisper about. Claims of favoritism. Special treatment. Perks for the neanderthal athletes.

Whatever they could come up with. Thinly veiled jealousy, tinged heavily with outright despisal for those of us who didn't have rich parents paying our bills.

In reality, it was a place that their parents – or board members who thought just like them – had set aside to make sure we stayed in our one little corner of campus. Accommodations that were barely a notch above meager, worse even than what I spent my first couple of years with the Navy in.

A place that we all loved because it also represented a way for us to stay far away from everyone else as well. A mutual disdain that both sides pretended to put away when it was rivalry week each fall before retreating back to our respective niches.

Class warfare there was no sign of inside the complex that my granddaughter called home.

Even less, the militaristic furnishings that I had once been saddled with, the interior of Cailee and Viv's room resembling a high-end hotel. Décor and design that weren't quite as nice as what we'd just rousted Everett and his paramour from, but were definitely better than any chain establishment in the country.

Space enough to house four or five, set aside for just two nineteen-year-old girls. The start of false expectations that I couldn't imagine was doing anybody much good, but wasn't about to point out.

Others might be the type to walk into someone else's home and insult them, but I sure as shit wasn't.

Especially when I was there because I needed their help to begin with.

"When was the last time you did see Cailee?" Quinn asked. A variation of the same question asked before we'd even all relocated to the living room comprising the central third of the apartment.

A three-person convoy moving from the doorway inside the apartment after the initial letdown by both sides of realizing Cailee wasn't with the other. Even worse, that neither had seen her.

A bit of disappointment followed by quick introductions. Forced niceties by my daughter as she attempted to keep the same voice used downstairs to gain entry, this time while trying to introduce me as her uncle.

A fictitious connection close enough to explain my presence, without spawning further questions.

Namely, about a grandfather I was sure she and Cailee had both said was long dead.

"Yesterday," Viv said. Leaving the sofa to Quinn, she took an armchair on the far end of the living room. A matching set in gray with peach throw pillows to match the rug on the floor, paired with a coffee table and rattan chair. Seating for as many as half a dozen, all grouped around a flat screen television larger than the windshield of my truck.

On the walls were collage picture frames of differing sizes and arrangements. Photos of Cailee and Viv engaged in various activities, often with many others included.

Faces I couldn't help but study, searching for anyone who looked like they didn't belong. Anybody in the background appearing to pay a bit too much attention.

Force of habit, pulled back to the fore in an instant.

"I have a late lab on Thursdays that doesn't start until five and goes until nine," Viv replied. "After that, a group of us were starving and hit the student union, so I didn't get back until almost eleven."

Lifting her palms toward the ceiling in a sort of shrug, she added, "By that time, Cai was long gone. I knew she had dinner plans, so I didn't think anything of it, but after you called, and I wasn't able to get ahold of her either..."

Again, she did the thing with her hands. A move that was almost apologetic, matching the oversized eyes as she glanced my way.

"Where'd she tell you she was going?" I asked.

"Said it was her dad's birthday, so she was going up to Lake Stevens," Viv replied. An instantaneous response, rattled off without pause or forethought.

A truth, told without needing to recall a shared lie.

Sliding my focus to the side, I fixed my stare on Quinn for a moment. A shared look, each of us recalling what was uncovered at The Fireside Inn barely an hour earlier.

The misdirection fed to both her and Everett, now expanded to include Cailee's roommate.

Subterfuge that was clearly done with a goal in mind.

"Did you believe her?" I pressed.

"Not at first," Viv admitted. Nodding toward Quinn, she added, "But then I remembered you guys always meet on Thursdays, so I figured it must be legit for her to miss."

Again, Quinn and I shared a look. A quick glance to ensure that the other heard what was just shared, registering the same inconsistency.

"Where did you think she was going?" Quinn asked.

"Truthfully? I figured she was going to see Lee again, but just didn't want to admit it."

"Who's Lee?" Quinn asked.

A question posed just an instant before I added, "Why wouldn't she want to admit it?"

Twin asks that came in from opposite directions, pulling Viv's attention both ways. A quick jerk from Quinn on the sofa to me standing in front of the television, her eyes growing a bit wider as she took each of us in.

"Uh..." she began. A low sound that resembled a grumble as she pulled her gaze away from me, returning her focus to Quinn.

A familiar face she focused on before explaining, "Lee is this guy we met at the football game last weekend. He was standing near us and they started talking, ended up kind of hitting it off."

Flicking her focus my way, she added, "I know they texted some for the next couple of days, and even went out on Tuesday. I thought maybe she wouldn't want to admit she was already seeing him for a third time, like I might give her guff or something over it."

Returning to Quinn, she finished with, "But then I remembered the thing about you guys on Thursdays, so I figured her story had to be true."

Just as she did when answering our first questions, she lowered her gaze when she was done. Guilt that wasn't hers to bear, manifesting more with each passing moment that she had to sit and ponder what had happened.

Details she had no reason to suspect in the moment, now seeming too great to be ignored.

A feeling I could empathize with in a thousand different ways, both in this moment and every single one for the last twenty-five years.

"Do you know where we can find this Lee?" I asked.

"No," Viv replied. Giving her head a shake, she sent the braid swinging out from either side of her neck. "He was sitting in the student section, but I don't think he goes here.

"I'm pretty sure Cai has a picture of him in her room though, if that helps."

Chapter Twelve

"You know him, don't you?" Quinn asked, barely making it out of the elevator – let alone the lobby – before launching the question. An ask loud enough, and with just enough of her patented assertive flair, to draw over a couple of stares as we exited.

A question I let linger without response as we crossed the sidewalk and climbed back into the truck. Determined strides, driven by what we had just uncovered and the next steps it was sure to spawn.

"No," I replied simply. My turn to do as she had earlier, and let a short response relay the underlying sentiment.

Absurdity that didn't need to be pointed out.

No matter what kind of background presence I might have kept the last few years, there was no way I would have known a random kid that just showed up six days earlier.

What I did know was all the signs of a situation that looked like it was by design.

A guy who wasn't enrolled at the university showing up at a ball-game and working his way into the student section, where there were no assigned seats. The first of three outings in a five-day stretch, the most recent of which had her lying to both her parents and her roommate as to where she was going.

Behavior extremely out of character, culminating with her texting Quinn for help and then disappearing.

Warnings that were already going off like flashbulbs in my mind, even before seeing the photo of them at the game. A shot taken at just the right angle, revealing something I guaranteed Lee did not want seen.

An item that shifted my entire way of thinking and – by extension – how we were to approach things moving forward.

Yet another transition, this time moving away from the building emotion and returning to my background. Training and experience that refused to be ignored, given the image Viv had provided, now tucked into the pocket of my jacket.

"Then...?"

Again, I didn't bother answering her immediately. Slamming the reinforced door shut to effectively block any noise from getting in or out, I instead reached for my phone tucked into the middle console.

Thumbing it to life, I pulled up the address book. A repository of names and numbers, most of which I hadn't reached out to or heard from in years.

Work contacts. Men and women I had been in the grind with for decades. People who saw things the same way I did. Had been taught to process information the same as well.

A repository of contacts and information that wasn't as helpful this far from D.C., though I still had a few I could reach out to.

Folks who had kept hurtling forward on the manhunt carousel even long after I stepped off, each additional day widening the gap between us. Acquaintances who never feigned being friends, our proximity to each other being for professional reasons and nothing more.

Matters that I could only hope this trended close enough to to earn me a free pass. A favor granted by way of shared history in the face of a topic of mutual interest.

And if that didn't work, offering up some markers I'd been banking with hopes I would never need to cash them in.

Letting my daughter's unfinished question continue to hang, I scrolled most of the way through my saved contacts. Names I hadn't looked at in ages. Attached people that I hadn't thought about in just as long.

Memories that I didn't really want, held onto in case a moment like this ever arose.

"Wha...who are we calling?" Quinn pressed.

"*We* aren't calling anybody," I replied, parroting the tone my daughter used earlier when I told her where I intended to start.

A hint that this part was going to be mine alone to perform.

Finding the name I wanted, I exhaled slowly, allowing my thumb to hover above it for an instant. A quick moment to consider what I was about to do. The cost that would likely be attached.

An instantaneous assessment that ended with me pressing the pad of my thumb down, no amount asked in return for what I needed to do too great. No expectation of reciprocation or demands of *quid pro quo* too high.

That was the reason Quinn had come to find me. Why she was insisting on riding shotgun, even as it was clear she hated it.

No longer was this simply a matter of not being able to get ahold of my granddaughter. Cailee hadn't stayed out too late or decided to go on a weekend road trip with friends or any of the other things college students were known to do.

This was something bigger. More malevolent. The type of thing that trended toward what I had spent a lifetime dealing with, no matter how much I hated to admit it.

That's why I was here. Even without Quinn knowing it, that's why she had come to see me.

This was my role, and I would play the damned thing until I brought Cailee home.

"Yeah?" a gruff male voice answered. One that I used to hear on a daily basis, though had only come in contact with twice since relocating to the west coast.

One, a funeral three years ago for Ben Carmichael, the last remaining member of our original team near the old stomping grounds we all used to haunt.

The second, a quick meeting much closer to where I was sitting that had gone better than my last encounter with Quinn, but still hadn't given way to any further interaction.

Just as we both preferred it.

"Can you meet?" I asked.

A simple question that caused my daughter to jerk her attention up from the passenger seat, her left eyebrow arched.

"Are you asking me?"

"Not really," I replied.

Coded speak which drew Quinn's eyebrow up higher. A look of disapproval, matching the purse of her lips as she stared at me.

Precursors to what were sure to be more smartass comments.

"One hour."

"Same place as last time?"

"I'll be there."

Saying nothing more, I ended the call. A single tap on the red button at the bottom of the screen before depositing it in the cupholder in the middle console between us.

A drop that was barely complete before Quinn said, "What the hell did you see in that picture?"

Fifteen feet away, the same two girls we spoke to on the way in walked by. Done with their class, they each had smiles on their face, tall paper cups of coffee in hand.

Liquid caffeine for the night of shenanigans they alluded to earlier.

"And don't you dare say it was nothing," Quinn said. "You wouldn't already be calling up old buddies and talking in FBI code if that was the case."

Chapter Thirteen

Most people hear the name Hattie and immediately have images of an older woman come to mind. A kindly sort wearing an apron dusted with flour and a kerchief with curls spilling down around the edges. A grandmother who insists on treating everyone she meets like one of her grandbabies, foisting whatever the air is redolent with the scent of upon them.

A conjured mental image so strong, it very nearly brings with it the scent of apple pie. Meatloaf. Any other such culinary delight that people yearn for, even if precious few still possess the requisite skill to recreate them.

This Hattie is nothing like that.

This Hattie doesn't wear aprons. Has never once cooked. Whatever hair remains is buzzed short, trending heavily toward silver.

Hell, this Hattie isn't even a she. A fact made apparent when he first picked up the phone and answered in a brusque voice, pushing Quinn's eyebrows up high on her forehead.

A tone that was already a deep baritone, made worse by seeing my name pop up on his screen. A moniker loaded with history, calling back to both of our early days on the opposite coast.

Time long ago, before tragedy struck both our homes.

His, to an even greater degree than my own.

"Who is this guy again?" Quinn asked as we strode forward, bypassing the sidewalk for a path through the center of the street. Asphalt damp with the omnipresent Seattle mist, leaving behind just enough residual moisture to turn everything into a reflective surface.

A mirror, causing the assorted lights and signage around us to glow, illuminating our forward path.

The question was a renewal of the initial barrage fired after I got off the phone earlier. One after another demanding to know who I had called. What that had to do with the photograph we got from Cailee's room of her and her new beau.

Where we were going and how it would get us closer to finding my granddaughter.

"His name is James Hattinger," I replied. Pressing my chin to my shoulder, I gave the answer just barely loud enough for her alone to hear.

A force of habit for me.

A professional courtesy to Hattie, this the sort of meeting he definitely would not want anybody else to know he took, for a multitude of reasons that would only grow once we sat down and I told him why I called.

A quick answer, followed by returning my gaze to the glowing red letters hovering fifteen feet above the ground not fifty yards ahead of us. Three rows of six capitals each, offset to make room for the glowing white face of an enormous manual clock.

An overall design that had managed to become iconic, relaying the time and spelling out the words **PUBLIC MARKET CENTER**.

A site otherwise known to the rest of the world as Pike's Place. A tourist destination that had become synonymous with Seattle, welcoming tens of thousands of visitors each day.

A crowd to serve as easy cover, perfectly situated to mask two old colleagues sitting down for a quick cup of coffee.

A reprisal of our only other meeting on the west coast. A quick check-in when he first moved to the area two years before to let him know that I was around. A professional courtesy, offered to a man who had been a part of my team during the early days before splintering off to oversee a crew of his own.

"Oh-kay," Quinn replied. "And you think he has information about this Lee?"

"Maybe not Lee specifically, but he'll know about that thing I showed you in the picture," I replied. A quick answer while continuing to move forward, each successive step quicker than the one before. Strides feeding off the situation, and an impending meeting with a contact from my former life.

One of the few vestiges of the opposite coast present in Seattle, conjuring back memories by the handful.

Recollections that I was sure were far from pleasant for Hattie as well, neither one of us having made the least effort to stay in contact since that lone encounter.

Less a manifestation of bad blood, and more an unspoken agreement that some things were best left in the past.

For both of us.

"And you think he'll just open up and share with us?" Quinn pressed. More stream of consciousness, unable to tamp down whatever thought popped into her head.

"Not us," I answered, reiterating my point while first calling him. Quinn was here because it would be disrespectful – and a waste of time – to try and hide her.

A presence that Hattie was aware of going clear back to the Marcel Bardette incident.

Still, that didn't mean he would be amenable to the three of us sitting down for a chat.

Increasing my speed once more, I pulled a step or two past my daughter and hopped up onto the curb lining the sidewalk. A clear demarcation point, taking us from the relative quiet and spaciousness of the street, into the fray of the lower levels of the marketplace.

Multiple floors, all bisected by aisle-ways and crammed tight with vendors of every imaginable type. Butchers and fish mongers. Bakeries and florists. Artisans and souvenir shops.

A bustling hub of voices and activity serving thousands of people and seeing many times as much money change hands each day, with all of the assorted scents and sights to match.

Sensory overload, making it easy for me to pull up just shy of the famed fish market. Rows of fresh catch packed in ice, arranged in a sweeping semicircle and stacked three levels tall. One of the few centralized hubs of Pike's Place, packed tight with tourists waiting with cameras poised for the next show by the employees in double-knit sweaters and rubber waders.

Part-time sales experts, part-time performers who would soon start flinging whole cod and salmon back and forth to the eternal glee of the gathered masses.

"Stay here. I'll be right back."

"He's here?" Quinn asked. Shooting a hand out, she pinched the elbow of my jacket, keeping me from moving away just yet. "Where?"

Tilting the top of my head to the side, I said, "The high-top over by the coffee shop. In the suit."

Following my gesture, Quinn leaned forward to peer around me. "You mean the old guy, with the cane?"

Chapter Fourteen

I knew better than to launch right into the reason I called and asked Hattie to meet. I may have made a point of stopping Quinn short and waving to the man from across the room, but that didn't mean I had fully explained who she was or her role in this.

Information he could easily speculate on, but he sure as hell wouldn't be giving me anything I needed until he knew for sure.

"You remember my daughter," I opened, flicking a hand toward the opposite corner of the open foyer. A gesture and an explanation both steeped in brevity, hoping that it would help stem any further pressing.

A goal that was immediately proven unfounded by his brows rising, causing a quartet of folds to appear in the soft flesh lining his forehead.

An unspoken question, tinged with the closest thing his features could manage to surprise.

"Yes." Dipping my chin in an exaggerated nod, I added, "I'm sure you already figured this out, but she was the reason I moved here when I retired four years ago. She's also the reason I'm here now.

"She needs my help. I need yours."

Cutting his gaze to the side, Hattie stared past my shoulder, toward the place where Quinn and I first made ourselves known to him. A spot I told her to vacate the instant I walked away, but knowing her, she was still fixed in.

Stubbornness, mixed with concern.

The desire to find her daughter, and at the same time stick it to me in any way she could.

Without a doubt, Hattie remembered what happened twenty-five years ago. A part of my five-person team at the time, he was one of the first people I called to help collect the pair of dead bodies that littered my kitchen in the aftermath.

He was there through the long and sleepless nights that ensued as we searched for Bardette afterwards, and he was a part of the strike team that helped me repay the favor by showing up in the middle of the night and arresting the bastard in front of his own wife and young son.

The last remaining member of the team, the others having succumbed to disease, or pressures of the job, or – as was what brought us together just a few years ago before Hattie moved out here – a car accident.

A team of five young agents brimming with vitality, now whittled down to the two men sitting at a table in Pike's Place, each broken in their own way.

Even if Hattie hadn't been part of all that took place back then, he for sure would have heard the cautionary tale that spread across the Bureau within moments, reinforcing everything they'd told us throughout our training.

The very real risks we were up against every day. The threats that could arrive on our doorstep if we weren't always vigilant.

A scarlet letter I bore the shame of wearing, up until it was snatched away by what happened to Hattie and his wife and daughter years later, once he was running his own team. The victims of an organization far larger and more ruthless than Bardette known as The Council who had attached an explosive device to the bottom of their car.

A vehicle all three were supposed to be in, but Hattie had jumped out to grab the newspaper when it exploded. A fiery eruption of glass and steel that had taken his family in an instant, along with his ability to walk without the cane Quinn had first commented on.

His induction into a shared brotherhood neither of us wanted to be a part of.

"Doesn't seem possible," Hattie muttered.

A statement that needed no further clarification for me to know exactly what he meant. A sentiment similar to what I still felt each time I looked at Quinn.

Even more so, Cailee.

A passage of time that didn't seem believable. Time that had slipped away, turning them into adults, and the two of us into old men.

A transition that must have seemed especially pronounced to Hattie, having not seen Quinn in decades.

An unwanted reminder of his own losses, forever frozen in time.

"No, it does not," I agreed.

"What kind of help?" Hattie asked. One of dozens of questions he no doubt had. Things he didn't voice, likely out of fear for equal amounts coming back his way.

Inquiries as to how he was holding up or how he was enjoying his time on the west coast. A relocation far removed not just from the chaos of the nation's capital, but from everything associated with what had happened.

Daily remembrances of what he had lost. A constant deluge of memories on every corner. Places where he and his wife had frequented. Spots that he had taken his daughter to play.

Omnipresence that he had somehow held onto for years, burying himself in the job. Finding and eliminating every member of The Council responsible for what happened, followed by many others just like them.

Work he poured himself into before finally having enough and doing just as my family had, running as far from it as possible. A new location for his last couple of years on the job before he could retire with a full pension, pushed out the door the instant he reached a quarter century served, just as I had been.

A career that had turned him into a walking repository of criminal data, which was the reason I had reached out.

An encyclopedia regarding matters such as what I first spotted on the photo in Cailee's room.

"Information," I replied. "Nothing more, and nothing that can come back on you."

Sliding his focus back over, he fixed his hound dog stare on me. A doleful glower under the bright bulb hanging down over the table, highlighting every crease and crevasse in his face. Unflattering lighting, solidifying the thought I was having just moments earlier about our losing war with time.

Years of hard living, exacerbated by physical injury and emotional torment.

Fifty-six, going on ninety.

"I don't think I need to tell you," he said, "even for an old colleague, only the first one is free."

"You do not," I replied.

Once more, his focus pushed to the side. Another long look, visibly weighing the present, remembering the past.

"I'll do what I can," he eventually said. "But I don't need to tell you who runs the shop out here these days."

"You do not," I replied, knowing fully well what he was alluding to. A man named Otis Herbert who was a thorn in both our sides for years before jumping at the first chance to run his own office eleven years earlier.

Someone who – like Hattie – I had also sat down with when first moving to the area, though it hadn't been nearly as lengthy or as amicable. A box checked, with no intention of ever crossing paths again.

By either of us.

"He still a pain in the ass?" I asked.

"And then some."

Letting one corner of my mouth curl upward, I held the smile just long enough to let it be known we were in agreement. A tiny bit of mirth to build camaraderie before moving into the reason why I had called. Why we're currently sitting in Pike's Place, instead of extending the streak of days since last seeing each other.

Raising both forearms to the table between us, I rolled my left wrist downward. With my right index finger, I pointed to the tan skin, tracing the tip of it across the sun-bleached hairs.

"I'm looking into a marking," I began. Running the finger toward the ulnar bone at a diagonal, I added, "A brand. Looks like a triangle."

Completing the imaginary marking, I kept the underside of my arm resting atop the table. A blank slate for him to stare down at, envisioning what I had just outlined.

Silent contemplation that lasted several moments before he rolled his gaze back up my direction.

A dour stare, even more pronounced than just a minute prior.

"You're looking into it?" he asked. "I thought you said-"

"I did," I replied, cutting him off before he could finish. A damned Bureau man to the core, seizing on the slightest misstep. One word added that shouldn't have been.

An error on my part, immediately grasped by him and used for leverage. An extraction of information I wasn't trying to hide, but didn't necessarily arrive looking to divulge if I didn't have to.

Leaning a few inches from the table, I reached to the inner pocket of my jacket. From it I extracted the photo Viv had supplied for us and placed it down on the table, using my middle and index fingers to slide it across.

An image that Hattie made no effort to reach out and accept, instead leaning forward to inspect it, a deep cleft forming between his brows.

Taken less than a week earlier, it was – to my knowledge – the most recent photo of Cailee in existence. A shot of her in a purple and gold Washington Huskies sweatshirt, with her sandy brown hair pulled back and a bit of flush on her cheeks.

At her side was a young man that looked like he could be anywhere between twenty and thirty years of age. A guy with heavily gelled hair combed back from his forehead, and several days of growth lining a chiseled jawline.

Handsome, in a slightly non-conventional sort of way.

A look that would have immediately started to set off warning lights, even without the marking that first caught my eye. The very same one I just outlined for Hattie, visible on the back of the wrist draped around Cailee's shoulder.

A blemish that was both too pronounced and too neat to be a mistake.

Bent forward at the waist, Hattie didn't move for more than half a minute. Nose aimed downward, he remained perfectly motionless, committing every pixel to memory, before slowly rotating back up to face me square.

"She looks just like her mother," he eventually said. "A little like you, even."

A statement of recognition that I let pass, replying instead with, "You recognize the marking?"

"I do."

"What about the kid wearing it?" I pressed. "I'm told his name is Lee."

Once more, Hattie slid his gaze away from mine. A move that this time I assumed was meant to check out our surroundings. Make sure that nobody else was nearby, paying too much attention to our conversation.

A glance much quicker than the previous, ending with him saying, "Leland. At one time, the crown prince of the Doone family. A name that – as you may or may not know – is Scottish for-"

"Mountain," I mumbled, vaguely recalling seeing the name once upon a time. A known associate to someone that I was chasing, not rising to a level to warrant investigation themselves, but known to run in overlapping circles.

A bad sign, causing the tension I arrived with to climb another notch.

Same for the number of mental connections being made, none of them leading anywhere good for my granddaughter.

"Exactly," Hattie said. "Which is what that marking you see there is. Like you said, it's a brand, made by heating the tip of a knife to look like the outline of a mountain.

"A show of loyalty on the back of their wrists that can be covered by a watch or a shirtsleeve if need be, unlike some of these punks in street gangs that insist on tattooing their faces or necks."

As he spoke, my focus drifted down to the picture resting between us. Winnowed down onto the kid's left wrist, I stared at the ridge of furrowed skin, superimposing it against the information Hattie was sharing.

A shape that I wouldn't have immediately figured out on my own, but now that it had been pointed out, could not rightly deny. A mar on the skin no larger than a quarter or – as Hattie just mentioned – the face of a watch, making what Quinn and I were up against much, much worse.

An escalation that did not bode well for the hours ahead.

"What do you mean *at one time* he was the crown prince?" I asked, flicking my attention back up to Hattie.

"In order for there to be a prince, there has to be a court," Hattie replied. "Which very much ended when the king died a couple years ago."

"Ended?"

"Mhm," Hattie grunted, dipping his chin in a nod. "The Doones weren't your typical family enterprise. The old man, Liam, *was* the enterprise.

"When he passed, his wife Careen didn't want any part of it. Sure as hell didn't want her son near it."

My brows rose in surprise. "So it wasn't one of ours?"

"Nope." Flipping his thumbs upward in a move reminiscent of Viv earlier, he added, "And as far as we know, they've gone completely dormant since. Few of the most loyal have stayed on as security, but otherwise, they're doing what most widows and their kids are these days, living off the inheritance."

What he described wasn't the usual path for how these sorts of things progressed, but it wasn't completely unheard of.

More often than not, a death at the top created a multitude of vacuums. Gaping holes both internally and in the greater market that incited plenty of infighting. A mad rush for new parties to stake their claim, taking what they felt was theirs.

On rare occasion though, it did play out as Hattie was describing. Parties who had no interest in the trade or, more likely, were tired of doing everything required to maintain it.

An opportunity for retirement dropped into their laps that they were smart enough to seize.

"Where do I find them?"

"You planning on going after them?" Hattie replied.

"No," I said, blinking myself back into the moment. Shaking my head to drive home the point, I added, "I do need to talk to them, though. If they're out of the game like you say, shouldn't be a big deal."

Exhaling slowly through his nose, Hattie took up the cane leaning against his thigh. Clutching the handle of it tight, he used it to slide himself sideways from his chair.

"No," he conceded, "it shouldn't. But be forewarned, I can't guarantee they'll see it that way."

Chapter Fifteen

"Grant, is everything alri—"

Now

The question gets no further, cut off by me stepping from around the corner in the hallway and driving the butt of the stun gun into the side of the woman's head. A shot she never sees coming, hitting her just above the ear.

My preferred point of contact as many have found out the last couple of days, sending her brain ricocheting from one ear to the other. Her eyes roll upward as her eyelids flutter. Her knees turn to liquid, her legs unable to support her weight beneath her.

A free fall I just barely manage to catch before she drops to the woven runner stretched the length of the hallway. A patterned design to match the one inside the main entrance to the guesthouse.

Right down to the unconscious thug dressed in black sprawled atop it.

Exactly as I did with her partner before her, I drop to a knee by her side. A shooting base with the taser extended before me, allowing me to jerk my attention in either direction. Quick checks to again ensure that nobody else heard what just happened.

No additional support is about to come running in.

Seeing nothing, I make myself wait several extra moments. Additional checks, ensuring that I don't succumb to the adrenaline seeping into my system.

The wrath underpinning it, and the thousands of malevolent desires it has spawned in the last couple of days.

A forced pause that lasts almost a full minute before I repeat the process from the front room. The sequence of releasing my grip on the taser and sliding the pack from my back.

Cobra cuffs for her hands.

Duct tape for her mouth and ankles.

The decision to go with the knockout shot instead of firing the taser had nothing to do with the narrow confines of the hallway. Not the sound of her approach or the optimal hiding spot around the bend in the walkway, allowing me to hide from view.

Sure as shit had nothing to do with her being a woman, my approach tonight one of equal opportunity. Every single person on this island is considered an enemy with the lone exception of my granddaughter.

The choice was one of logic. Tucked away in the rear of the guesthouse, there was no need to waste one of my precious taser cartridges. Already, the six I arrived with have been decreased by two. That leaves me only four remaining, with the possibilities of needing to clear the second outbuilding and any additional guards roaming the island.

People and places with a lot greater need for silence than right here.

Considering dragging her body out of the way, hiding it in a closet or the hall bathroom I just passed, I decide against it. Effort I don't need to expend. Time I don't have to waste.

Patience I am in even less supply of, the cocktail of elicited responses within me making such a thing impossible. A mash of anger and adrenaline and anticipation. Hope and desire fused together as I rise from the floor, giving her one last parting shot on my way.

A blow to the side of her knee, matching those given to both of her colleagues already.

A vicious strike against bone and tendon, ensuring that if any of them wake up, they won't be going anywhere.

Another example of my firm adherence to equal opportunity.

Bringing the taser out before me, I resume the path I was on before hearing her approach earlier. An unexpected intrusion adding an extra four minutes to the running tally.

Just shy of twenty in total since I first stepped onto Fawn Island.

Knees flexed in a combat pose, I can just barely feel the tendinitis starting to flare. Years of abuse that has been added to tremendously in the last couple of days. Sudden exertion that no amount of working out can match, leaving me sore before I even arrived.

Fatigue that the adrenaline has been able to mask thus far, each successive moment bound to make it more pronounced. Competing responses, causing my body temperature to climb. Sweat paints my features, stinging my eyes.

Small annoyances I shove to the background, my focus on the hallway as I push forward. To either side, décor matching the living room out front slips by. Tables formed from logs stripped of their bark. Faux pine trees wrapped in strings of lights. On the walls are art prints of mountain forests and whitetail deer in wooden frames.

Details that again call to mind my own home. A place sitting barely a hundred miles away, but tonight feels infinitely further.

A spot my granddaughter has never been, my entire goal to get her back there by morning.

Slipping around the same corner I used for the ambush, my attention goes to a door standing closed at the end of the hall. Almost definitely the place where the woman was just coming from. The last available spot where someone could be held captive, based on the general size and layout of the structure.

A master bedroom, now repurposed into something much more heinous.

A site I can only hope Cailee is waiting, saving us both the time and excess of having to go to the other outbuilding, or even worse, the main house.

Seeing the door looming ahead of me, my pace increases. A nod to what might be tucked behind it and the clock I know is moving ever forward. A full third of an hour now passed, growing since I first set foot on this godforsaken rock.

Time during which I may have been able to move without detection, but eventually somebody is going to notice the trio of guards having gone silent.

An initial window that I can't rely on lasting forever. A benefit of my surprise attack, meaning the faster I find Cailee, the more distance I can put between us and this hellhole before anybody notices she is gone.

Moving heel-to-toe along the narrow space, I pause at a doorway set into the wall on my right. A cavernous opening spilling light into the hallway, making it easy for me to peer in and identify it as another bathroom. A quick glance to clear behind the door and shower curtain before stepping out again.

Strides that grow quicker still as I aim for the door at the end of the hall. A solid plank of oak carved to look as if it is made of four slats lined side by side and lashed together. The hinges and handle are made from wrought iron.

Expensive touches in line with the rest of the house.

Details I notice only because of the heightened state of my senses. Adrenaline and anticipation surging through me as I keep the taser raised to shoulder height. Releasing my left hand from the base of it, I turn sideways, reaching out and depressing the spoon on the handle.

The instant I hear it click, the latch disengaging, I press the pads of my fingers against the door and push. A tiny shove sufficient to nudge it inward as I return both hands to the taser, keeping it at the ready.

A weapon that is proven unnecessary, as the only thing aimed back at me is the bright light from the chandelier overhead. A harsh glare that washes over me, causing folds of skin to form around my eyes as I stare in at a macabre scene that I immediately wish I could unsee.

I was right to assume that the suite was the master. A spread nearly as large as the living room, replete with a fireplace in the corner and a four-poster bed in the center. Another from the same motif, bare logs forming the frame, rising almost to the ceiling.

I was also right to anticipate the space having been repurposed. A holding pen of some sort that I hoped would include my granddaughter. Maybe another girl or two, given that there were multiple guards stationed to watch over the place.

Party favors for the host. Perhaps an honored guest.

A thought that alone was enough to make my stomach turn, but fit with the events of the last couple of days. The manner of her abduction, and the assorted people involved.

But even that paled to what rests before me.

Crammed inside the bedroom are no less than ten girls. Children not even old enough to be called young women. Kids ranging from no more than the front edge of their teens up through high school age at the very oldest.

Lined across the bed and on an inflatable mattress on the floor, they are stacked up like candlesticks. Children who for the moment look like they are sleeping, all tucked beneath blankets.

No doubt the work of sedation, preparing them for tomorrow when they will be forced into revealing dresses and adorned with copious amounts of stage makeup.

Garish appearances to match someone's idea of a doll collection.

Personal playthings all fitting a specific look, clearly done with intention.

Not one of which is my granddaughter.

Chapter Sixteen

Then

I knew the very instant that I stood up from the meeting with Hattie that nothing good was going to come from what happened next. A lack of options that meant I was going to have to do something very foolish, exposing myself in a way that was risky as hell, even if it was unavoidable.

The circumstances of Cailee reaching out to her mother had already made a quick and happy resolution unlikely. Never before had she used the safe word they established, this time doing so from an unknown number that immediately went dark.

What one might already call a worst-case scenario, made even more so by all of the most obvious explanations being checked off in short order. Not only was she not with her father or her roommate, but she had lied to both about where she was going.

Measures that made her invisible to her parents for a little long weekend fun, never realizing that the guy she was cavorting with was at one point the heir apparent to a local crime syndicate. A family that the Bureau had been keeping tabs on for years. One that, to hear

Hattie tell it, at a certain point had a finger in damned near every-thing moving through the largest docks in the Pacific Northwest.

Such involvement likely being why seeing the brand had initially rang a bell for me, even if I couldn't exactly pinpoint how or why.

Details that were lost in a sea of similar cases, all filled with people I wouldn't want my granddaughter anywhere near, no matter if they were supposedly dormant or not.

Facts all that were now making it that much harder for us to try and find her. Unforeseen dangers, manifesting in the worst way possible, to the point that she had almost done the hard work for her abductors.

A conglomeration of things now playing against us, leaving us with a dwindling timeframe and already down to calling in favors and weighing terrible options. Choices that were more like last resorts, such as marching straight from Pike's Place to the mansion of Careen Doone.

A home only in recent years, before that serving as the headquarters for the empire her husband oversaw.

Despite the last words I shared with Hattie about my going to visit the mansion not being an attack in any way, we both knew better. People like the Doones lived and breathed under a certain code. A standard of conduct that was ingrained in their being, imprinted after years of doing what they did.

A manner of operation that existed, even if they were no longer active participants.

A classic human example of the old expression about a leopard not just changing its spots.

Hattie was absolutely correct with his response to that last statement. Even if I meant no aggression, showing up at their home late on a Friday evening, unannounced and uninvited, was sure to be seen that way. A violation of every rule, both stated and unstated.

Transgressions enough on their own, only to get worse if we were to have the chance to speak and I revealed I was there to ask if they've seen Cailee or if they could put me in touch with Leland. Questions that could be seen as insults, evoking responses that could range from banishment to a bullet at the base of my skull.

Outcomes that weren't ideal for our search or for me personally, forced by the fact that already more than twenty hours had passed since Cailee reached out. A flare for help, letting us know that she was in need of aid and not to take our sweet-ass time about it.

Under better conditions, I would retreat back home. I would call Hattie again, or another old friend who owed me a favor. Someone with more tech savvy who could go online and dig through the Doone family finances. Scour for property holdings to determine if there was a secondary location where Leland lived. A third where he and Cailee might have disappeared to for the weekend.

Maybe even a credit card charge at some swanky hotel like Everett and Danila had been holed up in.

While that was going on, I would better prepare for what I was about to walk into. What almost certainly awaited beyond that.

Action that was fast starting to look like a certainty, any hope for a peaceful resolution having already dissipated.

A litany of additional entries on the list of things I should have done. A running tally, going all the way back to the night at the house when Quinn was still a teenager.

Hell, even long before that. A career path after finishing my tours with the Navy post college, using my degree and my experience to do damned near anything else.

More shit I couldn't do a damn thing about now. A lifetime of choices that had me about to walk into the Doone mansion, hoping to impart on people I'd never met why they should help me.

And if they wouldn't or couldn't, why they should also let me walk out to continue my search.

"He say anything else?" Quinn asked from the passenger seat. A variation of what she did with Viv earlier, and what I suspected was a trick pulled from her maternal toolbox. A way of asking the same question in multiple ways, hoping that each successive one might unearth a bit more information.

A tactic I myself had used more than once during my career.

"Not really," I said.

"Not really, or no?" Quinn pressed.

"Not really," I repeated, omitting the very thing I was pondering just a moment before. Hattie's warning about how my arrival would be received, and how that would impact things moving forward.

Adding nothing more, I checked both the rearview mirror and my blind spot. Quick glances to the late evening traffic that was mercifully thin, making it easy for me to drift a lane to the side.

And then another, following the indicated signage posted above the freeway.

Maneuvers made at a low rate of speed, despite every bit of me wanting to lean hard on the gas. Take the nearest exit and use it to get us turned around so we could go hurtling back north.

Urgency springing both from the information Hattie just shared and the place I knew I would soon be arriving.

The fear of what the inclusion of a family such as the Doones meant for Cailee.

"Where the hell are we going?" Quinn asked. Leaning forward in her seat, she turned and glanced out the side windows, for the first time since leaving Pike's Place registering where we were.

"The airport."

"The air..." she began, trailing off without finishing the full word. "Why the hell-"

"Because we need to rent a car," I said. Cutting her off before she could lob out the next question in order, I added, "Probably not a good idea to show up at this next place in this."

Snorting softly, Quinn said, "Oh, you mean a damned tank?"

Barely did the quip even register, my focus on the array of lanes splitting in various directions. "Yes."

"Why?" Quinn asked, any mirth already gone, replaced with the slightest hint of defensiveness. That same bit of indignation she showed before I left her to speak with Hattie.

Hell, even at the mention of me going anywhere without her back at my place earlier.

"You think they're going to search this thing when you show up?"

"Without a doubt," I said, knowing even without Hattie's final warning how the holdovers from the old regime would approach this, no matter how far removed they might be.

Provided, of course, that I even made it that far.

"And what do I do while you're off in your rental car?" Quinn asked.

"Find somewhere public to wait for an hour. If you don't hear back from me, call Hattie."

"Why? So he can call in the calvary to go get you?"

My turn to borrow Quinn's favorite response, I snorted softly. "Neither of you want that. But hopefully, he'll be able to help you find Cailee."

Chapter Seventeen

It would take more than the fingers on both hands to count the number of times I had approached places such as the Doone spread. Sprawling estates that looked like something from a billion-dollar blockbuster or the pages of a fancy magazine.

Palatial homes surrounded by gardens and landscaping. Personal oases patrolled by armed security, effectively cocooning them from the outside world.

Threats, as well as the rest of society. People they liked to look down on, oblivious to the fact that all so often their wealth was attained by leveraging the masses.

Places that would forever be out of reach from people making honest money. Lavish lifestyles that – with rare exception for athletes, music stars, and the like – could only be attained through illegal means. Nefarious actions that paid in cash and didn't bother with things like taxes.

Ill-gotten gains that allowed people to live well beyond the rest of society, solidifying whatever perverse mindset had put them there.

All things that Hattie didn't come right out and accuse the late

Liam Doone of as we made our way outside, only under the auspice of not speaking ill of the dead.

What was different from every last one of those previous trips was that I was arriving alone. I didn't have a team of fellow task force members, or even local law enforcement.

Backup that had been briefed on the layout of the compound or how much opposition to expect. Key data I was also without, to say nothing of my complete lack of firepower.

An overall difference in positioning that I could only hope would buy me some bit of leeway.

"What do you want?" a deep voice on the opposite end of the intercom demanded as I pulled up. A sidestep of the usual demand of how I was, going straight to know what I wanted.

A poor omen that was impossible to ignore, causing my grip to tighten on the wheel.

Rising directly out of the cobbled brick of the driveway, the intercom was affixed to a stand made of the same material. Pale stone that also matched the pillars framing the driveway on either side.

An imposing first impression. The kind of thing I wouldn't be surprised to find out had gun ports hidden within, able to unleash high-powered rounds with the push of a button.

Bullets that the reinforced plating and protective glass in my truck could likely withstand, but would have no trouble chewing through the rented sedan I was in.

A final layer to the security that made even the measures employed at my place pale by comparison. What they no doubt felt was necessary for the sake of maintaining such a prime location, just outside of Seattle proper.

Geographic placement granting them access to their various enterprises, without making them too obvious to anybody like my previous team who might be looking their way.

Stretched out wide from the pillars in both directions was wrought iron fencing. An outer perimeter for the property as a whole, matched by the gates standing closed before me. A design made of vertical poles extended nearly ten feet into the air. Separated by no more than a few inches, pointed spikes rose from the crosspiece securing them in place along the top.

A fence imposing enough, backstopped by rows of towering pine trees. Thick trunks with bushy boughs spread outward, creating a solid wall of green so dark it was almost black. An ominous shadow rising high, silhouetted against the cloud cover of night above.

A combined effect that was anything but decorative or inviting. A sight paired with the voice to let me know exactly where I stood.

How foolish this was.

What little choice I had in anything that had happened since my daughter first drove up the lane to my house.

"My name is Rand Bryant," I replied, bypassing my nickname for my actual first name in answer to a question that wasn't asked. Legal title that I knew someone would immediately plug into a computer, running down everything they could possibly find on me.

A process that took the better part of two minutes, culminating with the same voice snapping, "We don't know no Rand Bryant."

"No, you don't," I replied. "And you certainly don't owe me a favor, but I would consider it one if I could speak with Mrs. Doone for just a few minutes."

A sound that was a mixture of scoffing and chuckling found my ears. A response the man made sure I heard, enjoying his bit of momentary power, before replying, "If we don't know who you are, why the hell would we do you a favor?"

After spending the last five hours with my daughter, I knew the man was trying to bait me. Already, he had no intention of opening the gate. His goal beyond that was to coax me into doing or saying something foolish.

Anything that would provoke them into doing more than just barring my entry at the gate.

Incitement I would not allow. Escalation that would end badly for these men, and likely even worse for my granddaughter.

"You are probably correct," I answered. "But I need her help. I am trying to find my granddaughter."

Much like sharing with Hattie earlier that I was searching for Cailee, I knew that the next thing out of my mouth would radically alter the interaction moving forward. A redirect that I didn't want to walk right into, but knew there was no other way.

Not under optimal conditions, and sure as hell not with some inflated oaf on a power trip sitting at the controls.

A narrowed list of options and truncated timeframe, forcing me to do something I would really rather not.

"I think she might be in trouble," I said, pausing as I reached to the passenger seat beside me. A slow and methodical movement with my left hand in plain sight, fully cognizant of the possibility of the hidden guns I was considering just a moment before.

A reach for the lone item resting there, grabbing up the snapshot taken from Cailee's room and holding it up in front of the camera beside me.

"And I think Leland might be, too."

Chapter Eighteen

From what I could tell, the majority – if not the entirety – of the Doone's security team was lined along the porch on the front of the mansion to greet me. Six guys, all but one wearing some variation of the standard high-end security uniform.

A step up from the common henchman fare of cargo pants and spandex t-shirts, going instead for ill-fitting black suits and spandex t-shirts.

A show of force that was meant to stem any thoughts I might have had about trying anything. Open distrust, manifesting in the automatic weapons strapped to their hips and the glowers that graced their features.

Hostility that lingered as I stepped out of the rental and they broke into two groups. Half the men to move in and search me for weapons, while the others stood back with their bodies poised, hands cocked by their hips.

A two-team operation overseen by the largest of the bunch. The sole one not wearing a suit, and the one I assumed I spoke to over the intercom. A towering man in his early forties, with bare flesh that hinted at mixed parentage visible around his v-neck t-shirt and his scalp shaved clean.

All of the essentials for a man built like him, best for accentuating the extra thirty pounds of muscle that clung to his frame.

Musculature marred only by the triangular brand on the backside of his left wrist. A marking I imagined was hidden beneath the suit coat sleeves of each of the others as well.

Standing directly in front of me with arms crossed, he observed while his underlings pummeled the hell out of me, searching every pocket and bodily crevasse. An invasion that would make the most ardent TSA agent envious, taking both the photograph from my jacket pocket and even the car keys from my hand, ending with them demanding my belt and shoes before letting me pass.

Extreme measures that stemmed from watching too many movies that I had no choice but to agree to. The cost of admission, left sitting on the porch as the same pair of men flanked me on either side. Royal blue t-shirt on my left and dark red on the right, the three of us forming a marching formation.

A moving triangle used to follow the bald man into the home while the others descended on the sedan. The beginning of a second hunt that I had assured Quinn was coming. The reason for why we had taken the extra time to swing by the airport for a rental.

A deep dive that would likely make what was just done to me look minor by comparison. Another barrier to entry I was forced to accept, leaving the men to their work as I was led over the threshold into the home. A short journey that had me pad in stockinged feet across a foyer made of the same polished white marble as the front porch and columns.

Cold stone I could feel passing through my socks, serving as the central hub for the mansion, with offshoots extended in every direction. Spokes on a wheel, with some leading deeper into the cavernous home. Wide hallways with arched ceilings, extended well beyond my view.

Others came in the form of staircases, rising to the second level or descending into the subterranean.

Three different floors, all done in the same style. Marble flooring, offset by furniture of blonde wood. Designer pieces that rested along the base of the walls, giving way to artwork in silver frames.

Detailing put on display by the crystalline chandelier overhead, and the silver inlay of the Doone family crest on the floor. Refractive glow that gave an overall aesthetic making the place look light and airy, even at several hours after sunset.

Meticulous attention to detail I was given but a moment to take in before the overgrown leader of our convoy made a hard right. A quick turn from the open foyer into a much smaller space best described as a parlor.

A room with bookcases on the walls and a handful of settees and armchairs arranged around a circular rug in the center of the floor. The same attention to appearance that I noticed before, even if it was merely for show.

An area that was meant to be a buffer from the rest of the home. A physical barrier should anybody try to gain entry or even open fire from the outside.

A place to hold meetings like this one, with people they didn't trust enough to allow into their inner sanctum.

A category I undeniably fell under, as the security team was so intent on making clear to me.

"Mister...Bryant, is it?" a voice said the moment we were all inside. An unexpected sound that snapped my attention to the side to find a woman with dark hair standing alongside a wet bar tucked into the corner of the room.

Facing the side wall, a pair of tumblers rested on the glass countertop before her. In one hand was a crystal decanter, the bulky stopper clutched tight in the other.

A choice made from a vast collection lining the bar, the liquids housed within ranging from deep amber to completely clear. An alcohol collection I got the impression wasn't used often, but would still total more than most people spent on their vehicles.

"It is," I said. Turning to face her, I extended a hand before me. The start of an introduction that made it but a single step before being cut off by a massive hand clamping down atop my shoulder.

Weight alone that would have been enough to stop my forward progress, added to by the man squeezing tight. A vise pinching my trapezius muscle, causing the nerves to fire across the short distance to my brain.

Pain that nearly made me do the unthinkable. Snap my right hand backward with my thumb rotating out, driving it into the man's groin. The start of a sequence that would then see me driving my right knee up as he bent forward at the waist, doubled over the unexpected shot.

A means of disarming, done almost reflexively.

Training returning to the fore that I had to consciously keep at bay as Careen frowned, tilting her head to the side. "Mick, is that any way to treat a guest in our home?"

An admonishment that gave me both the man's name and a reprieve from his grip as she tilted a bit of the liquor into the pair of tumblers. Replacing the stopper in the decanter, she took the two glasses up from the bar and took a step my way.

The corners of her mouth tilted down as she paused and added, "Especially after you already took the man's shoes?"

Up close, Careen Doone looked a bit younger than expected. Said to be a retired widow and the mother of someone in his twenties, I had let stereotypes take over, expecting a woman who was every bit of fifty.

An assumption she looked to beat by at least half a decade, her skin still smooth, her hair noticeably void of any gray.

Byproducts of extreme upkeep, or – more likely – a man like Liam Doone having snagged himself a trophy wife long ago.

Extending one of the tumblers my way, she added, "I understand you may have information about Leland being in trouble. Is that right?"

A drink that I was not in the mood for, having no desire to numb my senses even the least bit, but knew better than to refuse.

"Thank you," I said, accepting the drink. "And yes, that is correct."

In my periphery, the guard in royal blue stepped forward, extending the photograph of Cailee and Leland taken from me outside.

A silent offering, with Mick filling in, "We found this on him."

Accepting the photo in one hand, Careen extended the tumbler in the opposite. "Cheers."

"*Slàinte Mhath*," I replied, tapping the rim of my glass to hers.

A reply that earned me a faint smile as we both drank, her gulping down more than half while I partook of just a sip. Enough to feel the warm flavor of it wash over my tongue and against the back of my throat.

A drink that as little as eight hours ago I would have drained, now taking down just enough to ensure I did not offend.

Keeping her elbow bent, Careen held the glass just a few inches from her lips. A pose poised to take another drink, even while her gaze moved to the photo in her opposite hand.

Fixing it there, she remained silent for several moments. An intense study of the image with her brow slightly furrowed, ending with her asking, "Your granddaughter?"

"Yes."

"And she is in trouble?"

"She might be," I replied, echoing the words I used into the camera earlier. Careful word selection, knowing full well there were three guns less than five feet away.

Weapons controlled by men looking for any excuse to draw them.

"But she's definitely missing, so we're just talking to anyone who might have seen her."

Raising her focus my way, Careen said, "And you think...?"

Again, I became very aware of the men to my rear. Types that I had encountered many times in the past, who were never above taking full advantage of a situation such as this.

An unarmed man, standing with his back to the men.

Courage that seemed to multiply when the odds were noticeably in their favor.

"Her mother's terrified," I said. "I am too. We were told that was taken at the game last weekend, so we thought maybe your son had seen her."

Extending the tumbler to the side, I continued, "I meant no disrespect coming to your home, but we didn't have his phone number, and this was the address that popped up when we looked online."

Even to my own ears, the story sounded thin as hell. The kind of thing somebody made up when they didn't want to reveal the real truth.

A fact that I was sure had the men behind me leaning forward, anxious to make a move. An impending threat that sent prickly heat the length of my neck.

My body braced to defend itself, while at the same time trying to focus on Careen.

Lowering her attention back to the photo, she studied it another moment. A lingering glance, as if checking the veracity of what I said against the evidence in her hand.

"Mick, have you heard anything?"

"Uh, not today, Ms. Doone," the man replied. Words and tone decidedly at odds with his little display over the intercom earlier.

A return to subservience that I almost wanted to smirk at, if not for the actions it would surely invoke from him and his team.

"Hm," Careen said, giving the image one last look. "Well, there is an easy enough way to find out, I guess."

Extending the photo my way, she waited until I accepted it and tucked it back into place in the inner pocket of my jacket before extracting a cellphone from the folds of her dress. Tapping at the screen a couple of times, she held it before her, balancing it on a flat palm as if a waitress with a tray.

Keeping it there, she waited as the line connected and a ringtone echoed out three times in order before being snatched up.

"Hey," a young male voice said. Somewhat muffled by the sound of conversation in the background, he added, "What's up?"

"Hey," Careen replied. "Sorry to interrupt your Friday night, but I'm here with a gentleman who can't seem to locate his grand-daughter and thought you might be with her."

"Huh," Leland replied. A non-committal answer, followed by most of the background noise dropping away. A relocation on his part, or a motion for the others in the room to quiet. "Well, I am here with some friends, but I doubt he's looking for any of them. Who's his granddaughter?"

"A girl named Cailee..." Letting her voice trail off, Careen looked a question my way.

"Coyle," I inserted.

"Cailee Coyle," Careen said.

"Huh," Leland repeated. What I guess was his standard reply. A way to buy himself a couple of seconds to concoct a response to each question posed. "Cailee Coyle. Name doesn't ring a bell."

"Are you sure?" Careen pressed. "I'm looking at a photo of the two of you together at a football game, of all places, just last weekend."

One last time, Leland replied with, "Huh." A word that was out before he knew it, followed by forced laughter. A shrill sound that caused Careen to visibly pull back from the phone, lasting several seconds.

"You know what, mom, that was for my buddy Keegan. We'd been drinking all afternoon and he decided we should go to the game, see if it was any more fun when we were hammered.

"Only problem was, we have no idea if it worked because we were so wasted, neither one of us could remember a thing the next morning."

Chapter Nineteen

Now

Twin thoughts roll up through me. A visceral response to what I found lining the master suite of the guesthouse, so palpable I can actually taste it. Bile that rises along my esophagus before spreading across my tongue, hooking my mouth downward in a grimace.

The first is that there is no way I can leave those girls like that. Children so young they make Cailee look middle-aged, all lined up for God only knows what.

Party favors for the event less than twenty-four hours away. A lifetime thereafter serving as fodder for the sick pleasures of evil people.

Endings that none of them asked for and sure as hell don't deserve. Outcomes that I spent a career trying to snuff out, wanting nothing more than to do the same now.

Call Quinn and tell her to bring the boat to shore as I start carrying as many as I can down to her. One trip after another until my body gives out or I am cut down by whatever opposition forces are lurking on the island.

A radical redirection that I know just as surely cannot come to pass. Not right now. Not with my granddaughter still stowed away somewhere, along with who knows how many more just like her.

She is the reason I am here. If, after she is secured, I can return to help the others, I will. But not a minute before.

That knowledge firmly rooted at the front of my mind, the second thought that takes hold is the desire to inflict as much damage as humanly possible on anybody I come across. Elimination of anyone who had a hand in capturing Cailee or any of the other children sleeping peacefully in that back room.

Wanton rage that bubbles up within, leading me to make a conscious swap of the stun gun for the MK3 that was strapped to my calf. A choice that is equally silent, but infinitely more lethal.

An instrument of death that is still far better than any of the assholes currently roaming Fawn Island merit.

Starting just seconds after pulling the master suite door shut, my first victim is the woman tied up in the hallway. A single strike that is as quick as it vicious, stealing her life without so much as her eyes opening in recognition.

A brutal slash exposing her throat to outside air. An open crevasse from which bright red blood bursts across the floor, pooling across the rug and hardwood.

With it comes the metallic scent of blood. A coppery tang that reaches my nostrils, further igniting long-dead synapses. Evoked responses that continue to mount, filling me with warmth and energy surpassing that provided by the adrenaline earlier.

Reactions that are completely reflexive – ingrained, even – though there is no joy in it for me. No relishing in the macabre or fetishizing over the violence.

Earned outcomes that I was content to spare them from before seeing what they were doing. Acts there are no way of rationalizing. No chance of trying to massage them away, claiming they were merely there as hired guns or to perform a very specific task.

Right now, more than a dozen families are going through exactly what my daughter and I have been the last couple of days. Fear and panic that is probably worse for them, left sitting at home or making phone calls, hoping for the best while suspecting the worst.

Forced inaction that I have been able to sidestep by virtue of my background.

The skills it provided and – more importantly for now – the detachment that came with it. The ability to distill things to their most basic level, seeing them as the purveyors of evil that they are.

Depravity that must be eliminated, by any means necessary.

Having already been through the guesthouse once, I know the layout. More than that, I know that there are only two guards present and that the blinds on all of the windows have been pulled shut.

Dual protections that allow me to stalk forward, clutching the MK3 in a backhanded grip. The blade still damp with blood, it juts out from my hip at ninety-degrees as I pass through the hall, chewing up distance in long strides.

Determined steps that exude the vitriol pulsating through me, carrying me directly to the bastard I encountered minutes before. The one I assume to be Grant, based off the comment the woman made right before I put her down.

The first time.

Planting my feet on either side of his head, I scythe the blade across in one clean movement. A vicious swipe across the length of my body, carving a trench into the soft flesh of his exposed neck.

A clean rip through the underlying muscle. The windpipe.

Both carotids.

Twin spigots that push arterial spray down his chest and onto the rug beneath him. The start of exsanguination that I leave his ass to as I circle wide and head for the door.

Chapter Twenty

Then

Even with the full onset of winter still more than a month away, the temperature was already starting to drop. A direct result of what ski towns and summer resorts referred to as shoulder season. That point on the annual calendar that didn't quite count as winter but hadn't yet started to see the snow fly.

A few weeks where it could still be quite pleasant under the afternoon sun, but the instant it went down, the ambient temperature plummeted with it. A nightly chill that wasn't enough for me to see my breath, but was definitely a dozen degrees or more below when I was sitting out on the end of my dock earlier.

An activity that felt so, so much longer ago than just a half dozen or so hours. A stretch of time in which a great deal had transpired, with precious little to show for it.

A series of dead ends promising that even more searching waited in the hours ahead, the only lead of any sort being a comment that wasn't supposed to have been made. An add-in to sell one lie, inadvertently walking into another.

"Jesus, where the hell have you been?" Quinn spat, picking up my call after just a single ring. "You know how many cups of coffee I've had to choke down to avoid looking suspicious?"

Rattled off fast enough that there was barely any separation between the words, I didn't doubt the veracity of her statement in the slightest. Heightened nerves made worse by copious amounts of liquid caffeine.

Anxiety's worst enemy, at a time when it could be least afforded.

"Are you still there now?" I asked, picking up that she had opted to go to a diner to kill the hour I had asked for.

A public place, where she could blend in without being noticed.

Fifteen feet away, the rental idled quietly. Left there with the intention of stepping out for only a minute, I didn't mind taking advantage of the red paint covering the curb. An impediment to anyone parking there for the night that didn't deter me in the slightest.

An open slab of concrete in front of a dry cleaners that had turned off the lights hours ago. A spot chosen at random, needed just long enough for me to step outside and make this call.

Instructions to my daughter, putting her in motion before getting to what I needed to do next.

A third consecutive task she could not be a part of, this one for even more grievous reasons than the previous two.

"Am I...?" Quinn began, letting her voice trail away. "I stepped outside, but where the hell else would I be? Driving around in that tank of yours? You told me to sit and wait for you, remember?"

Not bothering to let me reply, she added, "Where the hell are you?"

"On a sidewalk not far from downtown."

"Downtown?" Quinn asked. A quick repeat before letting the thought go. "You want me to come get you? Meet you back at the airport?"

"No," I replied. Casting a glance back in the direction I'd just come from, I peered down the length of the street, expecting a pair of

106

headlights to appear at any moment. The next step in the surveillance that started with whatever electronic gadgetry was hidden deep within the rental.

Mistrust that Hattie had warned me about, manifesting not in Careen Doone, but in her overgrown henchman Mick and his crew. A throwback from the previous regime, either now acting to cover Leland's lies, or not yet aware that their place in the life was effectively over.

Or maybe they were, seizing on this opportunity to rekindle some tiny bit of that old excitement. A single old man like me providing the perfect opportunity. A way to keep the team sharp, without fear of reprisal.

"But I do need you to do something else right now."

"Something else...?" Quinn started. Another round of repeating something I said, only to let it fall away. "Is that what this was? Just some excuse for you to get rid of me? Go back to your same old Lone Ranger bullshit?"

Even over the phone, I could feel the sheer incredulity dripping from every word. All of those same underlying emotions since she'd first arrived, now infused with caffeine and having the last hour to sit and stew.

Borderline hysterics I didn't have the time for as my gaze again drifted the length of the street in either direction.

"We have some shit to do, and it will go faster if we do them separate for a while."

Twice, I could hear her false start. The beginnings of further pushback that she forced down, neither amounting to even a single fully formed word. Sporadic thoughts pushed through a frenetic mind, needing several moments to come together in some form of a working order.

Processing that ended with her coming full circle and asking what should have been her first question.

"What happened?"

To try and tell her everything that had transpired since we parted would take too long. Details that would only get bogged down with more questions, or trip me up with rising anger.

Stumbling blocks that could not be afforded, now more than even just an hour ago.

"Leland lied out his ass," I replied. "Claimed he didn't know Cailee, and when his mom pressed him, he said he was drunk last Saturday night and didn't remember a damn thing."

Snorting loudly, Quinn asked, "And what about Tuesday?"

"Didn't even ask," I said. "Their goons were getting itchy and I already knew he was lying. No point in pushing it."

This time, my daughter replied with a string of mumbles. Comments and obscenities I couldn't imagine were aimed my way, for the simple reason that if so, she would have made sure they were loud enough to be heard.

Vitriol pointed at a third party that unspooled for several moments, ending with her asking, "What do you need me to do?"

"Go back and talk to Viv," I replied. "Ask her if she's seen or heard of a guy named Keegan. Supposedly, he is a buddy that Leland was with that night."

"And what are you going to do?"

Pushing away from my hiding place in front of the dry cleaners, I stepped across the sidewalk. Making my way back toward the rental, I again checked the street for the telltale flash of lights in the distance.

"I'm going to lose a tail."

Chapter Twenty-One

Four years ago, I relocated across the country to my current home. A move from hiding in the dense suburbs surrounding the nation's capital to the remote woods bordering on the Cascade Mountains.

Prior to that, I spent better than twenty years making trips to the Pacific Northwest. Repeated visits to check in on my ex-wife before she succumbed to breast cancer. My daughter. My granddaughter, once she was born.

Long commutes that they never knew the first thing about. Cross-country flights serving as a precursor to my eventual relocation. A vacation destination that became my landing spot in a place that I sure as hell would have never picked for either. A site on a map where everything was about as different as imaginable from the Alabama marshes where I grew up. Went to college. Met my ex-wife and became a parent.

Hell, the source of my inherited nickname.

Beyond that, it was a great deal different still from the Navy towns we bounced through for a couple of tours before landing in the greater D.C. area. Two young kids trying to make our way forward, at the same time attempting to raise one ourselves.

A path pockmarked with landmines that we mostly managed to avoid for a while. Toehold positions we were each able to make stick. Precarious balancing acts of every sort, whether they be professional, personal, or even financial.

Years of grinding that finally allowed that toehold to become a foothold. And then a steppingstone.

Ascents that were slow but steady, seeing my wife finish her CPA licensure and me enter the FBI. The beginning of what we thought was going to be more upward mobility that instead saw the bottom cut out from under us.

The classic American Dream ended prematurely by my work somehow following me home.

A landmark moment in my life. An incident that managed to simultaneously strap a rocket to my role in the Bureau and mark an abrupt end to my marriage. Same for any sort of relationship with the daughter who saw the whole thing happen. Sights and sounds that nobody should ever be forced to endure, let alone an innocent just past the cusp of being a teenager.

Vivid images that kept her up, screaming into the void at all hours. Night terrors that they both dealt with in the only way they could, fleeing to the far corner of the country.

One-way flights to Seattle that I wasn't supposed to know about, let alone follow them on. A background tagalong that neither of them asked for nor wanted. A presence that was more ethereal than visible. An observer from afar, vowing to never leave them unchecked after what happened that night.

A promise that I maintained, even after being told by my ex-wife not to.

A sentiment shared again by Quinn the last time we spoke after she spotted me in the crowd at Cailee's high school graduation.

Angry indignation ordering me away, somehow believing that any evil that lingered in their lives was a result of my presence. A direct connection that might have been easier for them to make in their minds, may have even made it simpler for them to sleep at night, but didn't change the realities of the world.

Dangers that existed in any moment at any place. Concerns that they always needed to be cognizant of.

Unseen risks that I was perpetually on the watch for, spending as much time scouting the greater Seattle area as I did observing the people I was there to look after. Force of habit, ensuring I knew their surrounding areas as well as I did my own.

Parts of the city where dangers lurked. Spots where crime and illegal acts specific to Seattle were occurring. Sites to be avoided if at all possible.

And, more importantly for my current purposes, the places where I could hide if ever I needed to. Dense urban pockets that I could disappear into, whether it be to make a hasty escape or to lose someone who might be following me.

The latter being my chief concern at the moment.

Back behind the wheel of the rental, a trio of different thoughts continued to work through my mind. Competing notions that played in a loop, each fighting for my full attention, only to be pushed aside before actually getting there.

Concerns addressing the past, present, and future all three, each needing to be addressed simultaneously.

For the former, I couldn't help but keep replaying what transpired at the Doone mansion. Not just the reception I received and the ongoing interest that was still being sent my way, but the genuine surprise Careen Doone displayed.

Truth that was almost as easy to spot as the obvious lies being pedaled by her son.

Confirmation both that Cailee's frantic text had something to do with her new love interest, and that whatever his angle was, it didn't concern his mother.

A relief in that it didn't involve the greater Doone family and whatever they might have previously been involved in, leading me to the question firmly rooted in the present. The ongoing attention that was being paid me by Mick and his crew, for reasons that were still unclear.

Interest that went beyond the excessive display in front of the mansion, including the various devices found in the rental after the fact, and even the headlights of the vehicle continuing to follow me a few car lengths back.

A nuisance that I could have attempted to sidestep by simply returning the sedan to the airport rental counter, but knew that wouldn't really rid me of their presence.

Not and give me the freedom of movement I would need to address the things that still remained in the future. A hunt that had shifted from Cailee and her father to Cailee and Leland, knowing that I likely couldn't find the former without the latter.

An ever-expanding search, in the face of a clock that continued to push forward.

A tightening crucible that was already beginning to shove bits of adrenaline into my bloodstream, the hits becoming stronger as I glanced into the rearview mirror one last time to ensure that my prey was still close.

Twin lights sitting high off the ground that I pretended not to notice as I flipped on my blinker, giving them plenty of warning as to where I was headed next.

A trap that I set over the course of more than half a block, coasting almost to a complete stop before making my last turn.

All under the watchful glow of the same bright red letters and white clock face that my daughter and I visited just hours before.

Chapter Twenty-Two

There was a reason why Hattie and I chose to go with Pike's Place earlier. A hallmark of the Seattle landscape, during daytime hours there was nowhere in the city that enjoyed more foot traffic. Tens of thousands of people hailing from dozens of countries and three times as many states providing the ideal cover.

A constantly changing demographic, all with some specific reason for being there. Locals in search of flowers or meat or produce. Foreigners seeking out the best tourist attractions in the area. Americans looking to see the show with flying fish.

Young people posing for images that they would throw up on the latest social media platform.

Scads of things for everyone to fixate on. A list that decidedly did not include two old men sitting at a high-top table outside a coffee shop.

Subterfuge while sitting right out in the open.

The complete opposite of why I chose to return just three hours later.

For all of the bustle and excitement of a day at the market, things began to slow down around seven. The normal standard for dinner-time, when most of the locals had procured what they needed and retreated home. Many of the tourists had also moved on, looking for the hottest restaurant spots or preparing for whatever the night might hold.

With a sudden drop in crowd size, there was no point in most of the vendors crammed into the lower levels staying active. People with their own families and lives to get home to.

A mass exodus, leaving only the restaurants and bars sitting up on the top floors open. A desertion of the lower levels, rendering them a labyrinth with minimal human interaction and even less camera coverage.

A place where my presence wouldn't be cause for suspicion, until it was too late.

An ideal spot to lose a tail, by any means necessary.

Parked just two rows over from the spot Quinn and I used earlier in the evening, I'd waited five extra minutes before exiting the rental, all of it spent continuing to cycle through the various matters circling in my head.

Pure torture, counting off seconds while trying to force everything into a working framework. A plausible backstory, buttressed by what was about to happen, and then conceiving a sound plan for moving forward.

Three-dimensional thinking, interspersed with occasional glances to the trio of small devices laid out in order on the passenger seat beside me. The very things I had told my daughter I suspected existed, uncovered through just a few minutes of searching after ending our call. A quick hunt while still illegally parked on the curb, the first two revealing themselves easily enough. A pair of listening devices that were nearly identical in size and make, the first meant to be discovered, the second taking nominally more effort.

Bugs that would be more than effective against someone who didn't have the background I did. Small round buds tucked into the push-button lighter and the driver's door speaker.

Placement that would border on insulting, if I didn't find it so amusing.

The third of the trio was the one that took a bit more effort. A few minutes of climbing around on the damp pavement, feeling the chill of the ground penetrate my jeans. Cold brought on by the damp film clinging to the pavement, staining the denim pant legs and elbows of my jacket.

Moisture that had released as steam on the drive over, momentarily fogging the windows before the defrost was able to drive it away.

Annoyances that were more than worth it to uncover the tracking device attached to the sedan's undercarriage. A standard relay model, affixed to the metal frame with a magnetic strip on the back.

A radio beacon of sorts, broadcasting my location to whoever was monitoring it on the opposite end. A short list of possibilities that I pretended to be blissfully unaware of as I climbed out and made my way back into the market.

Same as I did for the sound of car doors opening in my wake. The clear din of doors being slammed shut, echoing across the nearly empty parking lot.

The sound of footsteps rising and falling behind me.

Even the reflections of the pair of men in matching black suits who had first searched me out in front of the Doone mansion, spotted during a series of quick turns in the underbelly of the market. Tight corners that allowed me to use the glass fronts of the various shops and stalls as reflective surfaces, plainly revealing my old friends in royal blue and dark red.

Guys who seemed to have adopted the demeanor of their leader, their distaste for me having trended into outright despisal. Hatred that was obvious by the furrow of their brows and the set of their jaws as they followed me deeper into the recesses of the place.

A serpentine path, ending in the men's restroom at the bottom of a set of stairs on the northeast corner of the sprawl. A spot in the basement level, well beyond the reach of any surveillance.

Far removed from the traditional paths of foot traffic, the last person I'd seen was more than forty yards back.

The last open storefront, over twice that.

Space enough that would help to nullify any noises that might ensue. Sounds of close-quarter combat or cries of pain.

Calls that came to mind as I slid through the metal door to the restroom. Hallmark noises of battle that bounced through my head, causing my pulse to pick up.

Warmth rushed to my skin as I bypassed the obvious choice, going not for one of the handful of metal stalls, but instead slipped into the gap between the door and the side wall. A narrow wedge of space just wide enough for me to press my shoulder into the corner while staring out at the rest of the room.

A row of stalls, flanked by urinals and offset by ceramic sinks. Concrete flooring and dark green paint and tile, illuminated by the yellowed glow of overhead bulbs.

A snapshot from a different time, right down to the faint buzz of the lights and the competing scents of urine and cleaning products.

Details that came to my heightened senses as I stared out, counting off the seconds. A slow and steady climb, making it to eighteen before the first faint hint of footfalls could be heard through the door.

At twenty-three, they became more pronounced.

By thirty, unmistakable.

The heavy slaps of shoe leather against concrete as the two men bore down on the restroom. Speed helped by the downward trajectory of the staircase, allowing them to hit it just shy of a run. Forward momentum that snapped the metal gate back on its hinges, swinging it wide. A full arc that drove the front edge into the wall beside me, stopping it just inches from my nose.

An entrance with enough force to create a couple of gouges in the tile, showering the floor with ceramic chips.

Power that I planned to give right back to them, forcing myself to remain fixed in position as I heard the one who hit the door pass inside. Slapping footfalls and loud breaths, followed in order by his cohort.

A man not moving nearly as fast, making it just a step past the threshold before starting to slow.

As close to ideal positioning as I was going to get, I raised both hands. Putting them flat against the door, I jerked my hips back, pressing them into the tile behind me.

Leverage to help me drive forward, swinging the door shut even harder than it had been flung back a moment before. A metal battering ram hurtling forward, catching the second man square against his shoulder and hip. Unexpected contact that flung him sideways, tossing him into the first in the row of sinks.

Momentary flight, ending with him slamming into the ceramic fixture. Impact that folded him in half at the waist, wrapping his body around it as his hands both dropped to try to protect his core. A reflexive pose, leaving his head fully exposed for me to move in, whipping my right hand across my body.

Fingers splayed wide, I slapped my palm against his jaw, using it to drive his head sideways into the tile wall.

A second unexpected blow in as many seconds that rolled his eyes up in his head, causing his legs to melt beneath him. Supports that turned to noodles as he slumped forward, draping his upper body across the sink.

A precarious balancing act that I didn't bother to watch play out, my attention pulled away by the guttural roar unleashed from his partner. Royal Blue rushing my way, leading with the upturned sole of his shoe.

A straight heel kick that I did the only thing I could against, dropping straight to my knees. Tucking my chest against the front of my thighs, I felt the air move above my head as the kick whistled past, smashing into the wall just inches from his partner's backside.

A shot with enough power behind it to have knocked me cold on contact, sending a palpable jolt the length of his leg. Redirected energy I was not about to let go unused, immediately snapping my right elbow out to the side.

An improvised chicken wing, sending the tip of my ulnar bone into the soft flesh on the inside of his left knee, folding the joint outward. Impairment of both legs that sent him toppling backward, completely negating whatever advantages he might have arrived with.

Size. Age.

Even a partner.

Plusses that were rendered moot as I scrambled sideways, raising myself just far enough from the floor to raise my knee and fire it forward. A piston shot sent into his groin, causing him to make the same mistake his partner had.

A natural response, lowering his hands to protect his second-most vulnerable area, at the expense of what was most important.

Pressing both hands into the floor, I braced my toes against the concrete as well. Four points of contact used to spring forward, landing with my full weight upon the man.

A starting position, from which I began to swing. Heavy blows with both fists, driven by the animosity I felt for him, and his partner, and even his supervisor.

The anger for the punk kid they worked for.

The frustration of the last several hours.

And the fear that we still didn't have the slightest clue where my granddaughter might be.

Chapter Twenty-Three

"You're not really going to make me ask what happened, are you?" Quinn said. An opening seemingly without basis, her backside barely down in the passenger seat and the door closed before she asked it.

A quick shot, fired before I could do the same and ask how it went with Vivian.

Two people both with information to share, each more interested in what the other had to say first.

"I had a tail," I replied without glancing over. My focus, I kept on the network of streets surrounding the state's largest university. Nearly fifty thousand students wedged into an urban corridor never intended to house so many.

Narrow streets and one-ways, clogged with foot traffic and perpetually glistening with a coat of omnipresent Seattle mist.

A location that had gotten me a sideways glance from the cabbie when I told him where to drop me off after returning the rental. An offshoot, no doubt, of thoughts and assumptions that I'd rather not even consider.

"I lost it."

Snorting loudly, Quinn replied, "You had a tail and you lost it?"

Rolling her gaze my way, she added, "Don't you mean, you didn't have spots of blood on your jeans or a busted knuckle when you dropped me off, but now you do?"

"If that's how you'd prefer to phrase it," I replied. "I also had a tracking receiver and a pair of listening devices inside the rental, but don't have any of those anymore either."

Opening her lips to respond, my daughter pulled up short. A rare moment of restraint as her brows came together. Her chin turned slightly to the side.

"Doone?"

"Sort of," I replied. "While the old woman was wishing me luck and her son was lying to me, their head goon and his team was giving the car a good onceover."

Again, Quinn snorted. A sound even louder, more derisive, than the first.

One meant to make a point. A breadcrumb, wanting me to follow up. Ask her what it was supposed to mean.

Satisfaction I might have provided a few hours ago, but after the encounters with the men at Pike's Place, no longer had it in me to provide.

"You calling someone else old," Quinn muttered anyway, rolling her gaze back the other way. An inability to let an opportunity pass, even if I wasn't willing to play along.

Self-sacrifice that I no longer had available. Even less, the desire to point out that the phrase was meant to reference Careen as a mother, not as a person of advancing years.

Thoughts pushed aside by the growing senses of urgency and frustration within me. The former, due to the continued passage of time. Dead ends that were adding up at an alarming rate, with damned near nothing to show for the expended effort.

The latter, an extension of that very thing, and the fact that Quinn wasn't entirely wrong. After crawling around on the cold ground and wrestling with the pair of goons in the Pike's Place restroom, I was feeling a bit stiff.

Soreness that didn't exist twenty years ago. Accumulated mileage that I suspected would only become more pronounced as our search pressed forward.

"What about you?" I asked. Making a right, I turned away from campus. A move to get a bit more distance from the epicenter of Friday night activity. A hub of young people out and about, their hair and makeup choices made without concern for any chill or dampness in the air.

"I don't know how the hell you drive this thing," Quinn answered. "When I called this thing a tank earlier, I didn't know how right I was. And why the hell don't your windows roll down?"

The barb, I ignored entirely. The question that came after as well, not wanting to explain how the steel plating adhered to the body meant there was no room for the windows to slide down.

Details best left unsaid, only multiplying her quips about it being a tank.

"Were you able to get in to speak with Viv?"

"Obviously," Quinn replied, either not noticing or, more likely, not commenting on my sidestepping her previous question. "Said she'd never heard the names Leland or Doone. The guy in the picture only ever called himself Lee. Never gave a last name, and neither did Cailee."

I couldn't help but pull back the comment Viv made earlier, mentioning how Cailee had already taken to referring to herself and her new love interest as The Lees. Symmetry that could have been a completely coincidental product of Leland not wanting to give his real name, or a direct result of mirroring.

Giving her one more reason to be drawn to him. Matching names that he would use as some sort of common ground, acting as a gateway to further interest and interaction.

A not-uncommon move used in cons and scams of a variety of different types.

The bigger question here being what his goal was in doing so.

"Did you ask her about Keegan?" I asked.

"Yup," Quinn replied. "She said Lee – that's what she kept calling him – was definitely at the game by himself, though on their second meetup a couple nights ago, Lee took Cailee to a place where his friend – which turned out to be Keegan - was bartending."

For no less than the twentieth time, I pulled back up the phone call from the Doone's front parlor. The questions Careen posed to her son, and the answers he gave.

Responses that it was clear were fabricated, but were at least done with enough skill to be close approximations of the truth. Distorted facts, rather than wholesale recreations.

Signs of someone who had likely done so many times before.

"But she never met him?" I asked.

"Nope," Quinn said. "She did say that Cailee mentioned that the guy was kind of goth, not really what she pictured one of Lee's friends looking like, but that he was quote-unquote *super nice.*"

How he dressed or what his personality was like, I didn't much care. Superfluous details I cast aside, focusing on something Quinn said a moment before.

"She say where he was bartending?"

Chapter Twenty-Four

Now

The second outbuilding sitting atop Fawn Island is a boat shed. At least, it was at some point, most of the pieces housed inside it now battered beyond repair or covered in a thick layer of a dust.

A prior use by a previous owner that I have no interest in, having slipped inside just minutes after exiting the guesthouse. A destination I was headed toward anyway, pushed there faster by the sound of another guard approaching.

A conscious choice, sidestepping the desire to battle it out with him in the open in the name of maintaining some modicum of silence.

A secondary option that turned out for the best, landing me in the ideal hunting ground that is the boat shed. A contained space protecting me from any additional guards who may happen past. Insulation against the sounds sure to ensue.

Benefits that are enhanced by the unique interior of the place. A labyrinth of discarded boat carcasses and dismantled sailing pieces, creating pockets to hide in and shadows to slip between.

Plenty of distractions to make my newest opponent split their attention. Conscious focus that has to be alternated between their surroundings and seeking out the intruder they may or may not yet even know exists.

Movements that create plenty of noises, from feet scuffling over the dusty floor to grunts of exertion. Auditory signaling, letting me follow their progress as they work their way through the building.

Prey that has no idea it is such, still acting as if it is the predator.

An error in thinking I am more than happy to correct.

My body lowered into a crouch with one knee resting on the cold concrete floor, the MK3 is still clutched tight in an overhand grip. A tactical choice, better for delivering a strike than slashing.

Killing blows, coming in high and hard.

Barely did my heels cross over the threshold through the rear entrance into the building before the same sound that first sent me to cover again found my ears. A mechanized voice, matching the one I heard upon breeching the water just twenty-five minutes ago. A live human, filtered through a radio of some sort.

Communication on a closed circuit, asking for a status update. An innocuous enough question that was answered in much the same way as his cohort on the south shore. A response relaying complete boredom, not yet aware of what had befallen his colleagues.

Apathy more than a day ahead of any real excitement. Routine patrols that had been performed countless times, always in search of an enemy that refused to show.

In their mind, probably didn't even exist.

Unending passes that had caused malaise to set in. Corners to be sanded down, or even cut altogether. Regular patrol patterns winnowed inward, avoiding having to venture through the most treacherous terrain or the toughest environments.

Places like the boat shed where I was hiding, listening to the man just through the outer wall beside me. A guard with as much enthusiasm as his cohort out on the beach, content to continue wandering through the trees. Perhaps even find a spot hidden from view behind the weathered wood of the shed or the thick base of a pine tree where he could sit and stare at his phone. Maybe light up a cigarette and stare off into the darkness.

Alternative means of distraction I would have been content to leave him to, if not for the fact that I knew I would need to be passing by this same spot in the very near future. A frantic escape, possibly with an injured or even incapacitated Cailee in tow.

Much less favorable conditions that I could not allow.

Same for giving any sort of pass to what I'd just seen in the guesthouse. Heinous acts that already I had begun to mete out retribution for, though there was still plenty more to be done.

Twin facts that caused me to extend my free hand and pick up a small scrap of wood from the floor. A broken piece of a boat hull or an oar that had been cast aside and forgotten, left long enough for any color to fade and a layer of dust to form on the floor around it.

Debris that was no longer worthy of its original function, but fit my needs to the letter.

A projectile that I tossed across the room, sending it bouncing against the assortment of discarded objects stored inside. Thunderous reverberations that echoed throughout the enclosed space as I retreated to where I now wait.

Body crouched, my right hand clutches the handle of the knife tight. My left is pressed to the ground with fingers splayed wide. A sprinter's stance, ready to push off and send me hurtling at the first sign of the guard.

An impending victim who I know will show, content to remain hidden as long as necessary for them to arrive.

A wait that proves to be no more than a minute, ending with the whine of metal rubbing against itself. Rusted hinges that I was smart enough to avoid by sliding sideways through the narrow gap that the sagging door afforded.

Common sense that the guard is severely lacking, much like his cohort who answered the door at the guesthouse.

A colleague he will soon share a similar fate with.

Chapter Twenty-Five

Then

The name La Rosa Negra evoked a couple of distinct mental images. Immediate thoughts that jumped to mind the instant Quinn said it. Logical deductions that already had me planning the best way to approach the place long before we actually arrived.

Alternative plans put together on the fly, depending on what we rolled up to find.

The immediate visual that sprung to mind was of a high-end Spanish restaurant. A tapa joint or a wine bar, where men would be dressed in sports coats and women in cocktail dresses. A place with subdued lighting and flower arrangements on the tables. Hispanic wait staff with gelled hair and lots of bright red lipstick.

A play to stereotype for sure, but in my career, I had come to find that they often existed for a reason.

A joint that Quinn and I were both woefully underdressed for, and decidedly not the average sort of clientele. Two things that would make us stand out, leaving me hoping that what we would find fell under the second option that came to mind.

An alternative of a vastly different nature, trading in all of that for something substantially less polished. A salsa bar of sorts, with a live brass band up onstage and young people showing off their latest moves on the dance floor.

A pulsating sea of sweaty bodies, working to the latest Latin rhythms.

A place where I would still be visible by virtue of my age and ethnicity, but would also find it much easier to hide. A constantly evolving crowd that I could slip into, never committing to a spot long enough for anyone to get a good look.

A pair of possible sites that I went back and forth between. A series of ongoing tweaks to best practices that I riffled through while angling us away from campus.

Unending planning proven worthless as we pulled up to a place a couple of miles to the northeast that looked to be little more than a neighborhood bar from the exterior. An initial assessment that turned out to be overly generous as we stepped inside to find what was essentially a dive.

A place too far down the pecking order for anybody from the university to make the drive over, instead catering to a handful of blue-collar types in the area. Fishermen and dock workers who lined the nicked bar and surrounded the pair of pool tables in the corner.

A crowd with the smell of the sea clinging to them so strong it had saturated the walls around us.

The kind of spot that I could only figure had been foreclosed out of its original incarnation and reopened on the cheap, the only thing remaining being the name and signage.

"You gotta be shitting me," Quinn mumbled as we entered.

Casting aside the twin notions I had been working on just moments before, I instead pushed my thoughts back to the place I was just a couple of hours earlier. The posh Doone estate, replete with marble flooring and silver filigree.

A home in line with the title Hattie had assigned to young

Leland, dubbing him the prince of the once-flourishing Doone crime family.

An upbringing decidedly at odds with the place we now found ourselves. A spot that I couldn't imagine Careen even wanting her son to drive past, much less frequent.

One more on the growing list of inconsistencies. Items that confirmed that we were being lied to. Intentional misdirection that hadn't yet revealed its underlying motive.

And yet more reasons to be acutely aware of the ticking clock. More time that was about to pass as we continued trying to unravel where Cailee was.

Why someone had clearly gone to a shitload of trouble in hiding her.

"Agreed," I muttered. A statement that wasn't exactly in line with Quinn's initial assessment, even if I fully trusted she would understand what I was getting at.

A single word mumbled as my gaze cut to the battered piece of wood curling out from the front corner of the room. A hard edge for drinkers to post up at, extending nearly the entire length of the place.

A centerpiece so nicked and scratched it had to have been reclaimed driftwood or a chunk of a ship's hull. A source of the smell in the air, or brought in later as a way to lean into its new clientele.

Crowd awareness that had staggered over into blatant pandering.

"How much you want to bet...?" I asked, posing the start of the question before letting my voice drift off. An unspoken ask as I ran my focus the length of the bar, not wanting to be spotted blatantly examining the sole young man standing behind it.

A quick pass, taking in the four people scattered the length of the bar – one couple, framed on either side by guys even older than me nursing beers – before returning my attention to a kid who looked just barely old enough to drink himself.

A stick figure with pale arms, offset by a black t-shirt and matching hair.

"The skinny bitch with the bad dye job?" Quinn said, finishing my thought. "Gotta be him."

Grunting softly, I said, "Why don't you take this one?"

"Yup," Quinn replied. "Why don't you go take a piss or something?"

Doing as suggested, I moved straight ahead while she peeled off to the side. Divergent paths that led me to the backend of the place and the restroom carved out in the corner, noticeably smaller in both size and scope than the one I'd been in barely an hour earlier. A space I had to myself, allowing me to use the restroom and wash away the bits of blood still spotting my knuckles that I had missed earlier.

Cleansing followed by my face and neck, peeling away the sweat and grime that the last half day had produced. Products of both the unexpected workout, and the stress that we were both under.

Strain that still loomed large, threatening to extend well into the night.

If not further.

Five minutes after entering, I stepped out to find Quinn seated at a raised two-top matching the one Hattie and I had shared at Pike's Place. Her jean jacket peeled off, the sleeves of her flannel were rolled to mid-forearm.

A pair of beers rested on the table before her.

"Any luck?" I asked.

"Score one for Viv. Quote-unquote, *super nice*. Kid introduced himself before I even said a word," Quinn replied. Extending a finger, she wagged it between the two beers as she sat cocked in her seat, staring toward the bar. "Even gave us these for free."

"Free? Why?"

Sliding her focus my way, the corner of Quinn's mouth curled up in a lopsided grin. "I might have told him I was taking you out for a beer to celebrate your seventieth birthday."

Chapter Twenty-Six

La Rosa Negra looked no better from the rear than it had from the front earlier. A new vantage that included the pair of overflowing Dumpsters out back and the lone folding chair where employees would occasionally step outside for a smoke.

Quick exits that I suspected had more to do with needing a break from the smell inside and the crowd they were serving than with any sort of manners.

Especially when whatever smoke they emitted would only enhance the overall scent of the place. If they were really lucky, a burning tip might even ignite a blaze. The start of an insurance windfall or a real estate bidding war for the corner lot.

Outcomes I couldn't imagine the owners hadn't already considered a dozen times before. Far preferable outcomes to endless nights with thin crowds like the one my daughter and I interacted with earlier.

A Friday night bunch that was far from lively, evoking images of what Cailee and Leland must have been greeted by earlier in the week.

A place so desolate it was hardly worth opening. Air quiet

enough that they could actually hear the TV playing above the bar or even the ceiling fans turning lazily overhead.

More still for the number of irregularities that were fast piling up.

Finishing the pair of beers that Keegan had gifted to us – a birthday gift for a day almost a decade in the future that I was no more interested in than the whiskey with Careen Doone – we had exited and returned to the truck within a half hour of entering.

Having confirmed our target for the night, there was no need to linger. An obvious exit, followed by making a show of driving away.

Overwrought measures to quell any tiny bit of suspicion Keegan might have.

Using the time to make the short jaunt to a burger joint a few blocks away, we loaded up on grease and protein before heading back over. A quick retracing of our previous path, the only difference being our choice of parking spot. A swap of the place on the curb staring at the front door for a new post in the alley overlooking the rear exit and the string of vehicles lined beside it.

Spots clearly marked by a sign on the wall as reserved exclusively for employees. Spaces containing a quartet of rides, each easily iden- tifiable with the people manning the place inside. The world's simplest Rorschach test, solved in under a minute.

The dented Bronco on the far end was for the oversized man with graffiti tattoos lining his forearms that was working the door when we arrived. Unnecessary security in a subdued environment where Quinn comprised the youngest customer present.

A salt-stained Honda Civic with two hundred thousand under the hood was for the waitress with roughly just as many on her feet. A lifer, who expected the same from her vehicle.

The van that would never be allowed within fifty yards of a school belonged to the cook with long stringy hair and a makeshift sweat band visible through the window behind the bar. A guy who went through the motions with dead eyes, clearly counting down seconds until he could be free.

The start of what was likely the same in reverse, watching time tick by until he had to return.

Three easy choices, leaving the SUV parked closest to us as belonging to Keegan. A mid-size model with glossy black paint and free of rust, befitting the manicured look he maintained on his person.

Thus far, the only part of the night to make sense.

A man and a vehicle both at least somewhat in line with what I'd imagined Leland Doone interacting.

"You want the rest of these fries?" Quinn asked from the passenger seat. A question posed without forethought, easily qualifying as the nicest thing she'd said to me all night.

Which, by extension, made it the kindest gesture extended my way in decades.

A simple ask, free of underlying angst or barbed sentiment.

One I almost felt compelled to answer in the affirmative, if not for the fact that my stomach had contracted to the point that the single burger I'd eaten already felt as if it might come up at any moment. Growing tension throughout the course of the evening, becoming more pronounced on the backend of the adrenaline from getting rid of Mick's crew and now being forced to sit motionless.

Further inertia, when every part of me wanted to be on the move.

Climb out of the truck, march right back through the front door, and grab Keegan by his inky black hair.

"No, thanks," I replied, my gaze not once moving from the rear door to the bar. A pointed stare, practically willing it to open. "What time do you have?"

A quick flash of light appeared in my periphery as she flipped on the screen to her phone. A sudden burst, extinguished almost as fast as it arrived.

"Quarter-to," Quinn replied. "Probably making last call as we speak."

"When was the last time you checked the number Cailee texted from?"

"About every fifteen seconds while I was sitting in that diner, which was almost as often as Everett was texting for updates. Nothing."

Wadding the remainder of her food into a wrapper, she stuffed it all into the same sack we'd received thirty minutes earlier. A makeshift trash bag that we would get rid of later, deposited on the floorboard between her feet.

A burst of sound to match the light from her phone, also gone as fast as it arrived.

"You seem antsy," Quinn commented. A statement that pulled my chin an inch her way, without taking my focus away from the rear exit. "I'd think you'd be used to this."

"What's that?"

"Stakeouts. Manhunts. Whatever the lingo is for these sorts of things."

Tilting my chin upward, I returned my focus to neutral, facing the door barely forty yards away. A dark shadow, carved into a pale wall.

It wasn't surprising that what Quinn just shared was the mental image she was working with. An outcropping of what most people thought, planted there by television depictions.

Scenes of a couple guys sitting in the front seat of a vehicle, trading quips for hours on end. An entire night of laughs, carefully scripted out by a team of Hollywood scribes, always ending with the person they were there to see walking out just as one of them started to doze.

A trope that was almost laughable to anyone who had ever done the work themselves.

In truth, the bulk of what my team and I had done was electronic. Surveillance using every means necessary, the act of putting boots on the ground and subjecting anyone to potential danger an absolute last resort, especially in the last ten or fifteen years as technology continued to evolve.

A final step, once all else had been exhausted, or there was essentially no chance of failure.

This was something of a much different nature. A makeshift approach with extremely limited resources. Even more limited manpower.

With an end goal that was potentially far more harrowing than anything I ever faced in the Bureau.

"Didn't exactly look like this," I replied, leaving it at that.

An abbreviated answer my daughter seemed to pick up on, glancing my way as she asked, "No? How about with Danny Rivers? This how it went with him?"

The second allusion to him on the night, I flicked my gaze her way. A quick look to gauge her expression. Determine whether or not she actually wanted an answer.

A reply that rested on the tip of my tongue, pulled away before it could be stated by the rear door to the bar swinging open.

Keegan making his exit for the night, going not for the SUV as expected, but bypassing it in lieu of the battered Honda on the end.

Chapter Twenty-Seven

There were two ways we could go about things, which wasn't to say that we had two options. If it was up to me, we would have just grabbed Keegan's ass the second he stepped out behind La Rosa Negra. A drive-by with Quinn behind the wheel, myself doing the honors of snatching him off the sidewalk and shoving him sideways into the front seat.

A quick extraction, aided mightily by a couple of items from the bag on the rear bench seat, or even the compartments under and behind it. Things of a suggestive nature that would make any kind of pushback obsolete.

Same for giving him the chance to yell out or even draw his phone, dialing for aid or to warn Leland about what had happened.

A situation that would have taken but seconds, thwarted by the cameras affixed above the rear exit. A means of watching over the cars parked back there and – more importantly, I suspected – monitoring the workers who stepped outside to smoke.

Oversight to ensure they didn't do anything too bad or weren't lingering for too long.

Reasons that I could not have cared less about, only that they were there, and they appeared to be active.

Knowing that the most direct option wasn't available, we had no choice but to let him reach his vehicle. A transition that became a matter of tailing him, knowing full well that we couldn't let him get all the way to his destination.

A site that, at such an hour and in his line of work, could be anything from another lounge to while away the rest of the night or home to the place he likely shared with roommates, given his vocation and vehicle. Places that were even worse for us than behind La Rosa Negra, threatening to expose us or to extend the night even longer.

With the amount of time that had already passed since Cailee's text, and the time that we lost waiting for his shift to end, there was no way in hell we could let such a thing happen.

That meant we needed to dictate what came next.

Settling in three blocks behind the rusted Honda that was spewing some sort of noxious cloud from the rear tailpipe, I kept us as hidden as a large truck could be at such an hour. A task that I hoped would be aided by the young man's apathy, his thoughts and gaze pointed forward, without so much as a glance in the opposite direction.

Staying more than two blocks back, I tailed him due north, moving out of Laurelhurst and into the Ravenna neighborhood. A chunk of cityscape benefiting from the residual glow of the university system, with single family homes and public parks pockmarking the thoroughfare.

A place where young professors and middle-age professionals bought their first home and started to raise families. A suburb not unlike where I once lived with Quinn and her mom, before Marcel Bardette paid us a visit.

A nice, quiet suburb for us to make our move, just as Bardette had that night long ago.

A sneak attack, striking in a place where the threat of physical violence existed in books or movies, but never in person.

"What are you thinking?" Quinn muttered, as if snatching the thought directly from my mind.

A short, terse question, matching her body language as she sat poised in the seat beside me. A sprinter balanced in the blocks, aching to explode forward.

"I'm thinking it's quiet here," I whispered, flicking a glance in either direction.

"Yeah. And?"

Again, I was forced to recall that bucolic neighborhood three thousand miles to the east. The kind of place where kids played in the streets and families gathered for barbecues on the weekends.

A location with a soundtrack of dogs barking and children yelling during daylight hours that went completely dormant at night. Young kids needing their rest and exhausted parents collapsing just minutes behind them.

People unlike the hordes of college students we spotted earlier, who were still hours from sleep.

"Get into my bag back there," I said, leaning my body away so as to not block the gap between the front seats. "Grab my MK3."

Twisting sideways in her seat, Quinn dove up and over the console, her hip brushing my shoulder as she passed.

"Grab the what?"

"The knife. In the sheath."

One tiny hit at a time, I could feel adrenaline seeping into my bloodstream. Small bumps that were nothing like what I experienced while hidden behind the bathroom door at Pike's Place, but were enough to sharpen my senses.

My hands tightened on the steering wheel. The sounds of the road and Quinn shifting items around in the bag behind me became more pronounced.

My right foot flexed downward, pushing just a bit more fuel through the engine.

"What are you thinking?" Quinn asked a second time as she slid back into her seat, the knife in hand.

The same words, meant to evoke a much different response.

A question I let linger as I nudged the truck forward, narrowing the gap between us and the Honda by half. An open shift from a covert tail to a strike position.

"You ready to drive?" I whispered.

"Where am I going?" she asked.

"Just follow me," I muttered, waiting until I saw the flare of red taillights before giving the acccelerator one more nudge. A final burst to cover whatever distance remained between us, bearing down on the Honda.

A hard charge that Keegan had no chance of escaping, if he even saw it coming.

The collision between the front bumper of my truck and the trunk of the much smaller sedan was barely felt inside the reinforced body of my vehicle. A pause in forward momentum, but otherwise it went completely unnoticed.

A fate that the aluminum soda can Keegan was driving wasn't nearly so lucky to share.

Jamming the gearshift into park, I reached across the middle console, snatching the knife from Quinn with my right hand. My left snapped open the handle of the door and shoved it open, letting in a rush of cold.

Chilled air that felt especially pronounced as it touched the beads of sweat lining my forehead. Anticipation that drove me as I hit the ground at a jog. Even strides that increased in pace as the driver's door to the Honda swung wide and Keegan spilled out, his pale features striped with blood.

Red streaks, offset by chalky skin and black hair and clothes.

Injuries sustained by the airbag deploying on contact.

An initial blow that already had him staggering, making it easy for me to swing the knife in from the side. A shot not to kill him and not even using the blade, but a scything blow with the handle.

Blunt trauma, courtesy of the solid steel grip.

Impact that did to him just as the contact with the tile did to Doone's henchman earlier, causing Keegan's legs to buckle beneath him. A free fall to the pavement, where I was able to hook his slight form under either armpit and drag him the short distance back to the car.

A total time spent of under a minute, with another spent wrestling him into the trash-strewn backseat.

A third to extract the knife from its sheath and cut away the deployed airbag.

Thirty seconds after that I was behind the wheel, headed north, further away from the heart of the city.

Chapter Twenty-Eight

The shot I gave to Keegan was by design. A move I hadn't used in well over half a decade before tonight, returning through little more than muscle memory.

A skill picked up long ago, feeding off the adrenaline in my system and rising to the fore.

The default setting for most people in my position, stepping out of their vehicle to face an adversary who was already stunned and staggering, would be to curl up their fist and drive it straight forward. A piston shot to the bridge of the nose or to a distended cheekbone, looking to put them down. Knock them cold.

An ego move that might look cool on television, but was more likely to end with their own incapacitation.

Not through a loss of consciousness, but the loss of the damn hand. A dislocated knuckle, or a crack in one of the many, many tiny bones that form the fingers.

Small metacarpals linked through hinge joints, providing no real stability or support. A bundle of twigs, swung straight into a rock.

A solid plane of bone, backstopped by centuries of evolution. Ergonomic design, meant to insulate the brain from just such a blow.

One of the very first tenants that my training instructor at Quantico instilled in me. The omnipresent maxim that in our line of work, nothing put us at risk faster than the loss of a hand.

Especially when human nature was to punch using the dominant hand. The one needed for everything from writing to wiping an ass.

Holding and firing a gun.

A risk I had already undertaken in the bathroom against Royal Blue during a blind rage, not about to do so again.

In lieu of that, the better approach was to use some other part of the body for striking. A forearm blast. An elbow strike. Even a headbutt.

Large bones better adapted to absorb and distribute impact.

Options that still paled next to the best form of action, which was to use something else entirely. A weapon, real or improvised. A club or the butt of a gun or the stainless-steel handle of a knife.

A blunt chunk of metal, the impact of which was maximized many times over by coming in at an angle that neither the attacker – nor their anatomy – was expecting. A shot through the thinner skull flaps on either side, sending the brain ping-ponging back and forth.

Internal trauma that would scramble the circuitry, doing exactly as it had to Keegan. An overload of the neurons that caused his eyes to roll up as his knees melted beneath him.

A man less than half my age reduced to Jell-O, unable to stay upright under his own power.

An instant descent into unconsciousness that was quicker and easier than using one of the other implements inside the truck, lasting just long enough for me to get him loaded into his own car and driven outside of the city. A twenty-minute excursion to a state park I vaguely remembered having been to once before.

A remote location discovered during those same scouting missions that pointed me to Pike's Place earlier, situated just beyond the edge of the northern suburbs. A place that sat more than two miles from the closest town of any size, further insulated by the winding lane that took us through several hundred yards of dense forest.

A remote track carved into the trees, ending with a pad of concrete big enough to house a handful of cars. Parking for fishermen who might want to visit the pond not much bigger than my own, or picnickers stopping by to use the shelter house with a pair of charcoal grills and twice as many wooden tables.

An ideal fallback to have a very private conversation, without having to drive all the way back to my home more than an hour in the opposite direction.

A conscious balance of need and our most precious commodity, continuing to steadily tick away.

"Hey, wake up," Quinn said, stepping forward and thrusting out the bottle of water in her hand, sending a stream of liquid directly into his face. Chilled droplets that hit in the center of his forehead, splashing down over his features and sending eyeliner I hadn't even realized he was wearing streaming down his cheeks.

Black tears that streaked his features as he rolled his head to either side, using the point of his chin planted against his sternum as a pivot point. Pendulum swings in either direction before he was able to build the momentum to pull his gaze up to meet ours, staring out through hollow eyes.

"Wha..." he managed to gasp. A single sound before giving his head a shake, flinging water droplets in either direction. "What happened?"

Once more, Quinn snapped the water bottle forward, sending out a second stream of liquid. A move to help along the waking process, or done simply out of spite.

A fluid motion before retreating back to her previous spot on the opposite corner of the picnic table from me. Two points in a triangle, with Keegan's form slumped onto the bench between us supplying the third.

"You were in an accident. You'll live," Quinn said.

"An accident?" Keegan said, his features scrunching as he tried to

145

compute the answer. Confused thinking that lasted but a moment, his focus pulled away as he gazed out at our surroundings.

His usual dense cityscape, swapped out for trees and water.

A constant ambient glow, replaced with complete darkness.

"Where are-"

"Shut up," I said, stopping the question before it could be fully formed. A third since waking, which would only lead to a fourth, and then a fifth.

More time wasted.

Or worse, the confusion of what exactly was going on. The information he held and the pain that would soon befall him if he didn't share it.

"Tell us about Leland."

Folds of skin appeared on either side of his eyes. Small creases, made to look more pronounced by the ridiculous makeup smeared across his features.

Signs of confusion as he glanced to Quinn and then back to me.

"Who?"

"Leland," I repeated. "Doone."

Again, his gaze flicked to the side and returned.

"I don't know a Leland Doone."

Five feet away, I heard Quinn exhale through her nose. A telltale sign that her patience was waning.

Growing frustration to match my own as I reached to the inside pocket of my jacket. Extracting the same photo I'd been carrying for the last several hours, I held it at arm's length.

A visual I displayed in silence, not trusting myself to repeat the damned name a third time.

An image Keegan needed to look at for only a moment before whatever confusion there might have been melted away, recognition setting in.

"Oh! You mean Lee?"

"Yeah, sure, Lee," Quinn said as I pulled the picture back and returned it to my inner pocket. "Where do we find him?"

This time, Keegan slid his gaze from her to me and back, an inversion of just a few moments earlier.

"How the hell would I know?"

Balling her hand into a fist, Quinn jerked it up to her shoulder. A pose exactly like most would have used to go after Keegan getting out of his car, her body turned sideways as she shuffle-stepped forward.

One quick movement with her feet scraping against the concrete, cutting the space between them.

A move to attack, stopped by Keegan twisting his body to the side and yelling, "No, really! I barely know him! Never even met him before the other night!"

Pausing with her body still coiled, ready to strike, Quinn glanced to me.

"Go on," I said.

"Seriously," he said, keeping his eyes mashed tight and his body turned to the side, "some giant bald-headed guy came by the bar on Tuesday afternoon and said Lee was bringing a girl in later. Said he would give me two hundred bucks to pretend we were buddies."

"And you just went along with that?" I asked, giving no intimation that I knew exactly who he was alluding to.

Giant and bald being the two most obvious descriptors for a man like Mick.

"He wasn't exactly asking, and he was not a small guy," Keegan said, firing off the answers as fast as he could speak. "Figured it was easy money and beat the hell out of getting my ass kicked, so I played the part."

Sliding her feet forward a few inches, the sound causing Keegan to flinch again, Quinn asked, "And how the hell do we know this isn't all bullshit? You weren't in on it and this is just some story you're telling to save your own ass?"

"In on what?!" Keegan shouted, his voice rolling across the surface of the pond, unabated until being absorbed by the trees on the opposite side. Words that were becoming muddled by the tears beginning to leak from his eyes. "Look at me! Look at the piece of shit

I drive! You think a guy like that has anything to do with me, let alone brings some new chick to meet me?"

Again, Quinn glanced my way.

A look laced with dread, relaying that she too knew he was telling the truth.

"This girl," I said, "was she the one in the picture I just showed you?"

Chapter Twenty-Nine

Now

The smell of blood fills my nostrils. A scent that I first picked up in the basement restroom at Pike's Place and have carried ever since.

A scent that is primal in nature, harkening back to different times and places.

A different me.

Shades of a different life that come rushing forth, filling me with a feeling far beyond the traditional hit of adrenaline. A feeling that I imagine most junkies must have felt the first time they tasted their poison of choice, setting them off on a life of forever chasing that same euphoric high.

Riding on the surge provided by the metallic scent, it takes everything I have to make myself go slow. Forced deceleration as I slip between the trees. Silent padding over years of dead pine needles covering the ground, winding my way from the boathouse toward the main structure on the grounds. A towering three-story mansion that rises like a castle from the north end of the island.

A structure utilizing damn near every square inch of usable

ground, wedged tight between the granite slabs pushing up out of the water on either side. A home seemingly built for events just like what is set to take place tomorrow, with an obvious eye toward protection.

An impenetrable palace from three sides, using nature to do the heavy defense work.

A purpose decidedly at odds with the inviting façade of lights peeking through the trees before me.

The MK3 gripped tight in my right hand, my left is now wrapped around the base of a Heckler & Koch USP taken from my most recent prey. A gun that is not my particular favorite, but does come with the added benefit of a sound suppressor threaded down onto the end of it.

The reason why I opted to take it, leaving my preferred Beretta along with the rest of my supplies in the dive bag beside the rear door to the boathouse. A tactical choice, wanting to travel as light and fast as possible from this point forward.

As far as weapons go, the use of a suppressor is an interesting choice for a guard. A move to bypass the bark of the gun serving as an alarm, calling out a warning to others in the area, for the sake of silence. Quiet so as to not disturb anyone in the mansion tonight or – more likely – tomorrow.

Festivities that cannot be interrupted with unwanted reminders about the cost of protection going on outside.

From my purposes, the addition makes it a bit more unwieldy in terms of length, but provides the combined benefits of both the X26C and the knife.

That same lowered decibel, coupled with lethal stopping power.

Thirty minutes removed from first setting foot on the south shore, any lingering chill from the water is long past. A confluence of situation and natural chemicals have left me flush with body heat. Warmth enough that sweat runs down from my scalp and burns my eyes. The taste of brine is on my lips.

Sensory activation that mixes with the smell flitting across my nostrils as I pull to a stop against the base of a pine tree just shy of the southwest corner of the mansion. Old growth that has been around at least eighty years, making it thick enough to completely obscure me from anyone looking down from the balconies on the upper floors or the stone porch lining the ground level.

For any foot patrols, the wetsuit I wear renders me as nothing more than a smudge against the rough bark of the trunk. A slight discoloration that someone would have to be within a few feet to notice, and even then, only if paying close attention.

Concerns I need not worry about, knowing that the man charged with overseeing this area is currently looking up at the ceiling of the boathouse. Blood-stained fingers pressed to the trough carved into his neck, he stares up with sightless eyes, never to move again.

Weapons gripped tight in both hands, I put eyes on the full breadth of the southern face of the mansion for the first time. The one side of the massive structure that was completely obscured from the water on our reconnaissance run this afternoon.

A mix of architectural styles both old and new, with aspects of Cape Cod homes and palaces in the French countryside both present. Ornate columns and window framing, offset by a pitched roof and functional dormers.

An odd clash hinting of the varied owners it has passed through since first being built. People with money and outsized tastes who couldn't leave well enough alone, having to put their individual stamp on things.

Prior history that I do not give a damn about, my focus on the best form of approach.

Where to best slip inside without being noticed.

And how the hell to find Cailee amid all that space once I get there.

Chapter Thirty

Then

I had only been to Hattie's home one other time before. A holiday work function decades before that had been moved from the ballroom at a hotel in the greater D.C. area that we always used for such gatherings after a pipe burst the night before. A turnaround that was too short for the place to get back up to operation or for the office to find a suitable replacement.

A last-second thing that Hattie had been volun-told was moving to his home, due to his being the closest location with enough space to accommodate everyone.

A situation that was a distant second to merely canceling the event for everybody involved, though the powers that be had absolutely insisted it go forward. A bit of the typical corporate bullshit that the Bureau always liked to pretend it was above, but we all knew better.

Two hours of bad food and stilted conversation that we had all run for the door to escape, none happier to see it end than Hattie himself.

A night I couldn't help but call to mind as Quinn and I approached. Holiday merriment back when Hattie's wife and daughter were both still alive, at a magnificent home in Bethesda, in the northwest quadrant of the metro area.

A place befitting a family, overseen by his late wife with meticulous care. The fabled woman's touch, making sure that there were throw pillows on the sofas and fruit in the bowls on the counters.

Accents that were taken infinitely further by it being the holiday season, the place lit up like the lobby of a mountain resort. Garland and lights that started outside and grew more intense upon entry, culminating in a trio of trees in the main foyer.

A menagerie of gold and red that could serve as the setting for a holiday movie.

A harsh contrast to the squat cottage in Redmond that all but spelled out the words *piss off* across the front windows. A home made of dark brick that was a fraction of his previous abode in both size and scope.

Nowhere was there a sign of fall decoration, outside of perhaps the layer of dead leaves carpeting the small square of grass out front.

A place I would have driven right past without even noticing, if not for Quinn having the GPS up on her phone to direct us in after we finished with Keegan.

An address that, like my own, was probably known by – at most – a couple of people on the planet. One he sure as hell wouldn't have handed over to us if not for the fact that at more than an hour after midnight, there was nowhere else for us to meet that it wouldn't look exactly as such.

A couple of old guys meeting for coffee around dinner time at Pike's Place was one thing. A meeting that was almost clandestine by being so obvious.

Two of them sitting down with a much younger woman well after midnight didn't share the same good fortune.

Despite all that, he still only agreed to see us after I offered up an enormous marker in exchange for a few more minutes. A chip I was hoping to never have to play, forced into it by what took place with Keegan in the state park.

Another dead end.

More time wasted.

There was no mistaking the expression on Hattie's face as he opened the door to Quinn and me standing on the front stoop at ten minutes after one. A late hour that I was all set to launch into an apology about. At the very least, a thank you for seeing us again on short notice.

Words that were proven unnecessary by the realization that he was still wearing the same slacks and wingtips as earlier. The lower half of his professional attire, offset by his shirt and tie having been stripped away, leaving only a plain white undershirt.

A look that intimated he had been awake since we last spoke, with little intention of turning in anytime soon. Hints that were all but proven as fact by the tumbler of bourbon in his hand.

And the bags underscoring each eye, suggesting that it wasn't the first.

"Kennesaw, you say?" he began. Three quick words while glancing between either of us before fixing the same hound dog stare on me.

No attempt to make a formal introduction to Quinn, despite the two having only seen each other from across the market earlier.

"Kennesaw," I confirmed. A one-word reference to the origin of the marker I was there to cash in.

An assigned moniker much more appropriate for conversation than anything that actually took place there that night.

Again, his focus flicked between us. One last check, as if trying to determine the veracity of my statement. A second look to my daughter, to see if she might betray if I was being untrue.

A glance that was a complete waste of time, Quinn a better liar than I could ever be. A pupil of a far better teacher than anyone who had ever walked the halls at Quantico.

"Things with Doone went that bad?" he asked.

"Things with Careen Doone were fine," I replied. "Everything since has been a shitshow."

Starting right there, I ran him through the tail that followed me and our ensuing encounter in the Pike's Place restroom. The call with Leland and how it had led us to Keegan.

A brief overview that he listened to in silence, seemingly computing things in the same way I had been since leaving the park.

Long before that even, the growing pile of inconsistencies and false leads now well past unwieldy, threatening to topple over and bury us beneath it.

"We need to find Leland Doone," I said. A simple summation, leaving the rest of the narrative behind.

A single sentence, encapsulating everything we had been through. Every aborted attempt to find my granddaughter. Every conversation that had turned up nothing.

A lot of winnowing that now had us back on his doorstep, flinging ourselves at the only possible avenue that remained.

Leaning forward without having to reposition his cane, Hattie glanced past us. A quick look to the street, checking in either direction.

"Come on inside. The information I have is old, but it might be something."

Chapter Thirty-One

"Tell us about this cabin."

Perched on the front edge of the armchair in Hattie's living room, my elbows were braced on either knee. Fingers laced in front of me, I put my full attention on the man sitting a few feet away.

A being with frustration and exhaustion both seeming to roll from him. Envelop him, even. A combination that looked to be aging him in real time, leaving him with a complexion the color of ash.

Natural reactions to our arrival. The questions we were asking. The problems they could present for him.

Immediate matters, underscored by what my very presence must have represented. A different life and time, full of memories like the one that I was reliving about the holiday party just moments before.

Perhaps the only man I knew who not only understood what our family had gone through, but had succumbed to something even worse. A loss that could never be fully quantified, measuring much more than just the taking of life.

An evisceration of the soul, leaving behind a wrecked husk, both physically and emotionally.

"You realize this has all been a few years now, right?" he began.

"After we spoke last, I went back and checked the files. The Doone business wasn't an enterprise. There wasn't a pecking order, with generals and deputies all in place, ready to ascend if anything happened.

"Hell, it wasn't even a family affair. Their business *was* the old man. Careen never had any interest in the life, let alone keeping it running.

"Sure as shit didn't want her son anywhere near it."

With both wrists balanced on the arms of his chair, he gestured with his hands as he spoke. Subtle movements that caused the amber liquor inside his tumbler to swirl up either side, though not a drop ever made it over the rim.

Years of drinking in the wake of losing his family that had melded the glass into his hand. An extension of his body that he could deftly maneuver, even without conscious thought.

For the second time in the last hour, I knew that the person sitting before us was telling the truth.

Keegan did so because he didn't have a choice. Scared shitless and bracing for impact, he would have handed over his banking information if we asked for it.

For Hattie, it was something deeper. An inability to lie about something that had basically kept him on the clock after midnight on a Friday. The reason why he was still in slacks and loafers. No doubt, the glass in his hand that was far from his first.

"I was inside the mansion," I replied. "I spoke to Careen, told her what was going on. Her immediate response wasn't to call out for him, wasn't to tell one of her goons to go find him, it was to pick up the phone.

"He wasn't there."

"Tell us about the damn cabin," Quinn added, filling in the remainder for me. A pointed restatement of what I'd said just moments before, making it clear that it wasn't a request.

We were past the point of pleasantries. Light treading for the sake of past relationships or protecting egos.

Machinations that were only managing to let more time slip away. Extra hours, subjecting Cailee to people and places that I'd rather not delve into, preferring to keep thoughts of my granddaughter and the sorts of horrors I'd witnessed in my life far apart.

Mental images that would completely consume me. Mitigate any hope of clear thinking moving forward.

Whatever bit of posture Hattie might have maintained gave way. His body sagged further into the overstuffed cushion of his armchair, letting it wrap around him.

Lifting his left forearm, he raised the tumbler halfway to his lips. The start of a drink that made it no further, pushed away with a sigh.

Once more, his focus flicked from me to my daughter standing in front of the bookcases lining the back wall. Rows of volumes that gave the place the look and feel of a combination living room and study.

A utilitarian design meant to maximize the already small house, and the fact that Hattie probably only used half of what was available.

A hermetic home life, made even more pronounced by his physical limitations.

"Kennesaw?" he asked again.

One last check for affirmation. A way of letting us know the enormity of what was being asked.

"The slate is clean," I replied, pulling his focus back my way. "Tell us about the cabin."

"I don't know everything," Hattie replied, "because, again, it was before my time, but from what I gathered, there is a cabin northeast of the city that the old man used to use. A safe house, for when things got a little too heated and he and the family needed to disappear for a while.

"It's the only other location mentioned. If the kid isn't at the mansion, and I doubt he's still at his own place, wherever that might be, then he may be there."

Chapter Thirty-Two

The address Hattie gave us was to a spot deep within the Snoqualmie National Forest thirty minutes northeast of the city sprawl. A time and distance that might not have seemed like much on paper, but in reality might as well have been on a different continent.

A switch from the urban bustle of greater Seattle for the complete solitude of heavy pine forest. Old growth that was dense enough to create solid walls on either side of the road. Impenetrable barricades of pine boughs that stretched from ground level up to twenty or thirty feet into the air. Height that seemed to lean inward over the aging two-lane as it reached toward the heavens, blotting out all but a narrow corridor above.

A thin ribbon letting through the faintest bits of moonlight. The occasional fleck of a star.

Otherwise, there was nothing to be seen outside of the immediate cone of the front headlamps on the asphalt before us.

"You ever been up here before?" Quinn asked from the passenger seat. The first words said from either of us since leaving Hattie's home.

Half an hour of complete silence, each of us retreating deep into our thoughts.

Me, trying to put together the best way to approach things. A late-night arrival to what Hattie often referred to as a cabin, but was hard to imagine as anything other than the first term he used.

A safehouse.

A structure built with added security features, no doubt also featuring a small squadron of armed personnel, should that be where Leland was hiding. A team including anybody who wasn't at the Doone mansion earlier.

Probably even Mick and a few of the others as well.

A small army of branded men residing in a fortified position, called together the instant I left earlier. One of two different groupings put into motion, the other charged with staying on me. In-person surveillance by Dark Red and Royal Blue to match the bugs and transmitters hidden throughout the rental.

Foot soldiers who had by now woken up and reported back, ratcheting the awareness around the entire family. A heightened state of alert for some, coupled with a spike in animosity from their fearless leader.

A situation that blew right past delicate, landing firmly in the category of a shit show.

Enough to almost make me wish I had been less kind with those two in the Pike's Place bathroom, more than likely about to see them again under far less favorable circumstances.

Two feet to my right, I didn't want to even try to guess what my daughter was thinking. Arms folded, she stared straight ahead. Internal debate that had put an end to the litany of barbs and questions aimed my direction.

A tempest of thoughts centered around a parent's natural inclination to blame themselves, matched by a dozen others. Frustration at her daughter for lying to her. Hiding her new boyfriend.

Same for Everett Jory and Vivian Crane for not keeping better tabs on Cailee.

Hell, even Keegan for accepting Leland's money and costing us several hours.

Valid targets all, each of them almost certainly outpaced by whatever blame she levied at my feet. An assortment of possibilities, from me not doing the thing she told me not to, all the way to the very reason why she and Cailee were even living in Washington state.

A host of things I didn't have the time or energy to delve into, instead focusing on the immediate.

"Not really," I replied. "Little bit of hiking and such is all."

The answer was the truth, if not the entirety of it. I had spent time in the surrounding area, just as I had the state park we took Keegan to earlier, and even the labyrinth of streets around Pike's Place.

Scouting trips that were far from thorough, there simply no way to cover the vast spread of forest around us. Millions of acres of dense woods, crisscrossed with roads and trails, coated with a thick layer of moss.

Grunting softly in reply, Quinn dipped her chin. "And you're absolutely sure this isn't a setup?"

"No," I admitted.

Hattie was upfront about the fact that the information he was providing us was old. Intel gathered back when Liam Doone was still at the helm and the local Bureau outpost had a vested interest in ongoing monitoring.

Close tabs that Otis Herbert had determined there was no need to maintain after Liam passed and it became clear his wife had no interest in stepping in.

"I'm also not sure there will be anybody there at all," I added.

After the night we had had, it was hard not to consider the possibility that the excursion was another dead-end road. One more false lead, costing us precious hours, but showing no signs of Cailee.

Or really even usable data to help us get closer to her.

At the same time, it was basically all we had. Another check-in with Viv right before getting to Hattie's revealed she, nor any of their friends, heard from Cailee. Nothing had popped up on social media.

Everett was still getting stonewalled.

The cell number Cailee had texted from was off.

A veritable black hole that she had disappeared into, with the only viable lead being the sudden emergence of Leland in her life. An appearance that sprung up less than a week before, and now she was gone.

Timing that could not be by coincidence.

As I had told Careen Doone earlier, the only address that could be found online for any of the Doone family was the mansion. A central place that they probably figured most people knew about, and knew was monitored constantly by security.

A way to, as Hattie and I had earlier, hide in the open.

Information freely given, keeping anyone from delving deeper into the fact that no other locations were provided, even though it was clear her son no longer lived there.

"What if there is?" Quinn asked.

Flicking my gaze from the road to my phone balanced in the middle console, I estimated the short remaining distance between us and the safe house. An impending arrival that caused my pulse to pick up, anticipation beginning to mount for no less than the third time on the night.

"Then it could be ugly," I admitted.

"How ugly?"

Lifting my foot from the gas, I let the truck continue to roll forward. Forward progress down the center of the road, even as I turned off the headlights, plunging us into darkness.

An extinguishing of the sole illumination, seeming to pull the forest in around us.

"How ugly?" Quinn repeated.

My pulse continued to rise in indirect correlation with the speed of the truck. Slowing momentum that had us barely rolling forward over the level pavement.

"The body of the truck has reinforced plating and protective glass," I replied, sidestepping her exact question. "The tires are run flats."

Letting the truck drift to a complete stop, I tapped on the brakes just long enough to jerk the gearshift up into park.

"Keep the lights off and go slow," I continued. "And whatever the hell you do, do not get out of the truck."

Chapter Thirty-Three

Now

I do not care that the man is wearing slacks and a white chef's smock. It does not matter that his fleshy body is soft enough to hint of an extreme aversion to hitting the gym, let alone another human being. Not even that tears have filled his eyes, leaking out as he cowers before me, whimpering for mercy.

He goes into the same damn category as the dead guards littering the island.

He might not have been the one to nab Cailee. He may not be actively holding her.

But he is a part of this. He knows where she is.

And he will tell me.

Or he will die keeping his employer's secrets.

Wedged into a corner in the subterranean level of the Fawn Island mansion, his doughy form has melded into the surfaces behind him. Concrete block painted taupe behind his left shoulder. The stainless-steel door of a walk-in cooler behind his right.

Two firm surfaces that won't allow any further retreat, no matter how many times he slides his feet along the top of the tile floor beneath him. My hand clamped over his mouth, small noises slide out. Sounds to match the pleading in his eyes as he flicks them between me and the MK3 in my hand.

"You know I have a gun," I mutter. Weight balanced on my left knee, the same shoulder is pressed tight to the block wall.

A point of balance, allowing me to glance back the opposite direction every few seconds. Quick looks to ensure we are alone at the far end of a tangle of commercial kitchen equipment.

Tables and prep stations that, starting with first light, will probably be filled with men and women in outfits matching this man's. Chefs preparing for a massive gathering, and all the trappings it will entail.

Space enough for a team of a dozen or more, tonight rendered silent.

The proverbial quiet before a storm.

Raising my right hand before him, I let him see the six-inch blade on the MK3. Rotating it, I make sure the light catches the sawback blade.

"But I'm going to use this instead," I continue. "I'm going to go slow. I'm going to go after your most delicate areas. And I'm going to make sure you feel every last one of them."

With each sentence, I turn the blade a bit more. Deft movements, making sure to catch the glint of the light provided by the tube bulbs overhead.

Bright flashes that dance across his features, causing his eyes to grow as wide as the baby fat encasing them will allow.

"Unless you tell me exactly what I want to know," I add.

Once more, I bring the blade close. Resting the tip of it above his left temple, I pull it from left to right. A slow pass with the flat side against his skin.

Enough pressure is applied for him to feel the cool kiss of the steel. The drag of it across his forehead.

"Do you understand me?"

The little demonstration is nowhere near what I want to do to the man. Not even what he is owed. Seeing his complete lack of constitution though, I know it is all he can handle.

A single tendril of fear is sufficient to produce the same result as Leland Doone at the cabin last night. A complete emptying of his bladder that stains the front of his pants and will soon start to spread across the tile floor.

Bodily fluids to match the tears pooling at the corners of his eyes.

Unconscious responses that still do not answer my question.

"Do. You. Understand. Me?" I ask, slowly enunciating each word as I tap the tip against his brow. Tiny flicks that open up a handful of pinpricks in the pasty skin.

Microscopic punctures that are enough for dots of red to appear. Spots of blood that slowly grow, eventually becoming large enough to streak down.

Five of them in total, equally spaced so that two disappear into his brows while the other three stripe his cheeks and the bridge of his nose. Bright red that stands out against his pale skin.

More tears appear in the corners of his eyes. His fleshy features warble as he begins to sputter.

Signs that I may soon lose him if I don't hurry things along.

"Somewhere in this house is a girl," I say, the sound of my voice causing his features to scrunch tighter. Fear that has become overwhelming, threatening to start shutting things down. "Twenty years old or so. Sandy brown hair."

Extending my free hand, I slap his bulbous cheeks. Light swats using just the fingers, smearing his own blood over the clammy skin.

"Where is she and how do I get there?"

Chapter Thirty-Four

Then

The world slid by in a muted blur of various shades of green. A landscape of military camouflage, as seen through the night-vision goggles affixed to the top of my head.

Another of the items from what my daughter referred to dismissively as a toy box earlier. Supplies that I'm sure confirmed every preexisting notion she had about me. Conceptions going back to her own childhood recollections, enhanced by years of hearing my ex-wife chirp in her ear.

Constant berating that took on a life of its own when Quinn became an adult and a parent herself. A basis of comparison that probably guided most of her decisions, leaving her hellbent on doing the opposite of whatever she thought I would do.

A mythical monster that wasn't entirely without basis, but was nowhere near the beast she had come seeking.

Not that I was going to be the one to tell her such a thing. Not with where we were and the very real possibility of what we were about to do.

The whole reason I had opted to move across the country – and spent years making the trek before that – was to ensure the safety of two ladies. The only remaining vestiges of family I had. People whose safety was my responsibility.

If a beast was what was needed to ensure Cailee made it home, then a beast I would do my damnedest to become.

Not that the forces we were up against were making it easy. A series of stumbling blocks, now arising in the form of whoever had chosen the location for the safe house knew exactly what they were doing. Optimal placement that put it atop a knoll rising from the valley floor we had driven in on. A rise of more than a hundred yards, giving it the highest point in the surrounding area.

A spot that would simultaneously allow for the best viewpoint and firing lanes. High ground that was easy to monitor while forcing any intruders to climb the steep hillside leading up to it.

A hard hike over a forest floor that was damp with Pacific Northwest precipitation and laced with exposed tree roots. A combination that made for slow going as I pushed myself upward, fighting against the lactic acid burning in my thighs.

Pain enough, without the occasional stab of tendonitis in my left knee. The icy scratches of chilled air filling my lungs. The burn of sweat running into my eyes beneath the goggles, with no way to wipe them clean.

Underlying annoyances that I did my best to put out of mind as I worked my way forward, my hands tightening around the AR-15 gripped before me. A piece much like the pick gun earlier that never left the truck, this the first one taken from the compartment behind the bench seat.

Utensils of a much more lethal nature - ranging from firearms to explosives - always on standby for a call that I hoped was never coming.

Same as the go-bag in the hall closet. Or even the damned goggles resting atop my head.

Throwbacks to a different life I had hoped was far behind me.

More importantly, would never go anywhere near my daughter again, or my granddaughter even once.

Items that I was now equally split on, hoping to not have to use them, while at the same time praying they were necessary.

Items that would be essential if and only if Leland – and by extension, Mick and his crew – were here. The end of a hunt that had taken a good chunk of the night, finally providing some answers.

And, more importantly, a direct path to Cailee.

Clutching the base of the assault rifle in my right hand, my left was wrapped around the barrel. Offsetting points of leverage providing me balance as I leaned into the tilt of the ground beneath my feet.

Every last thing that wasn't absolutely essential, from my jacket to the photograph I'd been carrying around, was stripped away to make for quicker movement. Short, choppy steps, pushing the toes of my boots into the soft earth.

Head tilted down, I counted them off, only raising my focus on every tenth one. Quick glances up that revealed nothing on the first handful, finally rewarding my progress on the fifth such check with a pair of lights appearing in the distance.

Twin beacons that I took to be lamps on inside the cabin. Perhaps dome lights from a vehicle sitting outside. Faint glows that I used as I guide, lowering my ratio of steps-to-glances to five.

Spurred by the first signs of life in over fifteen minutes, my strides lengthened. My grip on the gun before me became firmer.

Natural reactions that took another step forward as sounds started to drift in from my left. The familiar moan of my truck's big engine as it began to climb. The crunch of the tires as they bit into what I guessed was a gravel road leading up to the cabin.

Noises I was sure that whoever was responsible for the lights burning up ahead must have heard as well. Signals they had been waiting most of the night for.

Hellbent on not letting my daughter arrive on her own, I increased my pace once more. Frantic scrambling that caused my legs to burn. Sweat to seep from every pore, saturating my hair and shirt. My lungs fought for air.

Indicators of my age. The toll of the last half day.

The amount of time that had passed since I last attempted any of this shit, no amount of time on a treadmill capable of mimicking the real thing.

Little by little, the bulbs burning up ahead grew more pronounced. Porch lights, backstopped by the thin glow of windows on either side. The outline of the cabin rising amidst the trees.

A singular target I put my full focus on as I churned forward, using the sound of the truck to mark Quinn's progress. Two points coming in at opposite angles, meeting at a singular site.

A convergence stopped just forty yards from completion, brought to a halt by the ground beneath my feet leveling out enough to reveal the pair of vehicles parked in front of the cabin. High-end sedans wedged tight into a narrow clearing at the foot of a set of stairs leading up onto the porch.

A wall of glass and metal, separating the front of the structure and the five men lined across their bumpers. Four figures clad in black suits, flanking a lone man in the middle with bare arms and a shaved head.

A crew I recognized in an instant, sending a ribbon of palpitations through my chest as my pace slowed. My weight rocked up onto my toes, making my footfalls land softer.

Unlike the last time, when I arrived at the Doone mansion to see them assuming a similar position, each of them already held their weapons before them. Small arms gripped with both hands, the barrels pointed at the ground.

Practiced stances with their gazes aimed straight ahead, watching as Quinn rolled closer.

Poses that changed to raise the guns before them, extending them parallel to the ground as she came to within fifteen feet and pulled to a stop.

"Rand Bryant!" Mick bellowed, his voice rolling through the silent forest. A sound that caused my chest to draw tighter as I shifted my grip on the assault rifle, turning it so the stock rested atop my right forearm. My left cradled the barrel, both ready to raise it and fire in an instant.

"Turn the engine off and step out!"

Little by little, I crept forward. Steps covering no more than six inches at a time. A painfully slow pace after practically sprinting up the side of the knoll.

"Now!"

A command of some sort, the moment the word was out, his team fanned wide into an arc. Five guns encircling the entire front end of the truck.

Movement readying for fire that I matched by easing up next to the upturned base of a pine tree. A clump of wood and mud that was the best cover I was going to get, at a location that was as close as time would allow.

I wasn't sure exactly what I was expecting to find by coming to the cabin, but never did I envision a firing squad standing outside. A singular sight that confirmed that Leland was involved and was likely inside, while at the same time bringing with it a whole host of other questions.

Namely, how the hell Cailee fit into any of it.

And why my asking earlier had evoked such a response.

Inquiries that would have to wait as I nestled the butt of the AR-15 to my shoulder. A weapon brought along in case it was needed or even as a means of deterrence, never once considering it would play out as it was.

A fight I would not initiate, but damned sure would not cower from.

Settling in, I rested my cheeks against the stock. The sights I settled on the closest guard, waiting for Mick and his team to act.

Movement that, to my unending surprise, didn't originate with them. One that instead came from my daughter, reading the situation and acting on my behalf. A way of giving me a temporary advantage by flipping on the front headlights for the truck.

A move that succeeded in momentarily blinding them, sending a couple scrambling while the others started to shoot at random.

As perfect a cue as there could be for me to do the same. Flipping the goggles up to rest atop my head, I took a half step away from the root clump.

Extending my knees, I rose to full height and began to fire.

Chapter Thirty-Five

I had to believe that the five men who came out and surrounded the truck were all that was present. It was possible that there were a couple more tucked away in the cabin, posted up right next to Leland Doone, but highly unlikely.

If anybody else was inside, they would have come running out the instant shots were fired. Human nature alone meant they would have wanted to see what was going on. Watch the carnage of their cohorts cutting down the old bastard who had the audacity to show up at the mansion earlier.

An ethereal figure they'd spent all night speculating on, wanting their chance to be a part of ending him.

Initial hubris that they might have been able to overcome enough to stay put at the onset, but sure as hell not once they figured out somebody was shooting back. Return fire that was cutting down more than half of their colleagues and sending the rest scrambling.

A Chinese fire drill that would have drawn everybody outside and had them close the door in their wake, making sure that nobody entered the house.

A facility fortified unto itself, meant to serve as a final line of defense.

Of those initial five, three were already gone. Shots to center mass from an AR-15 at a fairly short distance. Gas-powered rounds that had turned their torsos into mush, pounding them into the ground.

That left only two remaining.

One nameless, faceless thug wearing the standard uniform, and Mick. The guy I would have preferred to go after first, but didn't have an angle on from where I was firing.

"Kill the lights!" I called out from my spot behind the root ball. A shooting blind that had momentarily offset the advantages of the safe house and its location, rendering me virtually invisible. A specter, with only a few bright muzzle flashes to give away my position.

On cue, Quinn cut out the lights. An extinguishing of the bright glow as sudden as its appearance barely a minute before.

A total plunging back to the darkness, leaving only the porch lights and the smudges of glow on inside the cabin to illuminate the forest floor. A loss of light that I hoped had the same effect as flipping them on, causing my opposition to scramble.

Blind groping, making them susceptible to the uneven footing and unfamiliar terrain. Scads of things for them to focus on besides me as I returned to staring at the world through the muted greens of the night-vision goggles.

A monochromatic backdrop, punctuated by pinpricks of light still floating across my vision from the assorted muzzle flashes of the short fight. Bright orbs that spanned my field of vision as I lowered myself into a crouch, and took my first step away from cover.

Riding the adrenaline of what just took place, I could no longer feel the burn of lactic acid in my quads. There was no tightness in my knees.

Nothing to inhibit me as I moved in a combat stance, sidestepping from one form of cover to another. Swift steps with my weight balanced on my toes, taking care not to make any unnecessary sounds or give away my position while still going as fast as possible.

Extra caution, aided by the cover of wet leaves and moss underneath me, while still making sure to get to the last two before they could go up on the porch and through the front door. A fortified position that would mitigate everything that just took place, tilting things back in their favor.

Swinging in from the side, I passed from tree to tree. Quick cover that slid by as I moved closer to the truck still idling quietly, impervious to the onslaught of bullets that were just sent its way beyond some scratches in the paint.

Battle scars to be worn with pride, provided this all turned out as it was supposed to.

Using the truck as a point of reference, I put it in my periphery as I moved forward on the house. In the air, the scent of spent gunpowder tickled my nostrils. The acrid burn of smoke added to the sting in my eyes.

Hallmarks of a gunfight that I hadn't experienced in years.

Things that I couldn't deny the allure of, feeling the lightning of adrenaline surging through my system. Natural chemicals far surpassing anything that could be found in a pill or needle.

Stimulants that pushed me forward, emerging from between the last of the trees bunched tight around the cabin. A shift in field of vision that finally brought into view the two remaining combatants as they moved for the steps, using the two vehicles for cover.

A hasty retreat that would have been ideal, had I been inside the truck, or even approaching from that direction.

The problem for them being that I was decidedly not.

Seeing the two men who just moments before were threatening me and shooting at my daughter, my jaw clenched. My pace increased as I sighted in on the last of the henchmen in his cheap suit.

A target chosen for no other reason than he was closer to the door, and the most likely to get inside. A darkened silhouette that I fired twice on, putting a pair of rounds into his cloaked form.

Shots that struck him center mass, the power behind them flinging his body forward. Absorbed energy that carried him up and over the last step, depositing him flat onto his chest atop the porch floor.

The removal of a final ally that caused Mick to abandon any attempt at continuing to use cover. Any pretense of hiding behind the pair of sedans.

A deep and guttural roar erupted through the forest as he burst forward, charging up the stairs. Long strides that he used to clear the bottom few in a single step, looking to go the rest of the way with his second. A bounding leap that left him hanging in the air as he tried to hurtle the limbs of his fallen cohort.

Suspension that lasted just an instant too long, making for a clean target as I pulled back on the trigger once more. A shot fired from no more than a dozen yards away as I raced forward, matching his pace from the south.

Striking him in his right thigh, the bullet ripped through the meat, entering and exiting just a fraction of an instant apart. Combined force that caused him to rotate mid-air, dropping him hard onto his back.

A pirouette with an ungraceful landing, sliding to a stop just a couple of feet to the side of his colleague.

Combined traumas that left him stunned and gaping, unable to do anything to stop me as I leapt up onto the porch and kicked the handgun from his clutches.

Even less, as I drew the AR-15 across my body and snapped it downward, driving the butt of it into the bare flesh above his ear.

Chapter Thirty-Six

I knew the instant the front doorknob turned easily in my hand that we were wasting our time. Final confirmation of a series of things that had been present outside, I was just too preoccupied to put them all together.

Disparate points, such as there being two cars parked along the side of the cabin and Mick himself standing at the head of the firing formation.

Pieces that didn't coincide with the supposed purpose of the cabin. Movements and placement that wouldn't fit with a protection detail.

"He's not here," I muttered.

An audible thought as I released my left hand from the underside of the AR-15 barrel and nudged the door open.

"*What?*" Quinn snapped from a few feet behind me. Disregarding my request for her to stay with the truck while I cleared the place, I heard her boots thump against the boards of the porch.

A sound not unlike when she first approached on the dock half a day before. Footsteps that were closer to stomps, then trying to scare away any fish I might snag, now unable to contain the emotion hurtling through her.

Adrenaline from the drive up. Being fired upon.

Watching me destroy Mick and his assembled forces.

"How do you know?"

Not responding immediately, I instead returned my hand to the gun. A second point of support as I moved inside, swinging the front tip of the rifle across a living room that looked closer to a ski chalet than what was traditionally thought of as a safehouse.

Patterned fabric sofa. Solid wooden coffee table with crossed legs holding it upright. Antique skis and snowshoes on the walls.

Window dressing, in case any wayward hikers or curious park rangers happened by.

Cover that, more importantly, looked to have not been disturbed in some time. No cellphones rested on the arms of the couch. No bottles or cans or even coffee cups sat on the table.

Not a single scent was detectable in the air beyond the lingering smell of spent gunpowder.

"Nobody's been here," I replied, pushing through the living room into the attached kitchen on the backend. Separated from the living room by a bar extended from the side wall, it looked to be a continuation of the front portion. High-end fixtures and furnishings, all bearing a light film of dust.

Appliances and kitchenware that hadn't been used in some time.

Likely, since Liam Doone was still in charge years before.

"You've got to be shitting me," Quinn spat beside me.

This time, I didn't feel the need to respond at all. A question that was either rhetorical or simply her venting that I let go, peeking through the open doorway into what looked to be a pantry affixed to the backend of the kitchen.

A space matching the one before it in size, with rows of shelves lining three of the walls. Metal racks with canned goods and bottled water taking up the lowest levels, the plastic they were encased in frosted over with dust.

Items that I had no doubt were stamped with expiration dates that had passed long ago. Food that had been socked away in the past, long since forgotten.

Much like the place as a whole.

That alone bringing it with it a whole host of things to be considered.

And one realization that was too obvious to ignore.

"Look at this," I said, grasping the door to the pantry. Rotating it forward a few inches, I showed the outer edge of it to Quinn. "It's painted to look like wood, but it's actually steel."

Extending a finger, I added, "I bet if we tapped on the walls, it'd be the same."

Her lips drawn into a tight purse, her eyes flicked from to the walls. "Why...?"

"We used to call rooms like this The Alamo," I replied. "The safe room inside the safe house, where any final stand would be made."

Pushing the door back open, I added, "Stay here."

Retreating out of the pantry, I slipped past my daughter still attempting to process what was just shared. A simple order that she didn't feel the need to press me on for the first time all day, instead filing into the small alcove in my wake.

A check for herself that the space was more than just a pantry, and that it hadn't been used in some time.

A sight that sent a second spur of hostility through her, leaving her kicking the metal shelves and slapping at the top of the sealed plastic flats. Release of building frustration that echoed through the cabin as I turned my attention to the staircase rising perpendicular to the kitchen.

Steps framed on all sides by wooden walls, rising no more than a handful at a time before turning ninety-degrees. A design feature to take up the least amount of space, allowing me to ascend to the second floor while never going more than a few feet in any direction.

A confined area that normally would have my pulse thrumming, though I felt no nervousness as I climbed. No concern for who may be waiting at the top or any traps that the safe house might be equipped with.

Even the AR-15 I kept raised at shoulder height more out of habit than fear, finding no surprise as I arrived on the second floor to discover it was just as desolate as the one below.

Two bedrooms separated by a bath in between, all clustered around a small landing and done in the same décor as the first level.

None of which had been touched in ages.

Lowering the rifle before me, I rotated my grip to the same one I had used on approach earlier. Positioning better suited for carrying than impending action.

Letting it come to rest across my midsection, I followed the sounds of Quinn's continued thrashing to the first floor to find her having relocated from the pantry out into the kitchen. A space with more room for her to flail, and larger targets for her to strike.

Continued wailing that was now aimed at the countertops. Open-handed slaps, each one accompanied by a deep grunt. Primal sounds that reverberated through the house.

Frustration, fear, even a mother's love, all manifesting into a primal roar that continued as I slid past her and stepped out onto the porch.

A place I remained for the better part of two minutes, letting her carry on until whatever she was harboring was spent. Bottled emotion that I had been able to take out on the Doone goon squad more than once, this now her chance to finally do the same.

Needed release that culminated with her eventually exiting to join me with the sleeves of her jacket and the front of the underlying flannel still twisted up. Stray hairs hung lank around a face crimson with exertion.

Each breath was forced out loudly, pausing only to ask, "So we've got nothing?"

"Oh, we've got a hell of a lot more than that." Lifting my chin forward, I added, "We've got two vehicles, maybe some cellphones..."

Tilting my head to Mick's inert form still leaking blood onto the porch beside us, I added, "And we've got him."

To my left, Quinn snorted loudly. A sound meant to relay her displeasure, sent even before she rotated her focus to glare at me.

A pointed stare with her nostrils pulled back into a snarl.

"Please tell me that isn't supposed to make me feel better."

Matching her gaze, I shook my head just slightly to either side. "No, but it sounds a hell of a lot better than the alternative."

"Which is what?"

"Our asses were set up."

Chapter Thirty-Seven

Now

The MK3 is back in the sheath strapped to my calf, stowed away in lieu of the USP with the sound suppressor extended at shoulder height before me. A switch to give myself both maximum reach and stopping power as I inch my way forward, one stair at a time.

Just as I suspected, the bulbous bastard currently cooling his heels in the meat locker a floor below me wasn't lying about the layout of the house. Experiencing real pain for probably the first time in his life, there was no way he could concoct the gumption to lie.

Sheer terror that far outpaced even Keegan last night. A flooding of his system with adrenaline that made any sort of logical thought – let alone the ability to be devious – impossible.

Sputtering things out one syllable at a time, he'd told me where to find the entrance to the back stairwell of the mansion. A passageway tucked into a corner that I suspected was meant for servant use and nothing else. A way for them to get back and forth between the essential functions in the basement and the people paying for them up above without being seen.

An assumption all but confirmed by the brown ceramic tile with chipped edges underfoot. Construction materials that an owner of an entire island would never allow to be seen by family or guests.

Arranged in a winding path, the interior of the stairwell looks like something one would find in a turret, despite there being none visible from the outside. A unique feature meant to make the access way as small as possible.

Remote placement serving my purposes just fine, providing a lack of foot traffic from the thin crowd that might be present.

Insulated by stone and concrete, I am afforded complete silence as I ascend. Keeping my body pressed to the outside wall, I climb three steps at a time before pausing, the gun raised. A slow and methodical rise, punctuated every few moments by a quick turn the opposite direction.

A check to ensure I am still alone. There are no sounds bouncing through the narrow confines. No shadows thrown against the pale walls.

Opposition that would be especially grievous now, with such limited means of hiding or escaping. Two things that I still have very little interest in, but have to at least be cognizant of given where I am.

And, more importantly, the task I am here to complete.

Twenty-one steps after leaving the basement, I reach my first real trial. A landing with a thick oak door and wrought-iron fixtures, matching those found in the guest house.

An access point to the main level that I stop just shy of, sweeping my gaze around the outside of the door and into the corners of the entryway carved into the staircase. A quick check for signs of cameras that reveals nothing, followed by listening for any voices or footfalls on the opposite side.

Guards who may be aware of my presence or servants needing to gain access.

Opposition that I train the USP on the door in anticipation of.

Foes that never materialize, allowing me to push onward.

Raising my weight onto my toes, I use the textured grips on the bottom of my wetsuit to hop from the top step to the center of the landing. One fluid shift of weight, followed by another to match.

Forward momentum that carries me to the bottom stair of the next set, heading up to the second floor.

A simple movement, still sufficient to cause my heart rate to climb. Heightened anticipation that I can feel seeping from every pore, saturating the double-knit neoprene.

Raising the gun before me, I continue to climb. Steps that come a bit quicker now, my weight landing light on my toes.

Counting them off, I move higher. One after another on bent knees, pausing every few steps to swing the tip of the weapon back the opposite way.

Progress that is forcibly slow, while every cell of my being wants nothing more than to take off sprinting. Skip every other stair and get to the second floor, where my overgrown tour guide told me he knew a young woman was being held.

Information that I have to believe points to Cailee, even if he hadn't been there to confirm anything himself.

With each step I climb, flashbacks from the guesthouse return. Vivid images that are spliced into my vision, showing me the young girls all lined up in the master suite.

Snapshots that slowly morph as my mind replaces those sleeping children with Cailee in my mind.

A mental image that causes my teeth to clench, my every desire being to lift my chin and bellow into the stairwell. A release of agitation, and an open challenge to anyone within hearing range.

My own improvised Battle of Thermopylae, using the narrow confines to recreate Hell's Gate, daring any nearby guards to come for me.

An imagined battle that will have to wait a bit longer, as three minutes after locking the bleeding chef in the cooler, I exit the stairwell onto a second floor that is markedly different from the basement. Gone are the concrete floors and industrial appliances with everything done in assorted shades of gray.

In their place is polished hardwood underfoot, bisected by a colorful rug running the length of the hall. Wooden molding lines the top and bottom of the walls, lacquered to a mirrored shine.

Expansive light fixtures hang down overhead, bathing everything in a yellowy glow.

Furnishings that would seem inviting to a guest, though for my purposes present only obstacles. Bright light and an open layout leaving me completely exposed.

Same for the handful of doorways lining either wall. Potential hiding spots for guards lying in wait, or simply places where someone could spot me slipping by.

A total of more than twenty yards of open ground that I would gladly trade to be back in the trees between the boathouse and the mansion.

My body tucked into the corner of the entry to the staircase, I lower myself to a knee. Peering in either direction, I run a quick scan along the ceiling, scouring where it and the walls come together on either side.

A check for cameras that doesn't readily reveal anything, though that doesn't mean they aren't there. Fiber optics that could be too small to be noticed, or placement in other less obvious places.

Possibilities I can't do anything about as I rise from the floor. The base of the USP clasped in both hands, I keep it angled downward, pointed toward the floor.

One last moment to draw in a breath, steeling myself, before rolling to my left. Pressing my shoulder harder into the wall, I use it as a rotation point, swinging out from my hiding spot.

An emergence into the open, knowing that from this instant forward, I have no choice but to go fast. Cover as much ground as possible. Clear as many of the doorways on the floor as I can.

And, most importantly, find Cailee before anybody finds me.

Chapter Thirty-Eight

Then

The roll of duct tape hadn't come from the go-bag I always kept in the hall closet, or even the handful of special additions made for this evening. Items grabbed as I passed through the house, trying to balance the story Quinn had shared with me against what the night might hold.

Projections that had already proven woefully short, with the promise of much, much more to come.

The tape didn't even come from one of the special compartments my pickup was equipped with. Assorted carrying spaces all designed specifically with certain cargo in mind. A variety of tools I hoped I would never need, but knew better than to get rid of. A traveling arsenal that was always loaded up and waiting in the garage, should the need ever arise.

Just as it now had.

Having a much simpler origin than the other items employed throughout the night, the tape had been stowed away in a canvas bag

under the passenger seat. Part of the standard kit I carried in all vehicles, no matter how infrequently I drove them.

Jumper cables. A flashlight. Road flares.

Useful items should something happen along the side of a road.
Events far different from what took place at the cabin, but that didn't
mean the roll of silver adhesive wasn't still perfectly suited for what
we needed.

A useful tool, employed while we saw to another more pressing
matter first. Something with a very short timeframe, that being the
reason why there was now so much tape wrapped around the bullet
wound on Mick's leg. A rudimentary field dressing to keep him from
bleeding out, paired with more of the tape on his wrists, ankles, and
even around the lower half of his face.

Means of muting and immobilizing that were finished by bending
him backward and looping the last bits of the roll between his wrists
and ankles. A bow and arrow of sorts, with his arms and legs all
drawn back, rendering him unable to gain purchase or leverage in any
direction.

Final precautions to ensure he couldn't kick, lashing out or
making noise from the trunk of one of the two vehicles parked outside
the cabin. Anything to alert someone of his presence in the unlikely
event he was able to shake off the second shot I gave him with the
butt of the rifle.

A matching blow to the first coming in from the opposite side.
Congruent divots above either ear, striping his shaved head with dark
rivulets of blood.

But a fraction of the damage I wanted to inflict. Anger that had
been present through much of the night, matched by the feelings that
had been welling within since first encountering Mick's cohorts in
the Pike's Place bathroom earlier.

An initial taste of violence, awakening something long left
dormant within. A callback to times long ago.

My natural state, left untouched these last few years. Animal yearnings that had finally been acknowledged, leaving them craving more.

Predilections that, if the outburst in the cabin earlier was any indicator, had been inherited by my daughter as well.

Before handing out the second shot, I hadn't tried to so much as speak to Mick. Seeing how he had reacted to my presence at the Doone mansion and the little greeting party he'd put together for me at the cabin, there was no point. Anything he said to me would have been lies, or outright vitriol.

Hatred that would only piss me off, forcing me to give into my carnal cravings.

A removal of a chess piece meant to serve a far greater sacrifice a little later on.

Along those lines, I also hadn't even bothered trying to order him into the trunk. A request he would have clearly balked at, trying to muscle his way out or buy time by starting an argument that would have ended badly.

Wasted minutes, as a best case.

A shot from the other end of the rifle as a worst.

Outcomes I didn't have the desire to broach, instead leaving him perched on the top step and backing the rear of the sedan right up to the stairs. An elevated position so I could roll him into the open trunk.

A post from which it still took tremendous effort to get his ass moving, ending with his heft dropping the entire back end of the vehicle a couple of inches.

An uneremonious landing spot where I went to work with the tape before stripping away the single best source of information I knew the man possessed. Something completely dispassionate and without the ability to lie.

A simple burner phone, wedged into the rear pocket of his slacks.

The same one nested in the middle console beside me as I retraced the route south out of the mountains, following the square taillights of my truck up ahead. A device with call logs littered with unsaved numbers, the address void of a single known contact.

A phone that had clearly been in use since well before my visit to the Doone mansion.

And just as obviously had nothing to do with his post there.

One that couldn't tell me a great deal on its own, but would make an excellent basis for comparison. A data point that could be used for matching against a sibling that we were on our way to procure.

That being one of just many reasons for our return visit. One final swing past, this time armed with knowledge and leverage there was no way for us to have earlier.

And whatever gaps that weren't sufficient to cover, burning animosity would have to do the rest.

Sitting behind the wheel of the sedan, my weight rested on my right haunch. My left wrist was draped across the wheel.

A twisted position, allowing me to glance between my own phone and Mick's burner wedged into the cupholders on the middle console. Beyond them, the Beretta I had swapped the AR-15 for from the cache hidden in my truck.

My small arm of choice, after a career spent forced to carry a Glock. A preference for Italian over Austrian that had developed somewhere along the way, becoming more ingrained as the years passed.

One after another, I moved through the three-point progression dozens of times while continuing to play back the last couple of days. Everything my daughter and I had been through, superimposed onto what we knew about Cailee's experiences.

The danger she was in that had kicked off all of this, guiding our every decision since.

A mountain of disparate information that filled the drive back into the city, ending as I slid to a stop just inches behind the bumper of my own truck.

A parking spot nearly identical to the last time I pulled up in front of Hattie's home, this time with intentions of a far graver manner.

Chapter Thirty-Nine

The seating arrangement was largely the same as the last time the three of us were inside Hattie's living room, with only small modifications made in light of recent events. Adjustments to acknowledge the shifts that had occurred in the last several hours.

Realizations and discoveries after finding the safe house empty. Checking Mick's pockets to find not a regular cellphone with saved entries, but a burner with nothing but other like-kind devices listed in the call log.

Signs of a clandestine operation well outside the man's usual means of employment.

The overarching feeling I had left the Doone mansion with earlier – beyond the excess of the security measures and the self-righteousness of Mick – was that Careen was telling me the truth. While she might have resented my being there as a callback to a life she'd tried to leave behind, she empathized with the situation I was in.

A feeling I had been battling with ever since, trying to balance that belief against everything else going on.

A back-and-forth that now made infinitely more sense.

A narrative that wasn't without holes, but was starting to come together. A story still being processed, about to take a needed step forward by means of the largest remaining missing piece. One last question we had made the return trip for, ready to sit down for our third visit with Hattie of the night.

An ask I was going to make, even if I did have to sit directly across from someone who - if not ever a friend - was at least a colleague. A guy who had been in the same trenches as I, fighting against the same sorts of people.

A man who had had his home breached in the same sort of way, with an outcome that was even worse. A life shattering event that should have filled him with enough rage to dedicate the rest of his life to snuffing out criminals.

Not aligning himself with them, as he apparently had in the time since moving out west.

A question I would get an answer to, even if doing so required us both sitting just a few feet apart, weapons in hand. Automatic pistols that we each gripped tight, resting them along the tops of our thighs.

A face-off in the truest sense of the word, without a chance that either of us would miss at such range.

"Why?"

In my periphery, I was aware of Quinn pressing herself tight against the bookshelf along the wall. A spot well beyond the immediate line of fire. The furthest away she was willing to venture, needing to know the same answers I did.

A hunger for data that had overridden my repeated entreaties for her to stay in the truck. The warning from Hattie that she might be better served to wait outside after we accepted the unspoken invitation of the front door cracked open and entered the house to find him in this exact position.

Self-preservation, one of the strongest evoked emotions possible, superseded by the only one greater.

The ferocity of a parent looking to protect their own.

"I'm sure you've put together a good bit of it on your own," Hattie answered. "I mean, this was always your thing. Unraveling mysteries. Using clues to find people who didn't want to be found."

Shrugging his eyebrows, he added, "Christ knows we all got sick of hearing the stories about it around the office."

To that, I said absolutely nothing. Total silence, not about to succumb to letting him derail the conversation. Attempts to blame this on me that would take us far away from the reason why we had returned.

The simple one-word question I had already posed.

As open-ended an inquiry as could be made, letting him answer for why he had targeted my granddaughter. Lied to my face repeatedly.

Sent me and my daughter to a firing squad in the mountains.

"I knew from the first instant your name showed up on my caller ID that you were going to be a problem," Hattie continued. "There was no way in Hell you calling was a coincidence, which was the only reason I even picked it up.

"Just the same as I knew after we met the first time that you weren't going to leave this alone."

With each word spoken, the inward pinch of his brows became more pronounced. A glare heightened by decades of strain.

Twice, his right hand rose from the arm of his couch. Practiced behavior, meant to lift a tumbler of liquor that for one of the few times ever wasn't there.

"It would have been easy to just lie to you and say I didn't know anything about the brand you were referencing. Or to give you some bullshit story. But I knew if I did that, you'd just keep digging.

"You'd go talk to someone else. Flip over another rock. Make damned sure you got what you wanted, just like you always did."

Again, I remained silent, resisting the urge to ask any questions. Offer anything that might derail what he was sharing or detract from the simple question I was there for.

A cue that, for quite possibly the first time ever, my daughter followed, staying quiet herself.

"So I sent you to Careen, hoping you'd see that she was really out of the game and give it up. Start looking somewhere else, at least for a couple days."

Tilting his head to the side, his features scrunched. A look somewhere between a snarl and a grimace.

A mask of pain and anger that dissipated as fast as it appeared, his focus returning to meet mine.

"All I needed was a couple of days," he muttered. "Mick was supposed to keep you from even getting into the mansion. And when that didn't work, and you took out the guys he had following you, we decided to use the cabin."

With just a couple of lines, more dots connected in my lines. Pieces that I had noticed before, but hadn't yet put into a coherent framework.

Disparate items such as the overt hostility Mick displayed over the intercom. The clear unease that existed between him and Careen.

The makings of a scheme that Hattie was running with the Doone family, unbeknownst to the matriarch.

"They were supposed to grab you, keep you on ice up there through the weekend." Raising his free hand, he wagged his fingers my way. "Not this. Never did I intend this."

How exactly what took place in the mountains could be construed as just grabbing us, I didn't pretend to have the slightest idea. A show of force that had demanded I climb out of the truck and then opened fire for the mere offense of Quinn turning on the headlights.

Itchy fingers making it clear there were definitely ulterior motives at play, whether they be from Mick and his men, or handed down from Hattie himself, despite what he claimed.

Not that it really mattered much now, for them or him.

"What happens in two days?"

"The Council is back," Hattie said. A simple sentence, expelled with a sigh.

What I guessed to be a summation. A means to stop dancing through what happened and get right to the impetus behind it.

His way of finally answering my question.

"The Council?"

"The Council," Hattie repeated, extending his left hand and tapping the top of the cane leaning against the side of his chair. The reminder he had carried every single day for well over a decade of the case that had defined not just his career, but his life.

His version of Marcel Bardette.

"Their first meeting is Sunday night."

"We ended The Council," I said, ignoring the last piece while still trying to wrap my head around the first part, "after what happened."

"We did," Hattie answered, "but a few years ago, there began to be rumblings of them reforming under new leadership. Fresh blood that was going to pick things back up, starting over in a new location."

Again, he raised the same hand. His palm uplifted this time, he gestured not just to the tight confines of the room we were in, but, I suspected, the area as a whole.

His real reason for relocating a couple of years before, just as mine a few more before that was pressed to the bookcases along the wall.

"I mean, you didn't think I picked this place for the weather?" he asked. "My damn leg has hurt since I got here."

Still fighting to process what was being shared, place it alongside the information that I already had, I ignored the last comment completely. A quip that was supposed to be illustrative or even provide levity that I had no interest in.

Hell, I didn't care if his whole damn leg fell off.

"So that's why you've been running Doone," I said. "You knew Careen didn't want in, so you went to the kid, even got their security staff to jump in."

"Other way around," Hattie said. "I went to Careen, and when she wanted no part of it, Mick reached out, said he could deliver the kid."

"Reason being?"

"Because they're bored out of their minds, that's why," Hattie replied. His quickest, most forthright answer since we arrived.

Information that he almost flung at me, as if that part more than any other I should have already put together.

"Half of their staff have already left. The rest have been playing bodyguard since the old man kicked. They would have done this for free, just to have something to do.

"As for the kid, he took even less convincing."

Hearing it aloud, I had to consciously force down my initial reaction. A pang of anger that rose through my core, making me want to lift the Beretta and fire. Or rush forward and use it like I had the MK3 on Keegan earlier, mashing the butt of it into Hattie's skull.

Desires I pushed aside, forcing myself to focus on what was being shared.

Precious information that there likely wouldn't be another way of obtaining.

Looked on from the outside, it wasn't an impossible scenario to envision. I was around when The Council strapped that bomb to the underside of the family van. I attended the funerals of his wife and daughter.

More importantly, I saw what it did to him. The torment he was under. The amount of time and energy he spent in bringing them down.

I recall it vividly, because it mirrored – and arguably even surpassed - what I went through with Marcel Bardette. Efforts that Hattie had been there to help me with, and I made damned sure I repaid the favor.

I also knew what I would do if Marcel hadn't died in prison a few years ago and was suddenly rumored to be running free again. Extreme measures that would definitely include relocating to a satellite office. Even resurrecting a local crime family and convincing them to act as a mole for me.

An overarching scheme that clearly had all the fingerprints of the man I had worked with for so long.

What I didn't understand was how my granddaughter fit into this in any way.

"Why?" I snapped. One last time, reiterating the reason that Quinn and I had made the trek.

Not why he had sent me to the Doone mansion or planted an ambush – intended to be fatal or not – in the mountains, but why we were drawn into this at all.

A question to bring us back full circle, now that we better understood the machinations that had fed into it.

"Because they said they needed something from Leland. A show of faith as the price of inclusion," Hattie whispered.

"Meaning what?" I snapped. "You offered them somebody who helped take them down way back when?"

Twisting his chin an inch to either side, Hattie said, "They took my family."

"So you gave them mine?!"

The side-to-side movement continued, this time going a bit further in either direction. "Her last name is Coyle. I didn't even know she was your family."

Lifting the gun gripped tight in his right hand a few inches, he jabbed the tip my way. "What I do know is, I didn't offer her. Damned sure didn't pick her.

"*They* did."

With that, his final words expelled, he jerked the gun upward. One quick motion not to aim at me, but to plant the metal tip under his jaw.

A fluid movement that was the quickest I'd seen him move in years, ending with him jerking back on the trigger.

Chapter Forty

I wasn't sure which resonated louder inside the cavernous space that was Hattie's living room.

The gunshot that ended his life.

Or the final words he ever spoke.

In the immediate aftermath of the bullet traveling at an upward trajectory, starting in the soft skin under his chin before exiting through a much larger hole at the back of his skull, neither Quinn nor I said a word. Neither of us even moved.

We simply remained exactly as we were when he first jerked up his gun. A move that caused me to do the same with mine, extending it before me. A ready position to return fire with my index finger tucked inside the trigger guard.

Eight feet away, Quinn stood with legs flexed. Her own form of an alert pose, prepping to go diving for cover if need be. A stance that effectively made her a foot shorter than her actual height, frozen there by her hands clutching the bookshelf behind her.

Respective poses we both held, listening as the reverberations of the gunshot faded away. Sound waves that bounced from the arched ceiling above. Auditory ping-pong balls slamming against every wooden surface, slowly losing volume until finally dissipating entirely.

A soundtrack to the sight of Hattie's dead body in front of me. The fifth so far on the night, after a gap of many years before that.

A tally that promised to only be the beginning.

The force of the shot had torn away a good bit of the back half of his head. Blood and scalp and brain tissue that decorated the floor and wall behind his chair, most of it out of sight from where I sat.

A protected vantage that Quinn wasn't afforded as she stood rigid, her eyes wide.

Having driven him back in his seat, his body rested flush against the oversized cushions. His chin was pointed directly at the ceiling.

A single tendril of blood snaked downward from the entry wound an inch below his jaw.

For more than a full minute, neither of us moved. A long moment as the adrenaline slowly ebbed away, allowing logical thought to return.

Deductive reasoning, first registering in the burn in my right shoulder. Lactic acid from holding the gun extended parallel to the ground.

Muscular fatigue that Quinn must have experienced in her thighs as well, each of us returning to our stasis positions.

"What the hell just happened?" Quinn whispered.

A question I left unanswered as I placed my weapon down on the arm of the chair beside me and rose to a standing position.

"Did that asshole just kill my daughter?"

For the second time in as many moments, I let a question go without reply. The only sound was the wheeze of the cushions as they reinflated in my wake.

A faint hissing as I took a step forward, closing the gap between myself and Hattie. Shortened distance, making the assorted scents rolling from the man more pronounced. Smells of gunpowder and blood and even singed cotton from where the heated tip of his gun came to rest in his lap.

An acrid combination that flitted across my nostrils as I patted down either of his legs. A quick check that turned up nothing on the left before revealing what I was searching for on the right.

"And what the hell did that last thing he said mean exactly?" Quinn asked.

Once more, I remained silent. Quiet to let myself reason through what just happened, while affording my daughter the same.

Processing she took to audibly, needing a few extra moments to get to the question I knew she would eventually arrive on. The one I suspected she showed up with this afternoon, only now having the first shred of credibility to the theory.

The same damn one that was rattling around in my head.

Quite possibly the only thing that could take the assorted thoughts and emotions of the last half day and amplify them. Fear and worry and concern, potentially mixed with an even larger dollop of guilt.

"Did *you* do this?"

Uttered as more of an accusation than a question, I didn't need to look over to see the expression I knew was on my daughter's features. The same one she wore five hundred and now one days ago, standing on the front stoop of my home and telling me to keep my ass away.

A warning she probably wished she had heeded as well, leaving me to rot on that bench at the end of the dock.

"Huh?" she snapped.

Another question I ignored, pulling the phone wedged into Hattie's front pants leg free. A burner to match the one Mick had, the only difference being that his logs held just two numbers. Both unsaved, they were each present in equal amounts.

Listings it didn't take a lot of deduction skills to figure out.

One belonging to Mick, the other to Leland.

The only two people in his little scheme that he would need to speak with directly himself.

"Did you just kill my daughter?!" Quinn screamed, her shrill voice pulling my focus her way.

"I don't know," I whispered.

"What?!"

"I don't know!" I yelled, my voice raised for the first time all day to match hers. Hours of berating from her now coupled with the enormity of what was just shared.

The possibility that maybe this did somehow all connect back to me, just as it had decades before.

"I don't know who is doing this! Or why!" I said, letting the responses pour forth. Answers to every one of her questions, unleashed at a volume that echoed through the room.

Thrusting the burner phone out before me, I shouted, "All I've got is the name of some organization we snuffed out years ago that may or may not be meeting in two days, and a couple of phone numbers.

"That's all I know, so that's what I'm working with."

Across the room, Quinn stood quivering. Scads of emotions threatening to burst forth, barely able to be contained.

Even more, responses she wanted to shout back. Thoughts about what was happening and me personally, aching to be unleashed.

Verbal spears that she resisted throwing, instead taking a step to the side, and then another, drifting toward the door.

"Go to Hell. And this time, keep your ass there."

Chapter Forty-One

Now

The noise is little more than an inhalation. A quick breath drawn in, causing a slight whistle in the back of the throat. A sound evoked through sheer surprise, the arriving party not expecting to find anybody besides the same sleeping young woman that has been here for much of the last day.

Someone not much older than a child, lashed to a bed and fed drugs through an IV needle to keep her unconscious.

A sight that is both heartbreaking, and fills me with rage. Murderous wrath that means the instant the sound finds my ears, I raise the USP and tug back on the trigger.

No pause to wait for recognition as I whirl away from Cailee's bedside. Sure as hell not a chance for them to explain themselves or try to reason their way out of what I am seeing.

Not one part of me gives a damn that the arriving woman has been tasked with caring for Cailee. Checking her lines and changing her sheets and whatever the hell else. Making her feel as comfortable as possible.

Just like the guards outside and the fat ass in the basement and everyone else associated with this place, she is the enemy. She is personally responsible in one way or another for what I am staring at.

And she deserves to die for it.

The woman barely has a chance for her eyes to widen before the .45 caliber round slams into the smooth surface of her forehead. A red divot carved into the porcelain skin, exiting through a crater many times larger. Propulsive energy that sends a shower of blood and brain matter against the wall behind her. An amoebic mosaic visible as she melts to the floor, not to move again.

Barely has she done so before my attention swings back in the opposite direction. The immobilizing shock of moments before snapped, my mind begins to race anew. Patterned thinking, processing what I am seeing. What I need to do next.

How the hell I get us both out of here.

An escape that was already going to be the toughest part of all this, just made infinitely more so by the state of my granddaughter.

She is here and she is alive, and for those things I am thankful, but they are the absolute only positives to be found in this mess.

Passing the USP with a wisp of steam and smoke still rising from the front tip into my left hand, I pull the MK3 from its sheath with my right. Wielding it like a machete, I start with the leather straps binding Cailee to the bed frame.

Jerking the blade back past my hip, I snap it downward, flinging the razored edge at the inch-wide cowhide. Cleaving blows aimed just above the mattress, with enough force to rip through the straps without going anywhere near her skin.

The fastest possible way of freeing her from this makeshift prison, without expending the time to wrestle with the clasps encasing her ankles and wrists.

Unnecessary bindings given the amount of narcotics that look to have been fed into her system, shutting down almost all function beyond a slowed breathing pattern and even slower heartbeat. Essentials that ensure she is alive, but have rendered her little more than a rag doll, incapable of sending the needed nervous messaging to initiate movement, let alone the muscle response required to carry it out.

Again, those same urges I have felt repeatedly since entering the master suite in the guesthouse – or even stepping foot on the island before that – spike within me. Desires to go over to the corpse resting on the floor and lash out with feet and fists. Errant blows sent directly into joints and limbs, reveling in the sounds of their destruction.

Even more so, to spill out into the hallway and find whatever other guards might be around. Staff and servants too, if that is all there are.

Any target I can find to unleash the acrimony I am carrying. Complete annihilation of any breathing soul on the island, after which I will collect my granddaughter and carry her down to the south end to meet her mother aboard the fishing boat.

Desires that are little more than a pipe dream. Fantasy that will have to wait as I slide the MK3 back into the sheath along my calf.

"Come on, C. Let's get the hell out of here."

Chapter Forty-Two

Then

If people had any idea how dangerous cellphones were, they wouldn't keep the damned things clutched in their hands at all times. Attachment issues going far beyond Hattie's affinity for a tumbler of bourbon. A need to always be connected to the world as a whole. The deep-seated belief that if something occurred in some remote corner without them immediately knowing – and commenting – their life may somehow be rendered moot.

Unsecured points of access containing people's most prized secrets. Banking information. Social security and credit card numbers. Data about their spouse and children.

To say nothing of what I was now using Leland Doone's burner phone for. An around-the-clock means of locating someone, as easy as entering their number into any one of a hundred different websites out there.

A direct GPS system that nobody under the age of thirty had the common sense to ever turn off.

Not even when they were supposed to be deep in hiding.

A cheat code that I could only wish had been available back when I was doing this sort of thing for a living.

The only shared entry between Mick and Hattie's cellphones was an unsaved number with a local area code. A listing I had no doubt was attributed to Leland, he being the only logical shared link between the two.

The sole person outside of Mick in the entire Doone organization that Hattie would deal with once Careen had turned him down, wanting to keep the circle as tight as possible. A project that could have been in an official capacity, or performed even without Otis Herbert having the slightest it was going on.

A personal matter he was going to see to, regardless of consequences.

Almost certainly a burner phone, the device had likely been acquired by Hattie and handed out when everything began. Cheap models that didn't do nearly what most newer phones were capable of, but were still equipped with remote tracking. Satellite relay of its location at any moment it was turned on.

For some even if it was off, so long as the battery and SIM card inside were both connected.

A point of contact none of the men would be without, given the impending meeting of The Council. A means of communication that had fed me the location currently listed at the top of the screen of my own cellphone nestled into the cupholder of the middle console.

An arrangement that was a slight alteration of what I was used to, forced to make do after Quinn dropped my go-bag in the driveway and tore away from Hattie's place with my truck in a plume of smoke and the scent of charred rubber.

A hasty exit, managing one last outburst without her actually having to utter another word to me.

Anger that I couldn't blame her for, even if I didn't yet know if it was aimed in the right direction. Pressure that had become too much, needing to be released at the nearest possible target.

And since no clear options had presented themselves, she'd

resorted to the same punching bag she had been using for years. Hostility I was more than used to, dating back long before what happened at Cailee's graduation.

Not that it really mattered if I wasn't. Given what I was up against, the information Hattie had shared and the amount of time that had continued to tick away, I had far more important things to focus on than my daughter's feelings.

Hell, if anything, it might even be for the best. If her hatred for me kept her far removed, that just meant she was safe.

One less thing for me to worry about, each successive step promising to become increasingly hostile. Dangers that were going to continue to mount until I either found my granddaughter, or I died trying.

All before a hard deadline that was even more ominous – if not a little further away – than the forty-eight hour mark we had been chasing.

Flicking my gaze away from the street before me, I glanced to the red pin acting as a beacon on my screen. A locator resting near the bottom of a parabola dropping downward. A landmass of white, gridded with streets represented by gray lines.

A chunk of suburban life, surrounded on three sides by plains of bright blue.

A unique geographic feature that anyone who had spent even a little bit of time in the greater Seattle area recognized immediately as Mercer Island. A mass of ground rising right up in the center of Lake Washington, separating Seattle proper to the west from the enormous suburb of Bellevue to the east.

A corridor of land and water carved through the center of the metropolitan area, connected by a single freeway running across all three. Multiple lanes in both directions that were heavily congested during daylight hours with commuters trying to get to the office or tourists hitting the sights from their cheaper rooms outside of down-town, though at exactly halfway between midnight and dawn, was largely deserted.

Concrete lanes that were lightly dotted with truckers looking to dodge traffic or needing to make morning deadlines. Big rigs that paid me no mind as I slipped between them, passing over the open water of Lake Washington before hitting one of only a couple exits that existed on the island.

A ramp that extended away from the freeway at an angle, funneling me toward the center of the island. A southeastern direction I followed along a thoroughfare lined with fast-food restaurants and gas stations, most of their neon signage turned off for another couple of hours still.

Darkened buildings that filed by on either side as I continued onward, covering a couple more blocks before heading due south.

One last turn, taking me into the heart of the island. Streets that were entirely residential, littered with single family homes of one and two stories. Houses made of brick and stone, built to withstand the rain and cold of the unique setting.

Structures erected long ago, with towering trees filling their lawns and fall décor resting on their stoops.

Places that weren't the most posh in the city, but were definitely nestled in the upper middle class.

The kind of place I could definitely see Leland holing up. His idea of roughing it, compared to the mansion I'd been to earlier or the downtown penthouse he probably now called home.

A far cry in every way from La Rosa Negra, or even the young man with dyed hair who worked behind the bar.

Putting the wheels of the sedan taken from the cabin in the center of the street, I flicked my gaze between the glowing device beside me and the houses drifting past. Alternating glances, checking both my positioning on the screen, and the numbers affixed to front doors and mailboxes.

Digits made of wrought iron or brass that flashed under my headlights, guiding me through the last couple of hundred yards.

The final chunk of ground separating me from the young man I'd been chasing for what felt like days. The one who had magically popped up at a football game last weekend, and proceeded to turn my granddaughter's world upside down.

Which, by extension, had done the same to Quinn's.

And now my own.

Ripple effects that the little prick had never considered, thinking only about whatever enticing offer Hattie had made. The chance to rebuild what his father used to control. To ascend to what he likely believed was his rightful place.

Reasoning that probably made sense through his diminished worldview, about to be proven completely wrong.

Even if I didn't have both the address and location of the place up on my screen, it would have been easy to spot from the street. The sole home since I left Hattie's with lights blazing in every window, the single-story brick house was lit up like a jack-o-lantern.

A beacon along the street, calling me in as I dropped the turn signal and swung into the driveway, easing up behind a sedan that was the same make and model as the one I was sitting in. Another in a fleet, much like the burner phones they were using to communicate.

Rides possibly supplied by Hattie, but more likely as a part of their actual employment. Holdovers from Liam Doone's reign, when image was of the utmost importance.

Jamming the gearshift into park, I twisted off the ignition. Not planning to be there long, I didn't bother even pulling the keys as I reached for the Beretta resting on the passenger floorboard.

The same one I had been holding on Hattie not thirty minutes prior.

Tucking it tight to my right thigh, I slid sideways out of the vehicle. Turning my face toward the street, I jogged up the walk running the length of the house, careful to keep my features hidden from the residual glow passing through the windows lining the front.

Facing outward, I gave one last check of the area. A quick look to make sure there were no new lights on in any of the other windows. No dogs barking in the distance.

No super early risers, out for a bit of exercise.

Nothing to disturb the dead still of the night as I covered the last few strides and hopped up the pair of concrete steps leading to the door. Lifting a fist, I knocked twice, cut short before I could tap a third time by the door flying inward.

"Thank God you're here," a man in black slacks and a too-tight forest green t-shirt said. His body turned toward a television mounted on the far wall, a bag of chips was in his hands. "If I have to listen to those three in there go at it for-"

The start of a sentence that was cut short as he finally looked out to see the raised barrel of my gun pointed directly into his face.

Chapter Forty-Three

I didn't have any duct tape remaining, having used the entire roll previously to subdue Mick. Bindings that had done exactly as they were supposed to, rendering him basically immobile in the trunk of the car. Restrictions that had just minutes before been lessened as I slashed the tape around his ankles and the tether securing them to his wrists.

A small loosening from the human pretzel he had been so I could order his overgrown ass out of the trunk. A short journey on a wounded leg that took no small amount of effort, but was still better than having to try and wrestle him around by myself.

Bulk and heft that would have been damned near impossible, better served by letting him stagger along in a haze.

A state of semi-awareness that was still on plain display as he rested on the sofa in the living room of the same cabin Quinn and I drove away from barely two hours before. A location that was the best I could come up with on short notice after extracting Leland Doone from the pair of screaming ladies he was entangled with in the cottage on Mercer Island. Paramours that combined weren't as old as

219

me who took one look at the silhouette holding a gun in the doorway and immediately began to shriek.

Cries of terror that reverberated through the small house, threatening to reach the neighbors, cut short by light swats to the side of the head. Blows that might leave a small goose egg in the morning, but were mainly meant to silence them.

Shots that I would normally never levy on innocent young ladies, dealt under the auspice of where they were and who they were with. Guilt by association that made them my adversary, playing some small role in whatever had happened to my granddaughter.

Young ladies who would wake up with just each other before long and question if what they remembered really happened, or was merely a result of the empty mini bottles that lined the nightstand. Maybe even the faint lines of white powder that were sprinkled between them.

A confused discussion that would end with them feeling the knots on their heads and asking more questions before eventually stumbling home.

Provided, of course, that they didn't find the body of Leland's final guard stuffed in the closet with his bag of chips along the way.

The best I could do on short notice with Mick and Leland already occupying the entire trunk. A tight squeeze that required a lot of pushing, but was better than risking Leland waking up in the backseat and attacking me.

Even worse, getting pulled over for something innocuous like a busted taillight and trying to explain the bleeding, unconscious kid sprawled across the backseat.

Let alone how I came to be driving a stolen luxury sedan with a gunshot victim in the trunk and a loaded Beretta on the floorboard.

In and out of the small cottage on Mercer Island in less than fifteen minutes, it had taken another forty to get back to the cabin. A site I hadn't planned on returning to at all – let alone so soon – chosen as I was crossing the freeway over the open waters of Lake Washington.

Mental calculations done on the fly, coming to the conclusion that I needed a more remote location. A spot that was already littered with dead bodies, and clearly hadn't been used by anybody in months, if not years.

A far more suitable setting for what was planned next. A stark juxtaposition to the place tucked on a side street in a suburban neighborhood on a small landmass. Narrow confines that were deserted for the short time I was there given the late hour, but eventually would start to wake up.

If not by their own alarm clocks just a few hours away, then from the sights and sounds that were sure to ensue.

Anger that had been building for more than half a day. Frustration that was steadily climbing at the lack of progress in finding my granddaughter, finally cresting with the third visit with Hattie.

New information that had driven Quinn away.

Threatened to remove any lingering vestiges of control I had left if I came to discover that what my old associate had insinuated was true, and that this all somehow was caused by me.

No matter how unwittingly that might be.

Without the benefit of duct tape or the cobra cuffs I kept stowed in the truck to bind Leland into the lone armchair in the cabin's living room, I had resorted to what I had available. A pair of electric cords pulled from lamps in an upstairs bedroom to lash his arms to the wooden frame of his seat. A longer extension cord was used to secure both ankles to the bottom legs.

Bindings that looked just as effective as the duct tape enveloping his cohort as he too sat blinking heavily under the bright glow of the antler chandelier above. A return to firing of brain synapses after the blow given to him by the butt of my Beretta.

A shot that had ended any form of opposition before it even had a chance to begin.

The young man strapped to the chair before me didn't look exactly like the one in the photo I took from Cailee's apartment. In that image, he was clearly playing to type. A nice kid out for a football game, dressed in a baggy sweatshirt, his dark hair combed back in the middle with the sides left to curl around the sides of his forehead.

More suppositions of how lesser people looked and dressed, much like choosing the house on Mercer Island because he figured that's what it meant to be slumming.

In their place, he was now dressed in a matching set of black silk boxers and tank top. The only clothes he was wearing when I arrived, clearly showing up during a break between sessions for him and the pair of ladies.

Young women who were dressed in even less than him, all three strewn across the bed, still bearing a post-coital glow.

Around his neck was a handful of necklaces. Chains with gold links or oversized medallions, giving the impression of a young, white, Mr. T.

Despite his recent bedroom activities, every hair was meticulously in place, held there by copious amounts of gel.

"Mph," he muttered, squinting against the bright light from the overhead fixture. A series of faux deer antlers all laced together, hanging from a chain dropping straight down out of the exposed beams above. "Where-"

"Shut up," I said, cutting him off. Standing at the head of the coffee table separating Leland from Mick, my arms were crossed. Plainly visible in my right hand was the Beretta.

"Wha?" Leland said, rolling his attention my way. "Who the hell-"

Taking one single step to the side, I drew my left hand across my body. A windup in one direction, curling it past center mass, before snapping it back the other.

Centrifugal force that turned my arm into a whip, swinging the backside of my knuckles and fingers across his jaw. Contact that jerked his head the opposite direction and sent a plume of bloody spittle across the floor.

A blow loud enough to echo through the room, followed in order by Mick mumbling against the tape covering his mouth. Veiled threats of every kind no doubt, matched by him fighting to hoist his heft up off the couch with his hands tied behind him.

Performative measures I gave no mind, my attention firmly on Leland.

The little asshole I'd spent most of the night trying to find.

The one I would gladly spend the rest of it beating the hell out of if I had to to get what I needed.

"I told you to shut up," I said. Holding the Beretta up before me, I said, "Next time you speak out of turn, I hit you with this."

Turning it sideways, I worked the slide back on it, racking a round into the chamber. "And the one after that, well, ask your friend over there."

Leaving Leland to do as instructed and fix his gaze on the over-sized guard who had been watching over him - probably even cleaning up after him - for years, I returned to my previous position. Placing the gun down on the table so it was in plain sight of them both, I refolded my arms.

"Now," I said, "let's skip the part where you ask if I know who you are or what I'm doing. The answers to those are both yes. I know you are Leland Doone. I know your mother is Careen, and I know this piece of shit is Mick, your head of security."

Lifting my gaze, I glanced to the ceiling and added, "Just like I know that this cabin was a safe house your father used to have."

Lowering my attention back to him, I continued, "Now, let's go over what you should know. I am a man who has spent the last nine hours trying to find your ass. The same one who killed all those guards on the ground outside, and even the one at your little brothel there on Mercer Island.

"I shot Mick, and I will not hesitate to do the same to you."

Pausing there, I peered down at the kid, letting him feel not just the veracity in my words, but the pure loathing that underscored them. Hatred that had surfaced at moments such as the firefight earlier, or the bathroom at Pike's Place, or even the brief shouting match with my daughter. Simmering rage that was more than enough to rip him apart.

And enjoy doing it.

"I will ask you this once, pain free," I said. "After that, I will start to go to work, so I want you to think very hard about how you answer.

"Where the hell is Cailee?"

One at a time, I could see various thoughts work their way through his mind. Realization as to where he was and what was happening. Understanding of the threats I'd made.

Recognition of the question I'd asked.

Disparate items that landed, plainly resting on his features, as he tried to formulate some sort of response. No doubt a lie, or a smartass comment, or even a threat.

All of the usual first-round answers, needing at least a few more shots to come to understand that this wasn't what he was used to.

He was not in control.

And there was nothing he could do to change that.

It was a sequence I had seen play out many times, on every type of person I'd hunted down, in all sorts of locations. The universal belief by people of their ilk that they could be the outlier and talk their way to the upper hand.

Thought processing I could see at work, only interrupted by a flash of light outside the windows lining the front. Flares that presaged the low whine of an engine coming closer.

Signals that drew his attention over, needing a moment to resonate before his lips parted. A thin smile appeared, displaying teeth stained red with blood.

He managed to cough out a few chuckles.

Laughter that began to spill from him, causing his entire body to tug against his bindings. Muscle striations bulged along his bare arms and shoulders. Even the chains around his neck started to jangle.

Little by little, his voice rose as the vehicle came to a stop and the driver exited, stomping up the steps and onto the porch. Movements just barely audible over Leland's laughter. An impending arrival that he seemed certain was the calvary arriving to save him.

Noises I recognized as the furthest thing from it, remaining motionless as the sound of footsteps came nearer.

A late arrival, culminating in the front door bursting open to reveal Quinn on the other side. Wild eyed and windblown, she stopped just inside the threshold, taking in the spread before her. A quick pass from right to left, examining Mick and myself before ultimately landing on Leland.

A punk kid so certain of himself, of the victory he had envisioned, that the truth of things hadn't yet registered with him. Sanctimony, continuing to pour out as giggles.

Perceived amusement at what was happening. At what had already taken place.

At the arrival of Quinn herself.

Quite easily the worst possible thing he could have done. The proverbial last straw, coming on the heels of more than a day spent searching for Cailee.

Weight that was too much to bear, causing Quinn not to move on Leland himself, but to march directly for the table between us. Snatching up the Beretta, there was no pause. No empty threats. No questions or gestures or promises of what would happen next.

Nothing but a quick jerk to the side, aiming the weapon at Mick and pulling back on the trigger. A shot to the side of his skull, sending blood spatter across the floor and a thunderous reverberation through the cabin as the man's enormous body rocked sideways.

A descent that was still ongoing as Quinn turned the smoking tip of the gun on Leland.

"Where the hell is my daughter?"

Chapter Forty-Four

The change in Leland Doone was palpable. A visible switch that I thought all the dead bodies outside would have already flipped.

A visceral realization that he was no longer in his insulated cocoon. The protective umbrella he'd spent his life under was no more.

He was in a place where his father's name couldn't help him. His family's money meant nothing. Mick, and the guard from the cottage, and whoever else was paid to clean up his messes and keep his ass breathing, weren't coming through the door.

It was just him and two very pissed off people.

Family members of somebody he had set up. A pawn in a scheme predicated on his own self-importance. Misguided grandiose that made him an easy target for Mick and Hattie, deftly manipulating him to get exactly what they wanted.

The same way The Council – whoever the hell they and their new leadership might be – had.

Eyes widening to the size of plates, he sucked in deep breaths. Gasps of air that made his shoulders rise and fall. His torso draw in and out.

All the blood drained from his features.

A massive dump of adrenaline that, again, I would have already thought flooding his system. Chemicals fighting against whatever lingered in his system from the nightstand earlier, finally reaching his bloodstream. With it came a rise in body temperature, pushing beads of sweat to his skin.

Lips parting as his jaw sagged, he stared at Mick's limp form for the better part of a minute. A macabre show that he couldn't force himself to look away from, watching the man who had been the head of security for the family reduced to a corpse before him.

A man leaking copious amounts of blood from the open sieve in the side of his shaved head. Dark liquid pooling onto the sofa cushion beneath him, saturating the batting.

A deluge so heavy it had already turned the damned thing almost black.

"You crazy..." he muttered. The start of a sentence that instantly drew Quinn's arm up a second time. Raising it parallel to the floor, she squared the front tip between the kid's dark brows.

"Go ahead. Finish that sentence. I dare you."

To say I had never seen my daughter angry enough to do physical harm would be dishonest. An outright lie, even. The kind of thing a father might try to tell himself in the name of believing the best in his child, when in reality he knew the opposite was true.

Pissed off seemed to be my daughter's baseline state. A resting phase that could have been how she dealt with me, or just how she best faced the world.

A Teflon enamel that started that night at home twenty-five years ago, hardening into a shell that even a diamond couldn't breach.

Even knowing all that, it was the first time I had ever seen – or even known of – her to do something like that. An attack that wasn't just fatal, but without pause.

No grandstanding. No long speeches or posturing, making threats of what she would or wouldn't do.

A direct entrance with bloody intent, needing to only see what was playing out in front of her before attacking.

A parent's love, manifesting in that same animalistic way that I could feel bearing its fangs inside of me.

"Where the hell is my granddaughter?" I asked. Keeping myself rooted in place, I remained standing across from Quinn. Placement to ensure that I didn't do anything to draw away Leland's attention.

Nothing to pull his gaze from the very real threat of the gun still seeping wisps of smoke before him.

"Your wha?" Leland managed to get out. An incomplete sentence, shoved out between deep inhalations. His body's own physiology working against him, overloading his system with a dozen evoked responses simultaneously. "I don't..."

"You do, asshole," I spat. "Cailee. Where the hell is she?"

The middle of Leland's forehead formed a deep V as his brows came together. Confusion as he tried to flick his gaze my way.

Effort Quinn thwarted by sliding to the side, closing the distance between them, reducing it no more than a couple of feet. Positioning that was not just too close for her to miss if she pulled the trigger, but placement that made it impossible for him to look anywhere else.

Smell anything else.

"I..." he began to moan. A single sound sliding out from deep in his throat.

"You do," Quinn snapped, parroting my words. Keeping the Beretta extended in one hand, she reached into the pocket of her jean jacket with the other and extracted the photo we took from Cailee's apartment earlier.

The one I had been carrying before leaving it in the truck to slip through the woods the first time we were here.

"And we know you do, so start talking."

"Okay, yes, I know who she is, but I don't know where she is," he said, the words spilling out. "I swear, I don't!"

"Oh, now you swear?" Quinn said, taking another half step

forward, whittling the gap between them down further. "Is that supposed to make us believe you?"

"It's the truth!" Leland answered. Raising his focus from the gun before him for the first time, he looked to Quinn with wide eyes, his cheeks red and puffy. "I was supposed to meet her a couple nights ago, but she stood me up, and I haven't heard from her since! I swear! And I can prove it."

Ignoring his repeated use of the word *swear*, as if this was a courtroom and his being under oath magically meant every word was gospel, I went right for the last sentence. "How?"

"James Hattinger," he said, looking my direction. "At the FBI. He can tell you-"

"We already know Hattie," Quinn said, interrupting him before he could get the full sentence out. "And he ain't telling us anything, because his ass is dead."

His eyes widening even further, Leland kept his focus on me. "What?"

"Yep," I confirmed, raising my chin in a nod. "Shot himself in front of us right before I came to find you."

For the second time in less than five minutes, there was a visible shift in Leland's features. A downturn that occurred first at the sight of Mick being shot.

And now this one, at mention of Hattie being dead as well.

News that pulled away any remaining resolve he might have. Any strength. Even the ability to control his bodily functions, letting piss run freely, saturating his silk boxers and the chair he was sitting on.

A full bladder that quickly overtook both and began dripping to the floor.

The first of bodily fluids to leak, followed an instant later by on onrush of tears as he folded himself as far forward as his lashings would allow and began to sob.

Chapter Forty-Five

Now

The last thing on earth I want to do is use my granddaughter as a human shield. A flesh-and-blood replacement for a Kevlar vest, covering the front and back of my torso against any incoming fire.

Exposure that might end in one of the guards roaming the island doing to her what I just did to the woman coming to check on her. A shoot-first mentality that might end badly for the very person I am here to save.

It's just that right now, I don't have any other choice.

I have no idea what sort of chemical cocktail they were forcing into her veins via the intricate IV system in her room. Based on the low level remaining in the bag when I sliced it away and the complete lack of responsiveness from Cailee since, it was something potent.

A knockout elixir that is unlikely to wane anytime soon. What might as well be a paralytic, leaving her unable to aid in her own escape in any way. Not even to keep herself upright or run for the exit when I tell her to.

Dead weight that I don't just need to support, but have to carry. A load hefted over my left shoulder, her waist resting flat against the joint.

An unsecured mass that I curl my left arm up and over while keeping my opposite hand functional, hoping to keep her balanced in place as I make my way back down the same hall I traversed just minutes ago. A space that seemed a lot bigger and quieter on the previous trip, without the slaps of my feet.

Footfalls made louder by the cargo I am carrying.

The USP clutched in my right hand, my focus is on the opening ahead that I emerged from before. An entrance to the winding stairwell that will be a bit tight for the two of us, but will provide direct access to the basement.

A complete retracing of my prior route, bypassing the need to reinvent something that already worked once.

"Come on, C," I mutter between clenched teeth. Whispered affirmation as much for my sake as the unconscious girl slung over my shoulder. "Hang in there."

Race-walking down the hallway, I don't bother twisting to check behind us. Turns that would be unwieldy with her hoisted into place, slowing us down as we make for the exit.

Peeks back that I have to hope are unnecessary, my focus firmly on the opening up ahead. An open doorway that grows larger with each step. A portal drawing me nearer, pulling me forward.

Part two of a multi-pronged exfiltration that makes it into the stairwell and down just a single step before being brought to a halt. A sudden pause, caused by the sound of voices drifting upward toward us.

Light conversation, magnified by the tight confines and the stone walls on either side. A sound chamber that carries banter between two men our way, letting me hear every syllable shared.

A comment made by one, and the elicited laughter from the other.

Benign conversation that doesn't hint that they are aware of our presence, but still stops me where I stand with one foot raised. A precarious position with both hands occupied, leaving me with only a single point of contact.

Delicate balance, made worse by the ripple of palpitations rising up through me.

It isn't that I have the least qualm with killing these men. Just like the others who have come before them tonight, they deserve it.

Have earned it, even.

The problem, just as it was with the fish on the stringer at my dock only yesterday, is that doing so doesn't serve my purpose. Shooting them here won't only fail to benefit our escape, but it will actively make it worse.

Gunshots that – even with a suppressor – will carry through the tight confines of the staircase.

To say nothing of the logjam that two dead bodies will create in a confined space that was already going to be problematic.

Retracing the exact path that my foot traveled just an instant before, I place it back on the top step behind us. A second point of contact, allowing me to better balance Cailee's weight atop my shoulder.

Eschewing trying to merely walk backwards up and out of the stairwell, I instead push both heels downward and rotate my feet ninety-degrees. A sideways pivot that makes it easier for me to drive my opposite foot up off the lower step and climb back to the second floor.

At our back, I can hear the sounds of conversation growing closer. Ongoing repartee laced with mirth, echoing from the stone.

A soundtrack that spills out across the hardwood. Signs of impending arrival that spur me to move faster, using short, choppy steps as I carry Cailee back the direction we just came from.

Speed walking that I am already beginning to feel the effects of. Strain that is forming in the small of my back. Sweat that bathes my features.

Physical responses that already have me concerned about getting to the southern tip of the island, though fortunately for now we only need to go fifteen feet or so. A short jaunt, lasting just to the first doorway. A darkened entry I checked on the way past earlier, trusting my memory that it is just what we need.

A small half-bathroom, with only a sink and a toilet inside.

An unlikely destination for the pair of men approaching, making it an ideal place to hide as they pass.

Pace increasing one last time, I cover the last few steps and slip sideways through the door left standing wide. Going straight for the toilet against the far wall, I bend forward at the waist, letting gravity and Cailee's weight carry her forward.

A smooth transition from my shoulder to the porcelain seat, ending with her head and shoulder both braced against the wall beside it.

A resting spot I intend to leave her in for only a moment as I take a single step back the opposite direction. Distance enough to ease the door forward a few inches, blocking Cailee from view and creating space for me to hide in.

A repeat of sorts to what happened at Pike's Place just last night, right down to listening to the sounds of movement grow ever closer. A pair of foes who have no idea that I am poised in wait for them, ready to strike.

Bending my arm at the elbow, I raise the USP so the tip is pointed toward the ceiling.

My breath held tight, I wait as they finish their ascent. Stopping on the second floor, their voices grow louder as they come toward us, the hardwood groaning slightly beneath their weight.

Tucked behind the door, I put my focus on the narrow sliver afforded by the gap between the frame and hinges. A band of light that I stare intently at, watching, waiting, until it blinks out for but an instant as they pass.

The sign I have been waiting for.

A signal for me to slide out from my hiding spot and extend the USP to arm's length.

The instant my vantage moves past the edge of the doorway and I can clearly see both, I begin to fire.

Two rounds each into center mass, cutting them down where they stand.

Chapter Forty-Six

Then

Given the choice between the bodies littering the ground out in front of the cabin or the combination of Mick and Leland in the living room, Quinn and I decided to take the former. A choice to step out on the front porch, preferring to deal with the death scattered across the steps and around the gravel than what was waiting inside.

One dead man, and another returned to unconsciousness, soaked in tears and reeking of piss.

The two most responsible for what happened to Cailee. Targets for both of our ire, leaving us each wanting to do to Leland what Quinn had already done to Mick.

And once that was completed, start wailing on both of their corpses until at least part of the sheer rage pulsating through us was relieved.

The first to exit, Quinn stomped directly across the floorboards to the front edge of the porch. More loud footfalls, echoing through the desolate forest.

Quiet that allowed the sound to roll outward, unabated except for the dense pine growth pressing in tight from all directions. The very same cover that had saved my ass not four hours earlier.

A length of time that seemed unfathomable. A stretch during which I'd killed a handful of men, and witnessed the deaths of a few more.

Pressure that was starting to wear on us all, finally reaching a boiling point. Levels that could no longer be sustained in the face of such stakes.

Feelings that were put on hold earlier for the sake of our search. Level heads and best wishes ensuring that reasoning won out.

Logic that started to fall by the wayside around the time we spoke to Keegan. A combination of minutiae that wasn't making sense, culminating with the destruction splayed across the forest floor around us.

A fulcrum point, after which the truth of what we were up against had become obvious.

As were the things we would need to do to combat it, ensuring that we brought Cailee home again.

"You believe a word of that shit?" Quinn opened.

Standing with her thighs flush against the crosshatch supports of the porch rail, she dug into the inner pocket of her jean jacket. Extracting a pack of cigarettes, she tapped one out and thrust it between her lips.

A moment later, the acrid smell of tobacco smoke crossed my nostrils.

A habit I didn't even know she indulged in. Another thing that otherwise I would believe she was just using to bait me, though at this point I couldn't imagine even she had the strength for such a thing.

As I knew I sure as hell didn't.

The last thing either of us needed was a paternal lecture. A diatribe that wouldn't be well received, causing us to turn our angst at the one place we could ill afford right now.

Especially when our status was still a matter of some debate. A brief respite against a shared enemy, or round two of what began at Hattie's about to start.

Focusing instead on the question she asked, I thought back to all that I had just seen and heard during the last twenty minutes. A burst of activity on the front end, followed by a painfully slow start-and-stop conversation on the back.

Of everything that had transpired, the part I still least believed was that my daughter had taken a life. A shot to the side of Mick's skull without the slightest hint of hesitation.

A kickoff to all that came after that I opted to focus on instead, assuming that was the part she was actually referencing.

Once news of Hattie's demise was shared with Leland, the proverbial dam had broken. Just like Keegan earlier, any ability he had to lie, any skill at concocting subterfuge, was completely removed.

He was essentially reduced to an oversized raw nerve, soaked in piss and blubbering about how he just wanted to restore the family name and make his father proud. Drivel that we outright pushed him through until finally getting to some information that would help us.

And some more about how things had gone down over the last week that just infuriated us.

News that made us both wish Mick was still alive, so we could kill his ass again, having to settle for returning Leland to a state of unconsciousness instead.

More details I opted to skip past, putting my focus instead on the particulars of the weekend ahead. Things still yet to happen that could actually aid us moving forward.

"Timeframe he gave fits with what Hattie said earlier about Sunday night."

Glancing over, I saw her gaze fixed on the distance. Some darkened spot above the roof of the truck that she could focus on, even as her eyes glazed over.

"Also makes sense that they won't tell him exactly where it's going down until tomorrow morning. These kinds of people are paranoid as hell. They won't want to give anybody watching the time to get the drop on them, but they still have to give the other members enough lead time to get there."

A few feet away, Quinn cut a quick glance my way. A sideways stare while pushing out another zeppelin of smoke.

"Giving them twenty-four hours wouldn't really work. Nobody is going to get a message at ten o'clock on a Saturday night and take off.

"Depending how far they have to come, sending it out same day might not even be enough time."

I hadn't seen many gatherings like what was being described in the past, but I'd seen a few. Usually, the types of people who would attend something like The Council weren't the kind to play well with others. And even if they were, they would go to great lengths to avoid putting them all in the same room.

Too many targets, making teams like the one I was on practically salivate at the possibilities.

On rare occasion, though, meetings such as what was being described would happen. A gathering to negotiate a truce between warring factions. A memorial for a departed colleague.

The beginning of a new working partnership.

What could be going down now to bring so many together – or even exactly how many that may be - I had not a clue. Didn't sound like Hattie did either.

A completely new iteration, well beyond those we put away long ago, likely looking to tread on the old name. Stolen credibility that didn't much matter, it no longer my job to track down these types of people.

Now, all that mattered was finding my granddaughter.

Getting her as far away from this shit as I possibly could.

"These people," Quinn muttered. "This Council. You were there the first time?"

Grunting softly, I said, "I was."

"How bad are they?"

Long ago, I learned that words like *bad* belonged on a sliding scale. A rating system that had no absolutes, but dealt in quantifying degrees.

Based on the markets they worked in, the crimes they committed, The Council was nowhere near the worst. International traffickers of various forms who were more concerned with money than anything else.

A business mentality that pushed violence to the back burner. Last resorts in the name of protecting their interests.

Means steeped in efficiency, like what happened to Hattie's family.

"We beat them once," I said, not daring to utter a word of what Callie might be facing to my daughter. "We'll do it again."

Again, she glanced sideways at me. A lingering stare that weighted with no less than a handful of different motives, lasting several moments before she rotated her focus back to stare out past the truck.

"So now we wait," she muttered. A statement much more than a question.

Words heavily laced with dread. Disbelief.

"Just until morning," I replied. "Five or six hours from now, we'll either get a message telling us where the meeting is..."

"Or we won't, and then we'll really go to work on the kid," Quinn said as she snuffed out her cigarette on the top of the porch rail and cast it aside.

A white fleck, disappearing into the darkness.

"What about us?" I asked.

Making a point to look anywhere but at me as she turned away from the forest, Quinn smirked.

"I'll let you know."

Chapter Forty-Seven

The adage about the old requiring less rest than the young was only partially true. An expression based on observation, without actual testing or analysis. A belief that was semi-accurate, but didn't take into account that was largely because of lifestyle changes. A decline in activity level that decreased the need for rest.

A saying that I myself had found some limited truth in over the last couple of years, there only so many hikes and workouts one could do.

Especially when my afternoons largely consisted of sitting on the end of the dock catching dinner.

True as it might have been in general though, it sure as hell didn't apply in this situation. Not after the things that my daughter and I had already been through. The mad dash across the greater Seattle area. The firefight outside of the cabin. Nabbing Leland Doone from the safe house.

Witnessing Hattie take his own life.

Coupling all that with the host of interviews conducted and even the hour that was fast approaching when my day usually started rather than ended, the need for sleep was very real. Exhaustion that I

243

could feel deep in my joints, coming along with the aches of arthritis and the comedown from the assorted adrenaline surges throughout the night.

Weariness that meant within minutes of sprawling myself across the bed in one of the upstairs rooms of the cabin, I fell into a deep sleep. A darkened abyss through which there was no rapid-eye movement. No continued mental processing about everything that had transpired, and all that surely lay ahead.

A total disconnect, allowing me to completely black out. My body to grasp for every stray bit of replenishment it could.

A four-hour stretch that ended abruptly with the alarm on my phone sounding out at exactly eight-fifty. An intrusive wail that only needed a single tone before I was awake, shrugging off slumber and beginning to move again.

The start of a new day, spurred by the faintest glimmer of a working plan. A hope for how the next twelve hours or so would play out.

Having not bothered with a blanket, or to even remove anything more than my boots the night before, getting dressed took only a few seconds. A quick swap of the plain black pullover I had been wearing for a matching one in blue from the go-bag, while leaving everything from the waist down the same. Socks and underwear there were no point in changing without a way of showering, the only water in the place being the pallets in the pantry.

Plastic bottles that were plenty fine for brushing teeth or wetting down a washcloth to sponge away some of the stench of battle from the day before, but not enough to constitute actual bathing.

A lack of hygiene that was far from my biggest concern, needing only to ensure that it wasn't a public nuisance.

A reason for someone to take special notice.

Finishing by relieving myself in the empty toilet, I headed downstairs at exactly nine o'clock to find Leland awake. Eyes open, he stared intently out the windows lining the front of the cabin. A pointed stance meant to avoid the sight of Mick's dead body sprawled atop the sofa across from him.

A visual he could do his best to ignore, though there was no way to circumvent the smell. The metallic scent of blood and the caustic odor of gunpowder. The bitter ammonia tinge of Leland's own urine.

A potent enough combination, soon to include the slow start of desiccation. A process that would come faster as the sun grew stronger, penetrating the windows and warming the front room.

His features illuminated by the faint glow of sun, Leland seemed unaware of my presence. Complete detachment rendering him in a trance, trying to fool himself into believing none of this had happened. He was still back in the throes of passion with the pair of young ladies the night before. Or scouring local college football games for young coeds.

Even still back home at the family mansion with mommy.

Places where he felt safe and important, unaccountable for his actions.

Spots a hell of a long way from the safe house that had witnessed an untold number of people and crimes over the years. A backstory the kid could only guess at, his desires to add his own chapter being what had brought us all together now.

Me, awake only a few minutes and already antsy to be moving. Another headlong sprint with the goal of finding my granddaughter.

A forced stop that was fast drawing to a close, bringing with it a renewed sense of urgency.

Him, sitting across from a man he probably grew up thinking was invincible, the better part of his brain and blood now crusted to the couch. Piss-stained clothes. Cuts lining either arm from his straining against the cords keeping him pinned to the chair.

Upstairs, the faint sounds of Quinn rousting herself could be heard. Footsteps hitting wooden floorboards. An aging structure unused to movement, creaking and moaning under her weight.

"Here," I said. Twisting the top off a bottle of water, I took a step closer to Leland. Movement that he failed to register, continuing to stare out.

The separated state of mind, trying to insulate him from reality.

"Drink."

It wasn't until the midpoint of his rotation that he even recognized I was there. A natural response to noise that had made him turn, even without active thought.

An unexpected sight that caused him to jolt, visibly recoiling in his seat.

"Jesus," he muttered, glancing away and then back. "You scared me."

The number of things I wanted to reply were too many to list off. Comments ranging from the cliché that he doesn't know what scared is to threats of how frightened he should be.

How scared Cailee probably was, wherever she might be.

"Drink," I said once more, thrusting the bottle his way before he could get out another word. Shoving the top into his mouth, I tilted it upward, pouring water down his throat.

A steady stream he did his best to keep up with, even as it spilled out and down his chin on either side. Overflow that grew steadily larger until his parched throat could take no more and he began to cough, sending whatever was in his mouth down the front of his tank top.

A mess of hacking and sputtering that bent him forward. Continued coughing that expelled water droplets onto the hardwood floor as he fought for breath.

Sounds loud enough to mask Quinn finishing upstairs and coming down to join us, allowing her to move in silence until she was just a few feet away.

"Don't you dare sit there and choke to death," she muttered, pulling to a stop with her thumbs looped into the rear of jeans in my periphery. "We're not done with you yet."

Dressed in the same clothes as yesterday, the only visible difference in her appearance was her hair had been let down out of the ponytail. Locks that were wavy from having been cinched up the previous days, left to form a curtain around her jawline.

"You ready?" she asked, glancing my way.

Retreating back a few steps, I set the water bottle down on the bar and grabbed up my jacket. Riffling into the pockets, I extracted the only three items I took from the house where I found Leland the night before.

His wallet, a burner phone to match those carried by Hattie and Mick, and the battery I pulled out immediately upon finding it.

A device that hadn't exactly been a good luck charm for the latter two, likely to have the same effect for the third member of the crew as well.

"Wha?" Leland managed. Still folded forward in his chair, water dripping from his lips, he added, "You can't just leave me here."

"Don't worry," Quinn replied. "Like I said, we're not done with you yet."

Chapter Forty-Eight

The name of the joint was Stumpy's Place. A play on the thick pine forests that dotted much of the area, with the bottom foot of a tree that had been severed clean, revealing a dozen or so concentric rings, serving as the logo.

A diner that was a good fifteen miles from the cabin, resting right on the southern cusp of the Snoqualmie National Forest. A retro spot designed in the old silver dining car style that looked to mainly serve the men and women who frequented the surrounding woods. Folks in boots and flannel that lined the row of stools across the front counter and filled most of the freestanding tables in the center.

Large people who mostly thumbed their noses at the smaller booths across the front, making it easy for Quinn and me to commandeer a place in the corner. A vantage where I could keep my back to the wall and monitor everything going on around us.

Tasks my daughter was content to leave me to, the bulk of her focus going to the plate of sausage gravy and biscuits before her and the cup of coffee that never left her hand.

Her third such serving since arriving, with no sign of slowing.

Not that I begrudged her in the slightest, already working on a refill myself. Swill that tasted like boiled pine bark, but fulfilled the two main requirements of being hot and strong.

Liquid energy to break through the lingering soreness of the day before. Muscle pains that no amount of hiking or workouts in my basement could stave off.

The beginnings of a tonic that I paired with the protein and carbs of the Denver omelet and wheat toast on the plate in front of me. Food that otherwise I might find excellent, going down without much taste.

A loss of appetite brought on as my stomach tightened further with each passing minute. A slow march forward, with each second matched by my left leg bobbing up and down beneath the table.

Surging energy resulting from the anticipation beginning to mount within.

"What time is it?" Quinn asked through a mouthful of half-eaten biscuit.

Not trusting the cracked plastic Coke clock above the counter, I tapped on the screen of my cellphone.

"Nine fifty-three."

"What time are you going to turn it on?"

"Five minutes," I replied. "If anybody is trying to note locations, I want to give them as little time as possible."

Emitting a sound that was somewhere between a grunt and a growl, Quinn returned to her food. Head down, she used the fork in her right hand and her left index finger, shoveling the remains of breakfast into a heap.

A lead that I followed as I cut what remained of my omelet into thirds and began to fork them down. Oversized bites that I wasn't in the mood for, making myself eat them anyway. Nourishment that I knew I would need in the day ahead, much like the sleep this morning.

An old maxim that I heard going clear back to when I was a new sailor in the Navy, that being to always bank food and rest if possible.

One never knew when the next chance might be.

A mantra that served me well both there and later throughout my career, the last day bearing all the earmarks of a similar situation.

"When was the last time you checked the number Cailee texted from?"

"On the drive in," Quinn answered. A vague reply I took to mean it had yielded nothing yet again. "Squeezed in between more texts from Everett asking if we knew anything."

Three minutes after my daughter asked me to check the time, I dropped my fork down onto an empty plate and pushed it away. Sliding my phone over onto the same warm spot where the plate had rested, I tapped on the screen a second time, checking the white numbers against a bright blue backdrop.

Clear summer sky, giving way to vivid green pine trees, and below that the shimmering surface of water.

A snapshot taken from the end of my dock just a couple of months before. A place that seemed so disconnected from where I now was, though I couldn't help but wonder if ever I would look out from that spot without immediately linking it back to all of this.

A starting point that couldn't be dissociated.

Especially if things were to turn out badly.

A thought that held my attention just until the white numerals along the top ticked forward. A passing from 9:57 to 9:58, putting us exactly two minutes short of the hour.

"Here we go," I muttered, sliding my own phone away and replacing it with the cheap burners taken from both Mick and Leland. The former, scratched and beaten from abuse. The latter, a device so new it still had the peel-away sticker clinging to the screen.

A protective cover I left in place as I cast the other phone aside and inserted the battery into the back. Depressing the power button along the side, I held it until the screen flickered to life between us. Plain white, followed by a quick succession of words and letters.

Company names and model numbers I let pass as I slid my gaze up to see Quinn having assumed the same pose across from me. Her own interest in breakfast now gone as well, she stared straight ahead with her left cheek bulging outward, having not even gone the extra step of chewing and swallowing.

Both silent, we listened to the uneven cacophony of diner sounds around us. Utensils scraping plates. The drawer on the cash register sliding open.

Muted conversation and the low din of country music in the background. All of the expected sounds, matching the smells of bacon and maple syrup in the air.

Noises that grew more pronounced as the clock ticked a minute past the hour. And then another.

"Come on, dammit," Quinn said, the words slightly garbled through the wad of food stuck in her cheek. The last of breakfast she seemed to have forgotten about, forcing it down before adding, "I swear to God, if that kid lied to us..."

How that sentence would end, I had a few ideas myself. Notions I had entertained while listening to him share the story last night about how his scheduled meetup with Cailee on Thursday had gone. Vivid thoughts that had bordered on fantasy as I stood over his coughing ass this morning.

Plans that would have to wait at least a bit longer, interrupted by me reaching out and snatching up the second phone. Popping the accompanying battery into it, I started the same process of booting it up that we had just endured with Leland's phone.

A slog that seemed to last even longer the second time, the key difference between the two being the reward received at the end in the form of a new text. An incoming message I tapped on to accept, needing only a single glance before removing the battery from the back of both phones and grabbing up all four pieces from the table.

"What the hell?" Quinn asked, sliding out of the seat across from me. A question no doubt directed at the source of the text before moving on to add, "What did it say?"

The first part, I didn't even bother trying to answer.

Wouldn't know how to even if I wanted to.

"The meeting's happening. Fawn Island."

"Where the hell is that?"

"No idea."

Chapter Forty-Nine

Now

The total descent is supposed to be thirty-nine steps. Twenty-one separating the industrial kitchen in the basement from the main floor, with an additional eighteen needed to reach the second floor.

Our descent doesn't even make it half that far, stopping on the landing outside the door to the ground level. A dozen and a half stairs with the two of us wedged into the tight confines of the circular stairwell. A squeeze forcing me to walk sideways down, and even at that it leaves Cailee's hair and ankles brushing the walls on either side.

One step at a time, with our full combined weights slamming down onto my joints. Knees and ankles that are already feeling the effects of two days spent searching for her and the underlying arthritis beginning to flare.

Accumulated abuse that I can feel on each step down, with another floor and a couple hundred yards of open ground yet to cover.

An exit that will be anything but hasty, already straining my body in a way it hasn't been tested in ages. Exertion going back decades, well beyond anything I experienced throughout many of my years with the Bureau.

Physical struggle resembling some of the worst encountered during training at the Academy, or even boot camp before that.

Tests of strength and stamina, back when I had infinitely more of both.

Shortcomings that I now have no choice but to make up for through adrenaline and sheer force of will. Protective instinct over my family, and loathing for those who have endangered them.

Internal forces, aided by images like the ones of the children lined up in the guesthouse nearby.

Another horrific sight added to the catalog stored away in my mind. Snapshots I wish nothing more than to cast aside.

Visuals that I refuse to let Cailee become a part of, even if I die in the process.

Teeth gritted, my complete focus is on keeping us moving. Steady downward progress, after which things will level out in the kitchen. From there, a downhill sprint back through the trees, hopefully unimpeded after having removed a fair number of the guards earlier.

A mental sequence I am playing out in my mind, letting it drive me onward. Thoughts I am so immersed in, I almost miss the second appearance in as many minutes of someone ascending from the opposite direction.

Someone – whether male or female, guard or servant, I have no idea - stepping into the staircase from the entrance on the main level. A sudden intrusion, with only a single moan of a hinge as warning.

A precursor to a shadow flashing against the wall before a guard with dark hair combed straight back and a heavy shadow of facial hair appears. Unexpected opposition causing me to react through pure reflex.

A quick jerk upward of the gun in my hand, needing only to get it raised as high as my waist. A downward trajectory, aimed at his diminished elevation. Uneven heights, requiring me to raise it to a forty-five-degree before tugging back on the trigger.

Pure instinct, without thought of who might hear or fear of what may become of the body.

A short-range shot that isn't as clean as the woman on the second floor, hitting two inches lower and an inch to the side of the crater carved through the center of her forehead. Contact that drives through his left cheekbone, punching a clean hole straight into the skin and bone.

An entry point for an oversized bullet that spreads as it passes through the underlying soft tissue, exploding out the back of his skull in a plume of red and pink. Blood and brain matter that splatter paints the wall in a kaleidoscope of color far outpacing Hattie's display last night.

A mosaic left in plain sight as the force of the shot flings him backward. Propulsive energy that thrusts his top half down the stairs, folding him back at the knees.

Shoulders hitting first in the center of the landing, his feet come next. Whipping upward, they travel past his center mass and on down the top couple of steps leading to the basement.

A human Slinky sent toppling out of sight, leaving a trail of fresh blood spatter in its wake.

Chapter Fifty

Then

A close second to tracking capabilities on the long list of deficiencies with cellphones was the fact that they weren't well suited for doing any sort of reading or research. Deep dives that were far too difficult to navigate with a touchscreen keyboard and a viewing area no larger than a couple of inches square.

Dimensions that were fine for displaying the occasional map or looking up the odd phone number, but weren't going to be nearly sufficient for what we needed.

To say nothing of a lacking ability to print anything.

Not wanting to take the time to drive all the way home, the next best option was to find a nearby branch of the public library. An extension of the main Seattle system, with satellite locations all the way out to within ten miles of where I lived.

A place I was a member of under an assumed name and address and frequented at least once a week, said information coming as a surprise to my daughter. Initial shock that soon waned, pushed aside by a comment about proving my age once again.

A barb that was far from her best work, but I took to be her way of answering my last question from the night before, no matter how inadvertently. A return to status quo at least until our mission was complete that I let slide by without response as we entered the front doors to a facility that was less than half the size of what I was used to visiting.

A squat building made entirely of brick and glass nestled amidst a copse of pine trees, the interior laid out in a fairly standard formation. Essentially one large room, with different areas sectioned off by offering.

Up front were the new releases and adult fiction. Rows of metal shelves stacked five and six high, arranged in alphabetical order. Behind those were the non-fiction, with movies and music comprising the back.

In the far corner, a children's area was cordoned off by shelves that rose to waist height. Wooden units that enclosed a multi-colored rug and handfuls of miniature plastic chairs.

Seating almost filled to capacity by eager little ones listening to a librarian read a book aloud. A Saturday morning story hour to keep them occupied while their parents browsed about.

A source of noise and entertainment that provided plenty of cover for me and Quinn to slip unnoticed to the final quadrant of the library. The far front corner where a bank of public-use computers was located.

Machines that were roughly half full, manned by parents checking email and teenagers looking at whatever people their age devoted their attention to. Folks who barely glanced up as we slid around the far side and put our backs to the wall.

A vantage much like at the diner, where I could alternate my focus between the machine before us and the front door. A constant vigil that would be ongoing for the rest of the day, beginning the instant we powered Leland's phone to life.

Extra care that would need to be observed until we located

Cailee, no matter that the phone was now back off and the battery removed.

Measures I half expected Quinn to comment on, lobbing another caustic strike about paranoia my way.

A freebie she let pass more out of focus on the computer than any sort of benevolence as I jerked the mouse to wake the sleeping monitor. The instant it sprung to life, I input my library card and PIN numbers from memory into the corresponding boxes and hit enter.

Ten seconds after that, we were online, looking up Fawn Island.

A resident of Washington for only the last couple of years, never before had I heard of the place. A moniker that evoked plenty of visuals to mind, from narrow tongues of land sticking out into the Puget Sound or Pacific Ocean, to floating masses somewhere well off the coast.

Possibilities that would inform everything else moving forward, there no point in even looking at other information before starting there.

Going directly into a basic search engine, I input the name of the place. Bypassing the list of sites that came up in response, I instead clicked on the small thumbnail of a map along the right, bringing it up onto the screen.

An instant schematic that wasn't the absolute worst of what I'd imagined, but wasn't far off.

An assessment Quinn seemed to agree with, muttering, "Sonuvabitch."

"Mhm," I agreed, clicking on the plus sign in the bottom corner a few times to enlarge the image so it took up the bulk of the screen before us.

While technically one of the land masses comprising the San Juan Islands, Fawn was a nub of ground so tiny it couldn't even be seen on most maps without zooming in. A circle peeking out of the center of Deer Harbor, along the western part of Orcas Island.

One of the last toeholds of land that was technically American soil before crossing over into Canadian territory to the north or international waters to the west.

A place that The Council had clearly done their homework on, ensuring that if anyone was to get wind of the gathering, it would be a jurisdictional nightmare. A pissing match that would make any hope of prosecution moot.

Not that there was a high likelihood of that, the place appearing to be only accessible by boat and maybe helicopter, depending on topography and tree cover.

"What's it say online?" Quinn whispered.

A quiet request that I followed by reversing out and clicking on the first link in order. Overview information that told us the place was just a couple of acres in total and had been owned by a few Hollywood types over the years.

A celebrity playground before being purchased two years prior by an unknown party.

Details that fit with what little we knew from Hattie about the timeline of the reemergence of The Council.

Data that we spent the next twenty minutes trying to supplement, though any more details beyond that were scarce. A series of articles that were either too old to be relevant or were simply finding new ways to package the same information.

A hunt we kept at until nervous energy caused us both to be moving again, each armed with the same conclusion.

The only real way to get a handle on what we were up against was to go see Fawn Island for ourselves.

Chapter Fifty-One

My daughter went back to the same lie she pedaled at La Rosa Negra the night before. A made-up story about it being my birthday and this all part of a weekend celebration for the two of us. Long overdue time together, making up for the years when we were in different cities and couldn't be together.

A story with enough detail that the fellow with white hair and a whisk broom of a mustache behind the counter almost got moist in the eyes. Sentiment that caused his weathered features to curl up into a smile around the end of his unlit pipe as he glanced between us, nodding knowingly.

Or so he thought, not realizing that the last time I actually got so much as being told happy birthday from my daughter was a quarter century before on the opposite end of the country.

That being the same year I was last able to be a part of hers as well, her mother making it very clear I was not invited to whatever they were doing after moving away. Stonewalling that went as far as to even return any cards or gifts I sent unopened.

A concrete barrier that I threw myself against for a solid decade.

Long enough that Quinn had reached adulthood, and still my attempts at reaching out were brutally rebuffed.

A hint that I finally got, stopping altogether fourteen years ago.

More family history that the man didn't need to know as he handed over a key to an eighteen-foot Ranger fishing boat. A craft with two hundred and twenty horses on the back to get us where we needed to go, and a trolling motor off the side to provide plenty of cover once we arrived. Subterfuge that would be enabled by the stack of goods in the bed of the truck, picked up at a Walmart on our way over to the coast.

A small handful of fishing poles, with a prefab box of assorted gear and tackle. Stuff I could use later, perfectly suited for the pond out by my house, but not worth a damn on the waters we were venturing into.

Not that it much mattered. Every item was meant to be a prop in an act and nothing more. Just enough to keep any nosy overseers on the water or boat patrols around Fawn Island from getting suspicious.

"That everything?" I asked. My weight balanced on my knees at the stern of the craft, I turned toward my daughter behind the plastic shield protecting the steering wheel. A seating arrangement we had discussed beforehand, leaving me free to study our surroundings on the trip out, and – more importantly – once we arrived.

Complete focus on scouring the shoreline of the island, and the waterways surrounding it. Tasks that would be much more difficult if I also had to deal with marine traffic or nautical navigation, but would be easy enough while casting and reeling.

An arrangement that also suited Quinn fine, giving her something to do. A steering wheel to clutch, instead of being forced to pace across the short expanse in the center of the boat.

"Unless you think we need a cooler of beers or something to really drive home the act," Quinn replied without looking up. An offhand quip as she gave a quick check over the assorted gauges and switches lining the dash.

One final scan, ending with her cranking on the ignition. Three or four turns with middling success before finally the ignition caught, causing the engine to belch to life.

A begrudging start that coughed out a cloud of black smoke. A caustic plume that mixed with the brine in the air, tickling my nostrils as I leaned forward and unwound the nylon rope mooring the boat to the dock.

"I think we're good."

Leaving one end of the rope tethered to the cleat affixed to the edge of the craft, I flipped the opposite end into the boat beside me. Remaining bent forward at the waist, I pressed my palm into the side of the dock and pushed off, twisting the front a few feet to the side.

Space enough that Quinn could nudge the accelerator and begin to angle us away.

Using a slow and steady pace, we eased through the slips lining the dock on either side. Holding stations for boats of various sizes, representing everything from sleek rides like the one we were in to oversized pontoons to even a couple of small yachts.

Twenty footers that paled next to some of those parked closer to downtown, but probably got far more use from owners who wanted them as something more than status symbols.

"Is he still out there?" Quinn asked, her focus aimed straight ahead as she continued pushing us forward.

A vague question that I grasped instantly, turning and pressing my chin to my shoulder. A quick glance back to the shop we exited just moments before, complete with the old guy who had rented to us still leaning against the frame of the door.

His pipe lit, he removed it from his mouth with one hand, exhaling a billow of smoke that was promptly dragged away by the breeze. The other he raised over his head, spotting me looking back and offering a wave of farewell as we departed.

A gesture I matched, still standing with my hand upraised as Quinn punched the accelerator. A jolt on the throttle that thrust us forward, sending me back into the cushioned seats lining the rear of the craft.

A clumsy tumble that the old guy on the dock probably got a hell of a laugh from.

Just like my daughter beside me, letting loose a chuckle as the air whipped her hair around her head. A sandy brown flag beating rapidly to either side, framing a pair of dark aviator sunglasses.

One of a handful of purchases she picked up at Walmart while I was busy in the sporting goods department. A couple of non-alcoholic beverages and some snacks. A Seahawks hooded sweatshirt better suited for her to wear on the boat.

A tube of sunblock and the aviators, to protect her from the glare resting atop the surface of the water.

The old guy at the rental shop had given us an option. We could either rent by the hour, or go with a flat rate for a full twenty-four.

A choice we had pretended to debate for a couple of minutes, all the while knowing full well that we would be taking the entire day. Time enough for us to make a trip out this afternoon and scout Fawn Island before returning again later under cover of darkness.

Two trips in less than ten hours, knowing that if we let today seep into tomorrow, our odds of success dipped tremendously.

Day of, the security around the place would be heightened. Added measures to prepare for people arriving, as well as any guards that the other guests would bring along.

Trained personnel, along with the guests themselves, and the needed staff to assist them all. Caterers and servers and cleaning crew.

Potential obstacles in the form of people with eyes and ears that we would have to navigate.

To say nothing of the fact that already Cailee had been gone more than thirty-eight hours. A steady winding down, putting us well into the last quarter of the proverbial forty-eight if using that metric, and rapidly approaching the last twenty-four prior to the meeting if looking at things that way.

An allotment that was already pushing the outer extremes, there no chance we could let either clock continue to run.

A fact that we had both been trying to avoid stating since waking this morning, even if was plainly palpable from the sense of urgency between us.

Time strictures that would grow even tighter if she wasn't on the island and we had to continue our search elsewhere.

"If you're just going to stay down there," Quinn said, glancing my way, "why don't you make yourself useful and tell me where I'm going?"

"Just keep heading that way," I replied, extending a hand before me. "Eighteen miles. I'll let you know when we start getting close."

Chapter Fifty-Two

My fishing reel of choice was a spinning reel. A model I first started using with my pop way back in Alabama, having dragged it from one coast to the other with me in the time since.

Simple and durable, with excellent accuracy. Everything an old angler out looking for dinner like me could ask for.

A clear step down from the baitcasting or conventional models best suited for saltwater. A definite level up from the spincast models like the one that was gripped tight in my right hand, my left turning the lever on the side.

A very basic design that I couldn't imagine I would use a ton after today, chosen specifically for the task at hand. Ease of operation that let me work it without thought or even focus.

Full attention that I could put on the small landmass slowly slipping by off the port side of the boat. A chunk of rock rising directly up out of the sheltered bay on the western arm of Orcas Island. One of a handful of bodies of varying sizes filling the strait between the United States mainland and Canada's Vancouver Island.

One of the last tiny knobs of America before giving way to international waters.

A spot that, according to our library research, had been passed around for decades before finally falling into the hands of an unknown corporate buyer a couple years ago. A purchaser with very little public footprint, leaving a name and virtually nothing else that twenty minutes on Google could uncover.

Invisibility that was almost impossible in the modern era, except for those specifically aiming for it. Old paranoid types like myself, or those conducting illicit business dealings like The Council.

Approaching the rock from the southwest, I'd directed Quinn to steer us around the southern tip and take a counterclockwise direction. A choice based solely on the positioning of the sun, wanting to see all sides before they were cloaked in shadow.

Close inspection under the full light of day. Detailed views that I likely wouldn't be afforded later.

My eyes hidden beneath the thick lenses of polarized sunglasses kept in the middle console of my truck, I stared at the shore as we inched our way forward. A constant scan, letting my mind chronicle everything as my hands used muscle memory to work the reel.

A growing catalogue of information that I didn't even attempt to put into a working format yet, intent instead on merely gathering data. Inhaling as many details as I could, and letting them dictate how I acted next.

A mistake of rookie agents the world over that I too had fallen prey to long ago.

Based on what I had seen thus far, the island was exactly as reported online, no larger than a few acres. Room enough for a single main structure with a couple of smaller outbuildings nearby. Guesthouses or security centers or even a workout facility of some sort.

Buildings that bypassed the traditional cluster layout in favor of being strung through the center of the island. Placement based on what I guessed was the only usable ground, with much of the outside encased in rock formations.

Sheer cliffs and oversized boulders that resembled a table tilted downward. A peak on the northern end that gradually gave way to what looked like the only beach available on the opposite edge.

As a setting for a meeting like what Hattie and Leland had described, I could see it either being ideal, or a potential nightmare. A mix of positives and negatives that one would have to weigh, depending on what they felt most important.

For those who liked to show off, the place was far from the most lavish I'd ever seen. The main building where I guessed the meeting would take place was nice, but didn't hold a candle to many of the others I'd seen. Palatial spreads in the northern Mexico countryside or gracing the coasts of Malibu.

In truth, it didn't even compare to the Doone estate.

A modest spread when viewed through the lens of people like those on The Council, to say nothing of how far removed it was from anything resembling a metropolitan area.

A fact that led into the opposite side of the scale. Considerations that were tipped more toward privacy, as there was no place better than a remote island just minutes from international waters. A site that wouldn't require an excess of security, as anyone approaching by traditional means would be easily spotted.

Further, should anything happen – one of the guests getting ideas, or even a crazy bastard like myself trying to sneak on – the means of escape were extremely limited.

A crucible within which all sides were forced to get along.

Giving the crank on the side of the reel one last turn, I lifted the lure free of the water. Leaving a few inches of slack at the end, I swung it close enough to grasp, pretending to inspect it for a moment before tossing it back.

Another part of the ruse, giving me an excuse to raise the same hand I'd waved to the shopkeeper earlier over my head. A greeting to the man watching us from the rocks nearby, his body turned and his weight shifted so we couldn't see the automatic weapon strapped to his hip.

A friendly gesture he made no attempt to match, simply staring at us as we drifted by.

"How many is that now?" Quinn asked from her perch near the back. Handling the chore of working the trolling motor, she kept her focus on her task, making a point not to glance over.

"Three."

"Is that more or less than you were expecting?"

Pushing the lure back out before me, I took the rod in both hands, preparing to cast again.

"It's too many for there not to be something going on soon, not enough for anybody important to be here yet," I replied. "Guess Hattie and Leland were both at least telling the truth about that much."

"Hm," Quinn answered. A non-committal sound as she turned her head for the first time to openly stare at the guard, and even the island that he stood on. A pointed look it didn't take a degree in psychology to decipher, having had the same thoughts myself.

Notions that right now, Cailee could be barely one hundred yards away, stowed somewhere in that tangle of rocks and trees.

Or she could be far removed, and this was all just another grasping of straws that was burning precious time.

"Look away," I whispered, raising the tip of the rod to the sky and flicking it forward, sending the lure arcing away from us once more. "We'll be back soon."

Chapter Fifty-Three

Now

The reasons were many why I wanted to continue on down the back staircase.

The confined space served as a bottleneck for any opposition. Narrow walls on either side that ensured all future encounters we did have played out like the one just now. High ground for anybody who tried to ascend from below, and tough firing lanes for anyone pursuing from above.

Guards we could hear coming by means of the sound tube we were standing in.

Battle advantages that coupled with the fact that I had already traversed the route once before. I knew exactly how many steps it took to reach the basement. What the layout of the kitchen looked like once we got there.

Where the rear door exited and how to piece our way to the boat shed and the dive bag with the glowsticks behind it.

From there, the guesthouse and the beach where I could use them to signal Quinn.

A predetermined sequence I had been rehashing in my mind, trying to place my thoughts anywhere but on the strain of carrying a young woman down a tight spiraling stairwell, when the third guard in as many minutes had shown up.

An unexpected foe who obliterated all of those upsides in an instant.

Sudden shifts such as the sound of the gunshot snuffing him out, and the raucous tumbling of his body down the stairs. The spray of fresh blood and bodily debris painting the wall.

The blockade of his twisted carcass strewn across a path that was already tough to navigate, requiring I either attempt to leap him, or take the time and risk of putting Cailee down to push his ass to the side.

A host of things that I had to calculate in just a couple of quick moments before making the decision to exit on the first floor.

A choice that I recognized was far from optimal in the moment, but never thought it could be this bad.

A veritable shit show, forced into a firefight from the dining room floor while my granddaughter's limp form rests in a heap beside me.

Whereas the subterranean level of the mansion was essentially one open space, the main level is an intricate maze of rooms. Spaces designed for entertaining, with one flowing into the next.

No central corridor. No main foyer or hallway.

A piecemeal approach in line with the differing architectural styles on the outside, hinting that bits and pieces have been added on over the years. Rooms to fit a specific purpose, or designed to match the latest owner's unique tastes.

The first in order that we stepped out of the stairs to find was a trophy room. A space with thick carpets on the floor and leather sofas arranged in a semicircle in the center.

A staged setting for the copious number of animals adorning the walls. Everything from fish and deer taken from the surrounding areas to creatures like elephants and zebras found on the opposite side of the planet.

A collection representing nearly every species walking the earth, regardless of the legality surrounding the hunting of them. An over-sized display case in direct violation of that first rule my father drilled into me more than fifty years ago.

Excess and hubris that somehow managed to spike my loathing for all associated even more in just the short time it took to pass through. Hurried steps past the arrangement of sofas before exiting into a short connector that led us from the trophy room to a parlor of sorts.

A space that was a sharp contrast to the one before, mildly resembling where I met with Careen Doone last night in terms of scope and purpose. Any similarity, though, stopped there, with décor that was markedly different. A conscious swap of pale colors and textures for dark woods and accents.

An enclosed area that I cut a path straight through the center of. More of the same hurried pace, barely lifting my feet from the floor. An urgent race-walk, with each successive step magnifying the weight I was under.

Strain that caused my breath to grow shorter. Lactic acid to build in my thighs.

Fatigue that I absolutely refused to let derail us. Not after the last couple of days.

And damned sure not with a young woman I'd never actually met beyond a few staged interactions draped over my shoulder.

Working from nothing more than an outside visual as a schematic, I continued to move, keeping the USP in hand. Progress that was pointed in a southern direction, always in search of an exit.

An ongoing hunt that sent us through the only other point of entry in the room. Wooden double doors that rose to the ceiling, with no way of knowing what was on the opposite side.

A calculated risk, based on the good fortune that we had had since exiting the stairwell.

Luck that evaporated in an instant as we stepped into a third consecutive room of a disparate look and purpose. A dining room, set up for more than a dozen people. Chairs and place settings of fine China and crystal under the bright glow of pale white lights.

Interior design that didn't concern me nearly as much as the pair of guards standing in the open archway to our immediate left. A male and female team pulled from the throes of conversation, each looking as surprised at our sudden appearance as I was by theirs.

Three people frozen in place with eyes wide, visibly processing what was before them as palpitations rose through our chests.

Momentary paralysis that was snapped by me flinging myself and Cailee laterally away from the door we'd just passed through. Sudden movement, exacerbated by her weight and by my lifting the USP and firing off a single shot.

A confluence of actions, twisting my body to the side.

A loss of balance that sent us both tumbling to the floor and pulled the bullet higher and further to the right than I intended. An errant shot that still managed to make contact, spinning the man away from me as I landed flat on my back.

An abrupt end to my fall, felt the full length of my spine, causing no less than a handful of vertebrae to crack simultaneously.

More abuse that will no doubt be felt the instant the adrenaline begins to wane.

The same place I now find myself, raising both knees just far enough to plant my heels into the floor. Matching leverage points using the textured soles of the wetsuit to push forward, putting some distance between me and Cailee.

Extra space to protect her from return fire, and to improve my firing lanes. Angles that I measure with the gun extended by my side, my wrist raised just a few inches above the floor.

Using the thick slab of the tabletop above for cover, I put my full focus on the narrow gaps between the legs of the table and the chairs surrounding it. Chunks of wood that I work to navigate from my back as the sound of the woman's voice rings out.

Repeated questions asking if her partner is okay. Inquiries that keep rising in volume, bordering on frantic, reverberating through the small space.

One after another that all go unanswered.

Words that continue, inter-spliced with pops of gunfire. Shots from short range that are infinitely louder than the muffled round from the USP. Bullets that slam into the surface of the table and shatter the dishware covering it, sending sprays of glass and ceramic across from my body.

Chunks of shrapnel I don't even feel as they slap against the neoprene, my full focus kept level with the floor as I continue to inch forward in search of a target.

An ongoing hunt that continues for several moments, finally bearing fruit not from my own movement, but from the woman's rising hysteria. Emotion that causes her to tire from firing on me from above, instead trying to circle around to the head of the table.

Repositioning that does nothing for her, but gives me what I've been looking for. The clear outline of feet passing through one of the narrow openings directly across from me.

Two clean targets in order that I sure as hell will not let pass, tugging straight back on the trigger twice in a row.

Shots from no more than a couple yards away that rip through the canvas of her boot, the first shredding the toes of her left foot, the second the entire ankle joint. Cleaving blows that cut her legs from beneath her, causing her to cry out as she is pitched forward onto the floor.

Forward momentum past the end of the table that ends with a hard landing on knees and elbows. Impact that I can feel through the floorboards, firm enough to wrench the gun from her grasp and send it skittering across the floor.

An ungraceful fall, leaving her exposed for one last shot. A clear look at the tangle of red hair hanging like a curtain on either side of her head.

A waving target so close it would be impossible to miss.

Chapter Fifty-Four

Then

The same snowy-haired fellow who had rented us the boat was still leaning against the doorframe of his shop as we sidled up alongside the dock and drifted to a stop. His features scrunched in the same kindly grin, he shook his head at us, his internal monologue so obvious I could practically hear it as we tied off and headed for the truck.

Admonishments about how he'd told us we were packed too light for that type of trip. Not enough warm clothes. Nowhere near enough supplies.

Warnings that he'd gently nudged our way earlier, without trending into the territory of trying to upsell us.

Cautions steeped in the faux story we had handed him. A fabricated tale of familial merriment, with nothing but good intentions and the open sea ahead of us.

A contrived yarn that could not have been further from the truth. Drivel that was surpassed only by what we were going to tell him was our reason for returning should he venture any closer. More details of another fictitious outing that were proven unnecessary as the man simply raised the same hand to us in greeting before tapping whatever remained in his pipe into the ash tray by the door and disappearing back inside.

A retreat into the warmth of the shop, saving us from having to lie again, and more importantly the time it would take to do so. Minutes that were becoming more precious as the sun was already beginning its descent toward the western horizon.

A ticking clock, letting us know that our reconnaissance trip out to the island had taken longer than anticipated. Extra time to account for the myriad islands dotting the area, and the narrow lanes through which boats were left to pass.

Fishing and pleasure vessels both working their way through. Crafts that were almost all much larger than ours, giving them the right of first passage and leaving us to be tossed about in their wake.

An up-and-down ride that took more than half an hour in each direction, along with twice that to completely circumnavigate the island. A slow and methodical trip, during which I had cast and reeled in the same jig more than forty times.

Rhythmic action while scouring the razored cliffs on the eastern and western shorelines. The collection of boulders comprising the north end, forming just enough of an alcove to create a small marina. Tie-offs for a handful of crafts of small-to-mid size, serviced by a metal staircase affixed directly to the granite.

A trio of non-options, leaving only the southern tip of the island as a possibility. Thirty yards or so of beach that was sure to be patrolled, meaning getting too close with the boat was also out.

Topographical realities leaving only one choice that sure as hell didn't enthuse me, though there didn't appear to be another way.

A water landing it would have to be.

"Alright," Quinn said, her voice penetrating my thoughts. A single word that managed to cease my ongoing planning, pulling my attention her way. "You've had damn near an hour and a half now. What are you thinking?"

Splitting away from me as we walked across the parking lot, she slid down the passenger side of the truck. Matching her on the opposite side, I waited until we were both inside and the doors shut before replying, "We need to go shopping."

In my periphery I could see Quinn's hair brush over her shoulders as she jerked her attention my way. A reflexive reaction as she fixed her gaze, waiting for me to add more.

A pause lasting but a moment, ending with her prompting, "Shopping?"

"Unfortunately," I answered. "Makes no sense to go all the way home. We don't have that kind of time, and I don't even have everything we need."

"Don't have..." Quinn said, once more employing what had become a favored response and repeating part of what I said before tailing off. Glancing over her shoulder, she scoured the go-bag on the backseat and the row of drawers beneath it.

A bastion of items she could not begin to fathom the full extent of.

"What the hell else do we need?"

Shoving the key in the ignition, I brought the truck to life. Dropping it into gear, I swung out wide, looping around the scattered handful of vehicles in the lot.

Exiting onto the same street we'd come in on, I nudged the gas, running us past the small shop and a handful more closely resembling it. Boat rentals and fishing tours and even a couple of food stands, all still hanging on for the last days of the season.

A few final stabs at making a buck before shuttering things up and heading off to do whatever they enjoyed during the long winter months.

"From what I could see, there are only two places on the whole damn rock where we can come to shore," I said.

"Right," Quinn agreed. "The north end and the south end. The rest, you ain't making it up and over unless you're part crab."

Unaware she had even looked at the island more than to glare at the guard while we were out there, I couldn't help but smirk. A rare bit of mirth that she matched by adding, "What? You think it took my full attention just to operate the trolling motor?

"A freaking monkey could do it."

Unable to help myself, I let out a single chuckle. A reflexive response, likely to be my last of the day.

If not ever.

"The north end is too obvious," I replied. "They'll definitely have guards with the boats, if not cameras too."

"There's nowhere to pull up or tie off on the south end, though," Quinn countered.

"No," I agreed, dropping the blinker and drifting into the middle lane for an impending turn. A redirect onto the larger thoroughfare running perpendicular from the shore.

The site of a handful of big box and large chain stores that we had passed when exiting the freeway earlier.

Recollections that came back to me as we made the trip back from Fawn, a rough outline coming together in my head.

"But I'm not going to be approaching by boat."

Her focus still turned my way, her lips parted. The start of a response that made it no further. A pause to contemplate what was said, matching it against what she too saw on our trip.

Mental processing that took a couple of moments, culminating with, "That's why we're going shopping."

"That's why we're going shopping."

Turning back to face forward, she fell silent for a moment. More time to further contemplate what was shared.

"I hope you don't think you're leaving me behind again."

The truth was, I wished there was some way to breach the island alone. An approach that would get myself on, and then Cailee and me both away, without subjecting Quinn to any danger also.

An extension of what I thought when she drove off from Hattie's in a plume of smoke just last night. One less thing for me to worry about, so I could put my full focus on the task at hand.

If there was a way to make that happen now though, I damned sure wasn't seeing it.

"Nope," I replied. "You're my ride."

Chapter Fifty-Five

The salesperson at Sportsman's Warehouse was practically salivating. Eagerness that had ratcheted up with each additional item we discussed. Anticipation for a nice commission that kept growing the longer I was there, leaving him damned near giddy.

That very thing being why I had waited for the older guy with salt-and-pepper hair to move on to help someone else before swooping in. A pointed approach to the young kid in his twenties who would be more excited about his own impending windfall than analyzing what I was asking for.

Everything needed for an aquatic assault on the southern shore of Fawn Island that wasn't already stowed away in the truck Quinn called a tank.

The first half of what I anticipated being a multi-faceted evacuation this evening. An operation with many moving parts that would require another couple of stops just to acquire everything that was needed.

A nighttime dive leading to an island raid. And if somehow those both worked out, an evacuation of the same.

The sort of thing I hadn't attempted since I was in the Navy forty years ago. A much younger man in much better condition, not already carrying the stiffness of the last couple of days.

An action on short notice with supplies I didn't have the time to go all the way home to procure, instead picked up on the fly at a general outdoor supply store.

All the makings of an impending disaster. A lack of options that had us scrambling.

A position I had spent a career making sure to never be in, leaving my stomach pulled into a knot. A tight ball that I did my best to obscure from the kid across from me, forcing a smile onto my features.

A pained grin as he prattled on, more or less marveling at his own good fortune.

"Wow," the young salesman beamed. A guy who was roughly the same height as me, with dimensions swollen to almost twice my size. A juxtaposition of my own preference for calisthenics workouts and his inflated gym body.

A canvas for a host of other adornments, from thumb rings to hair gel.

More effort than any male should ever expend on grooming, decidedly at odds with the crowd he was trying to sell to.

"A SeaScooter," he continued, referring to the underwater craft I had just agreed to purchase. A handheld submersible, ideal for doing the hard work of pulling my old ass through the water.

A way to get from Quinn and the rented boat to the south shore of Fawn Island without expending every ounce of energy, or completely blowing my cover.

The first step in what felt like a cascading list of potential problems. A plan that was veering dangerously close to desperation, though we didn't have a choice.

Already, it felt like we were taking too long. More than a day and a half had passed since Cailee disappeared, with only nominal progress to show for it.

A precarious point, where desperation was likely to soon cause us to do something stupid.

"I wish my grandfather had been cool enough to buy me one of those for my eighteenth birthday."

Sticking with the current trend of pushing fake stories about a close-knit family, I bobbed my head. An attempted facsimile of the old guy at the marina, right down to the tight-lipped smile.

"It isn't cool to hear my daughter tell it," I replied. An allusion to the only part of the story that was true. A cause for my gaze to flick to the side to see Quinn working on her own shopping list a short distance away.

Items not intended for our impending mission, but for what would be needed in the slim chance it worked. Blankets and clothing for Cailee. A warm coat to wrap her in for the ride back, sure to be much colder than the last time we went across the water.

Items much like many I was there to purchase that Cailee already owned, but were stowed away in her apartment across the city. Too far off to be any good, or for us to go track down under such a tight timeframe.

"But that's the good thing about being a grandparent," I continued. "She has to say no, I get to say yes."

The grin the kid wore grew even larger. "My grandma has that exact saying on a magnet on her fridge."

"You don't say?"

"I do," he replied, oblivious to any bit of sarcasm that might exist.

Facetiousness I let fall away while adding, "Part of our agreement, though, was if I was going to get him this, I had to make sure he had everything he needed. The wetsuit, the dive gear, the whole deal."

On cue, the kid's eyebrows went up a fraction of an inch. An avaricious reply to the total tab just doubling. Expenses I didn't mind in the least, all courtesy of the cash found in Leland Doone's wallet.

A pittance compared to what his ass owed for all that had happened.

The kamikaze mission I was about to go on because of it.

"Sure thing," the kid said. Jutting a finger out before him, he pointed a couple of rows to the side and said, "Just follow me over here, and we'll get you all set up.

"We've got air tanks, glow sticks, dive bags. Anything your grandson could possibly need."

"Lead the way."

Chapter Fifty-Six

Now

The black jacket the woman in the dining room was wearing might be soaked in spots with blood, but it at least covers a decent chunk of the white gown Cailee is in. The neck is high enough to tuck her hair up under it. A zipper closes around her torso, blocking everything above the waist.

Far from total coverage, but sufficient to at least obscure the top half of her that is draped down my back. A bit of camouflage, ensuring that anybody who spots her at distance is out in front of me, giving us a fighting chance.

I have no idea how many people are guarding the island, though I have to believe that I have eliminated a decent chunk of the threat already. Two in the guardhouse, one in the boathouse, and what I discovered to be five in the mansion after rising from behind the table to find the shot I thought was errant actually struck the male guard in the throat.

A painful way to die that took a few moments to reach completion, but still got him where he needed to go.

Hell, along with the rest of them.

In addition to those, there was also the woman in Cailee's room, the chef still locked in the cooler, and the lone gunman on the south shore bound tight with cobra cuffs.

Eleven people already accounted for. A sizable force on hand the night before a gathering on a site that isn't much more than a handful of acres in total.

A landmass that seems to be getting bigger as I push forward, each step feeling like it is on a treadmill. Labored movement, without any real progress to show for it.

Under the extra weight of Cailee, the ground beyond the stone porch seems especially soft. The feet of my wetsuit keep digging deeper, leaving small divots in the damp earth.

I can feel soil clinging to the soles. Extra weight that exacerbates the fatigue in my legs. A burning sensation permeates my lungs, forcing me to consciously pull in each breath.

My knees are flexed. My back is hunched forward.

My body is starting to buckle beneath the added heft as I race-walk onward, willing myself to go faster. Get further from the back door to the mansion and anyone who might have heard the fracas in the stairwell or the dining room.

Added distance still from anybody who has entered either of the satellite structures and found the bodies left behind.

The USP with a fresh magazine from the man in the dining room gripped tight in my right hand, my arm is extended almost parallel to my body. A counterweight to help keep me upright as I work my way through the trees. Bushy pines with boughs that extend in odd intervals, their needles slapping me in the face and passing over my body.

For more than a minute, I push as hard as I can. Full exertion, depleting whatever blood oxygen levels I possess. Any stray bits of energy I might have stored over the last couple years of retirement that still remain after the past thirty-some hours.

Teeth clenched, I move as fast as I can. Short, hurried steps, even as spots begin to appear before me. Pops of light that dance across my vision, multiplying each time I blink.

Signs of strain that start to pull my body to the side, listing under the weight of my load.

Rather than try to fight against it, I lean in, turning my body in that direction, letting the added heft propel me. Combining with the downward slope of the land, my strides elongate. Our speed picks up.

Half sprinting, half staggering, my lips peel back over my teeth. A low growl rolls up from deep in my chest.

For the better part of two days now, my daughter and I have been flinging ourselves at this moment. A headlong sprint through the greater Seattle area, searching for the young woman now resting atop my shoulder.

My granddaughter. Barely more than a child, untouched by my past life or the mistakes therein. Errors that may or may not be why we are both here now.

Either way, a clean canvas, underserving of what has happened to her. A story yet to be told.

One that will damned sure not end here. Not like this.

Ahead of me, the boat shed emerges in the form of a solid vertical line. A darkened shadow that I put what remains of my focus on, pounding out a final few steps.

A last couple of strides, ending with my knees buckling beneath me. Combined weight that crashes down onto the sore joints, driving them into the soft earth.

Wrapping both arms around my granddaughter, I do my best to shield her from the spray of dead pine needless and soil that is kicked up. Loamy detritus that fills my mouth and nostrils, slapping Cailee's bare legs and clinging to the pale bottom of her gown.

An unceremonious slide that ends just a couple of feet from the side of the boat shed. Close enough that I can rock forward and place Cailee onto her bottom, much like I did in the second story bathroom.

A two-part unloading, setting down first her backside, and then the rest of her, leaning her shoulders against the side of the boat shed.

The instant her weight is off of me, I make no attempt to rise. No effort to grab the dive bag hopefully still waiting nearby.

Continuing the same forward movement, I lower my forehead to the ground. A classic tripod position with my ass in the air, best for maximizing oxygen intake.

One inhalation after another, I draw in as much air as I can. Deep breaths that expand my chest and lungs, beating back the fuzz resting on the periphery of my vision.

A much-needed rest that lasts nearly a full minute. Time enough to let the spinning in my head recede before I force myself back upright.

Weight rocking back onto my heels, I wipe the combination of sweat and mud from my forehead. My gaze goes to my grand-daughter resting peacefully against the side of the boat shed, bliss-fully unaware of everything that has happened.

What I suspect still needs to take place before we are in the clear.

"What do you say, C?" I whisper. "Why don't I go grab those glowsticks and flag down your mom so we can get the hell out of here?"

Chapter Fifty-Seven

Then

For the second time of the day, my daughter and I sat across from each other in a diner. Another eatery designed with a very specific décor and clientele in mind, this one trading out the retro theme and lumberjack patrons for a fisherman motif. Nautical intentions made obvious by the name The Sea Shanty stretched across the sign lit up above the door, taken further by the assortment of ship's wheels and fishing nets covering the walls. Items that looked to have put in actual time in the nearby Pacific, going until their usefulness was no more before retiring to the walls.

Accent pieces that doubled in perfuming the air, leaving it redolent with brine.

Shared commonalities between The Sea Shanty and La Rosa Negra, though any similarities ended there, right down to the predominant scent filling the air. A byproduct of a pared down menu comprised entirely of fried items. Fish, shrimp, and clams, all batter dipped and cooked in oil. For sides, there were fries or hushpuppies.

The lone outlier, coleslaw, had sold out earlier in the day, not to be remade until the morrow. A shortage the waitress hadn't seemed the least bit sorry about, delivering the information just as I suspected she did from early afternoon onward every day.

A matter-of-fact statement before taking our orders and disappearing into the back, returning just minutes later to set us up with more cheap coffee. A top off on the caffeine that had started to wane from earlier, helping to prep us for the night ahead.

Even if neither one of us really needed it, both thrumming with anticipation.

An entire stop that we weren't really up for, needing to do that the battery of the submersible could charge in the truck. A USB plug-in that was currently hard at work in the parking lot as we waited inside, forcing down whatever sustenance we could gather.

Protein and grease I wouldn't be surprised to see expelled into the water later if our return trip was anywhere near as choppy as the first.

"Alright, walk me through it again," Quinn said the instant the waitress was beyond earshot. Using a lowered voice for one of the few times in her life, she leaned forward and rested her forearms on the edge of the table. "Starting at the minute we walk out of this place."

Having been thinking of nothing else for the last couple of hours, I nodded in agreement. Matching her pose, I cast a sideways glance, ensuring we were alone.

There was no risk of being overhead. Nobody who might catch buzzwords like *submersible* or *stun gun* and become a bit too interested in what we were discussing.

"I leave first," I began. "Give me five minutes to go out and wrestle my ass into that wetsuit."

Already, I was dreading trying to wriggle my way into the double-knit neoprene. A full body covering, complete with feet, gloves, and a hood, leaving only my face and jaw exposed.

Protection against the frigid water temperatures, keeping hypothermia or frostbite at bay.

And more importantly, ensuring everything worked as it should when I arrived.

"Better make it ten," Quinn inserted. "I don't want to see anything more than I am right now."

Whether it was a barb or an attempt at levity, I wasn't sure. Possibilities I let slide by, merely nodding in agreement.

"Ten it is," I replied. "Assuming the battery is fully charged, you'll come join me and drive us back to the dock. The sign on the door of the dive shop said they close at seven, so we should have the place to ourselves."

"We'll park as close as possible, load our supplies in, and go. Everything in one trip."

"Shouldn't be hard," Quinn muttered. "Feel like I could carry the whole damn truck right now if I had to."

Grunting softly in agreement, I continued, "Same arrangement as last time. You drive and I'll navigate until it's time for me to go in the water."

"How far out?"

"A mile," I said. "Maybe a little more, depending on boat traffic this evening. Far enough that nobody can see or hear us, but sufficiently close that I can just point and go once I'm underwater."

Dipping her chin slightly, Quinn pressed, "And after you're on the rock?"

A question I knew was coming, I still wasn't entirely sure how to answer it. Part of that was because there were details included that I didn't exactly want to share with my daughter. Plot points that either solidified every worst impression she'd ever had of me, or conjured to mind horrors that she hadn't yet thought of.

Things that her daughter could be exposed to while we were sitting and waiting for our food to arrive. Mental images that could alter what was already a precarious state, making what she did to Mick this morning look mild by comparison.

Reactions that would be completely understandable, even if they could ill be afforded at the moment.

The remainder of any reticence I had was due to the fact that I didn't know exactly how it would go. One of the catchphrases that used to be bandied about the halls at the Bureau was the old Eisenhower standby about planning being everything, while a plan was useless.

A quote repeated so many times that it bordered on annoyance, hammering home the fact that no detailed proposal was ever really worth the paper it was written on. All we could do was create a strategy with the information we had, and try to best foresee any problems that might arise.

Pitfalls that this time were greater than on many of the previous raids I'd conducted. A litany of reasons that things could go awry, ranging from a lack of manpower to limited site data.

Operational pieces that paled compared to the worst possible outcome.

One that I didn't even want to consider, and was not about to mention to my daughter.

"I go find Cailee, and get her the hell out of there."

Chapter Fifty-Eight

Just as Quinn had requested, I left The Sea Shanty ten minutes before her. Pressing my phone to my face, I pretended to be taking a phone call, even going the extra step of holding up a finger while sliding sideways out of the booth.

Another lie told in what had been a multitude the last couple of days.

Twenty-five years of virtual silence, ended by us falling right into the traditional family tropes.

Keeping the device against my cheek, I'd swung around to the far side of the truck, using the time to disconnect the charging battery on the passenger seat and stow it in the bed before slipping into the bottom half of my newly acquired wetsuit. A struggle against space constraints getting out of my jeans, followed by a fight against the tight-knit material to get them up to my waist.

An inch-by-inch battle that claimed most of the hairs on my legs, reaching my midsection just as the driver's door swung upon. An unexpected entry that caused me to glance up in time to see my daughter's bemused expression spotlighted by the overhead lamp.

Another smirk at my expense, gone as fast as it arrived as she climbed in.

Only to return a second time as I fought to get my arms through either sleeve.

And then a third time as I grunted to zip it the length of my torso. A full-body compression sleeve that raised my core temperature several degrees, enveloping everything from my neck down.

Coverage that would later be extended to include all but my face, once the attached hood was cinched into place and the accompanying face mask fitted around the outside.

Protection against the chilled waters to be aided by the tremendous amount of adrenaline already spilling into my system. A culmination of more than a day spent sprinting in search of my granddaughter, the promise of finally seeing her again, bringing her home to safety, at long last within reach.

A length of time having evoked scads of other responses as well, ranging from the anticipation of what I was about to do to the sheer anger that it was happening at all.

Rage that had me questioning if I would be able to restrain myself not to go after the first guard I encountered. Just slide the MK3 from the sheath strapped to my calf, or bypass weapons altogether and use fists or rocks or whatever the hell else I could find as I wailed away.

Angst that was matched by my daughter in the driver's seat as she clutched the steering wheel in both hands, refraining from commenting on the size of the truck or the poor handling. Staring straight out, she wound us through a network of side streets, taking care to stay away from major thoroughfares.

A desire to avoid traffic in any form, allowing her to lean on the gas. Hard pushes on the accelerator, interspersed with only the occasional tap of the brakes.

Aggressive driving fed in no small part by the concentrated emotion inside the vehicle. Well over a day of pushing hard by me, surpassed by a wide margin for her.

Strain in the form of frustration and helplessness. The need to find Cailee. Bring her home.

Feel like at least one damn thing we were doing actually mattered, getting us closer to our goal.

"Was the battery charged?" Quinn asked as the glowing signage of the boat shop appeared in the distance.

The first words – or even sounds, outside of the engine revving – since we left. An especially loud ask, sending pinpricks of sensation through my chest.

"More than enough for what we need," I replied.

Grunting in reply, Quinn glanced to the darkened windows of the boat shop as we passed, aiming for the far entrance into the lot.

"Looks like the place is closed up for the night."

"Good," I replied, already running the list of items in the back seat that would need to come with me. Pieces taken from both the go-bag and the bench compartments, small enough to both fit inside the dive bag and not slow me down too much once I reached Fawn Island.

A full list that I worked through, letting my vision glaze as Quinn retraced the exact path we followed just hours before. A short journey, ending with us turning into the parking lot. An unceremonious entry at a high rate of speed, causing the front end of the truck to buck slightly before leveling out.

One last push on the gas shot us across the desolate piece of concrete to the front stall in the lot. A vantage staring past our rented boat and dozens more like it.

A view beyond even the reach of the reflected lights of the shore striped across the water, our gaze fixed on the inky darkness of the Pacific beyond.

"When I get out there on that rock and find Cailee," I whispered. The start of something I had been curious about since going to Cailee's apartment and being introduced to Viv as a great uncle, but had refrained from bringing up.

An inquiry that now seemed relevant given where we were and what we were about to do, for a variety of reasons.

One final question before we set off.

"Who should I tell her I am?"

Chapter Fifty-Nine

The total weight of the SeaScooter was roughly fifteen pounds. An anchor that was by no means heavy, but was more than enough to pull me directly under the surface of the water. A straight dive down into the inky blackness, aided by the dive bag tethered by a nylon cord around my waist. A waterproof pouch no larger than a foot square, plenty sufficient to carry an assortment of items from the truck, the go-bag, and our recent shopping spree.

A stun gun. Cobra cuffs. Duct tape. Glowsticks.

Beretta with extra magazine.

Heft that combined with the submersible to take me from perched on the side of the Ranger to an inverted plunge toward the ocean floor. A free fall into darkness I did nothing to fight against as my body seized from the sudden immersion into the frigid water. Icy shock that wrapped around my exposed jawline, sending electric pulses firing the entire length of my nervous system.

My body's natural warning siren, urging blood to rush toward my vital organs. Warmth that flooded through my chest and core as I continued to dive deeper, willing my fingers to remain clamped around the handles of the submersible.

A tight clutch, matching the squeeze my mouth had around the nozzle of the compressed air tank and the cinch of the dive bag around my waist.

A full body clench that I leaned into, forcing myself to continue drawing in even breaths. Controlled breathing to keep my heart rate from racing.

At the same time, I called to mind the plan as Quinn and I had devised it one last time. A point to focus on, demanding mental acuity. Sequenced thinking, ensuring I didn't slip into a state of euphoria from cold water shock.

One item after another, I rattled things off. My approach to the beach on the south end of the island. The guard I knew would still be posted there. The stun gun I intended to use on him.

The land assault that would follow.

The innocent young woman who hopefully waited somewhere therein.

The precious happy ending we had been racing for days in search of.

The very instant my progression reached the part of finding Cailee, I flicked the textured grip of my right thumb upward. A simple flip of the switch to activate the small craft, redirecting it from nosing straight down to swinging out before me.

A sudden start to the portable propeller that pushed it out ahead, jerking my back and shoulders into a line. A taut form dragged through the icy depths, clinging to the underwater craft as it pulled me forward.

During my years with the FBI, I had done many things. Stuff others had only seen in action movies. Things that many would label as flat stupid.

Prior to that with the Navy, I had been a part of missions and endured training that could be construed as nothing short of sadistic. Tests not just of the mind and body, but sometimes even the laws of gravity or physics.

Trials that I would have never thought existed, let alone could be successfully completed.

Tasks that I only came to understand later were there to serve as battering rams to mental barriers as much as anything. Proof to ourselves that we were capable of and could do more than our minds often realized.

Successive pummeling that we always emerged from, preparing us for whatever lay ahead.

Prior preparation that I wanted to believe still existed, even if I was now a much older man, decades removed from those same trainings and missions. It would come together and work one last time for me, because it had to.

Not for me, but for my granddaughter.

Running the craft wide open, I counted off the seconds. Silent calculations, using the position of the boat when I jumped and the rough estimation of the shoreline ahead as static points. Dots on either end of a straight line, making the arithmetic connecting the two fairly simple.

A straightforward process of dividing distance by speed, letting me know how long I needed to stay under. Time that was nothing short of torturous as I stayed submerged in the total darkness, fighting against the lactic acid in my shoulders and the strain of my grip on the submersible.

The first in what promised to be many escalating trials that lay ahead.

Chapter Sixty

Now

Cailee is exactly as I left her. Folded forward at the waist, I used the dark coat covering her top half to obscure as much of her bottom as possible. An impromptu cloak rendering her almost invisible, tucked between the side of the boat shed and the low hanging limbs of a spruce tree.

Still under the full effects of whatever sedation the bastards were pumping through her veins, her body is limp. Her arms flop as I slide in beside her, spraying chunks of mud and dead pine needles.

"Come on, C," I mutter, still panting from my sprint across the island. A path that this time took me due east, rather than going all the way to the southern tip.

A bit of misdirection for anyone who might have seen the green shine of the glowstick as I hurled it into the ocean. Sleight of hand to pull them that direction, trusting that Quinn still knows exactly where to go.

The only place on the whole damn island where an escape is even possible.

Leaving Cailee and me with one last bit of ground still to cover. "We gotta move."

Exactly the same as before, the words are more for my benefit than hers. Out loud commands that are just barely audible over my breathing. Desperate gasps for oxygen after the fire fight in the dining room. Carrying Cailee outside. Sprinting to the far side of the island and back.

Actions that have me completely oblivious to any chill in the air as sweat streams down my forehead, matting my hair to my scalp.

Just as I did before taking off, I allow myself a single minute. A few moments to try and catch my breath with my weight balanced on both knees. My body is pitched forward, allowing for maximum intake.

A last breather before taking off on this final run. One hundred yards to the shoreline and an aquatic escape.

A few hits of much needed air that are cut short by voices piercing the night. Errant shouts from whatever remains of the guard force. Noises that slip through the thick twist of trees surrounding the mansion, making it impossible to pinpoint where they are coming from.

Exact locations that don't concern me as much as the alarm permeating them. Urgency and confusion, making it clear that whatever cushion we had is gone. Any window for making it over the last chunk of land undetected before meeting up with Quinn on the shore has evaporated.

As has any chance of taking them on in ones and twos, whatever we encounter from here on likely to be the totality of whoever is left breathing.

"Now."

Pushing myself upright so I'm balanced on both knees beside my granddaughter, I hook my left hand under her armpit. Digging my fingers into the soft underbelly, I pull her forward while leaning in, sliding her back into position across my shoulder.

Limp weight resting flat on the forest floor requiring every bit of my remaining strength to lift her. Full-body strain that again brings pops of light to my vision. Flashbulbs of red and green that induces lightheadedness as I stand, my legs wobbling beneath me.

An uneven base forcing me to take a few staggering steps while continuing to pull in deep breaths. Extra oxygen to my brain as I list to the side, fighting to stay upright.

A battle against her weight and gravity that I am only able to win by jutting my left arm out. Mashing my palm flat against the side of the boathouse, I use it as an anchor point. A brace so I can pull my feet up under me.

A moment to center myself, listening to the voices growing ever closer. Louder.

A needed instant to steel myself before pushing off, again letting my load and the slope of the land carry us forward. Downward momentum that I make no effort to fight against, instead merely shifting my body a few inches to either side to navigate the forest.

A skier flying through a slalom run, needing only to get around each flag while continuing to hurtle our way forward.

A race of a very different kind, with far greater stakes.

A point that is hammered home as the sounds permeating the air begin to shift, transitioning from mere voices to the addition of the first pops of gunfire. Thunderous claps of released gas pressure that carry through the chilled air, sounding especially pronounced in the relative quiet of the island.

Telltale indicators that I would recognize anywhere, each one sending sensation through my abdomen and up into my chest.

Pinpricks that grow more pronounced with the realization that Cailee and I aren't being fired on. There is no hiss of bullets passing by. No miniature explosions of tree bark or pine needles as they strike.

Instead, the rounds are being aimed at the faint whine of a boat engine.

Shots fired at Quinn as she approaches.

Avoiding the main path through the center of the island, I stick to the trees as much as possible. Cover that lets us come in at an angle, from which I can see muzzle flashes erupting just forty yards ahead. Flashes of light that reflect across the surface of the water.

Streaks of orange and yellow, flickering into the distance. Bright colors that erupt one after another, silhouetting the pair of guards responsible for them. Two shooters standing on either side of the man I first met upon breaching the island.

A darkened lump still resting prone on the sand, not yet released from his bindings, unable to stand even if he was.

With each shot the guards fire, they shout into the night. Angry calls that begin to mix with additional voices drifting down from the opposite direction. Reinforcements, en route from the main house.

A cacophony that erupts from deep in their diaphragm. Noises that I'm guessing are meant to be menacing, daring the lone craft on the water to come closer as they continue to fire.

A shoreline game of chicken, with neither side backing down.

Using the rooster tails spouting from the backside of the boat as a guide, I abandon any pretense of trying to remain hidden. My focus goes to the men bouncing in place on the shore, firing shots one after another at my daughter.

More targets for the hatred I carry. Days of animosity, given one final chance at release.

Unfurling my right arm, I lift the USP before me, extending it straight out from my shoulder. An arrow pointing the way, I follow exactly where the tip is pointed, churning out just a handful more strides.

My lungs clench as my entire body tightens, willing every last bit of speed I can from my frame. Final steps as we approach the shore and the forest begins to thin around us.

A reduction of impediments giving me clear lanes of sight.

Starting with the darkened shape closest to me, I pull back on the trigger. My own addition to the light show refracting across the water. A single blossom of light, followed by another, and then a third in order.

Three consecutive shots that were not expected in the least, slamming into the shooter's back and flinging him face first into the ocean.

A forward fall that isn't even complete before I shift my aim to the side and do the same to his partner. Another trio of shots that chew through center mass as they start to turn my way, pitching them sideways into the water as well.

A second target eliminated as we spill down out of the trees, my feet crossing from soft earth onto the broken shells lining the beach. Loud footfalls that echo out as momentum carries us forward, drowning out the continued cries of guards at our back.

The last stragglers headed toward the shore, their calls now pockmarked by shots of their own.

Gunfire that I match by putting two rounds into the first guard splayed on his side on the beach. An inert target that I fire on as we pass, doing as I should have earlier.

Two final shots before flinging the gun to the side.

I don't bother with an attempt to turn and shoot at the onrushing guards at our back. Not with the chance of success so low, the more likely outcome being that we end up like the trio of guards already strewn across the sand.

Exposed targets that I have no interest in becoming, instead putting my full focus on the lead edge of the fishing boat as it swings into position before us. Throttling down, it tosses white churn in its wake.

At the wheel, Quinn shouts instructions. Words I can barely hear over the whine of the engine as she gets as close to shore as possible, looking to pull in broadside.

A convergence that I fling myself headlong toward, not even bothering to slow as we go plunging into the icy depths. Strides that go as far as they can before the resistance of the water is too strong.

A stumbling block that cuts my legs out from under me, sending Cailee and I both tumbling forward.

A tangle of limbs fully submerged in the frigid brine, blotting out the sounds of our pursuers to one side, and Quinn shouting instructions on the other.

Chapter Sixty-One

There is no way in Hell I can make it back to the boat shed to pick up the dive bag with the mask I wore on the ride in. Same for the remainder of the compressed air that I used to stay submerged the entire time.

Extra gear that would have only slowed us down as we ran for the beach, left behind at the first sound of opposition. Items cast aside without thinking that I would desperately need them later, my only concern being getting Cailee off the damn island and onto that boat.

A ride my ass was originally supposed to be on as well.

An initial scheme that I knew was not without holes, though I never saw this one coming. In truth, I figured I would have died long before it got to this point.

And if not, it would have only been by some miracle, meaning I eliminated whatever thin bit of resistance existed or was able to survive undetected.

Two things that are sure as shit not what happened. Quite the opposite in fact, which is why after Quinn and I were able to roll Cailee's unresponsive body out of the water and onto the boat, I sent them both away.

I didn't try to grab hold and go along for the ride. Didn't attempt to wrestle my own ass up and over the side.

Not with gunshots lighting up the beachfront like fireflies. Rounds that had already smacked into the side of the boat, it only a matter of time before they hit someone or something vital like the engine.

Both absolute worst-case scenarios, ending one or all three of us.

In the face of my daughter screaming for me to climb in, I did the only thing I could. My only action that was strong enough to make her do as I requested and get her and Cailee to safety.

I pushed myself away.

The start of a swim in the opposite direction that did as intended, causing her to rev the engine and begin to race off. A move that will almost assuredly get me chewed out by Quinn again, though I'll deal with that later.

Provided that things ever make it that far.

Also left sitting in the dive bag behind the boat shed is my Beretta. A backup weapon I could use to beat back the swarm of guards after casting aside the spent USP.

A choice I would make a thousand consecutive times again in the name of getting Cailee on that boat, even if it does now leave me without any way of fighting against the last remaining guards spread along the shoreline. Combatants standing in odd intervals with guns extended, their muzzle flashes lighting up the night with pinpricks of yellow and orange.

Rounds that pepper the water around me, aimed at my head bobbing above the surface and the tail of the boat as it speeds away. Miniature geysers that sprout up around me, leaving me just a few seconds to jerk the hood of my wetsuit up and over the top of my head.

One quick pull to allow for a tiny bit of protection from the icy cold I can already feel enveloping my body. A quick movement with both hands while filling my lungs before dropping below the surface, letting the frigid grasp of the water clamp around my face once more.

Cold that feels infinitely worse than it did just seconds ago, causing my entire body to seize. A full clench that seems to tighten my lungs, making it very clear that I have but one choice for survival. A single option for getting beyond the range of their weapons.

And that sure as hell isn't out swimming them.

Dropping myself down to just a few inches above the ocean floor, I fan both arms wide before me. Classic breaststroke technique with my body positioned parallel to the beachfront on my right.

Long, even strokes driven by adrenaline and urgency, propelling me forward.

Hidden several feet beneath the surface, sound has become magnified. In the distance, I can hear the faint whine of the fishing boat as it speeds away, widening the gap between us.

On my opposite flank, I can hear thrashing as the guards have started to become desperate. Even less prepared for the water than myself, they are beginning to make their way in.

Lifting their feet above the water, they drive their feet down with heavy stomp. Steps that sound like cannon fire where I am, no doubt water logging their boots as they continue hammering the surface with shots in my wake.

Tucked away several feet beneath the surface, there is no way the bullets could reach me even if they were firing in the right place. Simple physics that I witnessed many times during my years with the Navy, as the density of water is too great for the kinetic energy of a round to pass through.

Safety that is mine for as long as the air in my lungs holds out.

Precious oxygen that I will never again take for granted after this night.

Using the sounds of the guards as a barometer, I push onward, trying to envision my exact position as I move.

Based on what I saw earlier, the beach itself is less than thirty yards across. Under one hundred feet in total, cut by one third based on where Cailee and I entered the water, and another by the progress I've already made.

A diminishment of scope that leaves me with just thirty feet or so left to cover. No more than an additional handful of strokes to get myself out of their immediate sightline so I can surface.

A few quick breaths while checking my position against the enormous rock serving as the endpoint of the beach.

And, more importantly, the submersible I know is waiting there.

Chapter Sixty-Two

I can feel the warmth rushing back into my face. Blood flow forcing its way through capillaries that were nearly frozen to the point of destruction during my hasty retreat from Fawn Island.

Quite easily the longest breath hold of my life, clinging to the SeaScooter by nothing more than the textured grips of the wetsuit, putting space between myself and the remaining guards stalking the shore in my wake. Room to get beyond the range of their weapons, it only by pure luck that they were all using suppressed handguns instead of actual firearms.

An escape done almost entirely underwater, as that was infinitely preferable to giving them a whitecap to follow and fire at, to say nothing of having my wet features exposed to the rush of wind and spray against my cheeks. Additional windburn that I fought to stave off after climbing my ass up into the boat by curling myself into a ball in the center footwell.

Wound tight into the fetal position, I pressed my back against one side. Across from me, Quinn had curled Cailee up to do the same, both of our wet bodies shielded as much as possible by the seats rising up on either side.

Makeshift windbreaks, while Quinn got us back to the boat rental marina as fast as she could. A miserably interminable drive with her cursing the entire time, turning every few seconds to check our rear.

Repeated looks that I tried to keep track of for the first few minutes until the cold wracking me took over. Tremors that caused my entire body to jerk. Shivering that was a natural outcropping of my body pulling all the blood back to my organs, trying to retain vital warmth.

Violent quivering that remained until after we tied the boat off at the dock and Quinn ran to pull the truck up. Persisted still as we carried Cailee's limp form onto the dock and shoved my go-bag to the floor, turning the backseat into a makeshift cot, where we wrestled her out of the wet coat and gown and into the clothes purchased earlier.

Shaking that remained even throughout the first fifteen minutes after we left the shore, driving directly to a McDonald's with the heat at full blast. Stale warmth shoved through the quartet of vents lining the front, producing enough heat to surely have Quinn sweating in her Seahawks hoodie and jean jacket behind the wheel.

Discomfort she did nothing to voice as she ordered a pair of the largest hot coffees the fast-food joint offered and balanced them in the middle console between us. The quickest known way to bring up the core temperature, warming from within with hot fluids.

Rudimentary medical care that Cailee's state wouldn't allow, but for me came with the added benefit of caffeine I already knew I was going to need. Concentrated energy to help me get through the hours ahead, my night far from over.

Further actions that it had become brutally obvious while on the island needed to be done. Measures to complete what we had just started, ensuring that the momentary safety we had secured for Cailee would last.

An outcropping of something I had been thinking since Hattie's final words, now painfully clear.

"How you doing over there?" Quinn asks. The first words outside of ordering the coffee since we left the dock earlier.

No demands to know what happened. Not even any questions as to what occurs next.

Trusting my body to take in no more than a few sips at a time, I draw in a bit more of the beverage. My hands still enshrouded in the neoprene of the wetsuit, I clutch the cup in both hands with elbows bent, hinging at the shoulders to raise it to my face.

Numbed movement that serves its purpose, even if I must look like some sort of damned insect to anybody who might pass by on the freeway.

Not that there is a great deal of traffic to concern ourselves with, the midnight hour fast approaching.

"I may never go swimming again."

Snorting softly, Quinn replies, "Is that what that was?"

"Snorkeling or scuba diving either."

"Damn. However will you fill the days?"

My turn to snort, I let the sound of the vents take over. A few extra moments to draw in a bit more fluid, enjoying one of the few interactions we've had that wasn't laced with either underlying urgency or acrimony.

A pause to put down our respective knives while in the presence of Cailee, even if she can't hear a thing being said.

"It's getting better," I reply. A blanket statement, without mentioning that it feels like needles are running the entire length of my body. Hundreds of pinpricks along my extremities as the nerves reawaken and blood returns.

A process I am thankful for as it means that everything still works, even if I wish it would go a bit faster.

Keeping the cup clutched in both hands, I rotate at the waist and return it to the holder between us. Falling back into my seat, I unzip the front of the wet suit. The start of an undressing process that promises to be lengthy, exposing pale flesh to the rush of warmth being spewed from the vents.

Skin that is blotchy with the uneven distribution of blood that still exists, and clammy to the touch.

"You going to tell me what I missed out there?" Quinn asks. A question I'd been expecting since the instant I released the submersible and rolled up into the boat, spewing seawater across the carpeted interior. One that I can only figure she refrained from due to preoccupation.

Concern if not for me, then at least for Cailee.

Glancing my way, she adds, "Get all the traumatizing done at once?"

I know she is trying to add a slight touch of levity to things. A bit of mirth after two days with pretty much every other possible evoked response.

An emotional wringer, to match the physical one I just endured.

All I have to reply with is raising one side of my mouth. A half smile that may grow to full by morning, but I just don't have it in me right now.

"Call Everett first."

Whatever humor exists dissipates as fast as it arrived.

"Everett can wait five minutes."

"Not what I mean," I reply. Reaching for the texture fingers of the wetsuit enveloping my left hand, I add, "Tell him to go back to the Fireside Inn and book a room under Danila's name. Have her check in, and then meet us in the parking lot in half an hour."

Chapter Sixty-Three

To her credit, outside of a couple of prompting questions in the beginning, Quinn doesn't interrupt me one time as I share what happened during the hour-plus gap between my jumping out of the boat and eventually climbing back in. A detailed blow by blow with my gaze aimed straight ahead. Beside me, she does the same, only occasionally glancing over to check the screen of her phone between us.

A route to a destination we went to just yesterday. A hotel that was a first for both of us, this time coming in from the opposite direction.

Outside, the world has slipped into a state of quiet that so often accompanies the last few minutes before one day becomes the next. Most of the traffic that remains belongs to big rigs hauling timber or seafood from the coast. Many of the restaurants that lit the way earlier have closed for the night, their windows darkened.

Even a fair bit of the stars overhead have disappeared behind clouds rolling in.

A typical night in the Pacific Northwest, sure to bring the temperature down another couple degrees or more before morning.

One more thing for me to deal with in the hours ahead.

Start to finish, the story takes me ten minutes to share. Less than one-sixth of the time for the real events to unfold, relayed in excruciating detail. The thought processes that I went through and the actions they evoked.

No attempts are made whatsoever to sugarcoat anything. Vain efforts to obscure the truth that my daughter doesn't need and sure as hell won't appreciate.

The last twenty-five years have proven what she thinks of me. The types of things she believes I am capable of.

That's why she came to me in the first place.

No point in trying to soften any edges. Minimize the threat that was posed or the actions done to neutralize it.

If anything, even trying to do so will likely only lead to her manifesting something even worse in her mind. The long dormant monster she had created, finally roaring back to life.

A fantasy that is already close enough to the truth, there no need to sidestep it.

In the wake of sharing the full story, I fall silent. Quiet allowing her to process all that has been shared, and me to take continued stock of my body in the wake of our trip to the island.

Now out of the top half of the neoprene and back into the pullover I was wearing earlier, the feeling of numbness has begun to subside. A return to status quo, helped tremendously by the heat still being shoved through the vents and the pair of coffees sloshing around in my stomach.

Two enormous cups gulped down almost in their entirety, saving just a couple of inches for Quinn to top off her own energy reserves. Liquid caffeine that I hope she won't be nearly as in need of, though if I am to guess, she has no intention of sleeping the rest of the night either.

Her own self-appointed position of overlook, meant to post up beside her daughter until the moment the drugs in her system wane and she is able to open her eyes.

With the ebbing of the chill permeating my body, the full effect of everything I have been through these last couple of days becomes more pronounced. A total accumulation of abuse going well beyond just the assorted battles staged on Fawn Island, including what happened up at the cabin the previous night. The encounter in the restroom at Pike's Place before that.

Very little rest. Spotty intake of sustenance and hydration.

A sum total that rivals anything I ever went through in the Bureau. A fair number of the trials that I endured during my time in the Navy as well.

A grueling marathon that validates the effort expended since moving west years ago. All the hours in the basement gym, and the miles hiking through the surrounding forests.

Preparation for an event I hoped never happened, but now that it has, I'm glad to have put in.

The goal now being that there is enough remaining in the tank to go a bit further. One last piece to ensure it never happens again.

"There it is," Quinn mutters. Lifting her right hand from the wheel, she points to the glowing sign rising above the right side of the road ahead. One of a just a handful on at such an hour, calling out to any weary travelers who might be in need of a bed for the night.

Keeping the hand free, she reaches to the phone mounted beside her and kills the GPS. Mechanized instructions that are no longer wanted or needed as she slows.

"And there they are," I add, using the same gesture to point to Everett and Danila standing along the back bumper of a silver Range Rover. Facing toward each other, they cut short whatever conversation they are locked in, both turning to face our way as our headlights flash over them.

A freeze that lasts just an instant before they both start to walk toward us.

A desire to get closer, see to Cailee, that I can't fault them for in the slightest, having been driven by the same for the better part of a day and a half now.

"How many times has he called since we left here?" I mutter.

"About a hundred," Quinn replies. "Hell, maybe a thousand."

Grunting softly, I watch as they continue coming our way. Strides that pick up speed, climbing from a walk to a jog before turning into a sprint.

Everett in the lead, with Danila doing her best to keep pace behind, both racing right through the center of the parking lot. All the makings of a head-on collision, averted only by Quinn stamping on the brakes.

A sliding stop on wet blacktop, with Everett slapping both hands against the hood. Twin points of contact he maintains, crossing one over the other as he circles around the bumper and comes up the driver's side.

A worried father, finally able to take part in something that has probably kept him awake for damned near forty hours and counting. A painful stretch of time, with nothing more to do than send a barrage of texts to Quinn asking for updates.

Pure torture that is splashed across his features as the door is pushed open and he sets eyes on his daughter's unconscious form for the first time.

"Oh, Jesus," he whispers. Not bothering to even unlatch the rear door, he reaches past Quinn's seat and grasps Cailee by the ankle. "Is she...?"

Keeping his focus fixed on her, he adds, "What happened? Where was she?"

Questions that must have been playing on loop since we last saw him, rattled off without thought.

Asks that I bypass entirely for now, instead replying, "Everett, can you get her upstairs?"

Chapter Sixty-Four

Everett Jory isn't what I would call a physical man. That's one of the reasons why I was never that worried about him being with Quinn.

Hell, it's probably one of the reasons why she picked him. Another conscious choice to put maximum distance between herself and anything that reminded her of me.

As was evident when we surprised him earlier and he came to the door wearing only a sheet, it is clear that he works out. A few trips each week to the local gym, or maybe even some machines in the basement that we didn't notice when we were in his home earlier.

Dedicated care for his body that looks good, but as I've come to learn many times over the years, means nothing. Time spent on a treadmill or a bench press can have a great many benefits, but it can't instill a fighter's mentality.

Violence is something that comes from within. A willingness to engage in combat that some people can be pushed into, but most are either born with it or they aren't.

It isn't quantifiably genetic, but I'll be damned if I've ever met a good fighter who wasn't already showing the signs at any early age. A scrappiness that surfaced on the football field or after school in a parking lot somewhere.

To that end, I doubt Everett has ever once thrown a punch at an animate object. His affable demeanor and financial backing have dissipated any need.

Right now, though, I have no doubt that he could do it if he had to. His first ever foray into the former group, the anguish etched into his features displays pain that is very real. A father's worry that caused him and Danila to head home immediately after we left the first time, remaining there while bugging the piss out of Quinn for constant updates.

A need to be doing something that meant the second she called, he immediately made a reservation for another top-floor suite before driving right back over. At last, a task for him to focus on, completed without error or delay.

Accountability I hope can be trusted for the rest of the night and into the morrow as well.

Posted up at the end of the narrow hallway leading from the door past the bathroom and into the living room of the suite, he stands with hands clasped before him. A sentry guarding the only point of access to or from the outside, taken up once Cailee was safely tucked into bed.

His backside is balanced on the outside corner, making it easy for him to rotate his gaze between the front door and the suite where the rest of us are located. Security sweeps driven by nervous energy, performed every few seconds. Robotic precision from the neck up, with the rest of him remaining perfectly still.

A polar contrast to the mother of his child, who cannot stop pacing the length of the windows lining the side of the room. Long strides that eat up the distance before Quinn is forced to stop and turn back the opposite direction.

Constant movement that couldn't be helped if she tried, permeated with the same manic fuel as Everett, manifesting in a very different way.

People on either side of the room, leaving only myself in the armchair in the center and Danila on the opposite end of the sofa. Another pair of contradictions, my seat chosen for the purpose of ongoing recovery. An attempt to let my body rest, while continuing to fill it with whatever is on hand.

This time, the beverage of choice being more hot coffee from the maker on the back counter. Extra caffeine, taken with the benefit of continued heat. Warmth supplementing the hot shower I took when we first arrived and a return to my own clothes.

For Danila, her chosen spot and posture both give the impression of trying to make herself as unintrusive as possible. An outsider who only just met Quinn and me, pulled into what is clearly a family affair and trying not to overstep.

Having checked in as requested, she has now retreated to the sidelines, intent to remain there for whatever may – or may not – be needed next.

"You seriously think this isn't over yet?" Everett asks from his spot in the corner. A question that doesn't come off as a challenge so much as disbelief.

A valid ask after the nightmare of the last couple of days.

Flicking my gaze to Quinn striding my direction, I see her dip her chin just a fraction of an inch. An unspoken signal for me to share with him some small bit of what I told her on the drive over.

A retelling that won't be nearly as comprehensive for multitude reasons, the largest not being to protect myself against what I did out there, but the lack of the time needed to share it and answer the deluge of questions it would inevitably spark.

"I can all but guarantee it isn't," I reply. A launching point that I use to explain to him and Danila both what I found on the island. Not just the singular state of Cailee's confinement in the mansion, but the stark juxtaposition it created against the young girls in the guest house.

A dichotomy that has to mean something, even if I haven't fully unraveled it.

Questions that I have some working theories on, but nothing concrete. Nothing worth sharing yet.

Answers that I intend to spend the rest of the night in search of.

And tomorrow morning.

And however much longer it takes after that.

Chapter Sixty-Five

The ride down from the top floor is spent in silence. So too is the walk through the deserted lobby, the space looking markedly different than the last time the two of us were here.

Gone is the bright red receptionist or the gawking hotel guests, straining to get a look at Quinn putting on a show.

In their place is a quiet that borders on deserted. A lack of energy so common to spaces that are usually filled with people and movement, suddenly found empty.

Not until we are out in the parking lot, the asphalt wet with a recent downpour that must have occurred while we were upstairs, does Quinn ask, "Where are you going?"

I would have thought her first question would be to press me on what I shared about finding Cailee upstairs. The clear dichotomy between her and the other girls, done with intention.

An overview I gave to her in the truck earlier, without digging into the underlying motivation. A separation of both place and manner, making it obvious that she was meant to serve a purpose.

One that I don't know for sure yet, but can't help but keep bringing back to what Hattie – and later Leland – both said earlier.

Comments that didn't outright put the blame on me – or anyone else, for that matter – but suggested that there might be something to it.

And if there isn't, it is clear Cailee's inclusion was not by mistake.

"I'm going to start with the diner Leland mentioned last night," I reply. "The one where he was supposed to meet Cailee, see if it can tell me anything.

"After that, I need to go back up to the cabin."

"Why?"

I know better than to even try to repeat what took place upstairs and give a winnowed version of things. After everything that took place out at Fawn Island, there is no point in doing so.

She will see right through the bullshit. A woman forced to grow up much earlier than she should have, presaging a life of mistrust. A lack of naiveté that has left her always trying to smell out any inconsistencies.

A talent she has in spades, paired with a love of calling someone out.

Even in our limited interaction the last few years, that much I know for sure.

"Based on what I saw on the island, there is no way of knowing when Cailee might wake up and be able to talk," I reply.

On either side, vehicles wet with rain slip by, the droplets shining under the parking lot lights. Silent observers as we march down the center, headed for my truck.

"Which leaves Leland and whoever's phone that was as the next best sources of information," Quinn says.

Digging into the pocket of her jacket, she uses the fob to unlock the truck. One quick pulse that causes the parking lights to flash just a short distance ahead.

"The only remaining sources," I counter, holding out my hand between us. An upturned palm that she deposits the keys into, our respective heels continuing to beat out a steady rhythm between us.

"And what is it exactly you're looking for?"

This time I don't even try to answer the question. A conscious avoidance, knowing that she won't let me give a pared down answer, and I won't let myself tell the truth.

Popping open the driver's side door, I swing it wide. Doing the same for the rear door as well, I grasp the handles of my go-bag and heft it up onto the bench seat. A return to its previous spot before bringing Cailee here so I can access the storage compartments underneath.

A second trip to a very particular one that I last accessed just a few hours earlier. A return for the twin to the X26C taser currently sitting in the dive bag behind the boat shed on Fawn Island.

Sliding it free, I hold it close to my body, using the tail of my jacket to obscure it from view of any cameras that might be mounted on high.

"You know how to use one of these?" I ask.

Sliding her gaze down to my hands and back up, Quinn's shoulders visibly drop. A slight groan slides through her lips.

"Seriously?"

"It's either this or the spare Beretta. Which would you prefer?"

Shoving out a breath through her nostrils, she glances to the side. Crossing her arms, she runs through some sort of mental calculation, keeping her gaze averted for several moments.

A silent computation that ends with her snapping her right hand out. Snatching the stun gun from me, she returns the hand to its previous position, folding it under her opposite forearm.

A lightning strike that I barely saw, let alone anyone who might happen to be observing a grainy monitor from the front office.

"You really think this is necessary?" she asks, rotating her gaze back to meet mine. Tilting her chin down, she continues, "I don't just mean this, but all of it. You going back out tonight and everything?"

"It's the only way to keep her safe," I reply, relaying what I have been rolling around since the instant my anger receded enough after leaving the island to think clearly.

A shortened version of the complete truth, which is that I wish to Hell that this wasn't the case. I wish my body wasn't already beat up. That there was something more than coffee in my stomach.

Information about who I might be going up against.

"And the faster we do this, the better for her."

Again, her focus moves to the side. Resuming her previous stance, she stares past the hood of the truck, looking toward the trees lining the back of the lot.

"You heard Everett up there. If there is anything you need, he has money."

"I know."

"I'd go with you, but..."

"I know that too," I reply. An unspoken nod by her to the fact that she isn't leaving Cailee's side. And from me that I'm almost glad, feeling the same bit of the relief I did after leaving Hattie's last night.

So long as she is far removed, she can't be in danger.

One last time, she slides her gaze my way. Eyes narrowed, she says, "No radio silence. Stay in touch, keep us updated."

"I will."

Taking a step back, she adds, "And maybe don't die."

Chapter Sixty-Six

And maybe don't die.

For most parents, they can remember the first words their children said. Almost always mama or dada, with an equally high likelihood of it being said to the wrong gender.

After that, they can recall with total clarity a child's first full sentence. The first time they ever said they loved them.

A host of memories I don't have, each milestone somehow managing to take place while I was far removed. On a base somewhere on the opposite side of the world in the Navy, or some remote corner of the country chasing bad guys for the Bureau.

Career choices that meant I missed a lot of things during Quinn's first fourteen years.

Everything after Marcel Bardette and his crew showed up that night.

Absenteeism making the four words Quinn just said to me in the parking lot the nicest thing I have ever heard her say. A kind compliment that probably wasn't meant as one, though I will take it anyway.

A simple sentence that I can't help but play through my mind on repeat as I move east away from The Fireside Inn. A full tank of gas and another large coffee in the middle console, I push along the quiet highway.

Silence that allows me to replay everything that has come thus far. The sudden appearance and request from my daughter two days ago, so far removed from telling me she didn't want to ever see me again. A threat that had turned into a promise, if not for the actions of some as yet still unknown third party.

A secret evil that attacked the only thing strong enough to make the two of us not just coexist, but interact and work together for more than a day and a half. An unholy union that I would have thought ended with one of us killing the other.

And if that didn't do it, then surely the suicide mission that was the trip out to Fawn Island.

Phase two of what promises to be a third up ahead, meaning the words uttered by Quinn could be interpreted multiple ways. As a directive, ordering me off to do as I must, or a request, asking that I use care in whatever I am about to embark on.

Explanations either one that I will accept, even if for my purposes, I am choosing to look at what was said in a different way. A more metaphorical approach, meaning that in order for me not to die – or wish I had – other people must.

I have to ensure that nothing more happens to Quinn or Cailee. Safety that can only be guaranteed by finding and eliminating all who are responsible for what has happened.

Threats who singled Cailee out, and will continue to do so until whatever point they are trying to make is fulfilled.

An eventuality I cannot allow, marking this as a transition point.

A shift from a frantic search into a hunt.

Whether or not this all stems from something I did remains to be seen. Twenty-five years of cases and manhunts that no doubt pissed off a lot of people and created plenty of enemies.

Prior actions that now matter far less for their isolated details than the skills they provided. The tools and mindset required to now do what I must.

Chapter Sixty-Seven

The Half Moon Café is the restaurant equivalent of Keegan, the bartender from La Rosa Negra. A place that it is obvious at a glance Leland Doone has never and would never enter on his own. A joint open around the clock that probably doesn't do much more than nominal business between the breakfast crowd leaving and the late-night crowd showing up.

For the middle fourteen hours each day, a few locals and regulars might wander in for lunch or dinner, but beyond that, most of their money is made after dark. Drunks wandering home from the bar in need of some carbs to soak up alcohol or a place to make up an alibi to feed their wives. College kids up late playing video games or getting high, seeking something to eat and unable to make it themselves.

Predators like those who grabbed Cailee, requiring a place without cameras to conduct illicit activities.

Parked in the back corner of the lot, I can clearly see through the banks of windows lining three sides of the structure. A building sitting in the center of a corner lot in a neighborhood that has seen better days.

Down the street sits a mill of some sort that closed operations decades ago. Everything that could have been salvaged by the company was stripped away first, followed by scavengers looking to turn a buck.

What remains is a skeleton of the original. Wood and metal exposed to the harsh Seattle climate for years, leaving things rusted or rotted.

A pretty apt parallel to the handful of houses I passed on my drive in. Many of the cars sitting along the curb or on blocks in the front yards as well.

A harrowing sight even in the passing light of my headlamps, probably made infinitely worse under direct sun.

Never before have I seen this particular place, but it isn't unlike a lot of other diners across the country. Not so much Stumpy's or The Sea Shanty, both built to a very particular motif, but more like the numerous Waffle Houses dotting the landscape back home.

Bright yellow paint and signage, rendering the place visible from a distance. An oasis of light and movement in an otherwise darkened corner of the world.

A veritable punchbowl, making it easy to get a feel for the place, even while hiding as much as possible in a vehicle as large as my truck.

Unlike the other places my daughter and I have been recently, there appears to be no pretense in trying to separate the kitchen from the dining area. No need for swinging doors or a window inset high above the counter, providing just brief peeks at the back while food is shuffled out.

At the Half Moon, everything is done right out in the open. A layout that brings to mind images of a Japanese steakhouse or Mongolian barbecue, even if the food being prepared is much lower on the culinary hierarchy.

Serving as the centerpiece for the building is a flattop large enough to cook breakfast for dozens of people at a time. A slab of steel that at one point was probably polished and gleaming, having since been coated with a light layer of char.

Burn that has turned the top of it almost black, imparting flavor from thousands of previous meals into the eggs and hash browns currently sending up plumes of steam. Sustenance for the handful of patrons inside, overseen by a man in a dingy white t-shirt and even dingier apron.

Stains that, much like the griddle before him, have no doubt been earned by spending hundreds of hours in that exact spot doing that exact thing.

Extended out from the back wall of the structure, everything else is arranged in three-sided squares around it. Concentric rings, starting first with the counter, followed in order by freestanding tables, and finally booths affixed just below the windows.

Space and seating to accommodate several dozen at a time, tonight housing but a fraction of that. A crowd that could probably be serviced by one waitress if she was willing to hustle, instead split between a pair who look to have each taken half of the floor space.

A clean division through the middle, with no regard for where guests might be seated.

A game of chance that probably manages to balance itself out over time, tonight tilted in favor of the middle-aged woman with red hair. A ball of untamed frizz that extends from the top and back of her skull, the front just barely contained by a thick headband.

Assigned to oversee just a single table and a lone patron at the counter, she is content to post up next to the cash register. One arm folded across her midsection, her opposite elbow is braced atop it, her phone extended before her.

A stance she has assumed since I arrived several minutes ago, only occasionally looking up to check on her charges.

Malaise that is plainly evident on its own. Even more so as a contrast to the much younger woman in charge of the far half of the room. A girl who is donning a matching uniform, though any similarities between the two stop there.

At most a bit older than Cailee, the zip-up dress of yellow and black she wears hangs from a slight figure. Dishwater blonde hair is pulled into a ponytail at the base of her neck.

Not once has she stopped moving since I pulled in, servicing the remaining guests seated at the counter and multiple groups of four and five that have chosen her side to sit on. The closest I can imagine the place ever gets to a crowd, keeping her running in an endless loop of topping off drinks and fetching condiments.

Five full minutes, I sit and wait. Time that I use to merely observe, getting a feel for the place. A baseline of how it operates and the flow of customers.

Moments that I split with turning on Leland's phone to check and see if there is any word about what happened on Fawn Island earlier in the night. Any sudden cancelation of tomorrow's event, or words of warning to expected attendees.

Cautionary notes that never arrive.

Same for any activity from the phone that Cailee texted from.

Dead ends that pull my focus back to the establishment before me, trying to envision what might have happened two nights ago.

How many people might have been present.

Who Cailee would have seen as an ally enough to borrow their phone and fire off a message to her mother.

Chapter Sixty-Eight

I know where I am going even before the waitress with red hair gives me an appraising look and tells me to sit wherever there is an open seat. A directive I respond to with a nod and a mumbled thanks before heading straight for the booth that a gaggle of college students just piled out of. A short walk across a sticky floor, giving me a better view of everything I was able to plainly see from the outside.

An inverse of the fishbowl effect, putting me on display as I pass by the counter lined with stools on my right. The row of booths pressed tight against the wall to my opposite side.

The handful of freestanding tables filling the gap in between. Chipped and stained surfaces turned at odd angles and surrounded by uneven numbers of chairs.

Seats that I avoid as I wind my way through and slide into the standard arrangement of plastic benches separated by a tabletop that comprises a booth in the far corner. All three patterned with a veneer of faux wood, they are still damp from the cleaning I just watched the younger waitress complete not two minutes before.

Wet residue that is still likely better than whatever she just got done scrubbing away. Some combination of the same stickiness that sounded out as I crossed the room, clinging to the soles of my shoes.

Reaching to the stack of laminated menus wedged into the space behind the napkin holder, I pull one over in front of me. Another prop that I barely glance at, my focus instead going to the room around me.

A repeat of the sweep performed from the truck a few minutes prior.

A second look from a better angle, assessing those I am sharing the same air with. A group that looks no better up close than it did from afar.

At the counter, there are two strays. Both terrified they might have to interact with someone else, they are seated as far from each other as possible. Opposite ends of a sweeping horseshoe that puts them directly across from each other, each intent on avoided so much as eye contact.

Seated at the long connector piece forming the bottom of the shoe is a young couple in their early twenties that looks to have just come from a semi-formal event of some sort. Seated closest to me is a man in khakis and a dress shirt that is a size too large. Around his neck is a loosened tie that resembles the pattern of a couch my parents used to own.

On his far hip, a young woman with a mound of blown-out hair held together by a bow slumps against him. Donning a patterned dress, her shoes from earlier in the evening have been cast aside in favor of a pair of canvas sneakers.

Waiting for their food to arrive, they sit whispering between one another.

Quiet conversation that is unnecessary, as they could speak as loud as they wanted and still go unheard over the sound of metal utensils beating on the griddle in the back and the raucous laughter of the crew in the corner. A group as large as the rest of us combined in jeans and Mariners paraphernalia, looking to have closed down whatever bar they were watching this evening's game from before migrating this way.

A presence that most nights I might find intrusive, though tonight suits my purposes perfectly.

"Good evening," a voice says, pulling my attention away from the crowd in the corner to the waitress walking my way. A young woman who in person looks both younger and more exhausted than she did from afar.

"Evening."

"How are you?" she asks, coming to a stop at the head of the table, allowing me to see the plastic name tag affixed to her uniform for the first time, identifying her as Lila.

A small notepad and pencil already in hand, she holds both out before her, poised for use.

Practiced behavior, performed a thousand times before.

"Good," I lie. "You?"

Raising her gaze from the pad for the first time, she audibly sighs, her shoulders rising and falling with the effort. "One of those nights, you know?"

In reply, I can't help but smirk. A response borrowed from spending so much time with Quinn the last couple of days.

And in summation of everything I have been through since the sun last set.

"Do I ever."

The corner of her mouth flickers slightly. A natural response, there and gone before the automation kicks back in and her focus returns to her pad. "What can I get you to drink?"

"Coffee. Black."

"And do you know what you'd like to eat yet?"

"Well, I'm not sure," I reply, launching right into the story I was working on during the drive over. Another in what has been a litany of falsified tales the last couple of days, following what Quinn told Keegan and the old guy at the boat rental shop, and I in turn pedaled to the young punk at Sportsman's Warehouse.

"My granddaughter Cailee ate here for the first time a couple nights ago, and since she knows I usually work late, she told me I should try the place."

Again, her focus rolls up to meet mine. A slow and deliberate movement, ending with her barely whispering, "Oh, yeah?"

"Yeah, she even liked it so much, she grabbed someone else's phone to text me about it right then."

Chapter Sixty-Nine

"Hey!"

The single word is pushed forth in a hushed voice. A faux whisper that is still plenty to cross the empty parking lot, catching my attention barely halfway to my truck. No more than a handful of steps beyond the exit and the ongoing banter of the crew in the corner.

A group that apparently has no intention of leaving this evening, continuing their revelry from earlier in the night as long as possible. Boisterous delight at the good fortune of their favorite team and the promise of impending glories.

The kind of nonsense born in alcohol and fandom that I couldn't help but overhear as I was eating. A meal spent staring intently at my plate and making a point not to press Lila any further, acutely aware of two distinct facts.

One, that she was avoiding my table – and even corner – as much as possible.

And two, despite what she might have claimed, she knew exactly what I was referring to the instant I mentioned Cailee's name.

Unlike Keegan and Leland both, there was no imminent threat

staring her in the face. She hadn't been struck in any way. She was not bound or constricted at all.

The palpable fear she carried was a couple of days removed. Time long enough to have taken it from acute, overwhelming her circuitry, to more of an underlying level. A reduction from terror to worry that allowed her to concoct stories on the fly, insulating her from any potential threat.

A cocoon that I am still in the process of determining the best way to penetrate when the call catches my ear. Information I didn't press her on while sitting in a public space, but desperately need to know before proceeding.

Slowing my pace, my attention snaps to the side. Spun away from the roadside signage and the bank of windows framing the outside of the building, my gaze is pulled toward the back corner of the structure. Scanning the area, it takes a moment for my eyes to adjust to the drop in light before the faint outline of a yellow and black dress becomes visible.

Leaning away from the back corner of the building, the bit of color serves as a starting point, above which pale features and dishwater blonde hair materialize.

"Lila?"

"Shh!" she hisses, raising a finger to her lips. An urgent gesture she follows by using the same hand to wave me toward her. "Come here. Hurry!"

Doing exactly as instructed, I jog the first couple of steps. Momentum I use to carry me forward, even as I reduce my pace to a hurried walk. Long strides that close the gap between us, swinging me out of view from the windows lining the side of the building.

Maintaining her spot against the back corner, Lila folds her arms over her torso. A classic defensive posture that in her case makes her already slight form appear even skinnier.

Which, by extension, makes her look that much younger.

A scared child, not much different than how I imagine Cailee looked the last time she was here.

"I'm sorry," she says. Her gaze planted on the patch of cracked asphalt between us, she continues, "I didn't mean to lie to you, I..."

Stopping there, she swallows, sending a visible lump the length of her throat.

"Are you really her grandfather?"

Reaching to the inside pocket of my jacket, I extract the photo that Viv handed over last night. Holding it at arm's length before me, I wait as she lifts her gaze and leans in to study it before replying, "I am."

"Did she really text you?"

"She did," I reply, "though it wasn't about the food here."

Snorting softly, she retreats back to her original vertical position, with just a few inches separating her from the concrete block forming the back wall.

"What did she say?"

"That she was in trouble," I replied, bypassing the backstory of the code word, and even the intermediary of her mother before it got to me. Tucking the photo back into place, I ask, "It was your phone she used, wasn't it?"

"I...I don't know," she answers. "I mean..."

Letting her voice drift off, she turns her focus to the side. A quick glance along the back of the building, checking over the odd assort-ment of lifeless objects amassed there.

A veritable mess that makes the rear of La Rosa Negra look like an art exhibit by comparison. Stray trash bags and broken chairs. A stack of mangled pallets starting to mildew.

"She came in around 10:30," Lila says. A return to the beginning without prompting, seemingly as a way to better explain her last response.

The reasoning behind why she can't directly answer my question.

"Super nice. Super friendly. Said her name was Cailee and she was meeting someone, but she didn't know how long the bus would take and had gotten here early, so she asked if she could sit and wait."

Her confidence growing with each word shared, as if she is glad to be ridding herself of the story, she brings her gaze back to meet mine. Her brows rise as she continues, "We get all kinds in here, but friendly we don't see too often, so I told her to take all the time she needed.

"Well, 10:30 became 11:00. And then 11:15. At 11:30, two guys who it was pretty obvious weren't who she was expecting showed up and sat down in the booth with her."

As she speaks, I take care to keep any sort of visible reaction hidden. Complete neutrality, so as to not impact the story – or her willingness to share it – in any way.

No matter how much vitriol I can feel rising within.

Acrimony that climbs along the back of my throat, spilling across my tongue like the whiskey Careen Doone served me just last night.

"I knew right away something wasn't right when I saw one of them take her phone from her. After that, I went over and asked if I could get them drinks or if anybody wanted to order just to kind of check on things, but they didn't even look at me.

"Told me they weren't staying and to get lost."

With each syllable uttered, more questions rise to the fore. Details I want to pull out about what she saw or how Cailee reacted.

Inquiries that I keep silent for the time being, letting her get clear through the story without stopping her.

When she is done, if I need to, I can go back and ask about individual items. An after-the-fact approach that I have found is much easier than start-and-stop.

"I thought about calling the police," she continues, "but they hadn't really done anything. They were a little creepy for sure, and one of them still had her phone in his hand, but they hadn't hurt her or done anything to make a scene."

The skin crinkles around her eyes. Hints of guilt that she pushes through, continuing with, "So instead, I kind of caught Cailee's eye from over by the cash register. I held my phone up so she could see it, and then put it down on the counter.

"You know, like a signal that it was there if she needed it. Maybe she could fake needing to use the bathroom and grab it on her way by."

Having just exited the Half Moon, it is easy to put together exactly what she is describing. A visual for me to superimpose the details she is sharing, from the booth she was probably seated in, to the positioning of the cash register and the restroom right behind where Lila now stands.

"That was good thinking on your part," I offer.

"And it worked," Lila replies. "A couple minutes later, she did get up and walk by. She grabbed the phone on her way and made it to the restroom, but it wasn't thirty seconds later that the men both left the booth too. One went on outside, and the other back toward the restrooms.

"Right after that, they all three left."

The fingers on my left hand curl up into a ball. A fist so tight that I can feel the faint ridges of my nails against my palm.

"And your phone?"

Again, Lila glances to the side. A quick look that I can't help but feel like is a shift. Her story told, she is suddenly very aware of where she is and how long she's been gone.

A burden lifted that she now wants to retreat from as fast as possible.

A change meaning I am down to just my last few minutes. A few final stabs to get what I can before moving on.

"Found it and hers both in a toilet a few minutes later."

Grunting softly, I add the information to what I already know. The endless attempts by Quinn to call both numbers, and my own efforts to track their location.

Vain tries that never – and will never – turn up anything, both devices waterlogged beyond repair.

"Do you guys have any cameras here?" I ask. "Anything that I might be able to use to get a picture of the two guys or what they were driving?"

The same snort used when I commented on the food a couple of minutes ago returns. A derisive sound that is clearly reflexive whenever discussing her place of employment.

"We used to, but the new owners thought it was a waste of money."

"Can you describe them?"

"Angry," Lila replies, the word out without thought. "And furry. Thick hair, thick scruff, thick fuzz on their wrists and backs of their hands."

"What color?"

"Brown," she answers. "All of it was buzzed down short, so it looked kind of like...well..."

"Fur," I finish, grasping the same word she just used.

"Exactly."

"What about their car?"

Pressing her lips together tight, she shakes her head, causing the ponytail behind her head to peek out on either side. "No, sorry."

Once more, she flicks her gaze to the side. A precursor, letting me know that my time with her is finished, even before she says, "Listen, I should really-"

"Just one last thing," I say, cutting her off so I can squeeze in a final question. A relatively minor piece to check something said earlier, and to help shape what will come later. "The guy in the picture with her, was that who she was waiting on? Did he ever show up?"

A crease appears between her brows. A quick hint of confusion, as if she hasn't even considered this part before.

"He did, actually. Showed up around midnight. Walked in, looked around, and then walked right back out."

Chapter Seventy

Who the hell Leland Doone thought was behind the headlights that pulled up the steep drive to the cabin, I have no idea. Some sort of imagined threat that he had developed in his mind. A result of what must have been extreme hunger and dehydration in the wake of sitting tied up in the cabin for the last fifteen hours, leading to bouts of psychosis or hallucination.

Terrors that had caused him to scoot his chair more than three feet across the hardwood before hitting the edge of the heavy carpeting in the center of the room. A firm ledge that had sent him toppling to the side, pinning him to the floor with his head bent at an angle, most of his weight resting on a shoulder.

A pretzeled position causing him to belch out, "Oh, thank God!" at the sight of me standing before him.

A shrill cry that I don't respond to as I step inside. I also do nothing to acknowledge his current predicament or the pain it must be causing. Hours of agony leaving his face flush and his cheeks damp with tears.

A night that I can guarantee was still easier than mine.

Or Cailee's.

"Please," he mutters between lips dried to the point of cracking. "Help me up."

Again, I say nothing, taking two steps forward and stopping in the spot Quinn occupied earlier. Arms crossed, I start with Mick, surveying what twenty-four hours without a heartbeat have done.

His skin is chalky. The blood and brain matter that spilled from his head have crusted solid to the sofa. If it was any warmer, it would already be mildewing with flies circling about.

As it stands, he is starting to stink.

One hell of a sight and smell to keep Leland company all day.

"Give me some water."

Rolling my attention his way, I reply, "I see you've been well."

His chin wiggles to either side as if trying to shake off the comment. His features twist into a look of pleading. "Water. Please."

"My daughter didn't want me to come back," I say. Dropping my hands to my sides, I circle in behind him resting sideways on the floor.

Like my daughter a couple of days ago on the dock, I make a point of stamping my heels as I walk. Firm contacts he can't just hear, but feel coming up through the floorboards.

"Said we should just leave your ass here with Mick and the others, and that eventually you would get what you have coming."

A few feet away, a couple of ragged gasps escape. Pained sounds that are somewhere between a wheeze and a sob, though from where I'm standing, I can't tell which.

Not that I give a shit either way. In fact, at this point, the less I know the better.

Makes it easier to focus on the reason I am here. To place the image of Cailee or the young girls all sedated in the guesthouse at the front of my mind. The recent memory of Lila visibly trembling as she shared what happened at the Half Moon Café just a couple of nights before.

Anywhere but on the fact that he was telling the truth last night about thinking he was stood up by Cailee, and wasn't even there when she was taken.

Details that I can't let him know I am aware of, still needing a great deal more from him now.

Coming to a stop directly behind him, I let my shadow engulf him. Sudden darkness that causes his entire body to quiver. Trembling that is interspersed with tiny sounds sliding out.

A show of fear that lasts for several moments, ending with me bending down and grasping the back of the chair on either side.

"But I told her you would play ball and give me what I need to know."

Pulling in a form of modified deadlift, I lever him up from the floor, returning him to vertical. A load that is significantly more than Cailee's limp weight earlier, taking more effort than I care to admit.

"Right?"

"Yes! Yes," Leland replies, shoving the words out as gasps. "I'll tell you everything I know, just, please, water."

Flicking my gaze to the side, I look over at the half-empty plastic bottle that I let him drink from seventeen hours ago still resting on the counter.

"You want water?" I ask, rotating my focus back to stare at him full. "You have to pass a test first."

Still audibly pushing out each breath, Leland shakes his head to either side. "Wha...a test?"

"Friday night, when your mother called you and said I was there looking for my granddaughter, why did you lie?"

His chin drops to his chest. The sounds of his breathing become more pronounced as his shoulders begin to quiver. Slight tremors that grow until they are lifting and falling a centimeter at a time, driven by the crying that seizes him.

Tears that aren't quite sobs yet, but fast approaching.

A young man who is already broken, on the verge of becoming unrecoverable.

The exact state I need him in if he is to be trusted to help me with what comes next.

"Why!?" I snap, raising my voice so that it fills the interior of the cabin. A yell loud enough to draw him from his descent, causing him to jerk his face back up to meet mine.

"Why the hell do you think!?" he shouts back, his cheeks red and glistening. "My mom didn't know about any of this, sure as shit didn't want me involved in it! I lied so she wouldn't know!"

Remaining completely motionless, I let the answer hang in the air for several moments. Staring down at him, I hide any sort of response, watching as he continues to gasp with fluids leaking from his nose and eyes.

A free fall from his lofty perch that he definitely never envisioned when this all started.

Staying that way for the better part of a minute, my first move isn't toward the water on the counter. It isn't even to take a step in any direction.

Instead, I reach to the MK3 strapped to my hip after returning from Fawn Island. Washed free of the night's earlier events by my swim through the Pacific, I draw the gleaming steel from its sheath.

A sight that immediately causes Leland to begin to rock back and forth. Full-body spasms that push the chair across the floor as more tears rise to the surface.

"Come on! I told you the truth! I even told you everything I know about Cailee before that!"

"Yes, you did," I reply. Taking a step forward, I reach out and grab the arm of the chair, steadying it in place so he can't flee any further.

"Then why are you-"

In one deft movement, I slash the sawback blade against the outside of the wooden armrest. A cleaving strike, severing the lengths of electrical cord holding his left arm in place.

"And now you're going to tell me everything you know about the people who set her up," I add. Keeping my focus aimed on him still twisted to the side, cowering in his seat, I retreat a step. And then another.

Far enough that I can reach over and grab the bottle of water from the counter.

Tossing it into his lap, I add, "This could take a while, and I'm sure as hell not going to be feeding you the whole time."

Chapter Seventy-One

The remains of that first bottle of water didn't last longer than a few seconds. Long enough for Leland Doone to upend the bottom of it and pour out the last few inches, letting it free flow into his open mouth.

A damned baby bird with its head tilted up and jaws gaping, begging for vital nourishment.

A reaction that would have been understandable if it had been days since he last got something to drink or if he had been sweltering under the desert sun, but given the conditions, made it clear that he had never experienced the slightest modicum of discomfort.

Confirmation of my original thought that a life spent under the protective umbrella of his father's business dealings had effectively insulated him from the real world. Never before had he been faced with actual struggle or strife. Not once had he not had an army of guards or servants there to obey his every whim.

A manicured worldview that had now been shattered, likely to never return.

A hard lesson that had been imparted to Quinn twenty-five years ago. And Marcel Bardette's young son when I showed up to arrest his father. And even Hattie's little girl, had she survived the blast.

A casualty that eventually touched everyone who dealt with the kinds of matters we did.

Just the same as I feared might be the case for Cailee after she woke up.

The second bottle made it only nominally longer. Locking his lips around the top, he again lifted his chin toward the ceiling. Going the extra step of squeezing it in his hand to try and force the liquid out faster, he crushed the cheap plastic into a twisted heap. Disfigurement that was paused for an instant in the middle so he could take in a few deep breaths before going back for the remainder.

More than twenty ounces of replenishment taken down in under a minute.

Needed hydration, resulting in the two discarded empties resting on the floor near his feet and a return of some color to his features beyond just the flush of tears. Recovery that I am still not certain he deserves, but am willing to trade out for the time being in the name of getting the answers I need.

Provided that his ass continues to tell me the truth.

A momentary ally of convenience, in the face of something even worse.

"Tell me about the other night," I say, starting with the most recent piece of information. A story he first mentioned yesterday, now buttressed by an eyewitness account from Lila.

A known human interaction from which I can work backgrounds, while at the same time verifying that the truth Leland just told me about his mother wasn't just a breadcrumb tossed my way in the name of securing some water.

Standing with the backs of my knees pressed against the coffee table, I am effectively blocking Mick from view. A post chosen specifically to give Leland a bit of a break from what he's been staring at for almost a day solid now.

A respite that isn't an olive branch, but a benefit to be snatched away in the event I don't like what he has to say.

"Which night?" Leland asks.

With his right arm and ankles still bound to the chair, he sits with his weight twisted to the side. A natural lean, shifting toward his free hand, that extends all the way to his chin.

Turned partially to the side, he glances up at me through only one eye in quick glimpses.

"Thursday night. The night you set her up."

"Wasn't like that," he replies. "I already told you, she stood me up."

Giving no indication that I have been to the Half Moon or have heard what took place, I reply, "So what was it like?"

His brows come together as he turns my way. A quarter rotation that isn't far enough for him to look directly at me, but brings me further into his periphery.

"We were supposed to meet at midnight, but when I got there, she was nowhere to be found. I waited in the parking lot for a few, but she never showed, so I bounced.

"That was the last I seen or heard from her until mom called the next day."

Midnight fit with what Lila described, both for Cailee's arrival and departure, and Leland showing up later.

"Midnight?" I asked. "You routinely set dates for the middle of the night at cheap diners? Or was that just where you were stopping off on your way home from someone else? Maybe one of those girls I found you with on Mercer Island?"

The look of confusion grows more pronounced. Faint folds lines appear on the puffy skin surrounding his eyes.

The previous turn continues, moving so he could fully stare at me. "Date? That wasn't a date, and I didn't pick the time. We were supposed to meet at midnight. She didn't show, so I left."

"Did you think that maybe something was wrong? Did you even try to call her?"

His eyes narrow to the point that they are just barely slits. A look that goes past confused, landing firmly in the category of stupefied.

"How the hell could I have called her? I don't have her number."

I can feel my brows coming together. Misunderstanding that is now mine, fast starting to match the look on the young man across from me.

Two people clearly not in synch, trying to decipher what the other is saying.

A situation beginning to send up red flags about our respective positions.

"Don't have..." I begin. A thought I let drift off, replacing it with, "Then how the hell did you set up the date? Or meeting? Or whatever you want to call it?"

"I didn't," Leland replies. "I never set any of them up. I was just told to be somewhere at a certain time, so I went."

"Told by who?"

His gaze still fixed on mine, he tilts his chin forward. A silent reply that I don't understand at first, prompting him to then do the same again.

An exaggerated nod with his eyebrows lifted, aimed not at me, but the corpse a few feet behind me.

The man with the burner phone loaded with unknown numbers who had also received the text regarding when and where the meeting on Fawn Island was set to take place.

The same man Hattie had described as being bored out of his mind serving as Careen Doone's bodyguard, jumping at the chance to become active again.

The very same stiff who would be most beneficial to speak with now, if not for the tempestuous act of my daughter a day ago.

"Alright," I mutter. Exhaling slowly, I fold my arms before me. "Start at the beginning, and tell me exactly how your interaction with Cailee went."

Chapter Seventy-Two

I left Leland sitting in the armchair in the living room of the cabin with another bottle of water and the instructions not to even think about untying himself the rest of the way from the chair.

I needed to step outside for a few minutes, and I would be watching the entire time.

Orders that still dripped with malevolence that I was fast coming to realize wasn't his to be taking in anything more than a tertiary manner.

Anger that I wasn't ready to completely untether from him yet though, needing a few minutes to step outside and process all that was just discussed. New information that had me rethinking not only what had transpired and the roles of the various people in it, but how to proceed moving forward.

A classic example of there not being a best option, but rather a handful of shitty ones for me to choose from.

What happened at Fawn Island earlier was a pretty close approximation to how things usually played out back when I was with the Bureau. The details were obviously radically different - as not once did we ever pull off an underwater island landing – but the gist of things was almost always the same.

We were alerted to or uncovered a crime being committed. An investigation ensued, during which guilty parties and their location were identified.

A working plan was put together and then implemented.

In the matter of going to get Cailee, we didn't know with complete certainty she was on Fawn Island, but our investigation had narrowed it to a strong possibility. Process of elimination and deductive reasoning that told us if she wasn't there, the people who would know where to find her would be.

We were also able to go online and find out more about the island than we would ever want to know. Even made a trip out to see the place for ourselves.

A condensed version of what I used to do for sure, but still a fairly close approximation.

This is already promising to be nothing like that.

All the makings of a shit show, with odds far longer than what was pulled off earlier.

Two days of flinging myself headlong at this has produced plenty of aches and muscle soreness, but nothing concrete in the way of an identity beyond The Council. A semi-ethereal entity we put out of business years ago and that may or may not now be reforming.

The only known location that has been mentioned at all is the island I just scoured. The site of a meeting still the better part of a day away, begrudgingly handed over at the last possible minute.

A place with no signs of criminal activity beyond the girls piled up in the guesthouse, Cailee, and the handfuls of guards roaming the place.

No cameras covering the stairwells or hallways. No dogs roaming the grounds.

Hell, even their damn security used sound suppressors on their weapons.

As light a footprint as possible, with absolutely no presence of anyone who might be in charge. The new blood that Hattie alluded to, having resurrected the organization in recent years.

Nobody in suits roaming the halls. Definitely not a boat or helicopter to have brought them.

Not a single face associated with an organization as large as The Council outside of the pair of guys with buzzcuts that Lila mentioned. Thirty-somethings with glowers who could be two of a million such pairings along the western seaboard.

A sum total that is essentially zero. Every waking moment since Thursday afternoon spent in pursuit of something that has rendered almost nothing of use.

A lack of actionable data that is in itself telling. An indicator, pointing to only a single plausible course of action.

A last resort that no part of me wants to even consider, let alone pursue.

It's just that right now, I see no other possible way.

Not without letting today seep into tomorrow, and the vast assortment of problems that could bring with it.

Climbing down the short flight of stairs from the porch, I thread my way through the pair of sedans to my truck. Gravel crunches beneath my feet as I reach the driver's side door and pop it open, going straight for the middle console.

Grabbing up both of the burner phones, I insert one of the matching batteries into the back of each and power them to life. Twin reawakening processes that feel infinitely longer than what took place at Stumpy's.

Time spent that I already know will yield nothing, but need to invest before doing anything else, just in case. A final check to ensure that no word has been sent out regarding what I did earlier on Fawn Island.

A status update, or a warning, or even a damn trick question to see if anybody will reveal themselves. Any sign of acknowledgement about what took place.

And one last look to verify what Leland just told me. Something I should have done earlier but failed to in my haste to get him loaded up and away from the cottage on Mercer Island as fast possible, before anybody noticed the unconscious girls in the bedroom, the dead guard in the closet, or Mick stuffed into the trunk.

A list of concerns that might earn me a pass in the moment, but there is no excuse for having not circled back in the time since, especially after what happened at the diner this morning.

Springing to life within seconds of each other, my focus goes first to Leland's phone. Navigating directly to the recent call log, I find what is essentially a repeat of Hattie's phone earlier.

Just two numbers, with one showing up in far greater frequency than the other.

Mick, and then Hattie.

"Damn it."

Dropping the phone down onto the driver's seat before me, I move on to Mick's phone. A single tap on the screen that is nothing more than to check for anything incoming from The Council, or the buzzcuts, or anyone else he might have been in contact with.

A call or text message, of which there are decidedly none.

"Shit."

Taking up one of the phones in each hand, I retreat a step from the side of the truck. Swinging the door shut, I put my focus on the glow of the windows along the front porch, letting it guide me as I retrace my steps.

Slow, plodding strides, back through the sedans parked side by side, and up the wooden stairs.

A walk with a deliberate pace, used to milk out a few final seconds. Moments to consider things once more, hoping that some new angle, an as-yet-unseen option, will present itself.

Courses of action that fail to reveal themselves by the time I have climbed back up on the porch, assuming the same post I stood in less than a day before with my daughter. A place that worked well enough to have a conversation with her the first time, about to be employed to do the same again.

Stowing Mick and Leland's phones in the right pocket of my coat, I pull my own device out of the opposite side. Tapping on the screen a couple of times, I place it to my cheek, not wanting to risk putting it on speakerphone with just a pane of what is likely reinforced glass separating me from Leland.

After just a single ring, my daughter is on the line.

"Where are you? What's going on?" she opens, shoving the words out in a lump. Two quick questions, rattled off in order.

Asks that I ignore entirely, posing a pair of my own in reply.

"How's Cailee? She awake yet?"

"Not yet," Quinn says, "still sleeping. Now you're turn. What's going on?"

In short order, I rattle off everything that has happened since we last spoke. Information not to brag about my exploits, but to fill her in on where things stand.

Data that she may need if the next couple of hours go as I strongly suspect they might.

Omitting only the part about wishing Mick was still breathing so I could press him for answers – that being why I chose to shoot him in the leg instead of the chest on the front steps to begin with – I tell her everything else that I have uncovered.

A verbal dump that takes three full minutes, after which I fall silent. Complete quiet to let her process as best she can over the faint sound of Everett asking questions in the background.

A relay I trust will take place once we are done.

"Anything else?" Quinn eventually asks.

"Actually, yeah," I reply. "There are two things from the last couple of days that have been bothering me and I wanted to address right quick."

"What's that?"

"One, I didn't do anything to Danny Rivers," I say. "I wasn't even there. That bumbling oaf really did slip on some ice and break his own damn leg."

For a moment, there is no reply. No sound at all beyond more light voices in the background.

Everett, this time in discussion with Danila.

"Seriously?" Quinn asks. "That's what you've been thinking about all weekend?"

"One of them. The other is, I can take the blame for a great many things, Q," I begin, making a point to employ the moniker I have used to address her her entire life, with the exception of the last couple of days.

A concession to her little outburst about names when we first climbed into the truck that no longer feels relevant as I continue, "but I refuse to fall on the sword over your name. That was all your mother's doing."

This time, I can hear her snort. A bit of mirth that I lean into, adding, "It was her grandfather's name, and she was convinced she was going to use it whether you were a boy or girl. I knew better than to fight her on it, but I always hated him and the damn name."

Across the line, I can hear soft laughter. Muted chuckles that weren't the reason I called, but I will take. If what I have planned doesn't work and this is the last time we speak, at least it will be happy.

A rare high point in a lifetime of valleys.

The list of things I would like to add is too lengthy to even consider. Confessions and apologies and a thousand other things that I want to share with my daughter, but there simply isn't the time.

And right now, I'm not even sure she would be a receptive audience.

Considerations that I choose not to wade into, instead ending the call right there.

Clearing the screen, I exit back out to the homepage on the device. Pulling up a basic internet search engine, I type in my request. The start of a multi-screen sequence to find the phone number I need.

One more thing I need to see to before setting off again.

"Good evening, you've reached the Seattle office of the Federal Bureau of Investigation," a perky switchboard operator answers, oblivious to the hour as she rattles off the preplanned opening. "How may I direct your call?"

"Otis Herbert, please," I reply. "Tell him Rand Bryant is calling. I'll wait."

Chapter Seventy-Three

The pants Leland is wearing were pulled from the guard who took his final breath on the porch right outside the front door. The closest in size of the bunch, both of the shots that killed him were to center mass, meaning that his lower half was saved from anything more than some dirt and dust from the floorboards and an errant bit of blood.

A spot or two that had long since dried to match the black fabric.

The pullover he dons is the one I took off upstairs less than a day ago. Having been wearing it during the melee in the bathroom at Pike's Place and later still for the gunfight right outside the cabin, it smells like holy hell. The sweat of stress and battle that has had almost a full day of being stuffed into the go-bag in the back of the truck, baking into the fabric.

Odors that no amount of washing will ever get out, it's future up until ten minutes ago likely to be a garbage bin or an incinerator somewhere.

An overall outfit that is, like so many things over the last couple of days, a far cry from what I'm sure Leland is used to. Items that he would normally only put on if forced to play dress up like at the

Washington football game last weekend, though otherwise would never go near.

A costume that will have to suffice for what we are about to do.

Another on a long, long list of lies and subterfuge performed in such a short stretch of time.

One more thing I am not the least bit enthused about, but see no way around.

Cut free from his bindings, Leland paces across the short expanse of the cabin's kitchen. A short distance that is enough for no more than a couple of strides before he is forced to turn and move back the other way.

Frenetic energy that is spurred by the multiple bottles of water in his system, and a couple of granola bars taken from the stores in the safe room masquerading as a pantry. Foodstuffs that are more than three years out of date, taken down without the slightest pause.

Calories matched by the urgency and nervousness pulsating through him, and the freedom of being up and out of the chair after a solid day of being forced to sit. A potent combination that has eliminated any ability or desire to be still.

Motion that I afford him while standing on the opposite side of the counter, holding his and Mick's phones. The recent call logs of both up in front of me, I flick my gaze from one to the other, scanning the entries.

Unlisted numbers that are much easier to decipher for the former than the latter, with only the two in Leland's phone. Unsaved sequences corresponding to Hattie and Mick's burners, repeated at random.

An order that isn't quite as simple to unravel in Mick's phone, with more than a handful of different listings present. Entries that all have local area codes, but beyond that have nothing to differentiate them.

A task that would be much easier if the few incoming texts such as this morning's weren't all from blocked numbers.

Further proof that what Hattie said about Mick and his guards being bored and what Leland relayed about Mick handling most of the communication were both true.

A fact I am sure would be hammered home if I called Quinn again and asked her what Cailee's number is, it too no doubt present to set up the pair of meetings earlier in the week.

"Alright, one more time," Leland says, his voice drawing my attention, even as my gaze remains fixed on the screens before me. An ongoing sweep, matching timestamps on the various entries between the two phones. "What am I doing here?"

The question is valid. One that I have also been asking myself on repeat since stepping off the porch and heading down to my truck a little while ago.

That singular moment in the wake of our previous conversation when the rough outline I was putting together took a step forward. Evolution that could only exist with the inclusion of the young man before me.

Regardless how many times I pose that same inquiry to myself, not once have I settled on a definitive answer, always unable to account for the concern that the want and need to go quickly is clouding my judgment. If in the name of trying to protect Quinn and Cailee, I am setting myself up, and by extension leaving them completely exposed moving forward.

At the same time, I don't know any other way. The further removed from the events on Fawn Island we get, the greater the response will be. Answers that will come in one of two forms.

Overwhelming opposition that comes after us, or another disappearing act, going to ground for who knows how long.

Possibilities that are both shit for me and my family. Either a deluge that will swallow us, or a waiting game that eventually they will come out on top in.

Knowing that, I can't help but believe that the only course of action, no matter how tenuous it might be, is to take advantage of whatever chaos I managed to create earlier. Emergency response that must be occurring on the island, even if not a word has yet been shared with tomorrow's guests.

Using that as a baseline, the plan is to take whatever frantic behavior is ongoing, and pair it with what I just discovered.

From there, hopefully, maybe, I can circumvent an extended search by instead drawing the information I need to me.

A situation with as close to even odds as I can ever hope for.

A next-to-last step, after which I can finally finish this.

"You're going to call and ask to meet."

Pausing his march, Leland stares at me through widened eyes. "Just like that? *Oh, hey, this is Leland. Wanna get together for a drink?*"

Sliding my gaze up from the phones, I fix him with a stony glare. A pointed look, letting it be known that just because he is out of the chair and we are staring across at each other, we are not on the same level.

Sure as Hell aren't partners.

He is a means to an end. Someone who got drawn in himself, earning him a bit of leeway, but is still partially responsible for what happened to Cailee. A role that would have already gotten him shot, had he been on Fawn Island earlier.

Blanket recipients of my ire that he is avoiding for the time being, how long said reprieve lasts hinging upon how he handles the next couple of hours.

Dropping Leland's phone on the table, I reach to the sheath on my belt. Sliding free the MK3, I wrap my fist tight around the handle and place it next to Mick's phone on the counter.

A silent message that is received as Leland raises his hands, flashing his palms my way.

"You're going to say that shit has hit the fan. Some crazy old guy showed up at your house earlier tonight looking for you. He shot Mick and tore through most of your security force.

"You were just able to slip away during the battle and need somewhere safe to hide until the meeting tonight."

Now that I know how things were arranged, how the flow of information was being handled, it is clear that the better option would be to have Mick make the call himself. Phone whoever he had been speaking to on The Council directly and share what happened, saying he and Leland are together and moving.

A story that is infinitely more plausible, but isn't an option after Quinn's little explosion last night.

"You're scared and on the run."

Lifting his eyebrows, Leland replies, "That last part won't be hard, anyway."

Resuming his pacing, he reaches the stove in one long stride. Turning back the other way, he again looks over to me. "Who am I calling?"

"The waitress mentioned two guys in buzzcuts coming to grab Cailee before you got there," I reply. "My guess is, that's who Mick was talking to."

"No names?"

"Probably by design."

Winnowing my search to the time between when Lila said Cailee and the buzzcuts left the Half Moon and when Leland was supposed to meet her there, I pick out a pair of calls made within fifteen minutes of each other.

An incoming from an unknown number arriving at a quarter before midnight, and a second one arriving from Leland a few minutes later. A sequence I am guessing corresponds to the men calling Mick to let him know it is done, and Leland phoning to say he'd been stood up.

One educated guess, after which we will be left with dialing numbers at random, hoping to make a connection.

Tapping on the incoming call just before Leland's, I bring the number up on the screen and raise my focus. My hand tightens around the base of the knife.

For a moment, I consider pointing out that I have been to his family's mansion. I have met his mother.

And I have eliminated damn near everyone who might be there to protect her.

Threats that aren't nearly as effective as lifting my chin toward the pantry and saying, "Just remember, that behind you is essentially a vault. A sealed room with steel walls that I doubt anybody else in the world even knows exists.

"You try anything, and you'll get to run a firsthand experiment on just how long a couple cases of water and some granola lasts."

Paused with his body turned sideways in the alcove of the kitchen, his eyes flit down to the knife still grasped tight in my hand. A quick peek, followed by looking the other direction toward the pantry I just threatened him with.

A visible mental calculation that takes only a moment, ending with him asking, "Where do I tell them to find me?"

Chapter Seventy-Four

I can smell Leland sitting in the passenger seat beside me. A miasma of the assorted scents imbedded in the clothing he now wears, mixed with his own combination of odors. Terror sweats and piss and even some of the lingering pheromones from the amorous tryst he was in the midst of when I snatched him from the house on Mercer Island last night.

A plume of smells that is magnified by the heat coming through the front vents, threatening to choke out the cab of the truck, and by the first hits of adrenaline starting to seep into my system. A heightening of the senses that is fast beginning to feel like a baseline, having crested in a series of successive peaks over the last couple of days.

Rises that have built one on top of the other, reaching levels not felt in decades.

Seated behind the steering wheel, my left hand is positioned at seven o'clock. My weight rests on my right haunch, leaving my right hand free to grasp the MK3 in an overhand grip.

The quickest way to launch a strike in the event that Leland decides to try anything during the ride to the same state park where Quinn and I brought his buddy-for-hire Keegan just last night. An attack that I can't see him mounting, but don't want to make the mistake of letting whatever I might have uncovered in the last hour color how I see him.

A more favorable viewing, leaving me open and vulnerable to someone who no doubt has harbored as much ill will for me as I him the last couple of days.

A young man who we stripped of his pride, his most prized possession, and then forced to sit there stewing on it for nearly twenty-four hours. To make it worse, we even killed his greatest protector, and left the two of them together.

Reason enough for him to want to take a shot, before factoring in whatever reticence he might have about where we are going.

What we are about to do.

If given my druthers, I would have preferred to err on the side of caution and transfer him the same way as Keegan. A friendly tap to the side of the head with the handle of the MK3 to render him unconscious, and then throw him across the backseat, or even the bed of the truck.

Means of transport that would have completely freed me of concern, allowing me to put my full focus on what I hope is about to transpire. A generalized working plan, using the layout of the state park and who I imagine will soon be arriving to form a basic framework.

A more preferable approach that I had to cast aside in case I need Leland to answer the phone. A return call from whoever was on the other end of this morning's text, phoning to ask for clarification or to force a change of destination.

Having no choice but to leave him alert, I instead went with cobra cuffs to his wrists and ankles. Immobilization that he had accepted without complaint, seemingly just glad to be in warmer clothes and away from the sight of Mick's rotting remains.

Sitting in the seat that has been occupied by Quinn for much of the last couple days, he has also adopted her favored pose. Body twisted away from me, his right shoulder is pressed to the passenger door. His focus is aimed out through the same window.

Outside, the world has moved to the point where one day becomes the next. Not the minutes before and after midnight when the calendar date turns, but those instants when everything grinds to a complete halt.

All movement ceases as a collective breath is taken. A full pause, allowing but a moment of complete stillness, before things begin anew.

A begrudging recommencement of life that I can't help but feel is at odds with what I have planned.

A karmic violation of sorts to be added to my recent tally.

"Where are we?" Leland whispers. The first words from either one of us since we left the cabin and piled into the truck.

A vehicle I very briefly considered leaving behind in lieu of one of the sedans parked outside of the cabin. Vehicles that would better fit the story Leland shared over the phone about his hasty retreat from the mad man chewing through Mick and the others, though would provide nothing else.

No cache of weapons and gear in the back.

No lifted platform or reinforced body, should things go irrevocably awry.

A choice of invisibility versus capability that will always be won by the latter.

"North of the city," I reply, uncertain even myself about the patch of forest we are currently passing through. A stretch of dense pine and hardwood enveloping the last piece of road between the cabin and the state park.

Two remote points, connected through a series of backroads and state highways. A route dictated by the glowing screen of my phone, none of my previous trips to the park having been from this particular direction.

"Hm," he replies. A non-committal answer that is little more than a grunt. A single syllable that lingers for a moment before he adds, "You know, I never intended for her to get hurt."

Sliding my gaze sideways, I check the screen of my phone. A quick look to track the short remaining distance to the park.

A turn toward the passenger seat that I continue, moving just far enough to push him into my periphery.

"She was super nice. Seemed pretty cool."

Barely an hour ago, I heard the full story of how his and Cailee's interaction came to be. A completely staged meeting and courtship of sorts, with neither working with full information.

To Cailee, they were the Lees. Two people who met at a football game and hit it off, already sneaking away to clandestine meetings.

The beginning of something that wasn't anything yet, but she couldn't help but let her imagination run.

As is prone to happening with people her age.

For Leland, it was an assignment. A target that he was told was in the same position as himself. Another vestige from a once-proud family that was being recruited to The Council that he needed to get close to.

An act of espionage with Mick overseeing, arranging meetings and paying off unwitting accomplices.

A barrier to admission in the name of resurrecting the family business and carrying on his father's name.

As Hattie had put it, the price of inclusion.

"Not at all like most of the people I'm usually around."

One at a time, replies come to mind. Retorts from both ends of the spectrum, including telling him that I understood he was being manipulated and also that I don't care.

A multitude of responses that I am still working my way through, not yet ready to levy a decision one way or the other.

Answers I keep to myself as my focus moves back in the opposite direction, landing on the bright window of my phone's screen once more.

"We're here."

Chapter Seventy-Five

Once more, I am reminded of the sedans left sitting up at the cabin. Either of a pair that Mick and his crew brought up last night, looking to snatch me and keep me under wraps for a couple of days.

At least, that was the story Hattie shared, what Quinn and I arrived to find of a decidedly different nature.

Intentions that Mick never even pretended to hide, greeting us with a show of force that escalated without provocation.

Self-importance that Hattie had let run unchecked, to the point that their intentions were no longer aligned in the slightest.

For as much as bringing one of the sedans might have helped with optics, I can't help but again be glad to have brought the truck. A repository of supplies and weapons like my favored Beretta or the AR-15 I used on that very same encounter with Mick.

The former, I currently have tucked into the rear waistband of my jeans. The latter, I grip tight in hand while standing just off the center of the concrete floor of the shelter house.

Standing perpendicular to the same picnic table used last night, I stare out toward the parking lot and the lone concrete drive that feeds it. A vantage that confirms a secondary benefit of bringing what

Quinn kept insisting on calling a tank is that it makes for an ideal screen.

A massive wall of reinforced steel and glass, helping to shield Leland from the lane snaking its way through the trees.

A blind, forcing whoever approaches to have to come all the way to the small paved lot to even see him sitting in the exact spot where Keegan rested just twenty-nine hours ago.

Bait to draw them in, giving me a clear shot on their vehicle if they think better of it and try to reverse out and flee.

An even better angle if they do as I hope and exit their vehicle to speak with him.

"The waitress at the Half Moon said there were two of them who showed up the other night," I say. A comment I know I have already shared with Leland, stated this time more for my own benefit.

Audible thinking, working through the plan once more now that we are onsite.

Standing at the far end of the picnic table, I stare past him toward the truck parked fifteen yards away. Backed in so it is facing the lane, the doors are unlocked. The keys are in the ignition.

Everything to enable a quick getaway if things get ugly fast. If whoever shows up acts the same way Mick and his goons did and immediately start shooting, or if they roll up en masse, looking to snip loose ends.

"Groups like The Council usually have guys who are designated to handle odds and ends like that, and now this," I continue. More thinking aloud, bringing back information and details that I haven't actively thought about in years.

Snippets of data imbedded deep in the gray matter, drawn to the fore by recent events.

The information equivalent of my body responding to the adrenaline, reactivating synapses long thought dormant.

Tilting my chin forward, I say, "The truck is blocking the view from the lane, so they'll have to pull all the way in to be able to see you. That means they'll park to the left of the truck, both exit, and then walk out around it."

Clasping the grip of the assault rifle loaded with a fresh magazine, my arm is cocked at the elbow with the butt of the weapon nestled against my bicep. The barrel is pointed toward the exposed trusses of the cavernous ceiling above.

Unlike the knife I carried in the cabin and on the drive over, this is no longer for Leland's benefit, designed to ensure compliance.

From this point forward, it is an extension of myself.

"Where will you be?" Leland asks. His voice drawn taut, I don't need to glance at him to see the strain he is feeling. Yet another emotional shift in the face of a situation he never could have imagined just days ago.

Extending my free hand across my body, I point to a clump of trees just off the rear corner of the shelter house. A spot sufficiently far enough from the pond to be shrouded in shadow, away from any reflected glow that might kick up from their approaching headlights.

"Over there," I reply. "I'll wait for them both to exit and step out into the open-"

"And then you'll kill them?"

Snorting softly, I reach for the MK3 on my waist. Drawing out the blade, I reply, "Not if I don't have to."

"Not if..." he replies, his voice trailing away as his eyes widen, focusing on the blade coming his way.

"And even then, not both of them," I add.

Sliding the razored edge of the knife into the narrow gap between his wrists, I cut through the cobra cuffs holding them in place. A repeat of what took place when first arrived, freeing his ankles so he could get into position.

"Why not? Aren't these the guys who-"

"They are," I reply, stopping him short before he can get out the full question. An inquiry that I already know will just piss me off, the last thing I need being more anger. "But they're also the guys with the information we need."

Taking a step back, I watch as Leland pulls away the remains of the cuffs. Sliding them from his wrists, he holds them up, studying the thick plastic.

A quick examination, ended by him flinging them off into the darkness.

"And how do we get that?"

"*We* don't," I reply, using the same words I gave to Quinn just a day ago. Taking a step past him, I finish with, "I'm going to get into position. If you try anything, you'll be the first shot I fire."

Chapter Seventy-Six

The car they are driving must be one of those new electric models. Some damn space age thing that is completely silent, allowing it to make the turn off the road and get most of the way down the lane before I even know it is there.

Signaling done not by the sound of the engine carrying through the quiet night, but by the splintering of light passing through the trees. A flickering glow that steadily gets stronger as the vehicle approaches, moving fast despite the narrow and winding path.

"They're here!" Leland calls from his spot on the picnic bench. A warning that is much louder than need be, hinting of the chemical dump working its way into his system.

Adrenaline, mixed with fear and anticipation, matching the elixir that was present last night in the cabin, and again earlier when I first arrived back. Urgency that I can tell has him aching to jump up from the bench and go tearing toward the truck.

A course of action that I've already promised will end very badly for him, even if I can't blame him in the least for reacting to the potent cocktail in his system, my body starting to respond in its own way as well.

Another burst that is undeniable, even as I know this is likely just one more step along the way. A source of information, after which – hopefully – I will finally be able to put an end to things.

A multi-day odyssey far beyond anything I have ever incurred.

Or even imagined.

Saying absolutely nothing in reply, I push up from the seated position I'd assumed at the base of an ash tree just off the southwest corner of the shelter house. With my back braced against the thick trunk, I'd rested with the AR-15 balanced across my knees.

One hand on the stock and the other on the barrel, I'd sat and listened, positioned well below the traditional sightline. A vantage allowed by the high ground clearance of the ash tree, and the other hardwoods surrounding the shelter house.

A break from the thick pines resting on the far side of the pond, mimicking much of the western half of the state.

What I thought was a tiny victory, mitigated by the damned silent vehicle sliding into view.

Rolling forward onto my knees, I draw my feet up beneath me. Rising no higher than a crouch, I keep both hands locked around the rifle, rotating it into a firing grip as I take one step to the left.

A lateral movement, followed by two in retreat, putting the body of the tree between myself and the twin flares passing through the trees. Torches that become more pronounced as the vehicle approaches and the number of trees separating us dwindles.

Light that crawls steadily forward, hitting the edge of the parking lot, and then the rear of my truck.

Forward progress that goes until it touches the water's edge, setting the pond ablaze. Refraction that matches the sunset across the water at my own home that started all this a couple days ago.

"You still back there?" Leland calls, tilting his chin my way. Four words laced with fear, matched by his ass rising from the seat.

Signs of impending movement. One of the biggest holes that I knew existed in the plan, requiring his participation.

A third-party who hasn't been in these situations before. Doesn't have the requisite experience.

Sure as hell doesn't harbor the same acrimony that I do.

"Sit down!" I hiss, just barely loud enough to be heard. "Shut the hell up!"

Leaning forward, I press my left shoulder tight against the tree. A braced firing position providing maximum cover, with the barrel of the AR-15 snaking out from the side.

Pulse thrumming, I hear the slight crunch of tires biting into pavement as the vehicle comes to a stop. The last sound for several moments as whoever is inside sits and assesses the situation.

Seconds that seem to drag for hours as I press tighter into the tree, straining, aching, for movement. Complete focus, even while preparing to act myself.

Anticipation, in case they decide to reverse out and I need to fire on the run, or if they exit the vehicle with the intent of eliminating Leland.

Breath held, I focus on the narrow band of illuminated ground between the rear bumper of my truck and the corner post of the shelter house. A patch of rocky soil that I stare at, willing the two men with buzzcuts to appear.

Silent entreaties that pass through my mind for almost a full minute, at last answered by the sound of car doors opening. Faint sounds that are only nominally louder than the damn engine, preceding shadows striping the headlights left on.

Dark shapes that become full silhouettes, ultimately culminating in the pair of men Lila mentioned to me just a couple of hours ago. Guys in jeans with their hands stuffed into the front pockets of zip-up track jackets who are best described exactly as she did.

Angry. Furry.

Hair and beards shaved down to a uniform length, framing matching grimaces.

Hardened stares that I can tell Leland is fully aware of as he is unable to help himself and again starts to rise from his seat. Lifting his hands to either side, he exclaims, "Thank God you guys are here!"

A single sentence that sets off multiple events simultaneously.

The words are just barely out of his mouth, the sound still hanging in the air, as I shift my weight forward onto the balls of my feet. Keeping the AR-15 poised at shoulder level, I push off, the treads of my shoes digging into the soft earth, propelling me forward.

An initial burst of anticipatory action that reaches a full sprint within three strides while just twenty yards away, the two new arrivals both move as well. Tandem actions as they each pull their hands from their front pockets, both clutching small caliber handguns.

Nine-millimeter pieces that catch the light from their vehicle, flashing as they start to jog forward, raising the weapons to shoulder height.

A kill squad, sent to confirm and then eliminate Leland.

A method of cleanup, or simply the new leader of the revamped Council's way of dealing with anything that doesn't fit exactly to plan.

"Down!" I yell, letting the word roll up from deep in my diaphragm as I continue to charge from my spot hidden deep in the shadows. A command not issued so much for Leland's sake, but to buy both of us an extra moment.

One added instant that freezes both of the approaching men for a millisecond as they jerk toward the unexpected sound, perfectly framed in the gap before me.

Unmoving targets that make it easy for me to sight in on the closer of the two. The sacrificial lamb of the pair, who will hopefully enable me to get to his partner without having to shoot them both.

Planting my right foot as I continue moving forward, I tug straight back on the trigger four times in order. One time after another, squeezing my index finger as fast as the firing mechanism in the assault rifle will allow.

A quartet of booming shots at short range that chew through his center mass, ripping divots into his torso. Impact that lifts his ass from the ground, sending him wheeling into a blur of blood spatter and limbs.

A pinwheel tumbling backward, completely disconnected from the laws of gravity.

A sight I focus on as I sprint parallel to the shelter house, watching as his flailing body slams broadside into his partner. An unholy collision of blood and body parts that sounds out with a wet smack, sending both men toppling to the ground.

A hard landing that knocks the gun from the second man's hand as he slams into the rocky earth.

Passing by the front corner of the shelter house, I lower the AR-15 from my shoulder. Both hands still clutching it tight, I drop it from a firing pose to something more functional, rotating my grip to the underhand position.

An impromptu club that I wield on the second man as he fights to clear himself from beneath the remains of his partner. Pounding out the last couple of strides, I twist my body to the side and snap the butt of the rifle down, driving it into the soft skin of the man's temple.

A scything strike that splits the skin. Blood spills down into his beard, mixing with the droplets from his partner already striping his face.

On contact, his eyes roll up. His body goes limp, dropping him flat on his back.

A victory I don't even have a moment to enjoy before the front headlights of a handful more vehicles burst to life, spotlighting me in their shine.

Chapter Seventy-Seven

In the rush to get across the shelter house and clear the gun from the second attacker, I hadn't even looked up at the damned paved lane. Sprinting at the bastard with a buzzcut, all I could think about was taking him alive.

His partner was already dead. Whatever usefulness that could be provided, any information I could extract, had to come from the second.

After that, I would have absolutely nothing. No names, no descriptions, not even a way of contacting anybody.

I would be completely out of options, left hoping that Otis Herbert and his team – if he even took what I told him seriously – would be able to find something on Fawn Island. Reliance on an option that was far less than optimal, for reasons ranging from trying to explain why the island was dotted with dead bodies to knowing that any active role I might play was over.

A spot on the sidelines, reducing me to another of the family members of those girls in the guesthouse, left to fret and worry, without a damn thing to do about it.

Forced inaction that is about as far removed from what I am currently staring at as can be.

"Truck!" I bark without even glancing over to Leland still standing on the edge of the concrete slab comprising the floor of the shelter house, my gaze moving to the handful of vehicles that have spilled down the lane from the main road.

More of those damn electric vehicles like the first two men drove. SUVs and sedans that have moved into position in complete silence.

A damned army of a half dozen in total, pushed in side by side, filling the narrow gap carved through the trees.

"Now!"

Abandoning any thought of the man sprawled unconscious by my feet, I drop a couple of inches. Just enough to put some bend in my knees so I can rock forward and shove off the balls of my feet for the second time in as many minutes.

An inverted sprinter's stance, with both hands still gripping the assault rifle tight on either end. A weight that might slow me down a bit, but I am not about to cast aside in the face of what I am staring at.

My second shouted command breaks through the paralysis gripping Leland. An audible spike that smashes through the frozen veneer enveloping him, spurring him into action as well.

Side by side, we both go straight for the truck. No more than a handful of strides across the rocky soil before vaulting onto the asphalt.

Two more and we each reach our respective doors. Jerking the handles open, we pile back inside. A tight squeeze with the AR-15 resting against the steering wheel and the Beretta still wedged into my waistband, pinned between me and the seat back.

The instant the doors are shut, Leland mashes on the locks. One time after another, long after they are already engaged. Repetitive behavior, while audibly panting.

Breathing to match my own as I stare across the small concrete pad at the assemblage before us.

"Oh Jesus, oh Jesus, oh Jesus," Leland mutters, abandoning the locks in favor of spitting out a catchphrase on loop. His mind, over-flowing with adrenaline, unable to process more than one thing at a time and forced into repetition.

Background noise that I ignore, peering out as my hands tighten around the assault rifle.

A point to ground myself against my own chemical dump while trying to process what is stretched out in front of us.

From what I can see, there are six vehicles in total. One to transport the two guys I've already put down, and five additional strewn back along the lane. Two SUV's wedged side by side forty yards away, supported by two more parked at angles behind them.

A solid wall of four oversized cars, backed up by a single sedan in the rear.

A car parked a bit further back, which I have to assume is carrying whoever is in charge. The overseer, coming to ensure that things are finished.

My ultimate target unexpectedly delivered to me, though for now I have to focus on the vehicles in front of it. Space enough for more than fifteen men, a fair number of which are already starting to spill out from doors opening into the woods. Men clad in black suits like Mick's little brigade, with others to match the pair sprawled across the ground behind us.

Guys of varying ages and sizes, the only commonality being the handguns held before them. Weapons extended in both hands, barrels pointed toward the ground.

"What do we do? What do we do?" Leland rattles off beside me, his mind having moved on to its third iteration. Bits and pieces that can be snagged as they riffle across his consciousness.

Words that I again ignore, my gaze swinging from side to side.

My two biggest worries before coming out here were that they wouldn't believe Leland's little act on the phone and would ignore him entirely, or that whoever they sent would be too far down the pecking order to be of any use. More wasted time, like so many of our other endeavors over the last couple of days.

Energy expended with nothing to show for it.

And even worse this time, nowhere to look next. No way of reaching out to whoever is behind all this. No idea what to prepare against while figuring out a way to unearth them.

Worries that it is now obvious were only half right.

Based on the amassed force before us, it is clear that they didn't believe a word Leland said. They saw right through the weak story we put together, not for one second buying into the ruse about his escaping and going on the run, asking to meet at an out-of-the-way state park.

The part I was wrong about is how they would react to it.

A response in force, likely putting together the timing of his call with what happened at Fawn Island. A full mobilization, looking to crush the people responsible for what happened out there.

"What do we do? What do we do? What do we do?"

The situation staring back at me is not at all what I expected. At most, what just played out was the best case I had considered. Killing one buzzcut and keeping the other intact, so I could extract needed information.

Details as to who this new blood overseeing things is. Where I might find them.

One part of what I anticipated being a two-part finale.

A sweeping crescendo that has done me the favor of cutting things in half, bringing both parts to us.

A plan to draw them out that was worked even better than I could have imagined.

Releasing my grip on the butt of the AR-15, I slide my hand forward and twist the keys in the ignition. A quick turn that instantly calls the engine to life, the low rumble filling the interior of the truck cabin.

"What are..." Leland gasps beside me. The closest thing to a coherent thought since we climbed back into the truck. "You can't get through that many!"

This is not at all how I would have drawn things up. Bottling ourselves up like this was better suited for ambushing two guys, not fighting my way out against eight times that.

The stockpile of gear and weapons in the truck is sufficient, but not optimal against a force this size.

Nothing at all about this is what I was anticipating.

But I also wasn't anticipating my daughter showing up to tell me these assholes kidnapped my granddaughter either.

"We're not trying to," I mutter, jerking the gearshift down into drive and stomping my right foot on the gas pedal. Sudden acceleration that causes the tires to spin, sending up a plume of smoke and the angry wail of grinding rubber as they gain purchase, hurtling us forward.

To either side, little flecks of light appear. The start of the assault from our newly arrived enemy. Muzzle flashes that slip past, barely registering in my periphery as the burst of speed flings me back in my seat.

Leaving the rifle to rest across my lap, I extend my arms, grasping the steering wheel in both hands. Death grips that I maintain as I push us straight down the center of the lane for the first thirty yards before nudging the truck to the right.

On command, both passenger tires dip into the grass, tilting the truck to the side as I bear down on the SUV positioned to that side. A target I put my full attention on, keeping the accelerator pinned to the floor.

A motionless bit of glossy aluminum painted black that is no match for the enhanced build of the truck as we slam into it.

Without the burden of an engine, the front end crumples like an accordion. A mash of metal that reaches clear to the windshield, sending sprays of glass into the air.

Tiny shards that catch the lights of the vehicles behind it, glowing like crystals as they hang suspended before us.

Staying on the gas even after contact, I can feel the tires churning beneath us. Torque that pushes the busted remains of the vehicle into the one behind it, shoving them both toward the center of the lane.

The first half of the pile I intend to create.

A means to turn their attempted blockade into a damned bonfire.

Driving the first car on just a bit further, I switch pedals to stomp on the brakes. A momentary stop, just long enough to drop the gearshift into reverse.

A pause on the revving of the engine that makes the pinging of incoming rounds more clear.

"Jesus!" Leland yells. Pressing one hand to the dash, he wheels in his seat, turning to peer out behind us. "They're shooting at us!"

"They've been shooting at us," I reply, stomping on the accelerator a second time. Another abrupt surge that tosses Leland backward against the dash as we reverse out.

A redirect that is only half as long as the trip in. Twenty yards of distance before hitting the brakes, jerking us to another stop.

A momentary feeling of inertia, ended by a rocket start back straight ahead again.

A repeat of what just took place, this time coming in from the opposite side. A vehicular battering ram, pitting reinforced steel against a row of tin cans.

A matchup that the left side fares even worse than the right in, swinging inward, helping to form a massive twist of car frames.

The optimal target for what I have in mind next.

"Get into the bottom of the passenger-side compartment in the backseat," I say, ceasing our forward movement and dropping the gearshift into reverse. Glancing to Leland braced in the seat beside me, I add, "Grab the two plastic cases."

Chapter Seventy-Eight

The words that Quinn used just a day and a half ago are not lost on me. A derisive barb that was supposed to be dismissive. A way of telling me I was absurd. Paranoid. Any of a host of other adjectives that she couldn't quite formulate.

Ridicule that I almost wish she was here to eat, even if I'm glad she's nowhere near this melee.

"These?" Leland asks, thrusting a hard plastic case over the middle console between us. An offering made without looking as his stomach rests against the headrest. Folded in half, his ass is stuck up in air while he rummages through the compartment under the bench seat.

A frantic search made even messier by the adrenaline continuing to push through his system. Chemicals making motor function difficult, reducing him to little more than flailing.

Blunt instruments pushing things back and forth in a mad scramble.

"Yes!" I fire back, snatching the case out of his grasp and checking the label on the side. A quick look at what is stowed inside.

The second item needed for what I have in mind.

"Grab them both!"

Outside, muzzle flashes continue to ignite the night like flash-bulbs. Bright flowers that light up the forest on either side, fired from the cover of the trees. Orange and yellow blossoms bursting forth in uneven patterns, offset by the ping of rounds slapping against the body of the truck.

Shots like those fired by Mick and his goons that might scrape away a little paint, might even dent the outer shell, but are no match for the steel plating underlying it.

Taking advantage of the fact that we have again come to a stop on the edge of the tiny parking lot, the shooters push inward. Advancement based on what I guess they think is some sort of engine malfunction.

Damage from us ramming the shit out of their vehicles, rendering the truck inoperable.

An immobile target that they begin to swing in on. Two arms fanned wide, coming together like pincers.

Opposition forces more than a dozen strong who just watched what they believe was our attempt to escape. One futile effort after another to force our way through that resulted in wreckage blocking the sole exit.

A last gasp that has neutralized our own vehicle, and pinned us back against the edge of the pond.

Fallacious beliefs, falling for exactly what I wanted them to.

The battlefield equivalent of having Leland call earlier, serving to draw my opponent out into the open.

"Got it!" Leland says, jerking his top half back over the seat. Twisting himself around in the narrow confines of the front, he drops himself back down into his chair, both hands clutching the second plastic box tight. "Now what?"

To either side, our enemy continues to move closer. Creeping in from the woods, they begin to take shape. Dark silhouettes that are illuminated with each shot fired.

Bright bursts of light that completely expose them an instant at a time.

Knees bent into combat stances, their arms are extended in front of them as they inch forward.

"Give me that one," I say. A command Leland follows without dissent, passing it across the middle console.

Balancing it atop the first case resting across the barrel of the AR-15, I unlock the hasp on the side and pop open the top. A big reveal that Leland can't resist, leaning over from his seat to peer at the quartet of grenades balanced into notches cut into cushioned foam.

A macabre egg carton of sorts, designed to hold just four rather than a dozen.

A stockpile of handheld explosives that is more than sufficient for what I need.

"Are those...?" Leland mutters, leaning in an extra inch. A closer inspection that he abandons in the same instant, retreating back into his seat.

Outside, the sound of bullets striking the truck grows faster. Hard thumps from rounds imbedding themselves in the steel plating. The whine of shots skittering across the hood or windshield.

Noises that become louder as they push in closer on either side.

Sounds that I sit and listen to, steeling myself for what comes next. The narrow window I will have to pull it off. The even smaller chance of managing it unscathed.

Risks that I sit and weigh, grasping the wheel so tight that veins bulge along the backs of my wrists. The taste of sweat finds my lips.

"Put your seatbelt on," I mutter. "Now."

Twisting his body away from me, Leland grabs for the belt hanging beside him. A repeat of just seconds before, with the chemical elixir surging through him precluding most refined motor skills.

Another round of him fumbling and pawing, stabbing the metal end of the belt into the clasp a handful of times before finally it locks in.

A clear metallic click that can just barely be heard over the onslaught going on outside.

What might as well be a starting gun for me behind the wheel, telling me to go for what I have been chasing the last couple of days.

One last attempt to do right by Cailee, and those girls lined up in the guesthouse on Fawn Island. Hattie's deceased family and my own broken one and anybody else who has ever been violated by people such as these.

Assholes who will do no more harm after tonight.

Extending my right leg before me, I shove the accelerator nearly all the way to the floorboard. Another sudden jolt of fuel to the engine that causes the backend of the truck to fishtail as the tires spin, lifting a thin veil of smoke around us.

A precursor to the sound of tires squealing filling the air. The smell of scorched rubber infiltrating the cab.

The start of a third run that shoots us across the last couple of feet of the parking lot and up the lane. A short distance that we need just a few seconds to cover as I swing out wide to the left.

A route that matches the last one, only instead of taking it all the way to contact, I jerk the wheel to the side just short of the heaped pile of broken electric vehicles.

An impending pyre needing only a spark to set it ablaze.

The tires under us chew into the rocky soil as we make the turn, flinging mud and gravel against the wreckage. Earthly debris sprays across the pavement leading the way while I pump the brakes, dropping our speed.

A descent that doesn't make it all the way to zero, but is plenty slow that I can crack open the door and snatch up the first grenade from the box in my lap. A hot potato that I slide the pin from and chuck sidearm, bouncing it across the mound of the cars on the left.

The start of a three-second window.

Time enough to fling out a second offering to the pile on the right.

Two short-fuse detonators that I leave to do their work, turning my attention back to the path before us. Letting our momentum push the door shut, I give the wheel one more turn, angling us back toward the parking lot.

A hasty retreat with the front bumper aimed for the narrow bit of ground between the lane and the trees, sending our opposition scrambling to get out of the way. Men diving out into the pavement or back into the woods.

Frantic dives taking their full attention, leaving them all completely exposed as those precious few seconds tick away.

An inversion of what they expected barely a minute ago, making them the immobile targets when the pair of grenades go off within an instant of each other. Twin detonations that explode outward from amid the rubble, flinging chunks of metal and glass in every direction.

Shrapnel that works as well as any machine gun, slamming into the sedan parked in the rear and chewing through every man within fifteen yards of the pile.

An effective clearing of more than half the opposition before the spray of metal reaches the truck as it extends outward, smacking into the side of it.

My second signal in barely a minute.

The opening I have been craving.

"Here, take these," I say, flipping the lid on the grenades closed. Pushing them to the side, I slide them as far as the middle console before Leland reaches over and snatches them away.

"What are you-"

The rest of the question never materializes as I pound on the brakes one last time. Twisting the wheel back to the right, I bring the truck to a stop in the center of the lane, facing the smoking carnage that was previously their fleet of cars.

Jamming the gearshift into park, I unlatch the door with my left hand. Popping it open no more than an inch, I pull the same hand back and grasp the second plastic case.

With the opposite one, I grip the handle of the AR-15.

Despite the abuse it has undertaken, the door offers no resistance as I use my foot to shove it open, creating a portal to the outside that magnifies every last thing around me.

The smell of smoke and gunpowder in the air. The bright bursts of errant muzzle flashes from the handful of men who still remain. The sound of their weapons barking.

The chill of the air as it touches the sweat on my brow.

An assault on the senses that is almost intoxicating as I toss the second case to the ground and jump down to the pavement behind it. Raising the AR-15 to my shoulder, I start at the back of the line that was previously moving inward. Those furthest away from the explosions, and therefore posing the greatest threat.

Men who, despite the distance, are still scrambling to collect themselves. Desperate attempts to recover from taking non-lethal bits of shrapnel or having been slapped with the percussive wail of the explosions, many shooting at random into the night sky.

Targets I have been waiting all damned night for, a smile coming to my features as I begin to fire.

Chapter Seventy-Nine

In the wake of the short and furious battle that ensued after tossing the grenades into the pile of vehicles, the world is terribly quiet. Gone is the bark of automatic weapons. No more revving of my engine or the crunch of metal and glass.

I can't hear the cries of men calling out in pain or shouting instructions to one another as they move into position for one last push. A final offensive to bear down on my ass hidden in the bed of the truck.

Right now, all I can hear is a faint buzzing in my ears. Tinnitus from the blasts of gunfire that will get worse if things continue, but for now is just an underlying sound.

A distant distraction compared to the throbbing in my left side. A gunshot wound to the outer abdomen from the only damn shooter I missed on the first pass down the left flank. A lingering asshole who was able to squeeze off a couple of extra shots as I circled around the backend of my truck, looking to clear away whoever remained on the opposite side.

Bullets that were strafed at random, the last of which ripped across my ribcage. A glancing blow that entered at an angle, riding along the ridge of the bone. Fired from a fairly short distance, even such a small caliber was more than enough to tear through the muscular wall, cleaving a trench atop the cracked bone.

A divot stretched more than three inches in length, from which I can feel blood flowing. Wet warmth that saturates my pullover, shrink wrapping it to my skin.

Smacking me from behind, the force of it shoved me forward. An unexpected blow that stopped my firing, lifting the front end of the AR-15 toward the sky as I staggered to a knee.

A break in my steady onslaught, allowing the handful of men who remained in the trees to the right to begin shooting back.

Return fire, making me do the only thing I could, circling back in the opposite direction. A quick pivot with pulses of lightning pushing through every joint and muscle.

The body's natural reaction to pain, causing every nerve ending to fire at once as I snatched up the plastic case from the ground and tossed it into the bed of the truck.

A destination I followed it into, folding myself over the side. An unceremonious fall, made worse by landing on the Beretta still tucked into my waistband at the small of my back.

A place I still find myself, having made it as far as rolling onto my hip to remove the Beretta before falling flat with my mouth gaping. A battle to try and pull in enough air without over inflating my lungs and pushing against the searing pain in my side.

My eyes bulge as dozens of tiny lights flicker across my vision. A combination of the stars dotting the sky above, and the lingering pops of muzzle flashes.

Evoked responses that I fight to push past, knowing that I have to move. To remain motionless, even in a reinforced truck bed, means death.

The longer I stay here, the closer whoever is left out there gets. Steady convergence that at a certain point, I will be unable to stop. They will be too close, able to simply wait for me to show myself.

Or even worse, they will get to a point where they can fire over the side, ending me where I lay.

The proverbial fish in a barrel.

All of that assuming I don't lose too much blood and black out before then.

Lifting the back of my head from the truck bed, I press my chin to my chest. Careful not to lift myself too far from the rubber coating on the bed floor, rendering me an easy target, I peer the length of my body.

A quick assessment, taking in the AR-15 resting at an angle near my feet, the still-smoking tip pointed toward the tailgate. The blood-stained Beretta pressed against the wheel hump on my left.

Items I assess in an instant before moving to the second plastic box. A near copy of the first, the only differences being the label on the side and the cargo contained within.

A swap for the traditional grenades that I used on the vehicles in favor of flash bangs. Non-lethal explosives designed to disorient and incapacitate, sitting against the side of the truck bed after being kicked there by my frantic climb over the side.

My best bet for surviving however many men remain. A way to tilt things in my favor, granting me a few moments to reach the assault rifle at my feet and fire from an exposed position without fear of retribution.

A final push to snuff out these henchmen so I can go for whoever is in that last sedan, my hope that the explosion rendered it unable to flee.

The person I have to believe is in charge of all of this, having showed up with the same purpose as me, wanting to see this all put to an end.

Keeping my hips pinned to the truck bed, I swing my right leg outward. Bending it at the knee, I push it to the side, aiming for the plastic case.

A slow and stilted movement that sends more sharp pains the length of my body. Jolts of lightning that hurtle the length of me, causing my molars to come together. My lips peel back, exposing my teeth as I pull in bits of air.

An inch at a time, I drive my knee outward. A steady arc that passes over the bits of rubble lining the bed, traveling more than eighteen inches before it touches the closest corner of the case.

Solid contact that nudges it a few inches, rotating it against the opposite corner braced against the side of the truck. The fingers of my right hand splay wide as I reach toward it. The tips press against the textured rubber beneath me, fighting to go forward while being held back by the strain of the wound on my opposite side.

A fight between my own injuries and the precious seconds that are dwindling. Time during which my opposition are moving closer.

Backing my knee away, I come at it a second time. A harder push on the return pass, using the force to shove the case a few inches ahead. Continued rotation that brings it almost within reach.

A final stretch I am fighting to cover when an unexpected sound pierces the night, causing me to pause.

A man speaking.

Not the frantic call of one of the guards shouting commands, but a clear voice.

Addressing me by name.

"Rand Bryant!"

Pulling my attention away from the case, my head jerks toward the front of the truck. A pure reflexive reaction, twisting toward the unexpected sound as palpitations rise through my chest.

Shivers that touch the exposed wound on my side, setting it afire once more.

"You back there, Bear? Can you hear me?"

After walking the earth for six decades, I can't say that I've never heard the voice before. Interaction years ago, or a chance encounter in the recent past.

What I do know is it isn't familiar.

"Aw, come on, don't tell me after everything you've done tonight

– and over the last thirty years – that all it took was one little bullet to stop you."

Like Mick when I arrived at the Doone mansion, and my daughter before that, I know that the man is trying to bait me. Goad me into responding and giving away my exact position, or even worse into raising myself into view.

Options I refuse to give him.

The surprise of the moment broken, I roll my attention back the opposite direction. Focus I return to the plastic case, lifting my right knee one final time. A last try to bring the case up into reach.

Strain that I push through, even as I can feel my energy reserves beginning to wane.

"No? Don't feel like talking?" the man calls out in a voice that is threaded with something resembling amusement. "That's fine, you lay back there and collect yourself for a minute. We'll get to you soon enough. And then that little punk in the front seat. And his mother back home at the mansion. And your daughter and granddaughter wherever they're hiding.

"But that's okay, right now, you just stay where you are. It's my turn to talk for a while."

Bait or not, I can't help but feel the vitriol within rise. Wrath that pushes me forward.

With the wound ripped through my side, my opposite knee will rise only as far as my waist. What would be parallel to the ground if I was standing, but no further. A ceiling that I can't push past no matter how much I try, pushing with teeth clenched until water begins to leak from my eyes.

Gray fog appears on the edges of my vision.

"You've probably spent the last couple days asking yourself a lot of questions. Questions about why your granddaughter, a nice, quiet college student was kidnapped. How she let herself get mixed up with a little shit like Leland Doone. How James Hattinger and The Council and all that other stuff that you thought was long behind you just suddenly started popping back up."

As he prattles on, I push my leg back down to its original position. Both of them fully extended, I dig my heels in, using them as pressure points to lift my hips so I can rotate my body to the side.

Movement that causes my entire body to seize, stopping my progress after covering no more than a couple of inches.

A minuscule distance that is just barely what is needed.

Space enough so my fingertips can touch the smooth edge of the case.

"The answer to all of those questions actually goes back well beyond that," the man continues. "Clear back to the night we first met. A meeting I doubt you even remember, because why would you? You were the great Bear, and I was just a little boy.

"But I have to tell you, it is a night I haven't stopped thinking about since."

Pressing my fingers down onto the case, I drag it back toward me. A process that is slow at first under the uneven pressure, but becomes easier as I get it to within reach.

"Not once. Not during all those years spent going to visit my father when I was just a kid, asking him why he wasn't around like other dads. Talking to him over a damn telephone. Watching from behind glass as he got older, and then he got sick.

"Endless trips during which he always made me promise not to go after you or the other members of your team for putting him there. Begging me to leave it alone, that I was too young, that you guys were too good.

"Vows he forced me to make and that I did honor, up until he passed without ever breathing free air again three years ago.

"But after that, all bets were off."

Dragging the case up next to my hip, I unlatch the hasp along the side. Cracking open the top, I peer in at the quartet of offerings within.

Devices that are arranged much like the grenades, the only differences being small design changes.

"You can imagine how disappointed I was to find out that two members of your team that showed up that night were already gone. One from a heart attack, another died on the job. Those bastards got off easy, but that still left me with three.

"The first one, Carmichael, that was more like a trial run. My guys got a little too zealous during their chase. They were supposed to run him off the side of the road and then bring him to me, but they ended up wrapping the front end of his car around a telephone pole.

"Not ideal, but that still left you and Hattinger. And that's where things got fun."

Grabbing up the first flash bang, I pass it into my left hand. A second one goes into my right.

"See, you might have done a great job at completely falling off the map four years ago, but him? His name was all over the internet after his little run-in with The Council. A car bomb that killed his family? Left him crippled? I *knew* he wouldn't be able to leave the idea that they were back in action alone.

"If I was going to go to all that effort though, I had to know I could get you both. And, again, you had seemingly disappeared."

Resting flat on my back, clutching the flash bangs in either hand, I glance to the Beretta by my side. The AR-15 at the foot of the truck bed.

Weapons that are close enough I can move on them the instant the flash bangs hit the ground. A two-part sequence, performed in the brief opening I will be afforded.

"Which brings us back full circle," he says. "Like I said, never have I stopped thinking about that night we first met. Not you busting in the door with your team, and not the words you said as you arrested my father and took him away.

"Comments about how he never should have come after your family, which gave me the idea that that is exactly what I should do. I might not be able to find you – or your ex-wife, since cancer beat me to her - but I could find your daughter. And then it turned out, she also had a daughter.

"A full-on family reunion here in the Pacific Northwest that I knew you wouldn't be far from, so that's where I put The Council. Bought myself an island, called together a bunch of old cronies, filled it with party favors and guards, really went all in."

Lying prone, my gaze aimed straight upward, I can envision the few remaining opponents gathered tight around the bed of the truck. Men who have used the time afforded by this little monologue to inch closer.

A smaller version of the formation that was used earlier, forming arcs on either side. Arms to pin me in the second he is done speaking and gives them the word.

An asshole who could have stopped after the first sentence or two and I would have known exactly who he is. Why the call from Leland had worked as well as it did.

Details that I didn't need to hear nearly as much as he needed to share. Things he has been carrying around for decades, aching to finally get them off his chest.

Rambling that might have answered a couple of lingering questions, but the only reason I let it continue was because I needed the time to get my hands on the flash bangs, and to draw his men close enough I can use them.

Things that have now both been accomplished, removing any reason to hear another word.

"Hey, Lucien!" I call out to the son of Marcel Bardette. The only man stupid enough to have ever come to my home.

Ignorance proven hereditary, having repeated itself in his offspring.

"Ha!" Lucien replies, a slight tinge of surprise present. "So you do remember?"

Bringing my hands together, I slide the first safety pin from each of the flash bangs.

"You should have taken the advice I gave your father," I reply, completely ignoring his question. "And never gone anywhere near my family either."

Jerking the secondary pins, I snap the lower half of either arm in both directions. Flinging each of the projectiles over the sides of the truck, I close my eyes and roll onto my right haunch, covering my ears.

A protective stance needed for just a second and a half – a fraction of the grenades – before I can feel the thump of their blast.

Percussive force that pushes me into movement, fighting against the agony in my side as I bypass the Beretta, going straight for the AR-15.

A weapon with far more power that I use to eliminate every remaining person surrounding the truck.

A handful of men all sprawled across the ground or trying to stumble away from the truck. Targets I chew through one at a time even as my own energy continues to fade, ending with Lucien Bardette himself.

Chapter Eighty

The first thing to register is the bright light in the room as I crack my eyes open. A glow that isn't the filmy yellow of halogen tubes positioned above me, but the kind of luminosity that can only be created by the sun.

Natural illumination that streams in through the windows to my left, making everything radiate. An ethereal halo that is almost overpowering, causing my cheeks to bunch as I look away, rendering my eyes nothing more than slits.

Narrow openings through which I am able to take in the space around me. Condensed windows, revealing only small slivers of my surroundings.

The last thing I can remember with full clarity is standing in the back of my truck. The opened plastic case of the flash bangs resting between my feet, the discarded AR-15 was propped at an angle against the top of the tailgate. An impromptu landing spot once I had depleted the thirty rounds in the magazine and cast it aside.

Replacing it in my hands was the Beretta. Extended to arm's length, I was working my way back through the bodies of Lucien

Bardette and his men. Final shots for each of them to ensure their demise.

Added assurance that never would I – nor my family – ever encounter them again.

A process driven by pure animosity that I was still in the middle of when the adrenaline in my system finally waned, no longer enough to compensate for the physical abuse and blood loss I'd sustained. A fight between physiology and anatomy that the latter finally won out in, causing the fog that had been drifting into my vision to take over.

A complete cut to black that sent the world spinning as I toppled flat to my back for the second time in just a few minutes.

A place I fully intended to spend my final breaths, now making the questions of where the hell I am and how I got here especially poignant.

Still able to open my eyes to no more than a fraction of usual because of the harsh glare streaming through the window, the best I can surmise is that I am in a hospital bed of some sort. A makeshift space that isn't in a real facility, but has been repurposed into a close approximation.

The bed I am resting on is shrouded in white sheets and blankets. The back of it is tilted upward at an angle.

To my right is a stainless-steel pole supporting an IV bag connected to the line inserted into the veins traversing the crook of my elbow. Beside it is a matching table with a bottle of water and a couple of vials of pills.

Beneath the shrouded lumps of my feet at the end of the bed is a freestanding cabinet. A medicine chest with center-closing doors and glass fronts. On the shelves inside are rows of bandages and vials of various sorts. Clear cylinders filled with tongue depressors and cotton balls.

Staging that has to be by design, bringing to mind images from an era long since gone.

"Good morning," a female voice says. An unexpected sound

coming directly out of the sunlight on my left, jerking my attention that direction.

Squinting against the harsh glare, I force myself not to look away, blinking past the moisture that rises to the surface. A watery veneer that blurs that hazy silhouette forming before me.

An uneven outline that slowly fills itself in as my eyes adjust, revealing one of the last people on earth I expected to be sitting by my bedside.

A figure who tilts her wrist backwards to check her watch before adding, "Just barely, but still technically morning."

"Mrs. Doone?"

The words come out as little more than a croak. A faint gasp that travels up a parched throat and passes over cracked lips. Physical manifestations confirming that every memory I have from the last couple of days is real.

As will be the pain they evoke once whatever is currently coursing through my system subsides.

The corners of her mouth turn up as she chuckles softly. "I think we're a little past that, don't you?"

The dress she was wearing the first time we met has been swapped out for slacks and a sweater. Light colors that blend with the light pouring in around her, creating a bit of a halo effect.

"How did I get here?"

The smile grows a bit larger, matched by her eyebrows rising to match. "It turns out that things like security guards and safe houses in the woods aren't the only things that have lingered from our old life."

Lifting a hand, she motions to the space around us. "Though I have to admit, this is the first time we've used this room in a while."

The response isn't exactly an answer to my question. Information that allows me to make some connections, while leaving other things deliberately vague.

Word choice I have to believe is by design.

A tacit acknowledgment that she and her son are the reason I am alive, despite all that transpired over the last couple of days. The latter for having driven me back from the state park, and the former ensuring I received care from whatever doctor they keep on call once we got here.

Aid that neither one had any reason to provide.

Least of all, to me.

"Your son?" I ask.

Dipping her chin in a nod, she replies, "Not nearly as bad as you, but resting as well."

How much she knows about what has taken place the last couple of days – weeks, even – there is no way to be certain. Information encompassing not just what happened to Mick and his team, but going back to Hattie and The Council and all the rest.

Data I have to believe would have radically altered my reception. The state I would currently be in, if still breathing at all.

"Mrs. Do-" I begin, cutting myself off short. "Careen. I-"

"Leland told me what happened," she says, stopping me for the second time in as many moments. A pause as much from surprise at her words as from the insertion itself.

Reaching out, she rests a hand atop my arm buried beneath the covers. Leaving it there, she raises her gaze from me to the opposite wall. Her stare glazes as she focuses on it, saying, "Not just last night, but everything since that Hattinger guy first showed up here. Mick and your granddaughter and all the rest."

Flicking her attention down to me, her nostrils flare as she draws in air. "Thank you. Thank you for saving my son's life. For saving my life. For ridding us both of Mick and all his bullshit."

I have no way of knowing exactly what the story Leland shared with his mother was. Some amalgamation of truth and perception, shaped by recent events. A combination of things seen and heard and even imagined.

Reactions to being snatched away from the cottage. Tied up in the cabin. Witnessing the battle last night.

Acts that were done by my own hand and by others, further influenced by thankfulness for being alive. Guilt over dragging Cailee into things. Remorse for being seduced into taking part in the first place, trying to chase the approval of someone long gone.

Errors in judgment that could be his own realizations. Outcomes of listening to Lucien last night.

Realizations after showing up in the early morning hours with a bleeding old man and trying to explain it all to his mother.

"Thank you as well," I reply. "For saving my life. Welcoming me into your home twice now. Extending kindness to me that you have no reason to."

Her gaze still locked on mine, her mouth again curls upward. A wan smile tinged with sadness that lingers but an instant before falling away.

"I wouldn't say I have no reason," she replies. "I actually think you and I have a lot in common, both trying to shield the next generation from a past that refuses to leave us alone."

Chapter Eighty-One

The sun was fully up in the sky by the time I pulled the truck into the same parking lot I departed last night at The Fireside Inn. My third such visit in the last couple of days, each successive trip had been defined by a marked decrease in appearance. Physical manifestations of everything both me and the truck had been through.

Thursday night, we were both still whole. Just hours after being visited by Quinn, I hadn't so much as missed a meal yet. There were no scratches or bullet gouges in the body of the truck.

Unblemished forms that were definitely starting to show signs of wear by the time we returned last night. The effects of the trip out to Fawn Island for me, and the assorted dings from Mick and his crew along the truck.

Travails that had tested us both, and even left some marks behind. Battle scars that we both could wear with honor, proving what we had been through without sacrificing any functionality.

Points of pride that had morphed again, leaving the full effects of the last couple of days plainly on display for us both. A beating that took us to the brink of submission, survived only through adrenaline and a massive amount of luck.

Sheer will, mixed with hatred for the people I was fighting against even before I knew exactly who they were, and the love of those I was fighting for.

A potent combination of motivators that I had no doubt I would have died without.

Even with the care received at the Doone mansion, I could feel my energy reserves flagging. Weariness that was deep seated, likely to last for the next several days, if not longer.

Exhaustion that seemed to be shared by the truck as the hinges on the door let out a mighty wail. A pained cry that called across the parking lot as I pushed it shut, provoking a familiar voice to call, "Jesus Christ, what the hell happened to you?"

Standing with both hands pressed flat against the door, I raised my focus to the reflection in the window beside me. A quick peek that revealed Quinn coming my way.

Both hands buried inside the front pouch of the Seahawks hoodie, she jogged the remainder of the distance between us, only slowing as I turned to face her.

"Where the hell have you been?" she followed up with. A question that was pushed aside as she took in my appearance for the first time. A sight that caused her to gasp as her gaze slid to the truck behind me.

In that instant, I could see the rush of realizations that played across her features. A host of things that slid by in short order, landing on a single undeniable response.

A look of understanding that I had barely ever seen my daughter don, and sure as hell never aimed at me.

Understanding as to where I had been and what I had been through. Why our call last night went the way it did, and why I had been radio silent for most of the day.

The lengths that I had endured and the toll they had extracted.

On some level, I even wanted to believe she understood the thousand reasons why I had endured such hardship. The place that she and her daughter did – and always would – hold. The position of

overlook I would maintain until my last day, regardless what our relationship was.

The guilt I felt over everything that had caused said relationship
to deteriorate.

The motivation that had installed, propelling me to make it all
right, or at least as much of it as I could.

Dozens of thoughts that I had been having since talking to
Careen earlier. Parallels that might or might not have been apt to
draw. Things that I had wanted to say for so long, but never had the
chance.

Items that I wanted to believe were all encapsulated in that look
of understanding she wore. Quite possibly the deepest conversation
ever shared between the two of us, without either saying so much as a
word.

Falling in by my side, she had led me across the lobby and into
the elevator. Down the corridor on the top floor.

Even past Everett and Danila standing in the center of the suite
with mouths agape, staring at the man who suddenly looked and felt
every bit of the seventy years Quinn kept telling people I was, if not
older.

A real-time age progression they watched slip past as Quinn
marched me by. A direct path to the room attached to the backend of
the suite, closing the door behind us the instant we were over the
threshold.

Passage into a space that was roughly half the size of the outer
area, with all of the hotel bedroom staples. A king-size bed domi-
nating the floorspace. End tables flanking it. A dresser against the far
wall with a flat-screen television mounted above it.

Artwork in fancy frames. Floor-to-ceiling windows overlooking
the lake.

Items that, like those in the front room, were much nicer than
those found most anywhere else.

Stuff that I did not give a damn about, my entire focus going to
the young woman propped up in the center of the bed.

The same place it has remained in the few moments since as I stand rooted in place, staring at my granddaughter.

Confirmation more than anything else that my daughter does understand every last thing I hoped for the last couple days, and the decades preceding them.

"Cailee, I want to introduce you to someone," Quinn opens. Walking only as far as the corner of the bed, she stands perpendicular to it, able to see both me and her daughter without having to turn. "This is Bear. My father. Your grandfather."

Wearing a fluffy white robe to match the one Danila put on last night, Cailee sits upright in the center of the bed. Her back braced against the headboard, oversized pillows are stacked up on either side. A down comforter is pulled to her waist.

Not far removed from the shower, her wet hair is combed straight back. Her cheeks have been scrubbed so that they bear the slightest pink hue.

The sun streaming in through the windows strikes her at an angle.

An overall effect that makes her look almost ethereal as she rotates her focus from her mother to me.

An angel, worth every last thing done in recent days.

"Hi," I say.

For a moment, there is no response. Not a single word crosses her lips as she tilts her head an inch to the side, studying me.

If she is surprised by what her mother just said, she doesn't say it. If she is revolted by my appearance or angry for being told I was dead, she gives no indication.

Nothing at all for a full minute, ending with her saying, "I know you, don't I? I mean, I've seen you somewhere."

"Uh, yeah. You probably remember me from the incident at your graduation last year."

Shaking her head just slightly, wet tendrils of hair brush against the top of her robe. "No, not that. At the Starbucks, near campus."

Warmth rises to my face. The small of my back. Heat I can feel flushing my features as I glance to Quinn.

"That was me."

"And at the mall, last summer."

Pulling my focus away from Quinn, I slide it back to Cailee. Pressing my lips together, I nod in affirmation.

"Yeah, that too."

"I remember," she replies. "Because of your eyes. I always thought they looked like..."

Her voice trails away. An unfinished sentence as she looks to her mother, putting the connection together for the first time.

The recognition that in more ways than one, I've always been around.

Remaining fixed in that position, she keeps her focus locked on her mother. A pose she holds for several moments, lasting until a corner of her mouth begins to curl up.

Her gaze tracks back to me.

"I guess you're the one who gave her that God-awful name?"

To my right, Quinn belches out a laugh. A single sound that erupts from within her, causing Cailee to chuckle as well.

Laughter I can't help but join, even as it pulls against the bindings encasing my ribcage.

"No," I reply. "That was her mother's doing."

"Yeah, so you say," Quinn replies.

"It was," I say, raising my voice to be heard over the combined sounds of my daughter's and granddaughter's laughter.

Easily the most beautiful sound I have ever experienced.

"Why the hell do you think I always called you Q?"

Epilogue

For the second time in a week, the sound of the sensors at the end of my lane sent palpitations up through my chest. Natural responses so much stronger than those evoked the last time, coming on the heels of everything that happened just last weekend.

A whirlwind that I would have thought saw every bit of opposition wiped out, but there was no way of being certain.

Not considering who I was up against, with roots extended back for decades.

Going straight for the Beretta stowed in the bottom of my tackle box, I pulled it free and had it resting atop my left thigh by the time the images from the cameras overlooking the drive were relayed to me. Shots of a vehicle that was a far cry from the Honda that Quinn showed up in last time, but was no less recognizable.

Oversized SUV. Brand new tires. Spotless glossy black paint.

Windows tinted to match.

All of the telltale markers of an automobile I had been expecting since the minute I made that first phone call outside the cabin seven days ago. Hallmarks of a ride bought and paid for on the taxpayer dime, filling the motor pool of every government agency in the country.

None more so than the Bureau.

Much like that previous visit, once I saw who my unexpected visitor was, the trepidation vanished. Concern that was pushed away, replaced by the feeling of resignation.

An ending I knew for some time was coming, this way at least arriving while letting me get in a few final casts. The only way – short of another couple of minutes with my newly acquainted granddaughter – that I would want to spend my last bit of time as a free man.

Given the benefit of a forewarning, by the time the SUV pulls to a stop behind me, the Beretta is stowed back in the bottom of the tackle box. My phone is tucked away in the pocket of my fleece overcoat.

Nothing is amiss as I continue to cast and reel, listening to the sound of footsteps approach along the dock.

A process that is ongoing as Otis Herbert appears in my periphery. Dressed in dark gray jeans and a black Sherpa jacket, he walks to the edge of the dock. Hands buried in the front pockets of the latter, he stares out, crow's feet bunching around his eyes in the face of the late afternoon sun.

Glow that is misleadingly bright, the air temperature just a degree or two above fifty.

Another day in what continues to be a steady march toward an early winter.

Saying nothing, he waits as I reel in the last few feet of line. Watching it rise from the water, he sweeps his gaze along the length of the rod before finally settling it on me.

"Bear."

"Otis."

"Any luck?"

"Not too bad, considering the temperature," I say. Releasing my left hand from the reel, I gesture to the pole I picked up at Walmart a week ago resting on the dock between us.

The prop for the trip out to Fawn Island that I can't bring myself to throw away, even if most days I only carry it out, and then turn around and take it back when I'm done.

"You're welcome to join. Won't be too many more chances this year."

A full decade younger than I am, he could easily pass for his early forties. Cut from the same cloth as Everett Jory, he is a dedicated gym rat and health nut. Dedication to a lifestyle that looks and probably feels pretty good, but lacks the underlying demeanor to be useful for much more than aesthetics.

One of many reasons why, I suspect, he made a point of heading toward the administrative side of things once his time as a junior agent was complete.

A stark contrast to someone like myself, who was going out into the field until my very last days carrying a badge.

Outside of the faint lines framing his eyes, the sole signs of his age are a few flecks of gray in his sandy hair. A thick mane that is cut short and pushed to the side, framing a face that is shaped like a block.

Taking a step back, he exhales slowly as he bends and picks up the rod. Grasping the handle in one hand, he tilts it back, examining the chartreuse soft plastic lure tied to the end of the line.

A quick inspection that he finds satisfactory, swinging it out in front of him before raising the tip of the rod. Flicking it forward, he sends the line away at a diagonal, placing it near the far bank.

"How are your ribs doing?" he asks.

"Getting there," I reply.

Grunting softly in reply as he works the lure through the water, bringing it back to the dock, he asks, "And your granddaughter?"

The first time Otis Herbert and I ever met was now a little over twenty years ago. Running my own team at that point, he had come into the Bureau as part of the latest class.

A bunch of junior agents, bearing all of the annual hallmarks. Unearned ego and outsized bravado that I'm sure I showed up with the day I started. Just like hundreds before, and no doubt even more after.

Personality traits that are almost a requirement for the job.

The difference between most of us and Herbert being the entitlement that came with it. Self-importance that stemmed from his being a third-generation legacy.

A lifetime of proximity that made him a little too familiar with everything, which in turn rubbed me the wrong way.

Initial friction that eventually waned by the facts that he turned out to actually be pretty good at his job, and because our respective paths never took us near each other. Begrudging respect from afar that was the reason I went to see him when I moved up here.

Why I called and asked for his help last week.

Hell, why he is probably here to collect me now.

"Same," I reply. "Those first couple days were especially rough, but getting there, little by little."

Lifting my lure from the water, I consider raising it overhead again. One final cast that I think better of, instead content to leave it hanging over the side of the dock.

"The girls from the island?"

"We were able to track down the last family a couple of days ago," Herbert answers. "Jacksonville. How the hell she got clear up here is anybody's guess."

An image from that night flashes across my mind. A snapshot of those little ones lined up in the back bedroom of the guesthouse, pulled in from across the country. What Lucien Bardette referred to as party favors, about to be sent into places even more far flung.

A memory that still incites anger, even despite them having all made it home.

Probably always will.

"The other members of The Council?"

"They won't be going home anytime soon."

422

The answer is more vague than I would like, but considering our disparate positions – and the equally evasive answers I just gave him – I don't blame him.

"All in all, quite a score for our office," he continues. Pulling his lure up out of the water, he turns to glance my way. A quick look, as if considering stopping as well, before turning back.

Lifting the tip toward the sky, he sends out the line again.

"Not to mention, some of the other stuff we found out there. And at a certain state park north of the city.

Has a lot of people talking."

Staring straight out, I watch as the late afternoon sun dances atop the water. A surface with just enough chop from the breeze and Herbert's recent cast to create ripples moving in opposite direction.

Tiny breaks that breaks the glow into small pieces, making them twinkle up at me.

"That why you're here?" I ask, pushing the word out with a sigh. "To bring me in?"

"Bring you...?" he begins. Chuckling softly, he turns to glance at me. "Hell, Bear, I'm here to offer you a job."

I can feel my brows rise in surprise as I return the glance, my gaze meeting his.

"A job? I guess you don't remember that I had my office packed up for me four years ago."

"That you did," Herbert agrees, "but that was working as a direct employee of the Bureau. I'm here to see if you've ever given any thought to becoming a consultant."

* * *

Turn the page for a sneak peek of *Moonshine Creek*, A Standalone Suspense Thriller, or download now and start reading: dustinstevens.com/MCwb

Sneak Peek

Moonshine Creek, A Standalone Suspense Thriller

"Cort...you don't..."

Remington knows exactly the words he wants to say, though there is a disconnect that keeps them from coming out. A blockage existing somewhere between his mind and his mouth that has nothing to do with Tyrell and Val and Brady all standing nearby, their assault rifles still raised before them.

An audience that Remington is only vaguely aware of, much the same as the mansion littered with bodies behind them, or even the man with gunshot wounds to either knee laying nearby, audibly groaning in pain. Background noise that has been filtered out, his entire focus on his twin brother a few feet away.

A man who has not been baptized into this life the way Remington has. A divergent path that he would have never treaded anywhere near if not for the events of the last week.

Pausing his slow and stilted walk forward, his features twisted into a pained grimace, Cortland turns and looks at him. The over-sized M17 handgun hangs by his side, an anchor tugging his arm straight down from the shoulder.

"It's my turn," he mutters. "I got this one."

* * *

"Oh, my *gawd*," the woman exclaims, raising her voice loud enough to carry out into the central Texas evening. A declaration of amazement, altered by alcohol and delivered at a volume much louder than necessary. Sounds that roll well beyond the veranda extended from the back of the mansion, crossing over the stucco barrier and down to the compound below.

A space of more than twenty acres, all of it enclosed by a wall standing ten feet tall.

The bare minimum required for housing the very specific pets Leo Garcia keeps inside.

A landscaping feature that Garcia is certain the woman has not even bothered to notice since the small party moved outside just moments before. A planned march from the open dining room on the second floor, past the crackling fire pit and out to where they now stand.

A relocation prompted under the ruse of stepping outside to enjoy the sunset. The last few gasps of daylight still resting above the horizon, sending rays of neon orange outward like spokes on a wheel.

Stripes of light broken up by pockets of gases and wisps of clouds, turning the evening sky into a kaleidoscope of color. Vibrant pinks and purples, interspersed with shades of tangerine. A painting that people in other parts of the country will pay thousands of dollars to hang on their walls, playing out before them in real time.

A stunning visual firmly entrancing the woman by Garcia's side. Same for her husband on her opposite shoulder.

Maribelle and Johnson Kleese, otherwise known as Garcia's newest business associates. Owners of The Char Pit restaurant chain, with a pair of locations in the nearby Austin area and the promise of many more on the way. Expansion made possible by their acceptance of his offer for investment, the potential of cash infusions making them blind to what else might be attached.

Not that there is any reason for them to fear the worst. Nothing on Garcia's resume hints at the real source of his prodigious wealth. There is not a single hint of anything nefarious to be seen inside his home.

Never has one of his other various associates throughout the area been foolish enough to whisper a word about what partnering with him truly entails. Complete compliance ensured through displays much like the one that is now just minutes away.

A visual, bringing a stark end to the pleasantries of the evening. An abrupt halt to any pretense of this being an equal working relationship.

He now owns them, in every way. A fact that is the reason for their relocation to the veranda overlooking the grounds below. A display that will make the full extent of their hasty agreement quite apparent.

And will ensure their compliance with whatever Garcia dictates from this moment forward.

"Would you look at that view?" Maribelle gasps. A simple question eliciting a nod from her husband. Eagerness to please, mixed with stunned disbelief.

"Yes," Garcia replies. Turning at the waist, he raises a hand, pointing to the third floor of the mansion above. From it extends a pair of window panes, folded out to allow an unobstructed view of the grounds below. "When we built this place, we made sure the back of the home was facing the west so *mi madre* could watch the show every night from her room."

"Aw," Maribelle says, again raising her voice louder than necessary, drawing the word out to several syllables. More Texas excess, matching the overblown plume of blonde hair encircling her head, and the smear of bright pink lipstick on her face, and the absurd cowboy boots that have been clomping throughout Garcia's home all evening.

A walking caricature, matched by her diminutive husband beside her, desperately trying to overcompensate with a massive belt buckle and oversized hat atop his head. Lifts in his boots giving him an extra three inches.

Little Man Syndrome taken to the most extreme degree.

Baseline attempts at physical expansion made even more pronounced in Garcia's presence. An effect he has seen on multiple occasions, his own physical mass the sole thing his father ever gave him worth remembering.

"It is quite a spectacular sunset," Johnson adds.

"It is," Garcia says, "though that's not the show I am referring to."

Rotating back to face forward, Garcia waits as the sun continues to slip lower along the horizon, leaving just the top quarter of it visible. A steady descent pulling the residual light with it, casting long shadows across the compound below.

Darkened pockets form along the base of the outer walls. Long stripes extend from the clumps of post oak and pecan trees dotting the grounds. Old growth interspersed with low-growing shrubs and tumbleweeds.

The sole part of Garcia's estate not meticulously maintained, left wild for this exact purpose. Habitat playing as vital a role in his enterprise as the security staff roaming the property or the storehouses kept in secret throughout the area.

"Tell me," Garcia asks. "Have you heard about my nickname around town?"

The lead-in question for each of these displays, it is received much the same as usual. One of two evoked responses, the pair before him opting for one of each.

Pure confusion on the part of Johnson, offset by more faux mirth from his wife. Levity that again evokes her damnable cackle, extending a hand and placing it upon the sleeve of Garcia's tailored suit coat. Fingers that just moments before were eating dinner and holding a wine glass, not so much as washed before daring to touch the cream-colored linen.

"Oh, of course," Maribelle says. "Laughing Leo!"

"Yes," Garcia replies, flashing his gaze from her face down to her hand resting on his arm. An obvious hint that she completely misses, too entrenched in her wine and her ongoing display to notice. "That is correct. Though I must ask you, have you seen me laugh once this evening? Or in any of our previous meetings?"

For a moment, there is no response. The perplexed look on Johnson's face grows more pronounced. Maribelle pulls her hand back, her own smile fading.

The start of realization that Garcia relishes. People about to be impaled on the full weight of their new reality, made to watch it happen.

"The answer is, you have not," Garcia says. "Just as the sunset is not the reason I brought you out here this evening, at this exact moment."

Taking a step forward, Garcia brings himself up to within inches of the textured stucco railing lining the veranda. An optimal viewpoint allowing him to peer down into the compound below as a lone figure appears. Dressed in khaki slacks and a white undershirt, he is plainly visible in the semi-darkness of dusk.

Staggering along the dirt path carved through the center of the landmass, twice he falls to the ground, losing his balance as he turns to stare back in the direction he just came from.

A mistake they always make, as if looking toward the people who just released them for aid will somehow work out in their favor.

"I am a man with a great many business interests," Garcia says. "And for the most part, we get along very well. Just as if you do what I say, when I say, and how I say, you and I will get along just fine."

Extending a hand before him, he points to the figure fighting to regain his balance more than seventy yards away. A frantic flurry of hands and feet against loose soil, puffs of dust rising around him.

A vain try to rise and flee, as if there is a single thing he can do to save himself at this point, the time for such a thing long past.

"If you do not," Garcia continues, "if you try to renege on our arrangement, if you ever whisper a word of what really goes on here to anybody, you will find yourself in the same position as my former partner here."

Beside him, Garcia can hear Maribelle gasp. The first sounds of horror, bullying past the alcohol in her system and the shock of what they are seeing.

A few feet beyond, Johnson begins to huff, not yet aware of the pair of men moving in from either direction. Trained security who are Garcia's personal detail, a tiny subset of his larger staff.

Men who have watched the entire interaction this evening from afar, ready to insert themselves if need be.

A show of force that is unnecessary – the man of absolutely zero threat to someone as skilled as Garcia – but is a means to an end. Another layer to the spectacle put forth for the Kleese's benefit.

One final time, Garcia pauses. A planned break that lasts nearly a full minute before the sound he has been craving all evening pierces the air. A siren call that reverberates out into the night, passing through the compound and up onto the veranda.

A shrill whine that never fails to bring palpitations the length of Garcia's core as the narcotic release of adrenaline and anticipation surges into his bloodstream.

"You see," Garcia narrates, "the nickname is actually a misnomer. *I* am not the one who laughs. It is my friends down there."

On cue, a quartet of dark shadows move into view. Animals sitting low to the ground and moving fast in formation, following the exact same path as the man in white just minutes before.

"The spotted hyena. Average weight of one hundred and ten pounds, possessing a top speed of forty miles per hour and a bite force of up to eleven hundred PSI."

Letting that resonate for a moment, he adds, "Clan animals who prefer to hunt at dusk, and emit that sound you are hearing whenever they are agitated or smell prey."

It takes only an instant for the pack to disappear from sight. Speed and precision that Garcia admires for a moment before looking away, turning to stand perpendicular to the rail.

A change in vantage allowing him to watch the terror-stricken faces of the Kleeses beside him.

Maribelle leaning forward, bracing herself against the edge of the railing as she tries to pull in ragged breaths.

Her husband rooted in place, his jaw sagging, all color drained from his features.

A pose all three maintain until the first pained wail of the man below can be heard rising in the distance.

* * *

Continue reading *Moonshine Creek*:
dustinstevens.com/MCwb

Thank You

Hello, friends!

In my letter at the end of *Moonshine Creek*, I promised you all that, while that may have been the last we saw of Cortland and Remington, I still had plenty of other original ideas I'd been toying with. Stories that were outright standalones or would introduce new characters with room to expand in the future.

This was one of those in particular I was zeroing in on. A tale that began firmly in the former category, but as time went on, kind of grew into the latter.

The original notion for this story sprang from a phrase I first heard a couple of years ago. Someone was talking about the downtrodden state of their life, and kind of summarized it all with a sigh, stating, "I guess that's just the cost of it all."

For whatever reason, those last five words really stuck with me. It was a catchphrase that eventually became a working title before ultimately settling in as a character lens. A prism through which Bear could see the world and his place in it.

Essentially, a whole lot of questions without any definitive answers. The kind of thing that he could let drive him crazy, or he could accept what had been and work to improve what remained.

A work in progress that, as the book went on, I couldn't help but think we may want to watch come together a bit more in the future. 🙂

As for the non-linear storytelling pattern employed here, this was a first for me and, honestly, it was a blast. (Though, definitely tougher than the traditional format). Hopefully, you all enjoyed it as well, as if we do end up seeing Bear again somewhere down the line, there's a good chance this style will be making a repeat appearance.

With that, please allow me to close as always by saying thank you once again. I understand the unending number of books and entertainment that are available today, and really do appreciate you taking a chance on mine. (And if you're wondering, we'll be back again with our old friend Ham in the near future, followed up by some even older friends you might not be expecting... 😉)

Until next time, happy reading!

Much love,

Dustin

Free Book

Sign up for my newsletter and receive a FREE copy of my first bestseller – and still one of my personal favorites – *21 Hours!*
dustinstevens.com/free-book

Dustin's Books

Works Written by Dustin Stevens:

Reed & Billie Novels:
The Boat Man
The Good Son
The Kid
The Partnership
Justice
The Scorekeeper
The Bear
The Driver
The Promisor
The Ghost
The Family

Hawk Tate Novels:
Cold Fire
Cover Fire
Fire and Ice

Dustin's Books

Hellfire
Home Fire
Wild Fire
Friendly Fire
Catching Fire

Zoo Crew Novels:
The Zoo Crew
Dead Peasants
Tracer
The Glue Guy
Moonblink
The Shuffle
Smoked
Coming Soon

Ham Novels:
HAM
EVEN
RULES
HOME
GONE
Coming 2023

My Mira Saga:
Spare Change
Office Visit
Fair Trade
Ships Passing
Warning Shot
Battle Cry
Steel Trap
Iron Men
Until Death

Night Novels:

Overlook

Decisions

Twelve

Standalone Thrillers:

Moonshine Creek

The Exchange

The Subway

The Ring

Peeping Thoms

One Last Day

Shoot to Wound

The Debt

Going Viral

Liberation Day

Motive

21 Hours

Scars and Stars

Catastrophic

Four

Standalone Dramas:

Quarterback

Be My Eyes

Ohana

Just A Game

Children's Books w/ Maddie Stevens:

Danny the Daydreamer...Goes to the Grammy's

Danny the Daydreamer...Visits the Old West

Danny the Daydreamer...Goes to the Moon

(Coming Soon)

Works Written by T.R. Kohler:

Hunter Series:
The Hunter
Street Divorce

Jumper Series:
Into The Jungle
Out To Sea

Bulletproof Series:
Mike's Place
Underwater
Coming Soon

Translator Series:
The Translator
The Confession

About the Author

Dustin Stevens is the author of more than 60 novels, the vast majority having become #1 Amazon bestsellers, including the Reed & Billie and Hawk Tate series. *The Boat Man*, the first release in the best-selling Reed & Billie series, was named an Indie Award winner for E-Book fiction. The freestanding work *The Debt* was named an Independent Author Network action/adventure novel of the year and *The Exchange* was recognized for independent E-Book fiction.

He also writes thrillers and assorted other stories under the pseudonym T.R. Kohler.

A member of the Mystery Writers of America and Thriller Writers International, he resides in Honolulu, Hawaii.

Let's Keep in Touch:

Website: dustinstevens.com
Facebook: dustinstevens.com/fcbk
Twitter: dustinstevens.com/tw
Instagram: dustinstevens.com/DSinsta

Made in the USA
Middletown, DE
17 January 2024

48044570R00265